STARGÅTE

SG·1 ™

HOSTILE GROUND

Book one of the **APOCALYPSE SERIES**

SALLY MALCOLM &
LAURA HARPER

FANDEMONIUM BOOKS

An original publication of Fandemonium Ltd, produced under license from MGM Consumer Products.

Fandemonium Books
United Kingdom
Visit our website: www.stargatenovels.com

STARGÅTE
SG·1

METRO-GOLDWYN-MAYER Presents
RICHARD DEAN ANDERSON
in
STARGATE SG-1™
MICHAEL SHANKS AMANDA TAPPING CHRISTOPHER JUDGE DON S. DAVIS
Executive Producers JONATHAN GLASSNER BRAD WRIGHT
MICHAEL GREENBURG RICHARD DEAN ANDERSON
Developed for Television by BRAD WRIGHT & JONATHAN GLASSNER

WWW.MGM.COM

Print ISBN: 978-1-905586-66-0   Ebook ISBN: 978-1-80070-032-1

To my mum and dad, Tommy and Janie Harper – L.H.

For Jess and Ben – S.M.

Historical note:
This story is set in season three of STARGATE SG-1, between
the episodes
One Hundred Days and *Shades of Gray.*

"Vigil strange I kept on the field one night,
When you, my son and my comrade,
dropt at my side that day."
Vigil Strange I Kept on the Field One Night
– Walt Whitman

CHAPTER ONE

"TEAL'C, how far?"

The colonel's words were clipped, each one bitten off like a curse as he knelt next to Daniel in the mud. Sam couldn't see what he was doing, didn't dare take her eyes off the rain-sodden tree line, but she could smell the antiseptic and heard Daniel hiss in a sharp breath.

"We are now less than a kilometer from the Stargate," Teal'c said. He crouched next to her, staff weapon raised and his arm brushing against hers, making the most of the scant cover they shared — a fallen tree, rotting in the incessant rain. It wouldn't do much against a staff blast but it was better than nothing. She glanced up at the heavy sky, the clouds hiding a multitude of dangers. If those gliders came back…

Breathing hard, breathing through pain, Daniel said, "I'm okay. I can make it."

"Damn right you can." The colonel's growl made it an order as he ripped open another field dressing. Sam heard Daniel's shout of pain as the colonel pressed the bandage onto the wound. She didn't know how badly he was injured, but it had to be serious for the colonel to risk stopping their breakneck flight to the Stargate.

Movement — a fleeting shadow back in the tree line. She wiped rain from her face and eyes, squinting through the curtain of water that slanted across the open ground between SG-1 and the edge of the forest. Yes, there it was again, a glint of gold amid the trees. "Sir," she said, finger itchy on the trigger, "you might want to hurry that up."

"What do you think I'm doing, Carter?"

She ignored his sharp tone. "Teal'c, do you see them? Two o'clock."

"I do." He shifted his position, taking aim.

"Sir?" she risked a glance over her shoulder. Daniel was ashen, his jacket torn and dark with blood where the staff blast had hit, just above the hip and below his tac vest. She glimpsed a white compression bandage through the torn fabric. He grimaced as he moved, trying to stand.

The colonel put a restraining hand on his shoulder and looked over at Sam. She knew that look, the flat uncompromising expression that shut everything down. It meant they were in trouble. "Daniel and I are gonna head for the gate," he said, starting to pack away the med-kit with quick, efficient movements. "You and Teal'c hold them here as long as you can, then come after us." He stuffed his gear back into his vest and tugged the bill of his cap lower. "Don't leave it too long, Major."

She understood. If they were too slow getting back to the gate, there was a real danger they'd be outflanked. "Yes sir. Good luck."

His only reply was a curt nod before he turned to Daniel. "Ready?"

"Sure," Daniel said, teeth gritted. "How hard can it be?"

"Attaboy," the colonel said as he helped Daniel to his feet. "We might have to run."

Daniel nodded, turning from ashen to milky, but determined as ever. "Let's go."

Sam looked away, back to the enemy hiding in the trees, but not before she'd seen the bloom of scarlet on Daniel's dressing. She swallowed a hard knot of anxiety. It would be difficult enough to make it to the gate carrying a wound like that, let alone with a platoon of Jaffa on their heels.

"The enemy is moving," Teal'c murmured as several Jaffa emerged from the trees, keeping low as they scanned the scrubby clearing. Sam ducked behind their cover, not wanting to give away their position. "Go now, O'Neill," Teal'c said softly. "We will cover your retreat and hold this position as long as possible."

"Counting on it," the colonel said.

With Daniel's arm looped over his shoulder, he headed out into the sparse woodland that ran all the way back to the

Stargate. Sam winced at their slow, awkward pace. At that rate, they'd never reach the gate before the Jaffa.

A squall of rain blew into her face and she had to turn away, squeezing her eyes shut. When she looked back, Daniel and the colonel were gone, the rain at least helping to hide them from the advancing Jaffa, even if it did make the muddy ground slick and treacherous under foot. Wiping her face on her sleeve, she squirmed around and shivered as a trickle of rain slid down her neck and under her collar. "Daniel's moving pretty slow," she whispered, taking a bead on one of the Jaffa and switching her weapon to single shot. "Do you think they'll make it in time?" Even through the rain, she knew she'd hit her target. But not yet, let them come out a little further from the cover of the trees.

"It is possible," Teal'c said, "that one of us will need to precede them to the Stargate and hold it against the Jaffa."

"Yeah," Sam said, a beat of fear kicking in her chest, "that's what I figured."

Daniel was heavier than he looked and his feet kept slipping in the mud, threatening to send them both sprawling. He was doing his best, Jack knew that, but he was carrying a serious wound and he wasn't moving fast enough. He just couldn't.

From behind them came the rattle of an MP5 — Carter's precise bursts of weapons fire. But there were too many staff-blasts and, worse, they were getting closer. Teal'c and Carter were falling back faster than he and Daniel were staggering forward.

"Jack…" The grim whisper cut through the sounds of battle. "Need to stop… moment…"

One look at Daniel's ghostly face told him he didn't have a choice; Daniel was halfway to unconsciousness already. Lowering him to the ground, Jack braced him up against a tree, gleaning what little shelter he could from the thin canopy above, and considered the situation. It stunk. Still, they'd survived worse. Probably. He toggled his radio. "Carter, what's your position?"

He didn't get an answer right away, but he could hear her weapon discharging, so he figured she was busy. Couple of seconds later, her voice crackled over the radio. "We're falling back, sir. There's too many."

Damn it. He considered his choices for a moment, then made the decision and hit the talk button again. "Carter, you need to make a run for the gate, dial it up and hold it for us. Teal'c, I'm gonna need your help with Daniel."

"On our way, sir," was Carter's immediate response, which probably meant she'd already reached the same conclusion. "Carter out."

Daniel had a hand over his eyes, his bloodless lips pressed into a tight line of pain. "You should leave me here," he said, hand dropping into his lap as he peered up at Jack through rain-covered glasses. There was no bravado, no self-pity; he was just stating the obvious. "It would be the logical thing to do."

"Yeah, well," Jack said, reaching down and hauling him upright. "You know how I feel about logic."

"I mean it," Daniel said, swaying on his feet. "No point in us all dying here."

"No one's dying here," Jack said, as they staggered back into an ungainly hobble. "But maybe, just maybe, next time someone suggests a mission to study a bunch of ancient rocks instead finding of something useful, my objections won't get shut down."

Daniel didn't comment, but he didn't need to. Even semi-conscious, he managed to radiate indignation. Jack grimaced, but reminded himself that indignation was exactly what he needed from his team right now.

Sam darted through the trees, keeping as low and quiet as possible. She had to sacrifice most of her stealth for speed, but there was no point in advertising her presence if she could help it and so she breathed quietly and kept her ears open for sounds of pursuit.

She was traversing a hill, heading back to the Stargate,

through a sparsely wooded landscape. The rain had started last night and hadn't stopped since, transforming the valley below into marshland and the hillside into a mudslide. Not to mention soaking them all to the skin and turning what was meant to be a light mission into a grueling test of endurance. And that was before the Jaffa had shown up.

Behind her, but growing more distant, she could still hear the sounds of battle. Only staff weapons so far, which meant they hadn't caught up with Daniel and the colonel. Yet. Teal'c was doing a hell of a job holding the Jaffa back on his own.

Suddenly, the ground shifted and she stumbled, feet tangling and slip-sliding over tree roots washed bare by water streaming down the hill. Stifling a curse, she grabbed at a branch and caught it with one hand, but the weight of her pack swung her backward, slamming her shoulder into the tree, and she barely kept from face-planting into the mud. "Damn it," she growled, as she reached up to get both hands onto the branch. She scrambled back to more stable ground, getting her feet under her again. The dull throb in her shoulder promised it was going to hurt in the morning.

Sucking in a breath, she peered up the hill. She'd been sticking to the military crest for most of the way, but now it was time to head for the top. She had little but rain for cover as the trees grew increasingly scarce, but at least she had started to recognize the terrain they'd covered the day before — was it only the day before? — when they'd thought they were on a simple recon mission to an uninhabited world. A back-in-the-saddle mission, General Hammond had called it: SG-1's first trip off-world since the colonel had returned from his extended stay on Edora.

Not that Colonel O'Neill had exactly been thrilled at the prospect of trees, rain and artifacts. Then again, he hadn't exactly been thrilled by anything since they'd found him living the dream with Laira and her people. But that wasn't a place Sam wanted to go right now.

She tugged her cap lower against the rain and started to jog.

It was difficult going uphill in the heavy mud, and soon she was breathing hard. But it didn't matter because suddenly, over the ridge of the hill, emerged the stark metallic ring of the Stargate. At last. She couldn't wait to get home, out of the rain and away from the colonel's bleak mood.

She slowed before she crested the hill and left the last of the meager cover, catching her breath and assessing the situation. The gate stood in a clearing on the crown of the hill, the DHD and the three stone steps leading up to the gate lashed by rain that blew in cold sheets across the windswept space. She couldn't see any Jaffa, but that didn't mean they weren't already there, waiting.

She toggled her radio. "Sir," she said quietly, "I'm at the gate. It looks —"

A screech overhead cut her off, a pressure wave bending the trees and knocking her to the ground: Death Gliders, two of them, sweeping low and fast overhead. She stayed down, finger still holding the talk button. "Sir, did you see that?"

There was a crackle of static, then a series of detonations she felt through the ground as the gliders fired into the trees behind her. "Sir?" she barked into the radio. "Colonel O'Neill, come in."

Nothing.

"Colonel O'Neill, come in."

Gunfire rattled out from somewhere behind her: it was the colonel's MP5. She let out the breath she'd been holding. They weren't far — at least, not very far. Then the colonel's voice burst over the radio. "Carter! Open the gate!"

"Yes sir." She let her hand fall away from the radio and scrambled up to the edge of the tree line, dropping into a crouch as she gazed out at the DHD. It looked impossibly far away and who knew what else was hiding in the trees?

Taking a moment to settle her weapon in her hands, Sam scoured the area for movement. There was nothing. Maybe she'd caught a break and the Jaffa were still behind the thin line Teal'c and the colonel were holding. Or maybe they were sitting there, watching the gate. The DHD was about two hundred meters away, to the left of the Stargate and on the far side of the clearing, and there wasn't a stick of cover between it and the last of the trees. She'd be an open target.

Part of her wanted to wait for the rest of her team, so that she'd have someone to cover her dash across no-man's-land. But she had her orders and, besides, they'd be coming in hot. There would be no time to dial.

Taking a slow, steadying breath she held her weapon at port arms and started to run. She'd made it half way to the DHD when the Death Gliders made a second pass, screaming over the trees and peppering the ground in front of her with gunfire. She dived, rolled back to her feet, and kept running. Gliders were fast, but their targeting was lousy.

A hundred meters, fifty.

A staff blast arced from the trees, much too close. She felt the plasma scorch past her cheek. Dodging sideways, she started zigzagging toward the DHD, offering them a harder target. Another blast detonated on her heels, spraying mud high into the air. The impact knocked her forward, stumbling, but she kept her feet.

Forty meters, thirty. Almost there.

The gliders were back for another pass, but their aim was way off and she just ducked her head and started sprinting. The rain was sluicing off the DHD, running in little rivulets around the symbols. She was almost there, she could almost touch it.

And then another blast hit, right in front of her, knocking the breath from her lungs as she landed on her back in the mud. She struggled, turtle-like, until she could shift the weight of her pack sideways and get her feet under her again. And then there was a burst from an MP5, very close, and she spun around to see Teal'c racing from the tree line with Daniel slung over his shoulder and the colonel raking the trees with weapons fire as he backed up toward the Stargate.

She felt a fierce flash of relief; they'd made it.

"Dial the damn gate, Carter!"

Sam dived for the DHD and hit the first two symbols before Teal'c shouted. "Major Carter, get down!"

She threw herself sideways as the plasma bolt blasted over the top of the DHD. Damn it, too close. Half hidden behind the pedestal, she reached up and pressed the third and fourth symbol as Teal'c barreled into the scant cover of the DHD, dropping Daniel onto the ground and covering him with his body. Then he reached for his own weapon and fired over the DHD as Sam reached up and hit the fifth and sixth symbol.

"Teal'c?" Daniel's voice was weak, panicked. He clutched the wound on his side and his hand came away bloody, the sodden dressing falling to the ground. "Oh no…"

There was no time to help him. Teal'c fired again and Sam felt for the final symbol before she slammed her hand down on the central button.

Behind her, the gate began to spin. She risked a quick glance, only to see the colonel pinned down behind the spinning gate. "Sir!"

"I know!" he barked.

She could see the Jaffa approaching now, from all directions. And then the gliders were back, screaming overhead, mud spewing up as they hammered the ground around the Stargate. Several Jaffa went down, victims of friendly fire, and in that moment of confusion Sam jumped up and opened fire on their ranks. "Colonel!"

He bolted from behind the gate as the seventh chevron locked, diving for cover behind the DHD just as the wormhole exploded out of the Stargate, hissing into the cold rain.

Behind Teal'c, the gliders had swung around for another pass, their cannons strafing the ground in a direct line from the trees to the Stargate. Sam punched through their IDC as soon as the vortex stabilized, and the colonel dragged Daniel to his feet, hauling him toward the gate with one arm while he toggled his radio. "Med team to the gate room! Now!" And then he was gone, practically falling into the wormhole with Daniel in his arms as the oncoming gliders peppered the ground in front of the gate with cannon fire.

Two down, two to go.

Sam exchanged a swift glance with Teal'c. He nodded and opened fire on the Jaffa as she dashed up the steps, kneeling to cover him as he made his own run.

"Major Carter, now!" Teal'c yelled. Together, they threw themselves into the wormhole just as the stone steps exploded beneath their feet.

They tumbled in too fast, and yet somehow the passage through the wormhole took forever — an endless moment of nothingness, of being stretched and reformed and then spat out the other end.

Sam landed hard, hitting the floor with her shoulder and rolling over with too much velocity to get her feet under her. She wound up sprawled on her back — not exactly a dignified homecoming.

She opened her eyes, expecting to see Hammond's concerned face peering down at her. Maybe Janet's.

But what she saw was a low, snowy sky.

"What the —?" Scrambling to her feet, she looked around in shock. Teal'c was doing the same, in a low defensive crouch, his weapon raised.

They stood in a blasted landscape, nothing but rock and gray, ashy dirt. To her left, in the far distance, she could make out hills, their peaks shrouded in cloud. There was a sound too, a low roar like the crash of waves against the shore. Snow fell, thin and dirty, and Sam shivered in her muddy, rain-sodden clothes. It was freezing. "Colonel?" she called. "Daniel?"

"Over here."

She turned. Behind her, half hidden by the crescent of the Stargate, Colonel O'Neill crouched over Daniel who looked like he was out cold. The colonel's med kit was scattered on the ground and he was grimly pressing another dressing onto

Daniel's wound. It didn't look like the bleeding was stopping. He glanced up when he felt her eyes on him, his expression as bleak as the landscape. "Major," he said, "you wanna tell me what the hell just happened?"

She shook her head. "I don't know, sir."

"You don't *know*?"

"I —" Why did he always expect her to have the answer right away? She bit back her frustration, her rising panic, and peered up at the Stargate, searching for a solution. It was at an odd angle, tilted up and backward — which explained the rough landing — and it was scorched like it had seen some action. But it obviously still worked, so there was no reason they couldn't gate home.

She looked around for the DHD. It had to be... It was probably...

Oh crap.

"Yeah," the colonel said, returning his attention to Daniel. "We're screwed."

CHAPTER TWO

THERE were certain truths Colonel Robert Makepeace understood.

First, the world was in clear and present danger from hostile alien forces possessed of overwhelming military superiority and hell-bent on the enslavement of the entire human race. Second, the Stargate Program was run by a rats' nest of bureaucrats and politicians who spouted BS about building alliances and upholding American values, all the while keeping their beady eyes fixed on the budget, or the next election, and blind to the horrifying reality beyond the Stargate. In Makepeace's opinion, those two truths did not sit happily together.

Unfortunately, General Hammond — for all his Texan charm — had one foot firmly planted in the Pentagon. He'd drunk the Kool-Aid and seemed happy to bet their future on the friendship of their so-called allies: the Asgard, the Tollan, and the Tok'ra. But the truth was, if they couldn't use any of their allies' technology to take the fight to the Goa'uld, there was no damn point in sending good men and women out there to die in defense of those alliances.

Anyway, it was stupid to put that much faith in such tenuous relationships with creatures that weren't even human. Worse than that, it was damn dangerous. And he wasn't the only one who thought so.

Now, he was no fan of Harry Maybourne — he didn't even like the guy — but one thing Maybourne could do was make things happen. And Makepeace could get behind that. Besides, Maybourne had some good people working for him off-world, clear-sighted people who understood the brutal choices they faced. There'd be time enough for ethics when the planet had the weapons it needed to defend itself against the enemy, when the balance of power had shifted in their favor. Until then he intended to do everything he could to make sure that Earth was ready for the assault when it came, even if that meant breaking a few rules.

That's why he felt no compunction when he reached into the dusty alcove and picked up the package, wrapped in cloth and left there for him to retrieve. His team was still exploring, spread out and kicking up dust in yet another abandoned temple on a world destroyed by the enemy. There was nothing there of interest except the Tollan device — a phase-shifter, apparently — that he tucked carefully into the inner pocket of his jacket.

"Colonel?" Major Wade said, closer than Makepeace had thought.

He zipped his jacket closed and turned. "Major, what you got?"

"A whole handful of nothing, sir," Wade said. "This place is a washout."

He squinted up through the roofless temple, slipped on his sunglasses. "Yeah, I'm gonna call it. No point in wasting any more time here." He toggled his radio. "Johnson, Bosco — head back to the gate. We're moving out."

He jerked his head to Wade. "Dial it up."

As he watched the gate spin, watched clouds scudding over an alien sky, he resisted the temptation to pat his pocket. The tech was there, something concrete to help the fight against the enemy, something to make the eight hours they'd spent tramping about this dustbowl worthwhile.

"What's got you smiling, Colonel?" Wade said.

Makepeace shook his head, watching the gate open and the event horizon settle. "Just happy in my work, Major," he said and gestured toward the Stargate with his weapon. "Let's go home."

General George Hammond was not, by and large, a coffee drinker. After some repeated mutterings from Dr. Fraiser about blood cholesterol, he'd decided he was better off switching to fruit tea, both for his health and to avoid the stern gaze of the good doctor.

Yet here he was, in the SGC control room, watching a silent gate and holding his third cup of coffee in an hour. In all honesty, it was more about giving his hands something to do than the need for a caffeine hit. This job was usually enough to keep him up at night after all, the current situation being a case in point. It was just gone 2000 hours and there had been no radio contact from SG-1 since they'd left on what was supposed to be a standard recon to P5X-104. He shouldn't be worried. They weren't due back for another hour and, after all, this was SG-1. A little bit of off-world trouble often found them, but just as often the team would find their way out.

So why was he so antsy?

Maybe it was that word: team. SG-1's greatest strength could potentially become a weakness this time around. Hammond wasn't at all comfortable with the background to this mission, or the events which had preceded it. First of all, there had been those circumstances outside of his control: Edora, and all that had happened in the three months Colonel O'Neill had been MIA. Like everyone else, Hammond had feared the worst and SG-1's desperate efforts to reach their CO had been all the more painful to watch because there was no way to know if he'd even survived the fire rain. They were acting on faith alone, and on the principle they all lived by: no one gets left behind.

But bringing O'Neill back had turned out to be just part of the challenge. Hammond hadn't missed the tension strung out like barbed wire between the team on their return from Edora, most noticeably between O'Neill and Major Carter. Strange, after all she'd done to bring him home. Jack too had been strange, distant and somber in his rough-spun tunic and pants. At the time, Hammond had wondered what the hell had happened on that planet.

He'd found out later of course. Disclosure meant that O'Neill's report gave full details of his relationship with the woman from Edora, Laira. Then, of course, there was all that hadn't been written down. The lines of black and white text were narrowly spaced, but Hammond still managed to find plenty in between them. Turned out Jack had been ready to settle down, only to find himself pulled back into a life he'd started to accept was over. What would that do to a man's head? What would it do to the team he led?

And there is was again, that word: team. The natural thing would have been to give SG-1 time to strengthen their connection again, to rebuild their bonds as a unit. But circumstance hadn't allowed for that. There was the *other* mission to be considered now, the one only he, Jack and a handful of others knew about.

"One of our own, sir?" Jack had been dubious when Hammond had first informed him about the Tollan and Asgard suspicions.

"I know what's going through your head, Colonel," Hammond had replied. "I daresay they're the same thoughts I had when I met with High Chancellor Travell and Thor. It's hard to accept that someone you work with day in and day out could be a traitor."

"General, you're not saying that you think one of SG-1–"

"Not for a second, Jack. But there are other teams out there. Nearly all of them have had the opportunity to commit the crimes we're talking about here, and as much as it sickens me to accept it, one of our own *is* responsible."

Jack had shifted in his chair, as if he knew what was coming. "So I'm here because… ?"

"We need someone on the inside for this. Both the Tollan and the Asgard have requested you, and I can't say I question their judgment on that."

Jack had nodded slowly, his gaze flicking around the room, not agreeing as such, just considering. He, of all people, knew what it meant to go undercover. He knew that it meant changing who you were, that it meant lies and deceit for those closest to you. "Me," he'd finally said. "Just me."

"Yes. Just you."

"And what am I supposed to tell them, sir?"

No need to ask who he meant by 'them'. "No one can know, Jack. Not even your team. The future of the planet depends on the success of this mission."

"They won't believe it," he'd objected. "They won't believe I'd jeopardize our alliances just to get my hands on some alien gadgets. They know me better than that."

"It's not going to be easy, Jack, but you'll have to convince them."

O'Neill had shaken his head, looking unhappy. "Convince them that I'd walk away from the SGC? That I'd team up with *Maybourne*? How? How can I make them believe that without completely destroying their trust in me?"

There'd been a moment then when Jack had just stared, a slow and horrible realization dawning. Then his eyes had closed, his shoulders rising and falling with a deep breath. When he'd opened his eyes again, he'd already looked fractured.

"Whatever you need to do," Hammond had tried to assure him, "they'll understand." There was a moment's pause before he'd added, "I'm not making this an order, Colonel."

Jack had given a hollow laugh at that, raising his eyebrows, and Hammond had smiled ruefully in response. They'd both known he had no choice.

So Hammond had watched as O'Neill began his role in earnest, wedging a chisel into the cracks between himself and SG-1, cracks which had only just begun to heal, and widening them a little bit further every day. Destroying their trust in him.

And now he watched the silent gate, wondering where they were and what was happening to them, and he knew that O'Neill would still be working on those cracks. He could only hope that SG-1 wouldn't break apart completely before they came home.

CHAPTER THREE

STOP the bleeding. That was the first priority. Everything else could wait.

"Daniel?" Jack tapped his face and got a vague response, but Daniel's skin was clammy and cold and his pulse was thready. He was going into shock.

Working fast, Jack pulled away the sodden dressing and mopped out as much blood as he could from the wound. He could sense Carter hovering behind him and Teal'c further out, securing their position, but he had no spare attention for either. He grabbed the packet of FastClot from the med kit, tore it open and started pouring the granules into the wound until the blood was absorbed and not leaking to the surface. Packing the wound with more gauze, he reached for a pressure bandage. "Carter," he barked, "give me a hand with this."

Without a word, she took the bandage from him and started winding it around Daniel's abdomen while Jack kept the pressure on the dressing. When she was done she tied it off nice and tight and sat back on her heels. "That's the hemostatic agent they reverse engineered from the stuff SG-3 found on P3M-453," she said after a moment, nodding toward the FastClot. "I've never seen it used in the field before."

He peeled off the latex gloves and dropped them onto the ashy ground. "Your lucky day then, Major."

Lips pressed tight, Carter didn't reply. Instead, she reached up and touched a hand to Daniel's face, then to the pulse point in his neck. "He's shocky."

"I know. We need to warm him up."

"Here, sir?" She glanced around. "Shouldn't we hole up somewhere first? We're very exposed."

She had a point, they *were* pretty exposed, but Daniel's need was urgent. "Teal'c?" Jack called. "You see anything moving out there?"

Teal'c looked back at him from where he stood studying the misty hills. "Nothing, O'Neill. I see no tracks but our own, and nothing to indicate that the Stargate is in regular use."

"Well it wouldn't be," Jack muttered, "not without a DHD."

He sensed Carter shift uncomfortably, but didn't say anything to reassure her. Distance, he reminded himself. He was creating distance and undermining trust. Pulling a foil blanket from his pack he spread it out on the ground, kicking up a cloud of dirt in the process. Coughing, he waved the dust away from his face. "Carter, on three," he said, and together they lifted Daniel onto the blanket and wrapped the rest of it around him. Better than nothing, yet far less than he needed.

But at least the movement jostled some life back into him. He groaned, tried to lift his head. "Jack… ?"

"Hey, how're you doing?"

Daniel's eyes fluttered open and then closed again. "Infirmary… ?"

"Ah, not exactly," Jack said, casting a quick look at Carter. "Looks like we misdialed."

"What?" Her face was a startled picture of hurt and offence. "Colonel, I didn't misdial."

He gestured around them. "And yet… ?"

"No," she said, scrambling to her feet. "No, I dialed it right. I know I did…" But then she frowned, raking a hand through her hair. "I mean it was difficult, I had to reach up —" A flash of doubt crossed her face. "Oh God, what if I misdialed? It was hard to see from the angle I was at and the incoming fire was —"

"Carter!" He cut her off before she went any further, partly because he felt guilty for what he was doing — what he had to do — but mostly because there were times for self-recrimination and this wasn't one of them. "I don't care how we got here. I just need you to get us home." He jerked his head toward the Stargate. "Can we dial out manually?"

Biting down on whatever she was feeling — and it was always

difficult to tell with Carter — she said, "Maybe." She threw the cockeyed Stargate a dubious look. "It depends on whether it still has any residual power."

"Then go find out, Major."

She nodded, pulled one of her gadgets from her tac vest, and headed over to the gate. Meanwhile, Daniel was gamely trying to sit up. He still looked bone-white, but at least he was lucid. Thanking heaven for small mercies, Jack helped Daniel to sit, getting in behind to support him. "Teal'c," he said, calling him over. "You got some water there?"

"I do." Crouching before them, Teal'c pulled out his canteen and held it to Daniel's lips. "Drink what you can. You have lost a great deal of blood."

"Ah," Daniel said, sipping at the water. "So it's not a hang-over then… ?"

"If it were," Teal'c said. "You would feel worse."

In different circumstances, that would have made Jack smile, but not here with the snow falling and no damn DHD. He shifted a little, bracing Daniel's back while he took a moment to assess the situation. It was bad. They had no idea where they were, no idea what threats the planet posed, and no way to contact the SGC. But ultimately none of that mattered because, wherever the hell they were, they had to get home fast. He'd reached the limits of field medicine and Daniel needed a hospital.

He glanced over at Carter and hoped she'd pull another one of her famous miracles out of her… hat. But she'd climbed up onto the rim of the weirdly angled Stargate and was frowning down at her scanner. He recognized that frown and it wasn't a good sign. Given the beat-up appearance of the Stargate, things weren't looking good for a manual dial out. Which left what, exactly? Either they wait for a rescue that might never come or they find another way off this sorry-assed excuse for a planet. He didn't much like the odds on either option. "Carter?"

She looked up and shook her head, balanced on the rim of the gate and bracing herself against it with her free hand.

"Sorry, sir, there's nothing. The gate's dead. I don't think it's been used for decades."

"Damn it."

"I guess we're staying here for a while?" Daniel said, voice thin and his weight shifting slightly against Jack as he eased himself into a more comfortable position.

"Not for long," Jack promised. Daniel aside, he had a date with the Tollan Curia that he couldn't afford to miss. But first things first: they were cold, tired, and wet. They needed warmth and shelter and then he'd figure out the rest.

Dragging his pack closer, he helped Daniel settle against it and left Teal'c's canteen in his hands. "Drink," he said. "That's an order."

Daniel offered a wan smile. "You can't give me orders, Jack."

"Says who?" He squeezed his friend's shoulder and then stood up, looking out at the blasted landscape that stretched in all directions beneath low, heavy skies. "Teal'c," he said, "I figure we'll make camp here for now. I'm not sensing any immediate threats. You?"

"I am not," Teal'c agreed, but he didn't look happy either. "In fact, the lack of any apparent life is the most unsettling aspect of this world."

He hadn't noticed it before, too focused on stopping Daniel from bleeding out into the ashy ground, but now he paid attention he felt it too. There was nothing here: no birds, no insects, no vegetation underfoot. Nothing. He licked his lips; they were starting to chap in the cold air. "The sooner we get outa here the better," he said.

"I concur."

"Okay." He glanced back toward Carter, who was kneeling in the dirt near the Stargate and still futzing around with her scanner. "Carter! Unless you're about to dial us home, get the hell over here and help make camp. We're all freezing our asses off, let's not go hypothermic."

"Yes sir."

They didn't often use it, but Jack always packed a tent. It could fit four at a pinch, but it was more comfortable with three inside and one out on watch. Teal'c accused him of being soft, but it was at times like this when he felt its value — not even Teal'c could have rigged a shelter from a bunch of rocks.

Pulling the tent from his pack he dropped it onto the ground, raising a little puff of snow and dust. His hands were cold — he only had his fingerless gloves with him — and he flexed them a couple times to keep the blood flowing. He hadn't been joking about the hypothermia, they were all soaked through and the temperature here had to be close to freezing. It would be worse at night, no doubt. Shelter, food and dry clothes were urgent, especially for Daniel.

So, when he glanced up and saw Carter still crouched near the gate, messing with her scanner, he felt a flash of genuine impatience. "Major," he snapped, "I told you to leave that."

She shook her head, not looking up. "Sorry, sir, but —"

"No buts," he said, shaking out the tent. Teal'c grabbed the other end and they started stamping the stakes into the ground. "Get over here."

"No sir."

"Excuse me?"

"Colonel, you have to stop," she said, abruptly standing up. "Stop disturbing the soil."

Jack glanced at Teal'c who only lifted an eyebrow in query. "This better be good, Carter…"

She was walking toward them slowly, staring at the scanner which she held low down, close to the ground, and then high up over her head. "Sir," she said, at last stopping in front of him, "we can't stay here."

"On the planet?"

"In this location, sir."

"Because… ?"

She grimaced, like she was afraid to give the bad news. "I'm reading dangerous levels of radiation in the soil, sir."

He closed his eyes for a moment, absorbing the latest piece of crappy luck to come their way. "You have *got* to be kidding me, Carter…"

"I'm sorry, sir, I know it's not what you want to hear. But we can't stay here, it's not safe. And the more we disturb the soil, the greater the risk we run." She glanced down at her clothes, dusty with dirt where she'd tumbled out of the Stargate. "I think we're standing in a fallout zone, sir. Not a recent one, but at some point in this planet's past it looks like the Stargate was nuked."

"That would explain the absence of the DHD," Teal'c said.

"And the birds." Jack scratched a hand through his hair, shutting down his frustration and fears and focusing on the problem in hand; when circumstances changed, you changed your plans. He peered through the fine snow toward the hills. They were maybe two klicks away. "We'll head for higher ground," he decided. "There'll probably be less fallout accumulation up there."

"Yes sir," Carter said. "And if the gate was close to ground zero, which is likely, then the further we get from it the better."

It made sense, except… He looked over at Daniel and Carter's gaze followed his.

"We've got no choice, sir," she said quietly. "We have to move him."

"I know." But that didn't make it any easier. God only knew how Daniel would manage the hike; he should be in surgery already.

Jack rubbed a weary hand over his face. Just how much more crap was the universe going to throw at them today? In the pit of his stomach, the anxiety that had been churning since the first Jaffa attack tightened into a fist of fear. They should be home by now. Daniel should be safe in the infirmary, and he should be figuring out how to bring down Maybourne's nasty little off-world operation before Earth's allies abandoned them entirely. But instead they were stuck in the ass end of nowhere, with no way home — again — sucking in radioactive dust with every goddamn breath. "Damn it, Carter," he growled. "Hell of a time to screw up."

She stared. "I didn't—" But then she stopped, taking it like the officer she was. "Yes sir. I'll help Daniel get ready to move out."

And then she was gone, stalking past the Stargate to where Daniel lay wrapped in the foil blanket and propped up on Jack's pack.

"We do not know that Major Carter misdialed the gate address," Teal'c pointed out, disapproval chilling his voice as he crouched to pull up the tent stakes and refold the tent. "Indeed, it is more probable that an error occurred while we were in transit."

Jack didn't respond; he knew Teal'c was right.

"It is unlike you," Teal'c persisted, "to lay blame where it is not due."

Uncomfortable beneath Teal'c's scrutiny, he kept his gaze on the tent as he started repacking it. "Perhaps you don't know me as well as you think you do."

Another silence as Teal'c stood up. "I do not believe that is true, O'Neill. But whatever the cause of your ill humor, Major Carter does not deserve your anger."

"Yeah? Well maybe you should keep your opinions to yourself." He made his voice hard, angry, and didn't look up as Teal'c walked away in silence.

It hurt, deceiving his team like this. It twisted a knot of guilt in his gut. But, from the moment the Asgard and Tollan had laid down their highhanded ultimatum, his choice in the matter had been swept aside. Until Maybourne's SGC mole was uncovered, Jack was a puppet dancing to their allies' tune—and that pissed him off monumentally.

From beneath the bill of his cap, he watched Carter kneeling next to Daniel, encouraging him to drink some more water, touching her fingers to his throat and checking his pulse. He hated undermining her, it felt deep down wrong, but this wasn't the first time the job had demanded he walk a fine moral line.

The problem with Carter was her loyalty. She was the last person to believe him capable of deliberately contravening Air

Force regulations and stealing technology from the Tollan. Yet somehow, in just a few days, he had to make her buy it without question. He couldn't afford to have her raising doubts because, if Maybourne's mole got a sniff of a set-up, the whole mission would fail. And then the whole planet would be up the proverbial creek without a paddle.

Daniel was less of a problem, of course. They'd locked horns over the Stargate Program's purpose enough times that Daniel already believed him capable of almost anything. Daniel might not like it, but this wouldn't be the first time they'd been on opposite sides of the moral line. And it wouldn't be the first time Jack had disappointed him.

As for Teal'c, while he might not agree with Jack's actions, he'd understand that the end sometimes justified the means. And he understood frustration. Hell, why else had he turned his back on his own people for the chance to fight back?

But Carter? They were both Air Force and she knew exactly how much that meant to him, because it meant just as much to her. So if he was going to make the story stick then he needed to damage Carter's faith in him. And the way to do it was by ruthlessly undermining her trust.

Didn't mean he had to like it, though.

But he'd make it up to her. Once they were home, and the whole Maybourne screw-up had been squared away, he'd get things back on track with his team. Maybe he'd even invite them up to Minnesota, do a little fishing. No harm in that.

He shivered suddenly, a chill breeze picking up the snow and swirling it in harsh eddies. He didn't like this place. It was time to get moving.

Janet Fraiser finished writing on the clipboard in her hand and smiled at the young airman who was rebuttoning his pants in the infirmary while trying to avoid her eye. The newbies were always like this after receiving their standard inoculation shots and routine checkup. As if baring their ass to a female doctor was the most embarrassing thing they'd ever done.

I was a cadet once too, son, she often wanted to say. *I know what happens on leave.*

But mostly she just smiled in what she hoped was a motherly way or made a joke to alleviate their awkwardness.

Right now, though, her heart wasn't quite in it. She cast yet another glance at the clock, the clipboard and airman forgotten for the time being. Thirty-five minutes past due and still not a single word. Despite General Hammond's reassurances, it was hard to convince herself that there was nothing wrong. Probably because she'd known there was something wrong before the team had even set their boots on the metal of the ramp.

This mission, their first since Colonel O'Neill's return, was always going to be a tough one, but something just hadn't sat right with her, as if the entire team were going through the motions. And now she wondered, if something had gone wrong, whether SG-1 were in any shape to deal with it.

"Will that be all, ma'am?"

"I'm sorry?"

She turned toward Airman Wallace, who watched her expectantly. "Am I done? Y'know, with the shots?"

"Oh, yes. Yes, I'm sorry. Dismissed."

The young man sped from the infirmary, but stopped short by the door to snap a textbook salute to the man who entered.

"General Hammond," said Janet. She cast a glance at the coffee cup in his hand, but made no comment. By his expression, she suspected he needed it. "No word?"

He shook his head, worry and something deeper etched into every line on his face. His earlier confidence that everything was okay had clearly dissipated. "We sent a MALP, but the area around the gate is deserted. There's worse too. From the telemetry, there's evidence of a firefight close to the gate. Doctor, I'm going to order —"

The klaxon sounded. "Unauthorized off-world activation," declared Harriman's voice, and even over the loudspeaker

Janet could hear his anticipation. Both she and the general took off, speeding down the corridors until they reached the control room.

But Harriman looked crestfallen when they arrived. "I'm sorry, sirs. It's SG-3's IDC."

"Open the Iris," ordered Hammond.

Janet followed him down to the gate room, where Colonel Makepeace and his team were starting to hand off their weapons to the waiting SFs.

"What's going on, sir?" asked Makepeace.

"SG-1 are missing, Colonel," Hammond said. "I want SG-3 mission ready again within thirty minutes. You're going to P5X-104 and you're going to find our people."

Crouching close to the Stargate, Sam studied the small cairn of stones she'd built. It was off to one side, out of the path of the erupting event horizon, but close enough that a MALP would spot it immediately.

"Carter!" the colonel barked. "What're you doing?"

She gritted her teeth against a flash of irritation. "Leaving a marker, sir," she said, without looking up.

"Well hurry it up. We're about to move out."

"Yes sir."

The question was how to make it clear to anyone who came looking that they'd been here? After a moment's thought she reached around and pulled her SG-1 patch from the sleeve of her jacket.

She stared at it, caught by the insignia, at what it represented, and glanced up at her team. Teal'c stood poised and ready to move, while the colonel was helping Daniel to stand. Despite his injury, Daniel was smiling as the colonel tucked his shoulder under his arm to help support him. She felt a pang of melancholy as she watched them, as if she was witnessing the end of things, as if something indefinable was shifting between them all.

Shaking off the dismal feelings — this planet, she thought,

bred them in its cold, dank mist — she lifted a few stones and secured her patch inside the cairn. The top quarter poked out and anyone from the SGC would recognize it immediately. As long they kept within radio and visual range of the Stargate, they'd be able to open a channel to Earth as soon as they saw the MALP come through. And it *would* come through, she knew it. No matter how they'd ended up here, rescue would come.

Unlike Colonel O'Neill, she refused to forget that Stargate Command didn't leave its people behind.

CHAPTER FOUR

AS SOON as SG-3 emerged from the wormhole, Makepeace could see that O'Neill and his team had run into trouble. Craters, obviously from heavy Goa'uld artillery, pocked the ground and the rocks around the gate were charred by staff blasts. There had been a battle here, but whether SG-1 had come out on top remained to be seen.

"Stay alert, people," he barked as they descended the steps, weapons readied, boots squelching into mud. The only sound was the drumming of rain on the plastic of his camouflage poncho.

"You think they're still on this planet, sir?" asked Lieutenant Johnson, scanning the area through the sight of his P90.

"I guess that's what we're here to find out. By the looks of this place, they were under some pretty heavy fire. Let's sweep the perimeter. Wade, check out the DHD, see if they dialed out. Bosco, stay with him."

Makepeace and Johnson headed for the tree line, splitting up to cover more ground, while Major Wade opened up the front of the DHD and plugged himself in.

It was Johnson who made the find. "Sir, we got bodies!" Makepeace's stomach dropped, but when he reached the lieutenant it was the steely gray armor of a Jaffa that glinted dully in the undergrowth.

"There's another one over there," said Johnson, nodding further into the wooded area.

That, at least, gave him some satisfaction. Whatever had happened to the team, they'd at least managed to take a few of the bastards down beforehand. "Well, let's see who SG-1 had a tangle with, huh?" Makepeace wedged his toe under the body and flipped it over. The dead Jaffa's sightless eyes stared at the sky, rain washing the mud from his pale face. Hunkering down, Makepeace brushed away the remaining dirt from the corpse's forehead.

"You recognize it, sir?"

Makepeace pursed his lips and shook his head. The tattoo was unfamiliar, a horned circle with a strange looking cross underneath. He pulled the tiny camera from the side pocket of his BDUs and snapped a shot. Let the experts back at the base take a look at it and figure out who they were dealing with. If SG-1 were being held captive, they'd need all the intel they could gather, and if this was a new snake on the block, they'd need far more than that.

As they made their way back to the gate, Makepeace scanned the area. The place was a washout, the rain having spoiled any real chance they might have had of picking up a trail, but there were spent bullet casings everywhere. Whatever had happened, the team had obviously been balls to the wall and Makepeace saw three possible outcomes.

First, SG-1 had been cut off from the gate and then taken prisoner by whatever snakehead had attacked them. If that was the case, then he didn't like the odds of finding where they'd been taken.

Second option: they'd dialed an address and made it through, but wherever they'd ended up it wasn't Earth. And given their current MIA status, they'd possibly landed in a situation that was just as hot as the one they'd escaped. Makepeace didn't much like that option either.

The last option was one he could work with: they'd dialed up, but had to take cover before they could reach the wormhole itself, which meant they were still in hiding somewhere nearby. But why not come out when the coast was clear and dial home?

He knew O'Neill and he knew what sort of a strategist he was. In fact, O'Neill and he were similar in many ways. Jack always sought the practical answer, not necessarily the one that conformed to the rules, but he was a man who got the job done, regardless. A fine leader and one for whom he'd always had a lot of respect. Who else could take a scientist, a civilian geek and a goddamned alien and turn them into a formidable unit?

Makepeace also knew that he wasn't the only one who was watching O'Neill as a potential asset — which just made it all the more important to get them back in one piece.

"Anything?" he asked Wade, who stood squinting at the hand-held unit he'd plugged into the front of the DHD.

"It's the darnedest thing, sir. As far as I can tell, the last address dialed was Earth."

"How is that possible? There was no incoming wormhole at the SGC."

Wade shrugged. "Maybe it skipped to another gate? Wouldn't be the first time. But if that's the case…"

Wade didn't need to finish his sentence. If SG-1 went through a wormhole that had skipped to some other random gate, they could be anywhere in the galaxy. How the hell would they have any hope of finding them? And if a Goa'uld had them, then the clock was most definitely ticking.

"Okay, people," Makepeace said, "there's nothing more to find here. Let's move out."

But as he turned to head up the steps to the gate his eye was caught by something lying in the mud. A USAF standard issue field dressing — and it was soaked in blood. Wherever SG-1 was, one of them was injured and bleeding badly.

The climb up the hillside was slow going. The mist made visibility difficult and often they had to backtrack on themselves after finding their path cut off by jutting rocks that had been hidden in the low light.

Teal'c took point, stopping frequently to ensure that Colonel O'Neill, upon whom Daniel Jackson was leaning heavily, had not fallen too far behind. Major Carter walked alongside Teal'c, taking regular soil readings.

"Radiation levels are dropping," she said at last. "Not much further and they'll be within safe parameters."

"The temperature is also dropping. We must take care not to climb too high."

Major Carter glanced behind her. "Yeah, we need to keep Daniel warm especially. I'm concerned about the blood he's lost."

It was true that their friend was looking ashen. The FastClot had stemmed the flow of blood from the wound, but he needed medical attention. Teal'c worried that his condition would worsen before they had discovered a route off this planet.

"Once we have established camp, I should return to the Stargate," he said. "The DHD may be buried beneath the rubble. My symbiote should prevent the radiation from affecting me." Major Carter nodded, but Teal'c could see that the issue troubled her. "You are not at fault for our current situation, Major," he said.

She gave a humorless laugh. "Try telling the colonel that."

Teal'c frowned. It was true that O'Neill had been unduly harsh on her since arriving on this world, but this was just one more aspect of the strange mood that had fallen over their commander since his return from Edora. "He is concerned. His words are not meant in earnest."

"Maybe not," she said, "but I just… I feel like this has been going on for a while. Ever since he got back, it's been different. *He's* been different."

"I too have noticed a difference in Colonel O'Neill. His behavior is not what it was."

"You have?" Major Carter seemed relieved at this, as if glad that she was not alone in her observations.

"I have wondered what could have brought about such a difference. Perhaps his time on Edora changed him in some way?"

Teal'c did not miss how Major Carter's shoulders sank. "Yes," she said. "That's what I was thinking too."

"Rest assured, however, he has faith in your abilities and would not judge you over something in which you are blameless."

She shrugged. "It doesn't matter now. All that matters is figuring out what brought us here so I can find a way home."

There was nothing Teal'c could say to refute that. Blameless or not, Major Carter would take the responsibility for getting them home upon her own shoulders; it was simply her way. "Perhaps there are people here who can help us."

She shook her head and looked around. "I don't think so, Teal'c. Look at this place. There's been some sort of devastating event. If there's any life on this planet, it could be hundreds, even thousands of miles away. It would take some serious exploration to get any idea of the geography. We can't even see the horizon. The planet could be vast. No, even if Daniel wasn't hurt, our best bet is to stick close to the gate."

"Carter!" Both Teal'c and the Major turned at O'Neill's call. "We gotta make camp soon. Daniel can't go much further."

By his side, Daniel Jackson stumbled on. "I'm fine, Jack," he said, though his pallor and pained expression told them otherwise.

"There is some level ground up ahead, O'Neill," said Teal'c. "A good place to camp if the radiation levels aren't too high."

They all looked at the major for confirmation. She nodded. "We're good, sir."

But as they dropped their packs on the ground and set up camp in sullen silence, Teal'c scanned the fog-shrouded barren landscape and knew they were anything but good.

It was hard to tell when the sun finally set; the gloom of the low hanging sky meant the switch from day to night was almost imperceptible. The only real thing that Daniel was aware of was pain and more pain. Despite his repeated claims that he was fine, the hole in his side burned and he'd have given just about anything to see the inside of the infirmary, Janet Fraiser standing by his bedside with an IV of some lovely morphine. That, it seemed, was not to be, and the best he could hope for was the improvised ministrations of Jack or Sam and whatever they had left in their field kits. Despite the severe chill of the air, he could feel the fever start to take hold of him and knew it wasn't good.

"How're you feeling?"

Daniel opened his eyes to find one of his interim nurses standing over him, one not quite as pretty as Janet and with a less pleasing bedside manner.

"Um, not the greatest I've ever felt, if I'm being honest." His throat was dry and his voice a croak.

Jack dropped to one knee by Daniel and started to unzip one side of the sleeping bag into which they'd bundled him before propping him against this rock. "Tent should be up in a few minutes and we'll get you where it's warmer. Let me take a look."

Daniel raised his arm and immediately regretted it, as waves of pain and nausea gripped him. He sucked in a breath and squeezed his eyes shut, trying not to throw up as Jack peeled back his dressing.

"The bleeding's stopped at least," he said, though Daniel could tell from his tone that there was still plenty to worry about.

"I'll be fine," he said. "I just need some sleep."

Jack caught his eye and nodded, both of them complicit in the lie. "Think you can handle another shot?" Jack asked, pulling a sealed hypo from one of the pockets of his BDUs.

"If it's something to take even the edge off, then you jab away."

As Jack stuck the needle in his side, Daniel took the opportunity to have a look at their surroundings, something he'd been too out of it to notice on the climb up. "Do you think we're safe here?"

Jack shrugged. "As safe as we can be, I guess. I haven't seen any sign of life at all. If Carter's right, and there was some sort of nuclear strike here, then it could be we're the only things breathing on this entire planet."

Truth be told, it was the lack of life that spooked Daniel the most. There wasn't even a wind blowing, just this interminable mist and the occasional snowfall that drifted, listless, from a bleak monochrome sky. This whole world had the feel of something spent, used up.

And Jack's current mood did nothing to alleviate that feeling.

"Tent's ready, sir," called Sam, and Jack acknowledged her with a brusque jerk of his chin. She turned away, but not before Daniel caught the look on her face.

"It wasn't her fault, you know," he said, as Jack helped him out of the sleeping bag and to his feet.

Jack didn't look at him. "She misdialed."

"You know she didn't."

"Well, the SGC sure needs a paintjob, don't ya think?"

Daniel swallowed against the rasp in his throat. He'd done too much talking, too much thinking. He wasn't up for an argument and the shot had started to kick in, dulling his senses. Sleep, that was what he needed, just let his eyes close for a little while. As Jack half carried him across the craggy hillside towards the tent, he could feel his mind swimming again. "It wasn't her fault," he repeated, though his words had started to sound a little slurred. "Something's... gone wrong. We're somewhere else... somewhere bad."

He was vaguely aware now of being inside the tent, Teal'c by his side re-zipping his sleeping bag, Jack's frowning face by the opening. And just before he lost consciousness once more, he looked beyond Jack, further down the hillside. There, cloaked by mist and drifting snow, he was sure he saw something: the silhouette of a silent, solitary figure. Watching.

Then his eyes closed and, for a while, he saw no more.

CHAPTER FIVE

IT WAS late and the base was quiet. Well, *quieter*. The SGC never slept, but the bustle of the day's duty shifts were over and only those who watched and waited through the night remained.

Hammond should have been long gone, but leaving the base when any of his people were in trouble was always impossible and, somehow, more so when it was SG-1. He admired all the officers and teams he had the privilege to command, but he couldn't deny that Colonel O'Neill's team held a special place in his heart. Maybe it was because they'd been the first to step through the gate; maybe it was because they'd given the most in service to the planet. Or maybe he just liked them. Whatever the reason, the thought of going home to his safe and comfortable house while his people were in trouble was anathema to everything he held dear. He simply couldn't do it.

SG-3 had reported back a couple of hours earlier, but with no good news. All Colonel Makepeace's team had found on P5X-104 were dead Jaffa, spent ammunition cartridges, and a bloody field dressing. Things weren't looking good for SG-1, but O'Neill's team had come back from worse than this and Hammond had learned over the past three years never to count them out. Not unless he saw the bodies, and sometimes not even then.

So he watched, waited and prayed for another SG-1 miracle.

He wasn't lacking work to keep him occupied during his long vigil — his in-tray was always glad of a little extra attention — but there was another pressing matter keeping him awake tonight, and it wasn't unrelated to the most recent disappearance of Colonel O'Neill.

The Tollan Curia required an update on the SGC's investigation into the theft of allied technology, and the only news he had to give High Chancellor Travell was bad. Both races — Tollan and Asgard — had made it clear that their relationship with

Earth was contingent on O'Neill uncovering Maybourne's mole within the SGC. How they might react to the colonel's disappearance was a question Hammond feared to answer.

Would they suspect SG-1 of complicity? Nonsense, of course, but the whole debacle had already damaged their trust in Stargate Command. And what if, God forbid, O'Neill didn't return at all? Would that mark the end of Earth's relationship with their allies? That prospect frightened him and he wasn't ashamed to admit it. Without their allies, they were extremely vulnerable.

The thought made him antsy and Hammond got up from his desk to pace over to the window that separated his office from the briefing room. He could just make out the arc of the Stargate in the gate room below, still and silent. Waiting, like the rest of them.

He didn't enjoy thinking about worst case scenarios, but in this job it came with the territory and he didn't shy away from it. If O'Neill didn't make it back, then Earth was in trouble. Period. And he took some of the responsibility for that himself. One man should not have been allowed to become so critical to the fate of the planet. And their alliances should not — could not — rest entirely on the shoulders of Colonel Jack O'Neill. More than that, the security of Earth could not depend entirely on those fragile alliances. It was untenable and it was something he was determined to change, no matter what had become of SG-1.

Struck by a thought, he walked over to the bookcase behind his desk, scanned the narrow spines, and pulled out a report. It was a proposal for a permanent off-world Alpha Site that would provide both operational support for the SGC's front line teams and a refuge of last resort in the event of enemy incursion. He flicked through the pages, reminding himself of the detail. O'Neill had written it over a year ago and it was a damn good piece of work that spelled out, in O'Neill's pithy style, the strategic and tactical necessity for a permanent off-world base. Hammond had been happy to sign off on it and to start the preliminary work on establishing the Alpha Site. They'd even got so far as locating a suitable planet and starting to consider personnel. Hammond had been minded to give O'Neill the command. He was more than ready for the challenge and Hammond had suspected that the colonel wouldn't be averse to a slight sidestep in chain of command.

But then the Pentagon had pulled the plug — for budgetary reasons — and the whole thing had been shelved.

It was difficult for men like him and O'Neill not to feel undermined by those kinds of decisions, made as they were by people so far away from the sharp end that they couldn't even begin to see the point. But that point was getting clearer to him by the day and he was under no illusion what it would mean for Earth if their relationship with their allies broke down, most especially with the Asgard. The truth was, without the Protected Planets Treaty, Earth was a sitting duck in a vast and hostile pond.

They'd grown complacent, Hammond realized. They'd relied too heavily on the protection of the Asgard and too deeply on O'Neill's ability to garner their trust. Now, with both those struts weakening, the whole edifice of Earth's security was teetering on the brink of collapse. And they had no Plan B.

"General?" Captain Austen popped his head around the door, making Hammond jump.

"Son, I thought you'd gone home hours ago."

"No, sir," Austen said. "Just catching up on some email, but I was about to leave if there's nothing else?"

"No, there's nothing else. Get yourself home."

The captain nodded, then said, "Ah, General, don't forget that High Chancellor Travell is expecting you to contact her tonight." He glanced at his watch. "The working day on Tollana starts at 0330 hours, mountain time, sir."

"Thank you, Captain," he said, repressing a smile. Keen as mustard, this one. "I'll be sure to contact the High Chancellor before I leave." Not that he was planning on leaving. Not that he knew what to tell her.

"Yes, sir," the captain said. "Major Lee is on duty in the control room tonight, sir. I've briefed him."

"Sounds like everything's in hand, Captain. I'll see you tomorrow."

When Austen had pulled the door shut behind him, Hammond sank back into his chair to think. He had to talk to Travell, of course, and he'd have to do it in person; this wasn't a conversation he could have in the middle of the control room. But he didn't want to travel to Tollana alone — he needed backup, someone else in his camp. But with SG-1 missing, who else could he bring? More importantly, who else could he trust? Someone inside the SGC was Maybourne's mole.

He ran through some possibilities, but one name came consistently at the top of the list: Colonel Robert Makepeace. He was a good man, a good soldier. Solid in the field and dedicated to Stargate Command and everything for which it stood. He was no Jack O'Neill, of course, but he was a damn fine officer and he'd pulled O'Neill's butt out of the fire more than once. And Hammond had to trust someone.

So, Makepeace it would have be and if the Curia didn't like it then they were out of luck. It wasn't that he distrusted the Tollan, but he'd certainly feel more comfortable with someone watching his back while he broke the bad news. If nothing else, they could discuss tactics.

With that decision made, he turned back to his in-tray. But before he could so much as reach for the next report, his phone rang. With none of his aides on duty, the call came straight through to his desk. It was Dr. Fraiser's number and he picked up immediately.

"What can I do for you, Doctor?"

"Sir," she said, "I have the results of the tests on the field dressing Colonel Makepeace retrieved from P5X-104."

Her tone of voice settled a heavy weight in his chest — this wasn't a conversation he wanted to have over the telephone either. "I'll be right up, doctor."

At that time of night the elevator ride to the infirmary didn't take long and Hammond was walking into Fraiser's office just a couple of minutes after she'd called. He wasn't surprised to see Colonel Makepeace already there, perched on one of the plastic chairs with his hair still damp from the shower.

"Sir," Makepeace said, getting to his feet.

Hammond waved away the formality. "As you were, Colonel. Thank you for coming so promptly. It's been a tiring day."

Makepeace shrugged. "Daresay I've not had the worst of it, sir."

On the other side of the desk, Fraiser sat with a single sheet of paper in front of her and a serious look on her face. Hammond took a seat. "Doctor, what have you got?"

Fraiser kept her fingers pressed lightly on the desk, taking a breath before she slid the paper toward Hammond. "Well, for a start," she said, "I can tell you that the blood on the dressing belongs to Dr. Jackson."

Hammond gave a curt nod. There'd been a chance that his team had been treating someone else, but it had always been more likely that one of their own had been wounded. "Is there anything else?"

"Not much," she admitted. "From the volume of blood and the fact that the dressing had been removed — I assume in order to replace it — it looks like a severe wound, possibly arterial. I can't say for sure, of course; there are a number of reasons why he might bleed heavily."

None of which were good, Hammond supposed. "Very well. Thank you, doctor."

"Sir?" Makepeace shifted in his chair; he looked too big for the small room, like he was chafing at being so tightly confined. "It's significant that they were changing a wound dressing in front of the Stargate. O'Neill would never do that if they were about to gate home."

Hammond couldn't argue with him. "Then the question is, if they weren't about to gate home, where were they about to go?"

Makepeace scratched his head. "Maybe they were captured, sir, and held there while the Jaffa decided what to do with them? If Dr. Jackson was wounded they might have taken the opportunity to change his dressing." He frowned. "There was a lot of spent ordinance there, General. Whatever happened, they put up one hell of a fight at the gate."

"And yet," Hammond said, "when your team examined the DHD they found that the last address dialed was Earth."

"That's correct, sir."

"But the gate here didn't open."

"I can't explain it, sir. Maybe something happened before it could connect? There was a lot of damage close to the gate, some impacts that look like they came from a staff-cannon or a glider. Maybe that interfered with the wormhole? It wouldn't be the first time we've seen something like that."

"No," Hammond agreed, "it wouldn't." He thought for a moment. "Colonel, can you identify which Goa'uld we're dealing with here?"

"I made a note of the," he gestured toward his forehead, "marking on the bodies, sir. I didn't recognize it, but I've taken it up to Dr. Rothman and he's looking into it."

It was a pity, Hammond thought, that Dr. Jackson wasn't here to look into it himself. Instead, it was his blood that had been spilled on a distant world and Hammond's job to get him home. He sighed, feeling helpless in the face of so many dead ends. "Then we're at an impasse," he said. "Colonel, do you have any suggestions? I'm open to ideas."

Makepeace sat forward in his seat. "Send my team back to '104, sir. We only searched the vicinity of the Stargate, but if we headed all the way out to the site Dr. Jackson wanted to investigate we might find out more. It's even possible they're being held on the planet. We didn't find any evidence of Goa'uld transport rings being used. Either that or they've taken refuge somewhere and ended up cut off from the gate."

"That's a good idea, Colonel," he said, although he'd be sending a different team. He needed Makepeace to travel with him to Tollana.

He was about to say as much when Dr. Fraiser interrupted. "General, how about contacting the Tok'ra? They're bound to recognize the Jaffa insignia and they'll know a lot more about it than Dr. Rothman — with all due respect to the doctor."

Makepeace snorted. "The Tok'ra? Come on, Doc, they only help us when it's in their own interest. One of our teams going missing won't mean anything to them."

Hammond didn't appreciate his dismissive tone and Fraiser's eyes took on a distinctly flinty expression. "I'm sure it'll mean something to General Carter, Colonel."

Makepeace shrugged, but remained unconvinced. "The general's only one of them, Doc. I'm just saying — I've never known a Tok'ra do anything without an ulterior motive. And there's nothing in this for them." He looked over at Hammond. "It might be worth asking them, General, but I wouldn't hold my breath waiting for an answer. For something this important, we're better off relying on our own resources."

"Really, Colonel?" The chilly look in Fraiser's eye belied her mild tone. "Even when our own resources aren't adequate to the task?"

"They're good enough," Makepeace said, getting to his feet. He was doing a poor job of masking his irritation. "One thing you learn out there is to trust no one but your own people. It's the only way you'll get home alive." He towered over the doctor as he spoke, but if he was attempting to intimidate her, he was out of luck. Fraiser simply regarded him with a cool, appraising gaze and it was the colonel who looked away first. Glancing at Hammond he said, "Sir, permission to prep for a return mission to P5X-104?"

Hammond considered the request for a moment, taking in the man's hard face and harder attitude. Unfortunately, he couldn't ignore the alarm bells that had started ringing in the back of his mind and he realized that, for all his admirable qualities, Colonel Makepeace was not the man to take into his confidence about the Maybourne situation. In fact, Hammond was forced to admit that he probably shouldn't trust any of his off-world teams. However unlikely it might be, each of them had had the opportunity to steal technology from their allies.

Swallowing down the sudden sour taste in his mouth, he shook his head. "Permission denied, Colonel. I'll send SG-2."

"What? But, sir —"

"Robert, your team has just finished two back-to-back missions. You're all exhausted. Go home and get some rest and report back here for 1000 hours tomorrow."

"General Hammond —"

"That's an order, Colonel."

Makepeace's jaw clenched and he straightened. "Yes sir," he said with obvious reluctance. He threw Fraiser a dark look, and then turned back to Hammond. "SG-3 will do whatever it takes to bring them home, General."

"I know, son. Now go get some rest."

After Makepeace had gone, Hammond sat for a while in Fraiser's silent office. She was staring at the closed door, her thoughts drifting far away. SG-1 were her friends too, Hammond reminded himself. She and Major Carter were especially close, but her history with the colonel went right back to the beginning of the Stargate program. It was sometimes easy to forget that Doctor Janet Fraiser was one of the indomitable rocks upon which Stargate Command had been built. He respected her, admired her, and valued her judgment more than almost anyone else on the base.

Maybe sensing his eyes on her, Fraiser shook herself out of her thoughts and looked over at him. "Despite all his bravado, sir," she said, her tone almost apologetic, "I hope Colonel Makepeace is right. I hope he finds them."

"So do I." Hammond gave a thin smile. "Makepeace is a

good man, doctor, but I'm afraid his manner can sometimes be a little… abrasive."

"Ah," Fraiser said with a smile of her own. "Abrasive — that's what it's called." After a pause, she added, "For what it's worth, General, I think he's wrong about the Tok'ra. They may be stand-offish at times, but I believe they'd help us if they could — especially Martouf and General Carter."

He nodded. "I agree."

"And despite what the colonel may think, we can't survive out there alone. Even Colonel O'Neill admits that, and you know what he thinks about the Tok'ra."

Hammond smiled at the picture she was painting. O'Neill had never been backward in coming forward with his criticism of their allies, but he was prepared to give them credit too when it was deserved. Maybe his frank honesty, Hammond reflected, was why they trusted him.

"Well," Fraiser said, getting her feet, "with your permission, sir, I'll get on with my rounds." She nodded toward the two occupied beds in the infirmary. "I've got half of SG-5 in with a nasty case of bacterial gastroenteritis."

"From their last mission?" He didn't remember hearing about it.

The doctor gave a rueful smile. "Leftover Chinese takeout, sir."

Hammond chuckled. "I guess not all the dangers are to be found off-world, doctor."

"No sir," she said, but the smile slipped from her face. "Only most of them."

He nodded as his thoughts also returned to SG-1. "I'll be sure to keep you apprised of any progress."

"Thank you, General. I appreciate that."

He stood up and headed to the door, but he'd only just grasped the handle when a thought struck him out of the blue. It was perfectly formed and perfectly right and he wondered why it hadn't occurred to him before. "Doctor," he said, turning back around. "How would you feel about taking a little trip?"

Fraiser cocked her head, curious. "A trip, sir?"

"To Tollana," he said. "I've a feeling I'll need a friend by my side."

CHAPTER SIX

"SAM?"

Daniel's voice roused her from a light doze and she was awake at once. She never slept deeply off-world, and even less so when the situation was this precarious. It was dark in the tent, but much warmer than outside with the three of them crowded in together. Daniel lay in the middle, inside his own and the colonel's sleeping bags, Teal'c lay flat on his back and unmoving on one side of him and Sam had been curled up on the other. She could hear the slow, deep breaths that meant Teal'c had entered *kel'no'reem,* and moved quietly so as not to disturb him.

Sitting up, she pushed her sleeping bag down to her waist and reached over to find Daniel's forehead. The colonel had ordered them to observe light discipline, so she had to make her way by touch alone.

"I'm here," she said quietly. His skin felt fevered, which sent a coil of disquiet spiraling up into her throat. On the plus side, at least he hadn't gone into full-fledged shock. "You want some water?"

She could feel him nod under her hand, so found the canteen — which was now less than half full — and held it to his lips. He took a few thirsty sips and then lay back down with a hiss of pain.

"Bad?"

"Um, yeah."

She squeezed his shoulder. "Hang in there."

"I'm hanging."

She smiled at his quiet stoicism. He'd always been like this, right from day one when he was still reeling from the loss of his wife. "You want me to ask Colonel O'Neill about a morphine shot?"

There was a rustle of movement as Daniel shook his head.

"Save it for later."

She knew what he meant, of course — later, when the pain was more intense. "We'll be home by then," she said, smoothing her hand over his forehead.

He made a soft sound that might have been a laugh. "Optimist."

"Try to get some sleep," she said, stroking her fingers up into his hair. She remembered her mom doing the same for her as a child and felt a sting of old, old pain.

They were quiet for a while, the sound of Teal'c's steady breathing filling the tent. Outside, she could hear the colonel moving about on watch. He was probably trying to keep warm. They'd not lit a fire, for obvious reasons, so there was nothing to do but keep moving. She peeked under her Velcro watch cover at the glowing face — twenty minutes until she had to relieve him. No point in trying to go back to sleep. Not that she'd been sleeping.

"Sam?" Daniel again.

"Shh," she soothed him, stroking his head.

"No, Sam, there's something…" She looked down and saw his eyes glint in the almost total darkness. "I… I think I saw something, before."

Her hand stopped moving. "What kind of thing?"

"A person," he said. "I thought I saw someone out there, watching us, right before I passed out."

"Right before you passed out?"

He caught the skeptical tone of her voice. "No, I'm sure it was real," he persisted. "A girl in the mist."

"Okay," she said, stroking his head again. "But we did a thorough recon of the area, Daniel. There's not much here."

He scrubbed a hand across his face, brushing her fingers. "I know what I saw."

"Okay," she said again. "I'll tell the colonel. We'll keep our eyes open."

"Girl in the mist," he muttered, more drowsy. "I saw her…"

Sam sat with him a few minutes longer, waiting until he'd

drifted down into a feverish sleep. Then she struggled out of her sleeping bag, leaving it for the colonel to use, and crawled to the door of the tent and unzipped it slowly, quietly. She shoved her feet into her boots, tied the laces tight and slipped her tac vest back on, as much for the additional warmth as the protection.

Closing the tent, she picked up her weapon and glanced around in search of the colonel. They'd camped just into the tree line, looking down over what she'd named in her head as the Stargate Valley. Before the light had failed she'd still been able to see the gate in the distance, and beyond it she'd glimpsed a gunmetal gray strip of water at the far end of the valley. Not the sea, but maybe an estuary of some kind. Behind the tent, hills rose up high but not quite into mountains. It was all lost in the darkness now, though. If this planet had a moon, its light wasn't visible tonight.

They'd found no fresh water, but she'd rigged one of the tarps to catch whatever snow or rain fell overnight, although she wasn't entirely sure it would be uncontaminated. She crouched and peered inside the tarp. There was already a thin covering of slushy water. She'd test it in the morning to see if it was safe to drink.

At least the ground here was free of the ashy fallout that had gathered in the valley. She'd insisted they all brushed as much of it off their clothes and belongings as possible as soon as they'd left the valley and started heading up to higher ground. Colonel O'Neill had grumbled about the delay, but only half-heartedly — almost as if he was going through the motions. He knew the danger as well as anyone.

Once they'd made camp, they'd all changed into dry clothes and packed their wet — and probably contaminated — clothes away into their packs. Sam had been keen to just discard them, but Colonel O'Neill had insisted on keeping them. An extra layer could be the difference between life and death.

Standing up again, she glanced around, but had to take a few steps away from the tent before she saw the colonel. It was marginally lighter outside, the thin snow cover reflecting back what little brightness the sky had to offer, and she could just make him out sitting on one of the rocks that littered the hillside, gazing out in the direction of the dark water.

Bracing herself for a brusque reception — he was always brusque these days — she walked toward him making enough noise that he'd hear her coming. It was never a good idea to startle an armed man on watch. "Sir?" she said, when she was close enough to talk quietly. "Time to turn in."

He didn't move, didn't respond right away. Then he said, "I thought I saw a light."

"Where?"

He pointed out toward the black horizon. "Way, way out. And then it was gone."

She took a few steps closer, the icy air making her nose run. She sniffed. At least the snow had stopped falling, although that wouldn't do much for her attempt to collect drinking water. "What do you think it was?"

"No idea. Boat? Could have been anything."

"But if you're right, sir, it means the planet could be inhabited. At least, part of it."

"Inhabited by the people who nuked the gate."

She conceded the point without argument and instead said, "Sir, Daniel told me he thinks he saw someone."

That got his attention. He turned around, looking at her from beneath the bill of his hat. She couldn't see his face at all in the shadows. "When?"

"Right before he passed out."

"Ah."

"But he's convinced it was real," she said. "And if you saw a light… ?"

"Teal'c didn't find any tracks," he said, getting to his feet and stamping his feet, trying to knock some heat into them. "Teal'c's pretty thorough."

"I know, sir. But I told him I'd tell you."

He nodded. "How is he?"

No good news there. "He's still got a fever, sir. I'm afraid he's developing an infection."

"Yup," the colonel said, tight and clipped with concern. "I gave him an antibiotic shot, but God knows what kind of alien bugs were on that planet — or this one."

"Yes sir."

"He needs to be in hospital."

"I know."

He turned, kicking irritably at the rock he'd been sitting on. "God, we need to get out of here."

Sam felt his accusation hanging there in the air between them. *You misdialed, Major. This is your fault.*

There was a time, before Edora, when he'd never have been so unjust, and she couldn't help wondering if he blamed her for dragging him home when he didn't want to leave. Was he punishing her? It wasn't like him, but the colonel hadn't been himself since he got back and that was the only explanation she could find. She just wished he'd talk about it, but of course he never would.

"This can't be easy for you, sir," she said, taking a sideways approach to the subject. "I mean, it's your first off-world mission since Edora and we're stuck. Again."

"Some dumb luck, huh?"

Gritting her teeth, she decided to face it head on. If he was pissed she'd brought him home then she'd rather he told her so upfront. Anything was better than this bristling tension. "Sir, I'm sorry if —"

"No, *I'm* sorry, Carter," he interrupted, still scuffing at the rock with the toe of his boot. "I'm sorry I jumped to conclusions about what went wrong today."

"Oh."

"I kinda bit your head off back there."

"Um," she said, taking a moment to switch tracks. "It's okay, sir. You're worried about Daniel. We all are."

He nodded. "Yeah."

She took a step closer, shoving her cold hands into her jacket pockets. "Sir, I've been thinking about it, actually, and I honestly don't believe I misdialed."

"Okay." He threw her a sideways look. "You got a better theory?"

"Yes sir." She'd been pondering it as they walked up out of the valley, running through the problem over and over. If she hadn't misdialed, then what had happened? She thought she had the answer. "Sir, just at the moment we left P5X-104, the Death Gliders made another pass. They were firing at the gate as we went through."

He looked at her and she could see comprehension dawning in his eyes. "You're thinking just like Antarctica?"

"Yes sir. I think the energy transfer caused by the impact might have caused the wormhole to skip to another Stargate."

"This doesn't look much like Area 51."

"No, but the wormhole could have skipped to another gate, one close to Earth within the Stargate network."

He shook his head and pulled his cap back on. "Close to Earth, you say?"

She knew what he was thinking. "Sir, I realize that 'close to Earth' is a relative term —"

"Without a DHD, Carter, we might as well be on the other side of the galaxy."

She frowned, studying him for a moment and trying to decide whether he really didn't get it or was just pretending to be obtuse. But he only played dumb when there was someone to misdirect, and he wasn't about to convince *her* he was stupid. Which meant he really didn't get it. "Sir, you do realize that General Hammond will be looking for us?"

He fixed her with an unreadable look. "Of course I do."

"So… ?" she said, testing to see if he was following her logic. "So?"

"Sir, if I'm right, the gate will have connected with Earth

before the energy from the weapons strike caused the matter stream to skip. So the SGC will know we tried to dial in. And if they reach the same conclusion about what's happened, which is very likely given that we've encountered this exact scenario before, then they'll narrow the search to the planets between P5X-104 and Earth. Which means it won't take them long to find us. Maybe just a couple of days."

"Lots of 'ifs' in there, Carter."

She shook her head, but didn't answer; she didn't know what to say to him. What had happened to the indomitable Colonel O'Neill who never gave up and never questioned the capacity of his team — or the SGC — to bring their people home? She wondered if he was still on Edora, because this wasn't him, this wasn't him at all.

Maybe he could see what she was feeling, because an expression flickered across his face that she couldn't reconcile with the officer she knew. It looked like self-doubt or indecision. "Carter," he sighed, "this whole situation sucks."

"Yes sir."

"Not just —" He broke off and shook his head. "We *really* need to get home."

"We will, sir," she said, surprised by his vehemence. "General Hammond won't give up on us. We don't leave our people behind, remember?"

"Yeah," he said, but he didn't look any happier. "I remember."

"Do you?" She didn't meant to sound pointed, but it had apparently only taken him three months on Edora to give up on them.

He skewered her with a sharp look. "What's that supposed to mean, Major?"

"Nothing, sir."

"Nothing?"

"No sir." She looked away, squinting out toward the horizon — a slight hint of gray was emerging through the murk of mist. "You should get some rest, Colonel."

He was silent, but she could feel his eyes drilling into her and she braced herself for a reprimand. But he said nothing and after a while moved past her toward the tent. She let out the breath she hadn't realized she was holding.

A couple of steps behind her, the colonel stopped. "Carter?"

She turned. "Sir?"

He looked at her as if he might be about to say something reassuring, something more like the old Colonel O'Neill. But in the end he just said, "When it's light, make coffee. We all need something warm in our bellies."

"Yes sir."

With another nod he turned back to the tent and she turned back to studying the horizon. Soon she heard the tent unzip and zip up again, and she was alone with her thoughts on this cold, bleak planet.

She hoped the sun rose quickly here; she was yearning for a little warmth.

The ritual of *kel'no'reem* was beneficial on many levels. Rest and restoration of the body was but one advantage. A more profound gain, if practiced with discipline, was a heightened level of self-perception that allowed a great deal of insight into one's own motivations. A Jaffa so trained could not be surprised by his response to any situation, and the self-command thus gained was of incalculable value, not only in battle but in many other walks of life.

Teal'c had long observed that there were many among the Tau'ri who would benefit from the meditative discipline of *kel'no'reem* — O'Neill first among them. He had suggested this once, but his attempt at tutoring O'Neill in the art had proven… challenging. And, ultimately, futile.

Rising out of the deepest levels of meditation, Teal'c was slowly allowing consciousness to return when O'Neill crawled into the tent, bristling with tension. Teal'c, in his heightened state of awareness, could feel it as surely as the static charge of an open wormhole.

It was a pity that O'Neill had proven so resistant to the calming art of *kel'no'reem*, for this aura of unease had surrounded him almost from the moment Teal'c had first seized his hand through the rocky surface of Edora, and had only grown more intense since their return to Earth. Its cause, Teal'c could not guess, but its effect was evident.

O'Neill doubted himself, and increasingly, Major Carter and Daniel Jackson doubted him. It was a dangerous position for a commander and Teal'c was surprised that O'Neill, whose ability as a warrior he valued second only to Master Bra'tac, would allow such a situation to develop, let alone endure.

He was minded to challenge him about his behavior, but was hesitant to do so until they had returned to Earth. It would do no good to provoke a confrontation here, where all their lives depended upon cohesion.

At his side, Daniel Jackson stirred, feverish. His condition was a matter of great concern and it was his care that must be their first priority.

"Jack… ?"

"Hey."

"Are you touching my head?"

There was a moment's silence. "I'm checking your temperature."

"I've got a fever."

"I know. Go to sleep."

"Yeah…" He hissed a little as he moved. "Turns out that's not so easy with a hole in your side."

O'Neill shuffled about, getting into the sleeping bag and settling down to rest. "I can't give you morphine yet," he said. "You have to stay with us a little longer. We might need to move again soon."

"I know."

There was another silence. Teal'c opened his eyes and, through the thin walls of the tent, he began to see a faint light that promised dawn.

After a while, Daniel Jackson spoke again, his voice containing that slight teasing edge it often did when talking to O'Neill. "You know, Sam was stroking my hair earlier, to help me get to sleep…"

But O'Neill did not rise to the bait as once he might. He simply said, "Good for her. Now go to sleep."

A longer time passed, the walls of the tent slowly becoming visible, gray shadows among gray shadows. Teal'c let his eyes close again, hoarding his energy against the day to come.

"Jack?"

O'Neill sighed. "What?"

"You're being pretty hard on her, you know."

"Daniel—"

"I'm just saying—you're being hard on Sam."

O'Neill did not answer immediately, but Teal'c could sense the way he lay tense and unmoving. "Carter's an Air Force major, Daniel. She can take it."

"Yes, but I don't understand why—"

"Daniel, stop."

Another silence, this one brittle. "I just wish you'd tell me what's wrong."

"What's wrong," O'Neill snapped, "is that you're hurt, we're stuck in the backend of nowhere with no way to get home, and I need to— *We* really need to get back. That's what's wrong."

"We both know there's something else," Daniel Jackson said, sounding weary and defeated. "But if you don't want to talk about—"

"What I *want*," O'Neill said, "is half an hour's sleep. So just shut the hell up, will you?"

Daniel Jackson said no more, but Teal'c could hear him moving and shifting in pain. Teal'c did not think all his discomfort was caused by the injury he carried.

CHAPTER SEVEN

THE pristine gardens and immaculate walkways that surrounded the Curia building on Tollana did nothing to settle General Hammond's spirits as he and Dr. Fraiser were led from the Stargate to their summit with the High Council and the Asgard. He knew that the news he brought would not be welcome, but he saw no other way to deal with the situation other than being completely forthright. Deceit was what had gotten them into this situation, and where he came from a man was judged by his honor and his sincerity. His father had always said that a man who couldn't bear to hear the truth wasn't a man worth trusting. It didn't make the task ahead any more appealing, however. He gripped the handle of his briefcase, hoping that his alternative tactic would not be in vain.

He could sense that Janet was just as uneasy as him, but she said nothing as they were led to a large, comfortably furnished lounge area and advised that they would be summoned when the summit was due to begin. As the door closed behind the young Tollan representative, Janet let out a breath and sat down on one of the low couches.

"Thank you for agreeing to accompany me, Dr. Fraiser," said Hammond. "I know this isn't the best of off-world excursions."

Janet shook her head. "I'm glad you felt you could trust me enough to brief me on what's been happening, General. I just find it hard to believe that we're in this situation. That some of our own people could be responsible for this. Maybe I'm just being naïve."

Hammond sat down across from her. "In my experience, there tend to be objectionable elements at all levels of the government and military, no matter how hard we try and weed them out. I suppose I feel more than a little responsible that it happened on my watch."

"You're not at fault, sir. I think we all prefer to think the best of our colleagues. And personally, I can't say I've been suspicious of anyone at the SGC. Either the Tollan and Asgard are wrong… or the rogue personnel are very good at their job of blending in."

"Exactly how good is what Colonel O'Neill was supposed to find out. But now…" Hammond trailed off. But now… but *what* now? He had nothing else to offer on that point and, by his watch, it was a question he would have to answer in a little over ten minutes.

"You're not so sure?"

He was about to say no, he wasn't sure, that it was ridiculous that their allies were resting the fate of the whole planet on their trust of just one man — even if that man were Jack O'Neill. But this was neither the time nor the place. It was down to him and Dr. Fraiser to represent Earth and they had to demonstrate that they were in support of this operation if they were to salvage anything from the alliance with the Tollan and Asgard. His concerns could wait.

The door opened and their Tollan guide stepped through. The young man couldn't have been more than twenty. "General Hammond, Dr. Fraiser, you may follow me now. The Curia is about to commence."

"Some hospitality," muttered Janet, as they were led from the room. "Do they use interns to greet all their interplanetary allies?"

Hammond couldn't help but agree with her. This whole exercise felt as cold and clinical as the gleaming white corridor down which they were led to the Curia chamber. The atmosphere within the room did nothing to alleviate his anxiety.

As a newly promoted Brigadier General during the age of Perestroika and Glasnost, he'd sat in on many diplomatic meetings between US and Soviet ambassadors and military representatives. On the surface, the purpose of those meetings had been to end the mistrust and menace engendered by the Cold

War, to strengthen new relationships and put aside grievances. But always, *always*, beneath the veneer of diplomacy lurked the ugly suspicion of old battles: handshakes above the table and loaded guns below. It was that same suspicion that permeated the Curia.

"General Hammond, Dr. Fraiser," said High Chancellor Travell, not rising from her seat on the dais. "Thank you for agreeing to our request for a meeting."

Resisting the urge to point out that it was less of a request and more of a summons, Hammond said, "It's my pleasure, High Chancellor. I just hope that we can move forward in resolving the issues at hand."

"That too is our hope, General Hammond," said another voice. "Please know that we are most glad to see you here."

Hammond turned to find Thor also seated behind the dais, flanked by two other Asgard representatives. For the first time since he arrived on Tollana, Hammond felt a modicum of relief. He'd worried about who the Asgard might send as their representative, but the presence of Thor, whom he considered a true friend of the SGC and of Earth, bolstered his hope that the meeting would not end in disaster after all.

He and Fraiser took their seats and the proceedings began.

"We are disappointed that Colonel O'Neill is not here with you, General. We had hoped to speak with him before the summit. I hope he is still committed to the investigation?" asked Travell.

"We have encountered a setback in that respect, High Chancellor. It's my unfortunate task to inform you that Colonel O'Neill, along with SG-1, have been missing in action for two days. We have launched a full search and rescue but, as I'm sure you understand, this is no small task. Our enemies are many."

There was silence. The Tollan officials exchanged looks that made Hammond's blood boil and beside him Fraiser shifted in her seat. He glanced over at Thor, who said, "I am truly sorry to hear such news, General Hammond. Colonel O'Neill and his team are nothing if not resourceful. I am confident they will find a way back to Earth."

"We are also most concerned to hear the news of SG-1's disappearance, General," said Travell. "We hope your search for them proves fruitful."

"Thank you, High Chancellor," replied Hammond, although he doubted their sympathies were entirely unselfish.

"Can we take it that your investigation into your people is on hold while this search continues?"

"It seems we have little choice in that regard," said Hammond, trying to ignore the way she'd said 'your people', as if all of humanity had been judged by the Tollan and found wanting. "Both yourselves and the Asgard have stipulated that no one other than Colonel O'Neill may conduct the investigation," he continued. "But, under the circumstances, I would like to request that you reconsider that condition." He withdrew a pale blue manila folder from his briefcase; a card to be played which he hoped would at least prolong the game. He looked around the Curia, towards Thor, his best hope of gaining the agreement of the room. "There are several people under my command whom I'd like to offer for consideration–"

"Our judgment on that matter has not changed, General. No one but O'Neill will be acceptable to carry out the mission." This came from one of the other Tollan officials, a man whose face was not familiar to Hammond. The arrogant disdain which he conveyed in just a few words, however, was entirely recognizable.

"My government is just as eager to find these criminals as you are," he said. "But with this restriction, you're making it very difficult."

"Might I remind you how much is at stake for our planets, General Hammond?" said the nameless Tollan, leaning forward in his seat, his voice rising. "For many generations we took great steps to ensure that our technology was protected, yet within a short time of treating with Earth we find ourselves in the position of having that which we have defended, often at the cost of our lives, stolen from beneath our noses. And you *dare* to tell us that we are making this difficult?"

High Chancellor Travell turned to her fellow official and made a gesture, just a slight movement of her hand, but enough to calm him. "I'm sure General Hammond is fully aware of what is at stake, Chancellor Morrel. Let us remember that this is not a Triad and accusations have no place here."

Hammond closed his eyes and took his own calming breath. In truth, this was becoming more like a trial by the second, except that he and Dr. Fraiser were sorely underrepresented. "I can assure you, Chancellor, that Earth comprehends the stakes entirely. If, as a result of these thefts, we are excluded from the Protected Planets Treaty…" At this he looked meaningfully at the Asgard, who remained silent. "Then we have much more to lose than a few gadgets."

The Tollan stiffened, offended by his flippant tone.

He spread his hands in apology. "All I'm asking is that you allow someone else to investigate this crime," he said. "Hell, I'll do it myself if you'll let me."

But Morrel only shook his head. "Our word on the matter is final," said the Chancellor, eyebrows raised to forestall further challenge.

Hammond tensed his jaw. "Then we have a problem."

"Yes, General. We do."

And that's when he knew he was beaten, because those words came from the Asgard to Thor's right — and Thor said nothing to contradict him.

Just like that his trump card was tossed on the floor, rendered useless.

Janet could feel her hackles rising the moment she entered the Curia chamber. As honored and flattered as she was to know that General Hammond considered her worthy of his trust and of handling this mission, she was a doctor, not a diplomat. Her game face extended as far as her bedside manner, and even then she knew that sometimes you had to be just a little bit ruthless to make sure the patient took his medicine. The Tollan had always struck her as a people who didn't like being told when they needed their medicine.

The general was much better at this than her — all part of the job description, she supposed — so she'd been content to offer silent moral support and let him do the talking. She suspected that anything she had to say on the subject might end up causing an interplanetary incident.

Nevertheless, even General Hammond now seemed on the brink of losing his cool.

He jabbed a finger at the folder in front of him, pressing it down right in the middle of the SGC logo. "The people named in this file, I trust them implicitly. I would trust them with the lives of every member of Stargate Command. Hell, I would trust them with the lives of my *family*. If you can't take my word on that, then I don't see where we can go from here."

"Your word is not the issue, General Hammond," said the Asgard seated next to Thor. Even his serene voice had started to grate on Janet's nerves, though she knew they were their best hope of salvaging anything from this summit. "But you must understand that our prime goal as a race is our genetic survival."

Suddenly, Janet found she couldn't remain silent. "Isn't that the goal of every race? We *all* want to survive."

Thor turned towards her, but his shiny black gaze gave away nothing. If he disapproved of her interruption, he gave no outward sign. "Forgive me, Dr. Fraiser, but I believe Tyr is correct. My own observations of humanity indicate that you do not fully consider the future of your species. Often, you have demonstrated that other principles take precedence over survival. Principles such as friendship, or the love one human feels for another. On Earth, these can often be given value above life itself. And, just as often, the selfish needs of the few take precedence over the good of all."

Janet had no choice but to agree. "Yes, of course that's true, but that doesn't devalue our worth as a species. It doesn't mean we can't be trusted."

"Of course it doesn't," said Tyr. "But it does mean that often personal loyalties can cloud your judgment. How can you be sure that those you believe you can trust haven't succumbed to those selfish needs? For the Asgard, genetic survival is all. It is everything, not just of our own species, but of every species. Science guarantees survival, and so the science must be held above all else. We are facing great threats in our galaxy, Dr. Fraiser. We cannot risk our technology being compromised."

It was hopeless. Between the cold arrogance of the Tollan and the simple mathematical logic of the Asgard, there was no way she and Hammond had a chance of convincing this counsel to let them continue the investigation without Colonel O'Neill. But there was another solution, and Hammond had clearly thought of that too.

"Then help us find SG-1. They're out there somewhere, but our attempts to trace them have been fruitless so far. With your help —"

"That's out of the question, General," said the High Chancellor. "Given current relations between Tollana and Earth, any sharing of technology would contravene every statute in our Charter of Government. We are already occupying a very gray area of our law by meeting with you today."

The general spread his hands, clearly just as exasperated as Janet, and turned to the Asgard. "Thor?"

"I am sorry, General Hammond, but as Tyr has said, we face other threats in our galaxy. We simply do not have the resources to help with a search for SG-1."

"So you won't help us find SG-1, but no one other than O'Neill is acceptable to you. Will you at least allow us the time to conduct a thorough search ourselves?"

Before either the Tollan or Asgard could answer, there was a knock at the door and the young guide who had brought them here entered and approached High Chancellor Travell. General Hammond turned to Janet, using the momentary distraction as a chance to regroup. She couldn't remember the last time she had seen him so somber.

"I'm afraid we're fighting a losing battle here, doctor," he said, glancing over to where the Tollan were deep in conversation.

"I don't understand why they're so being so unrelenting. Don't they understand that we're trying to help them?"

"The Tollan have never been the easiest of bedfellows. It's taken years of negotiation to establish any solid kind of relationship with them, and now I'm afraid all that hard work is being unraveled by the actions of a few." Despite his obvious frustration at the current impasse, General Hammond still seemed inclined to give them the benefit of the doubt, although Janet wasn't sure she could be so magnanimous. "Neither the Tollan nor the Asgard need to answer for their actions," he reminded her. "They haven't committed any crime."

"And neither have we, General!" Janet struggled to keep her voice down. "Travell said herself that this isn't a Triad. So why do I feel like we're being judged and made to defend ourselves?"

"Because whoever is responsible for this is one of us, and we are responsible for them. Until we get SG-1 back, and O'Neill can find out who is doing this, then all of Earth will be held accountable, no matter how much we might dispute that fact."

"And the Asgard? I would have expected Thor at least to have our back."

At that, Hammond frowned and looked over her shoulder at where Thor and his people sat. "Yes," he murmured, "I'm concerned about that myself. This threat he and Tyr have mentioned, I wonder..."

Before he could say anymore, High Chancellor Travell called the summit to order, having apparently finished whatever business was important enough to warrant the impromptu interruption.

"High Chancellor," said Hammond, his mask of diplomacy in place once more, "Dr. Fraiser and I have discussed your comments on the matter at hand, and we fully understand both your and the Asgard's position. We would like to offer you our full assurances that we will commit every resource to the search and rescue of SG-1. I'm confident that Colonel O'Neill will be back and ready to continue his investigation very soon."

Travell's expression, if sober before was now downright severe. "I'm afraid the situation is no longer as simple as that, General Hammond. SG-1 went missing two days ago, you say?"

Hammond nodded, but his face echoed the feeling of dread that had dropped like a stone into Janet's gut.

"Well," continued Travell, "we have a report of yet another technology theft from a Tollan outpost on one of our nearby planets. Less than two days ago. Perhaps SG-1 is not so guiltless as you would have us believe?"

CHAPTER EIGHT

DAWN broke on a morning not dissimilar from the preceding day. A few flakes of snow drifted down from a disconsolate sky and the air felt sharp and chill as Teal'c left the warmth of the tent. He drew in a deep breath and stretched his arms and back, shaking his muscles loose.

Major Carter looked up from where she crouched near a small fire, feeding a few sticks into the flames. "Hey Teal'c," she said with a wan smile. "Get some rest?"

"I did."

She nodded toward the fire. "The colonel wanted coffee and I figured we should save the Sterno for emergencies." She held out her hands toward the growing flames. "The heat's welcome too."

"It is prudent to conserve our supplies," Teal'c agreed. "Have you conducted an inventory, Major Carter?"

She rose to her feet, keeping one eye on the burgeoning fire. "We've got about three days of food, a week on short rations. But water might be a problem if the snow's contaminated. Our radios should last at least a week, though, if we limit their use to emergencies. I figure we'll just hole up here until we see the gate open. We're still within radio range if the SGC try to contact us via the MALP."

He raised an eyebrow in surprise at her confidence. "You expect us to be recovered quickly then, Major Carter?"

"Yeah," she said, starting to rummage in her pack and pulling out a tripod which she erected over the fire. "Someone has to stay positive."

Unsure how to interpret the slight edge to Major Carter's voice, Teal'c decided not to comment. Although he had every faith in the Tau'ri, it was by no means certain that rescue would come soon. Or even at all. It was, after all, a very large galaxy. "I will make a circuit of the area," he said, reaching for his staff weapon that lay on the ground tucked between the flysheet and inner tent.

"Good idea," she said, pulling her scanner from her pocket and walking over to the tarpaulin in which she had collected snow. "Oh," she added, in afterthought, "Daniel thinks he saw someone last night, watching us. It might just have been the fever, but… keep your eyes peeled?"

He simply inclined his head in agreement and made no comment on the macabre eye-peeling idiom.

Staff weapon in his hand, he left the camp and headed down and to the left, following the path they had travelled the previous day. He could see their tracks clearly: his own long stride, Major Carter's close behind, followed by Daniel Jackson's limping gait and O'Neill's footsteps next to him. He crouched for a moment, to make sure that no other tracks were imposed over theirs, but he was confident that no one else had passed that way.

After walking down and across the hillside for five minutes he stopped. The trees were behind him now, and his view over the valley below was uninterrupted. The Stargate sat at its far end, close to a wide-mouthed bay cluttered with rocks and debris that might once have been buildings or other manmade structures. He could hear the distant rush of water, taste a slight salt tang in the air. Strange, without the accompanying cry of seabirds.

On the other side of the valley rose more hills, a green blush halfway up mirroring the tree line on his side of the valley. But all between was desolation, a bleak and colorless landscape. Whatever battle had been fought here, it had happened long ago and this planet had done its best to scour away all evidence of the ordeal. But life had yet to return. He stood for a few moments, scanning the valley and hills for movement. There was none.

Turning right, he moved off parallel to the slant of the slope. His feet crunched over stone and he used his staff to help him balance on the rugged ground. Eyes and ears open, he heard nothing but his own footsteps.

After ten minutes he turned again, heading up the slope and

back into the trees. He smelled coffee in the air as he passed level with their camp but did not stop, pressing on higher into the trees to complete his circuit. Even here there were no birds, although there was evidence of life. He crouched again, turning over small animal droppings with his fingertips — perhaps something like an *unat*? They would have food, at least, if their stay was longer than Major Carter anticipated. He also spotted rocks protruding from the dirt that were too square and regular to be naturally shaped. Bricks then, which meant that, at some point in the past, this area had been inhabited by humans — or some other intelligent species.

It was as he crouched on the slope above their camp that he heard the sound — a subtle movement, the careful tread of careful feet. He held himself still, breathed shallow and silent. He could see little, so relied upon his ears alone.

Footsteps, more than one set. Light, balanced. A hunter, further into the trees, stalking prey. A soft hiss, barely a sound — wood against wood, perhaps? And then a low whistle and a solid thud. A scrabbling of movement to his left, away from their camp, the death throes of some small animal. Then silence.

Carefully, Teal'c rose to his feet. There was a tree to his right, broader than most, and he moved silently toward it. From above, he could hear the footsteps again. Less careful now, and with them came a whisper of voices. Two men.

Teal'c ducked behind the tree as the hunters cut across his path, heading downhill toward their kill. They did not see him, but he had plenty of time to observe them. Young men dressed raggedly, capes of patched furs hanging from lean, rangy bodies. These were hungry men. One had an animal dangling from his hand — as Teal'c had surmised, it was an *unat*. The Tau'ri would call it a 'rabbit'. The animal looked as skinny as the man who had killed it. The other man held only a bow in his hand, a couple of slender arrows tucked into his belt.

Something fluttered in the trees above, the first bird Teal'c had seen in this place. But the effect on the two men was remarkable. They both dropped to the ground in fear, eyes scanning the sky. Neither moved until the bird broke cover, flapping off and higher up the hillside. Then one of the men laughed, nudged the other as if embarrassed, and said, "Ah, only a skua", before they climbed back to their feet and continued down the slope. Teal'c wondered if there was some species of predatory bird on this planet.

He watched the hunters stop a little further on and retrieve the arrow and another *unat* from the undergrowth, before they disappeared into the trees, walking parallel with the hillside.

When he was certain they were gone, and that there were no others close by, Teal'c hurried to complete his circuit of their camp. It appeared that Daniel Jackson had been correct, there were people here. Whether that improved or worsened their situation remained to be seen.

By the time he returned to their camp site, Colonel O'Neill was also awake — if he had slept at all. He sipped from the steaming mug cradled in his hands. Major Carter was crawling backward out of the tent and climbing to her feet.

"His fever's definitely lower," she said as she walked back to the fire and picked up her own mug from a rock close by. "He's trying the coffee."

"*He* can hear you…" Daniel Jackson called from inside the tent.

Major Carter smiled. Then she saw Teal'c and said, "Hey, want some coffee?"

"O'Neill," he said, by way of answer, "there are people on this planet. I have seen them."

"What?" Coffee forgotten, O'Neill reached for his weapon. "Where?"

"Hunters," Teal'c said. "Two men armed with bows and arrows. They headed that way." He pointed past their tent, up into the trees.

"Bows and arrows?" He understood O'Neill's disappointment; this was not a technologically advanced people and it was unlikely they would be able to assist them in opening the

Stargate.

"Told you I saw someone." Daniel Jackson's disembodied voice sounded rather pleased.

O'Neill just frowned, thinking. "Did they see you?"

"They did not."

He nodded. "How much gear were they carrying?"

"Nothing but their weapons. I do not believe they were hunting far from home."

"You can track them?"

"Yes."

"There must be a village or something around here," O'Neill guessed, glancing about as if he might be able to see it from where he stood. "Maybe they know what happened to the DHD?"

"That is possible," Teal'c conceded. "But it is most likely that the DHD was destroyed, or buried, in the nuclear attack on the Stargate."

"It's also possible they have it in their town square and dance around it singing songs at Christmas." O'Neill finished his coffee in one long swallow. "Let's not make any assumptions here."

A shuffling movement from the tent revealed Daniel Jackson, milk-faced as he edged his way out. "Ah, actually," he said, "I think we can rule out the Christmas scenario."

"Bad example," O'Neill said. "The point is, these people — whoever they are — know one-hundred percent more about this planet than we do. So, pack-up your stuff. We're gonna go say hello."

"Sir?" Major Carter looked uneasy. "Is that a good idea?"

"You got a better one?"

She shrugged, shook her head. "Sir, SERE protocol recommends holing up until—"

"Major, are you trying to lecture *me* on survival and evasion protocols?"

"No sir, it's just—"

"Good," he said. "Now get ready to move out."

Teal'c could see the concern playing across her face. Major

Carter had a great deal to learn about maintaining a soldier's impassive façade.

"I'm sorry, sir, but I don't think it's a good idea," she said, proving that she also had much to learn about the wisdom of remaining silent. "We don't know how far away these people live, or whether or not they'll be hostile. And if we move out of radio range we won't know if the SGC have come looking for us."

O'Neill's face, on the other hand, remained inscrutable. Only the sharp edge to his voice betrayed impatience. "Carter..."

"Sir, the SGC could dial the gate at any moment. We have to give them time."

"We don't *have* time!" It was unusual, although not unprecedented, for O'Neill to momentarily lose control. But it was never a good sign. He scowled, jamming his cap onto his head and tugging it low over his eyes as if hiding in its shadow. Angry silence filled the space between him and Major Carter, and Teal'c felt his concern about O'Neill's behavior ratchet up another notch. It felt amiss in a way he could not adequately define.

"What about Daniel, sir?" Major Carter said at last, coldly professional. "One of us could stay here with him, to keep an eye on the Stargate, and—"

O'Neill shook his head. "We don't split up. Besides, I need Daniel to talk to these people."

From the mouth of the tent, Daniel said, "Actually, I'm feeling better, Sam. The rest did me good, I think."

"See? It'll be fine."

Major Carter was shaking her head, but it was clear she knew the point had been lost. "For the record, sir, I think leaving the vicinity of the Stargate is a mistake."

O'Neill glowered, but said only, "Duly noted, Major." Then he gestured at the equipment — most of it Major Carter's — outside the tent. "Get your crap together, Carter. And *that's* an order."

"Yes sir." She clamped her mouth shut and Teal'c could see her jaw muscles twitch from the effort of saying no more.

Snatching up his empty coffee mug again, O'Neill shook out

the dregs as he stalked back to the tent.

"We should at least leave a marker, sir," Major Carter said as he walked past her. "Like I did at the gate."

"Knock yourself out," O'Neill said. "Just be ready to go in ten."

She watched him disappear into the tent and then shook her head as her eyes met Teal'c's. "*This* is a bad idea."

Teal'c wasn't sure that their current predicament allowed for any good ones.

It wasn't that Daniel had been exaggerating when he said he felt better, it was just that 'better' was a relative term and he'd been starting from a very low point.

Walking was possible, so long as he didn't jostle the wound in his side. The pain was always there, and he could bear its base level, but if he twisted sideways or bent over or — His foot jarred on a stone and, *God, just like that*, agony flared. He gritted his teeth, sucked in a breath.

"Daniel?" Sam touched his arm.

He gestured that he was fine, rode the wave of pain until it started to recede, and then forced himself to start walking again. An hour into their trek through the woods and he knew he was slowing the pace. Not that anyone was complaining. Not that anyone was saying much of anything.

Teal'c had taken point, following the trail left by the two hunters. Well, trail was a loose term, but to Teal'c's skilled eye it was, apparently, very clear. Jack was stalking along at Teal'c's shoulder, silent and bristling with whatever was bugging him. He and Teal'c were so alike it was comic. For all Jack's offbeat humor, he was as guarded as any Jaffa when it came to something important.

"Hey," Sam said. "Doing okay?"

"I could ask you the same thing…" Daniel said, diverting the subject from himself. He was bored of his own problems and Sam had been fuming wordlessly since her confrontation with Jack — an event which, in itself, was strange. He'd never seen them openly disagree like that, and never in the field.

"We're too far from the gate to get a radio signal now," she said and gave a bemused kind of shrug. "For what that's worth."

He studied her pinched expression. "I don't suppose you know what's been bugging Colonel Jackass recently?"

Sam smiled at the moniker, but it soon faded. "I think it has something to do with Edora," she said, glancing at Jack and lowering her voice. "I overheard him telling —" She stopped dead, her hand suddenly gripping Daniel's arm.

Up ahead Teal'c had signaled a halt and both he and Jack were dropping into a crouch. Sam did the same, helping Daniel down too. He tried not to hiss in pain as the wound in his side compressed.

After a long few minutes of him trying to be silent while in fairly excruciating agony, Teal'c and Jack rose to their feet again and walked on. Daniel shared a look with Sam, who just shrugged and helped him up.

But they walked in silence now, and through the trees Daniel could see that the ground ahead was starting to fall away. Teal'c and Jack stopped just at the point where the ground plunged downward, dropped to their stomachs and crawled forward until they could peer over the edge. Slowly, Daniel and Sam caught up.

Keeping below the ridgeline, Sam stopped him while they were still out of sight of whatever lay below. He was breathless, his wound was throbbing, and he didn't object when Sam maneuvered him toward a fallen tree so that he could rest. Not that sitting hurt any less — in fact it was worse — but his legs were feeling decidedly gelatinous and his head was starting to spin. Sam pressed half a power bar into his hand. He smiled and hoped it would help.

Teal'c and Jack lay still, watching. Then, on some unspoken signal, they squirmed back down the slope and stood up, trotting downhill to where Daniel and Sam were waiting.

"Looks like there are some caves down there," Jack said, as he got close enough to talk. "We saw Teal'c's guys head inside."

"How steep's the descent?" Sam asked, her tone excruciatingly cool.

Jack matched it exactly. "Not bad if we go around the side." He'd found his sunglasses, despite the dour weather, and Daniel couldn't see much more than his straight, uncompromising mouth.

"I will assist Daniel Jackson," Teal'c offered. "It is not far to the cave entrance. With luck, you will be able to rest there."

Jack frowned behind his sunglasses and said, "I'll take point. Carter, cover our six."

"Yes sir."

With Teal'c helping him walk, Daniel moved faster. Which was good, because Jack looked like he was in a hurry. He loped downhill with his loose-limbed stride, weapon held casually in both hands — if you could ever hold a semiautomatic machine gun casually.

Behind him Daniel could hear Sam's careful footsteps, but whatever she was thinking she kept her thoughts to herself.

Ahead, the trees started to thin as they descended into a shallow valley. The air was dank and misty, but despite that he could still make out the caves, a natural formation of blocky rocks that rose out of the scrubby grass in a low, elliptical lump.

Jack slowed as he drew near, casting a glance over his shoulder and waiting for the rest of them to catch up. "Okay Daniel," he said, "let's take this nice and easy. We don't want to surprise anyone."

"Yeah just… give me a moment…" He was feeling decidedly woozy, a slow and steady thumping building inside his skull. Not that he was going to admit it, but he was starting to feel a lot worse.

"Daniel?" Sam touched his forehead. "You're hot."

"I'm fine."

Jack just said, "Let's do this."

With O'Neill up front and the others ranged behind him, they cautiously approached the shadowed entrance to the cave. Daniel had been in enough dark, damp caves in his life to be expecting a familiar fusty aroma, but there was none beyond the muddy, grassy scent of the ground. He peered into the gloom, past Jack's head, and realized at once that they were looking at —

"A door," Jack said, stopping dead. "It's a goddamn door." Moving closer, he pressed his hand against it. "Iron."

"That's… interesting," Daniel said. "So now what?"

For a moment they all looked at each other. Then Jack said, "I guess we knock?"

It felt a bit silly, them standing there in front of the door and knocking like trick-or-treaters in search of candy — or a way home. With a 'what-the-hell?' shrug, Jack lifted his hand and rapped on the door. It rang like a bell.

But as the echo faded Sam said, "Colonel?" Her weapon was raised, trained on the top of the rocks. A man stood there, a silhouette against the white sky.

"Oh… hello…" Daniel began.

But then another man joined the first, and then a second. Jack lifted his gun, taking a step back, covering his team as Teal'c's staff sprang open.

"O'Neill," he said, turning slowly. "We are surrounded."

"Yup," Jack said.

From all sides, men and women emerged from the misty valley. Dressed in a mishmash of clothing — animal skins and heavy woolen fabrics — they regarded SG-1 with wary curiosity. But the most remarkable thing about these people, as far as Daniel was concerned, wasn't their clothing or their long, braided hair. It was the smattering of sophisticated weapons they were holding, all of which were aimed firmly at him and his team.

"Teal'c?" Jack said, not lowering his weapon. "I distinctly remember you saying 'bows and arrows'…"

CHAPTER NINE

STANDING on the ramp, Dr. Fraiser at his side, Hammond could see the open wormhole behind him reflected in the window of the control room. It stayed there, shimmering and beautiful, for a second or two more before it dissipated and left the gate room a darker, more somber place.

"I don't know about you, sir," Fraiser said, "but I'm glad to be home."

"You're not alone, doctor."

"I've been in warmer morgues than that place," she said as they started to walk down the ramp. "Metaphorically speaking."

"The Tollan have never been known for their warmth and hospitality," he said, although in truth it was the Asgard's attitude that really troubled him. But this was neither the time nor the place for that discussion.

However, it seemed that Dr. Fraiser's thoughts were running along the same line. "I'd like to go and check in with the infirmary, sir, but if you'd like me to stop by your office later… ?"

They'd reached the bottom of the ramp and behind the doctor he could see the blast doors open. Harriman headed straight toward him like a man on a mission.

"I appreciate that, doctor," Hammond said. "Give me a call when you're done in the infirmary."

"Yes sir." And with that, and a smile for Harriman, she was gone.

"Sir," the sergeant said, turning to walk with Hammond as he headed out of the gate room. All around them the SF's were standing down and the air had that static fizz he would forever associate with the Stargate. "You have a visitor waiting, General."

He stopped. "What kind of visitor?" If it was Kinsey—

"It's General Carter, sir. He arrived about an hour ago."

Of course. He'd contacted the Tok'ra a couple of days back

and wasn't surprised Jacob had come — the question was, did he come officially or unofficially? And would the Tok'ra offer any help locating SG-1? "Did he come alone?" Hammond said, heading through the blast doors and out into the corridor.

"Yes sir. He's waiting in the briefing room."

Hammond nodded and headed up the narrow stairs and into the control room. If Jacob had come alone, then he'd probably come unofficially, which, in turn, probably meant that the Tok'ra couldn't, or wouldn't, help — just as Colonel Makepeace had predicted. However, Hammond wasn't about to rule them out just yet. Jacob Carter had a powerful motive to find SG-1, and help was help, whether or not it was officially sanctioned by the Tok'ra High Council.

"Sergeant?" he said, as he crossed the control room to the stairs. "Bring me everything Dr. Rothman has on the Jaffa symbol Colonel Makepeace retrieved from P5X-104."

"Yes sir."

He stopped, one foot on the lowest step. "And Sergeant? See if you can rustle us up some coffee and sandwiches. Common hospitality doesn't stretch to lunch on Tollana and I haven't eaten since 0600 hours this morning."

When he reached the briefing room, he found his old friend sitting at the long conference table, staring out pensively into the gate room. Jacob turned when he heard Hammond enter and rose to his feet. "George," he said.

"Good to see you, Jacob. Although I wish the circumstances were different." They shook hands and Hammond took his customary seat at the head of the table, gesturing for Jacob sit back down.

He did, hunched forward and with his hands clenched tight on the table in front of him. There was tension in every line of his body. "I take it there's no news?"

"No, I'm sorry. We've searched P5X-104 but found no trace of SG-1. As far as we can tell from the DHD, Earth was the last planet dialed but the wormhole never connected with our

Stargate. Or with the secondary gate, currently in storage in Nevada."

Jacob nodded. "You have a theory?"

"We have two," he said, just as Harriman entered with a file tucked under one arm and balancing a tray with two coffees, several sandwiches, and a couple bags of potato chips. The man was a miracle worker.

"Thank you, Sergeant." Despite the situation, his stomach was growling and only his good manners stopped him from digging in right away. He gestured to Jacob to help himself as he took the file from Harriman. It was a thin file; Dr. Rothman hadn't managed to find out a great deal, but at least it contained the photographs Makepeace had taken.

Once they were alone again, and he'd taken a couple of bites of sandwich, he turned back to Jacob. "So, I was saying—we have two theories."

Jacob wasn't eating. He just sipped his coffee, looking dour and concerned. "Go on."

"Theory one," Hammond said, wiping mayo from his fingers. "We think the gate on '104 may have been hit by staff-cannon fire which caused the wormhole to skip to another gate somewhere between P5X-104 and Earth."

"You've set up a search?"

"We have teams out right now—it'll take a week to check all the closest addresses."

Jacob nodded, frowning. There was an inward-looking expression on his face and Hammond realized he was communing with Selmak. He took the opportunity to finish his sandwich. After a moment, Jacob looked up and said, "What's your second theory?"

This one, Hammond liked even less. "That the dialing sequence was interrupted before it could connect and SG-1 were captured by the Jaffa on the planet. There was quite a firefight at the gate."

Jacob rubbed his hands over his face. "There's a third theory," he said, meeting Hammond's eyes with a bleak look.

But the third option wasn't even worth considering. "If the wormhole collapsed while they were in transit," Hammond said, "then they're gone and there's nothing we can do about it."

For a moment they sat in silence, but then Jacob sighed, as if rallying himself, and said, "Whose Jaffa? Who was on the planet?"

"We were hoping you could tell us."

Hammond pulled the file closer and took out the photo of the fallen Jaffa, the symbol tattooed onto his forehead stark against his deathly skin. He passed the picture to Jacob, who looked at it briefly before passing it back. "Hecate," he said.

Hammond nodded. "Yes, Dr. Rothman had gotten that far. What do you know about her?"

When Jacob spoke again, it was in Selmak's resonant tone. "She is a minor Goa'uld of whom we know very little. It is likely that she is allied with a more powerful System Lord however, or she would not risk such an open attack. We will endeavor to find out more."

"Thank you," Hammond said, although it was little enough to be thankful for. "In the meantime," he added, since he had Selmak's attention, "are the Tok'ra able to help us look for our people?" He lowered his voice even though they had the room to themselves. "Major Carter notwithstanding, you're aware of the urgency to retrieve Colonel O'Neill?"

Selmak nodded. "We are. The Asgard and Tollan are both in contact with our High Council. Unfortunately, the Tok'ra have also suffered thefts of technology and, because of that, and because of our ancient alliances with both the Asgard and the Tollan, the Tok'ra cannot offer you any help."

It was a struggle not to vent his anger and, for a moment, Hammond said nothing, clamping his jaw against words he knew wouldn't help. But it was Jacob Carter sitting there, and it was his daughter who was lost. Keeping his voice as even as he could he said, "You have to know that this mole in the SGC is just one person — one person among the billions on this planet. You can't punish us all for their crimes."

Selmak retreated, letting Jacob come forward. Perhaps, wisely, he felt that this was something best discussed between old friends. "Look, George," Jacob said, "God knows I agree with you. And I don't for a minute think that anyone in SG-1 had anything to do with this..."

"SG-1... ?" That news had spread fast.

Jacob gave a wry smile. "Oh yes, we heard about the most recent theft. The Tollan were very quick to point out that it happened while SG-1 was AWOL."

"Missing," Hammond corrected.

Jacob conceded the point. "The Tollan don't trust the Tau'ri, George. They never really have. We're too... unpredictable. The Asgard persuaded them to trust Jack because — Well, for some reason the Asgard like him and the Tollan trust the Asgard. But with Jack out of the picture? I gotta tell you, it's not looking good."

"You don't need to tell me," Hammond said, poking at the remains of the sandwiches. His appetite had suddenly vanished. "But Jacob, we're talking about Samantha."

"I *know.*"

And for a moment, in that tight voice and anxious frown, Hammond glimpsed the man he'd once know, a man grieving for his lost wife and struggling to parent his children.

"Believe me," Jacob said, "I'll do everything possible to help find Sam — unofficially. I'll talk to my contacts, see if anyone's heard anything, and find out what I can about Hecate. But there's nothing I can do to move the High Council on this. And don't think I haven't tried." Then he let out a long, controlled breath — it sounded like the prelude to bad news. "And George," he said, "there's something else."

"Go on."

"Rumors," he said. "We've heard them from a couple of different operatives now."

Hammond didn't speak, just sat back in his chair and folded

his arms across his chest. Waiting.

Jacob held his gaze for a long moment. "They say the Asgard are close — and I mean *close* — to withdrawing Earth from the Protected Planets Treaty."

It was the worst news, but far from unexpected. "All because one man is missing?"

"It's not just that," Jacob said. "There's something odd with the Asgard — something going on that they're not telling us about."

Hammond thought back to Thor and Tyr, to their uncompromising insistence on O'Neill's involvement. "What do you mean?"

Jacob shrugged. "We don't know exactly, but they've been pulling ships out of our galaxy for over a year now. From a military standpoint," he said, "it looks a hell of a lot like they're falling back to defend a safer position."

Mind racing, and not at all happy with the conclusions he was reaching, Hammond said, "At the negotiations today, Thor mentioned something about a threat in their galaxy."

"Yes," Jacob said. "That's all they'll say. But whatever this threat is, I'm beginning to wonder if they've still got the capacity — or even the will — to maintain the Protected Planet Treaty at all."

"So this is just an excuse? A way to fall back without losing face?"

Jacob spread his hands. "Perhaps. Like I said, we don't know any more than you do."

"In which case," Hammond said, starting to make the connections, "they've got no good reason to help us clear up this mess, have they? And that might just explain why they're so damned insistent that Colonel O'Neill is the only man who can solve the problem."

"They're certainly making it difficult," Jacob agreed.

"Sonofa —" He swallowed the curse, outraged, yet somehow unsurprised by the turn of events. "So what do we do?"

"Find Jack O'Neill," Jacob said. "Find my daughter. And don't give the little gray bastards a reason to pull the plug." Then he leaned closer, across the table, and dropped his voice to a harsh whisper. "Because there are plenty of Goa'uld out there looking at Earth with hungry eyes, George. And the only thing holding them back is that damn treaty."

Crap. Crap, crap, crap.

They'd seen them coming. Of course they'd seen them coming. Daniel had already told them they'd been spotted the night before. Damn it. What had he been thinking?

Furious with himself, Jack backed up another step and tried to cover his whole team while figuring out how the hell to get out of this.

Everything, *everything* was going wrong.

There were people all around them, forming a loose but complete circle. They didn't look aggressive, but the kick-ass weapons they carried — and what the hell *were* they? — definitely meant business. To his left, one of the men stepped forward. He was young — they were all young — but he had the swagger of a leader. His long braided hair was pulled back from his face and he wore a coat stitched together from the skins of whatever critters lived on this rock. A dark, close-cropped beard framed narrow features and a pair of piercing eyes marked him out as both smart and dangerous.

He looked like he knew what to do with the weapon he was aiming at Jack, but, despite the high-tech gun, he also had a bow slung across his back and a knife hanging from his belt next to two scrawny rabbits.

"Listen," Jack said, keeping his weapon leveled and his finger hovering over the trigger. "We don't want any trouble. Daniel — tell them."

"I… uh…" Daniel sounded vague, distracted. "We're explorers. We… oh…"

"Colonel?" Carter's voice was urgent and he didn't need to look to know that Daniel was about to hit the deck. Or the mud.

He had no choice; they couldn't fight. Lowering his weapon, he lifted his hands away from it and said, "Stand down, Major. Daniel — probably lie down."

"O'Neill?" Teal'c said.

His unease was obvious and Jack shared it. But there was no helping it — against this many armed people, with Daniel too sick to run or fight, they didn't stand a chance. "You too, T."

After a moment, he heard Teal'c's staff weapon power down. Risking a glance over his shoulder, he caught a glimpse of Daniel's white face as Carter helped ease him to the ground.

Should have left him at the camp, he thought. *Should have left Carter with him at the camp.*

But then maybe they'd have been picked off two-by-two and it wouldn't have made a blind bit of difference? At least this way he could keep an eye on them.

Shelving the fruitless second-guessing, he turned back to the stranger. "My name's Jack O'Neill," he said. "This is Carter, Teal'c and the guy down there is Daniel. We're explorers. Actually, we're lost explorers."

The man didn't lower his weapon, but he did speak. His voice was heavily accented, but the words were recognizable. "I am Aedan Trask," he said. "I speak for my people. Why are you in our lands?"

"Like I said — we're lost."

"And where have you come from?" His sharp eyes were full of suspicion. "One of the southern camps? You dress and speak strangely."

"Oh, much further than that," Jack said, gesturing vaguely toward the Stargate. "Way, way over there…"

The girl standing next to Aedan — barely twenty, bony, with wide, earnest eyes — reached up and whispered something in his ear. He nodded. "Elspeth said she watched you walk out of the valley last night. Did you cross it?"

"Ah…" Jack glanced over at Daniel. Carter had dropped her pack and propped him up against it. He was still conscious, though ghostly white. Jack swallowed a fresh knot of concern and said, "A little help here?"

Daniel licked his lips. "We're far from home," he said. "And we need your help."

As he spoke, a big drop of rain landed on Jack's cap, another hitting the side of his face. Just when he didn't think this damn planet could *get* any worse. The universe, he decided bitterly, was having a laugh at his expense.

Aedan looked up at the sky, then back at Daniel. He still didn't lower his weapon. "The valley is poisoned," he said. "Is that why you're sick?"

"Ah… poisoned?" Daniel said, frowning. "No, I was wounded. Shot."

"Actually," Carter said, "that's probably not true anyway. About the valley?" Aedan looked at her, confused, so she plowed on; sometimes Carter just didn't know when to shut up. "While prolonged exposure to the radioactive fallout — that is, to the dust in the valley — is dangerous, you could probably cross —"

"Carter?"

She glanced up at him. "Sir?"

"Not now."

Jaw clamped shut, she nodded and fell silent, but he didn't miss the flash of wounded pride in her eyes — and this time he hadn't even been *trying* to knock her down.

Another drop of rain landed on his face, followed by more and heavier. Quelling his frustration, he took a breath and tried to be diplomatic. "Look, Aedan," he said. "Daniel's right, we need your help. He's badly injured and we really need to open the Stargate and go home."

Aedan looked blank. "Stargate?"

"Big stone ring back in the valley?"

There was a palpable shifting among the group, half amusement and half unease. Neither was encouraging. "You're head-sick," Aedan said, aiming his weapon more sharply. "Only Devourers come through the Eye."

"Devourers?" Jack echoed. Who, or what, were Devourers? And, more importantly, how did they open the Stargate without a DHD?

He cast a quick look at Carter, but she just shrugged: *no idea.* Daniel had his eyes closed and didn't seem to be responding at all. Crap.

"Not only Devourers," the girl next to Aedan piped up. "They aren't the only ones."

"Hush up, Elspeth."

"I won't," she said. "The old gods lived beyond the Eye. Everyone knows that." Turning to Jack she fixed him with a searching look. "Do you serve them? The old gods?"

He opened his mouth to respond, but Teal'c got there first. "We do not."

"There *are* no gods," Aedan said irritably, "old or otherwise. Now give over your blethering, Elspeth."

She backed down, but didn't appear cowed and continued to regard them steadily — especially Teal'c — with her large, curious eyes.

The rain was heavy now, a steady downpour. And the wind was picking up too, driving rain down the valley in long, cold sweeps. Their only dry clothes were about to get soaked through. Jack decided to cut his losses. These kids might not own a DHD but they did own a warm, dry cave. Besides, he needed to learn more about the Devourers — whoever they were — and how they used the Stargate. Hell, he'd be happy to hitch a ride home with the Goa'uld at this point.

"Aedan," he said, trying to sound reasonable and friendly. "It's raining. My friend's injured and we need shelter. We're willing to trade for it." He eyed their lean, hungry bodies and the couple of skinny rabbits dangling from Aedan's belt. "We have food," he said, "medicines, weapons…"

Aedan shifted as the wind tugged at his hair, ruffling the furs of his coat.

"We can't bring armed strangers inside," a male voice objected from behind them. Jack glanced over his shoulder, but he couldn't tell which of the men had spoken. They all watched him with the same overt suspicion.

"Their weapons are primitive," Aedan said. "And we can take precautions."

Jack turned back to face him. "Precautions? What kind of precautions?"

Aedan just smiled.

"O'Neill!"

Teal'c went down first, convulsing beneath a snaking sheen of blue energy. Spinning around, Jack barely managed to grab hold of his weapon before he was hit too, a nerve-numbing shockwave radiating out from his right shoulder. He pitched sideways, legs giving way, and saw Carter fall, sprawling across Daniel before the world went black.

CHAPTER TEN

DUSK was a hint of purple in the western sky by the time Makepeace swung his Dodge SUV into the visitor center parking lot and killed the engine. Though sunset was while off yet, the sun had already dropped behind Pikes Peak and, according to the dash, the temperature had cooled to a pleasant sixty-five degrees. Makepeace scanned the few cars that remained in the lot. The park was close to closing, but there were still a number of minivans and station wagons occupying a few spaces — family cars, their occupants the remnants of what had most likely been a busy day. Come Labor Day, the lot and the center would be deserted at this time, the few tourists who visited having long since departed. There was no sign yet of the man he had come here to meet, and none of these vehicles looked like they'd be his preferred mode of transport. Harold Maybourne was a man who liked to keep other people waiting, a message, Makepeace thought, about who was in control.

It had taken Makepeace longer than usual to get here. His conversation in the infirmary with General Hammond had left him antsy, though he couldn't pinpoint why. Perhaps it was the general's refusal to let him take SG-3 back out on the search and rescue, but Makepeace sensed that something more was going on. Of course, working for the Stargate Program, he was used to there being secrets to which he wasn't privy. He wasn't always on the need-to-know list and that was just fine by him, but today... Hammond's expression had turned guarded, as if he'd been about to share something with Makepeace, but then changed his mind.

Maybe he was just being paranoid. Or maybe he shouldn't have mouthed off about the Tok'ra, but dammit he hadn't said anything that wasn't true. Either way, he'd left the base with a distinct feeling of unease, the Tollan artifact a heavy weight in the gym bag he carried. Instead of heading straight to the rendezvous, he'd swung south on 115, keeping an eye on the rearview, then took a few random lefts and rights, before doubling back on himself up I-25. Not until he'd hit North 30th, did he shake the notion that he'd been followed. The sooner he offloaded this damned tech, the better.

Makepeace picked up the bag and got out of the SUV, taking a moment to survey the towering red rocks that surrounded him: The Garden of the Gods National Park, Colorado Springs. Given the delusions of grandeur held by the very sons-of-bitches who threatened the planet, the irony of the name did not escape him, and he wondered if Maybourne had chosen it as a rendezvous point deliberately. He doubted the man appreciated its majestic beauty. Then again, Makepeace also doubted whether Maybourne had that sophisticated a sense of humor.

He headed into the visitor's center and made for the coffee shop. He hadn't yet followed Hammond's direction to grab some shut-eye and the toll of two back-to-back missions was starting to weigh on him.

"What can I get ya?" asked the waitress — Trish, by her name badge — with a sunny smile, though Makepeace caught the way she flicked a glance at the clock behind him. Evidently, it had been a long day for her too and she no doubt wondered at a visitor arriving so late.

"Coffee, please. Black, and throw in an extra espresso shot."

"The coffee I can do, hon, but we ain't no Starbucks."

Makepeace gave her a smile and nodded, then pointed to the 'Theater' sign suspended from the ceiling. "Is the movie still on?"

"It sure is," said Trish. "Five minutes until the last show of the day. That'll be five dollars for the ticket and a buck seventy-five for the coffee."

Makepeace thanked her, handed over a ten and told her to keep the change.

"Well, thank you, honey." Apparently, a decent tip was the very thing to make a late visitor less objectionable. "You go on in and enjoy the show."

He'd only just settled into his seat in the darkened theater, when he heard the door open and close behind him. Harold Maybourne sat down a row in front just as the screen brightened and the first bars of America the Beautiful drifted out of the speakers.

"You're late," said Maybourne.

"I had to make a detour," said Makepeace, resisting the urge to ask where Maybourne had been hiding that he knew when he'd arrived. The colonel loved his subterfuge too much and it wouldn't do to encourage him.

Maybourne glanced over his shoulder. "You were followed?"

"No, but I wanted to take precautions. General Hammond is worried about something."

Maybourne turned back to the screen. Old grainy footage of Native Americans was playing now, their feathered headdresses incongruous with their weskits and collarless shirts. "Well, of course he is," said Maybourne. "His precious SG-1 is missing."

Makepeace narrowed his eyes. At no point during their phone conversation earlier had he mentioned that. "You know about that?"

"I know about a lot of things."

A thought struck Makepeace then, unpleasant but all too credible. "And just how *much* do you know about *this*, Maybourne?"

Maybourne paused and inclined his head towards Makepeace again. "Is that what you think me capable of, Colonel? Striking against our own people?"

"I think you're probably capable of a lot more than I'd consider reasonable."

"Tell me, Makepeace, how's the view from that moral high ground? Because last I checked your hands aren't exactly squeaky clean."

Makepeace clenched his jaw. "There's a line —"

"Which you cross repeatedly."

Makepeace said nothing. It was hard to defend the indefensible.

"For the record," continued Maybourne, "no, I had nothing to do with what happened to SG-1. Interested parties have been watching O'Neill and it wouldn't be wise to have him disappear. That said…" He trailed off, as if considering his next words.

"What?" demanded Makepeace.

"It wouldn't be the worst thing in the world if the good colonel and his team were to, let's say, take a little longer to return."

"What the hell are you talking about, Maybourne?" His BS and double talk were starting to get on Makepeace's last nerve. At least with men like George Hammond you knew where you were; he was as slippery as a fresh caught catfish. And his comments about Jack O'Neill didn't sit well with Makepeace one little bit.

"I hear the Asgard are threatening to remove the Earth from the Protected Planets Treaty."

Makepeace started forward in his seat, his eyes flicking to the gym bag on the floor. "You're not serious."

"I'm perfectly serious," replied Maybourne. It was hard to read his expression, dark as it was in the theater, with only the side of his face visible. He seemed unconcerned.

"Because of what we're doing?"

Maybourne snorted a laugh. "Of course, because of what we're doing. You don't get to steal from your neighbors and not have them build higher fences."

"Then we need to stop."

That prompted Maybourne to turn in his seat and fix Makepeace with a stare. "You really have no idea, do you, Robert? We don't *stop*. We never *stop*. They can't beat us this way."

"We're not at war with them, Maybourne," hissed Makepeace.

"Aren't we?" the colonel asked, his tone mildly amused. He turned and settled back in his seat, watching the images of red rocks towering amid the pinyon pine that flickered on the screen. "You're a native Coloradan, aren't you, Colonel? How well do you know this park?"

Makepeace frowned at the tangent. It was getting late and he hadn't been prepared for the curveball Maybourne had thrown. He wanted answers, but he also just wanted to go home. "Pretty well. My old man used to bring us climbing here."

"And I bet you had a swell time. There're all kinds of regulations now of course. Rules to stop you climbing where you want, that just take the fun out of the whole thing. You know the big rock just north of here? The one they call the Tower of Babel?"

Makepeace knew it, but he said nothing. Maybourne continued anyway. "It's named for the tower that humanity, speaking a single, united language, decided to build to try and reach heaven. 'And the Lord, who came down to see the city and the tower which the children of men built, said, Behold, the people is one, and nothing they plan to do will be impossible for them. So the Lord scattered them from there over all the Earth.'"

"I didn't come here for Bible study."

"You asked me a question, Colonel, now let me ask this of you: do you think we speak a single language now, Makepeace? Is humanity united?" Maybourne didn't wait for him to answer. "No, Robert, it's not. We're scattered, and none of us speak the same language. Looking to the skies for salvation won't help our cause. The only thing the skies will bring us is a shiny ha'tak ready to rain destruction over all the lands. People like the Tollan don't give a damn about our planet; they don't care what happens to the people living here, the small people like your friend Trish out there. No one is going to save us but ourselves. So, we don't stop. We keep going. We do more. SG-1 might come back, or they might not. But regardless, when the Asgard and their buddies decide that we're no longer worth the risk, the Pentagon will realize that it's time we looked to our own backyard for help. And by that time people like you and I will have made sure that we've got the might to take care of ourselves."

The screen turned to black and the theater went silent.

"Don't get squeamish on me, Robert. Stick to the plan."

Makepeace stood without a word, retrieving the gym bag from the floor. He hesitated a moment before dropping it in the empty seat next to Maybourne. Then he was through the theater door and out of the dark, into the clean air of the park as Trish's call to 'come back real soon' echoed in his ears.

Pain woke him, jangling nerves crawling back to life, limbs heavy and unresponsive and his mind sluggish. His mouth felt dry, tasted foul, and someone was using a jackhammer inside his skull.

"God…" Jack dragged a heavy arm across his eyes, blinking and dazzled by flickering yellow light. The world was blurry and it took a moment for his vision to clear. When it did, he found himself staring at a rocky ceiling. And then he remembered — cave.

He was a prisoner.

Stifling another groan, he forced his uncooperative arms and legs to work and pushed himself up so that his back rested against the wall. He stayed there for a few moments, catching his breath, using the time to assess his position.

First, he was unarmed: both his MP5 and Beretta were missing.

Second, he was in a small cell, there was some kind of straw or grass on the floor, and in the corner a lantern hung from a crude iron hook. It cast enough light to reveal a rough-hewn wooden door — shut — and Carter. She was a couple of feet away, flat on her back and out cold.

Third, Daniel and Teal'c were missing.

"Carter?" His voice was no more than a croak, but his limbs were recovering from what felt like the world's worst case of pins-and-needles, and he managed to drag himself over to her. "Carter." He pressed clumsy fingers to her throat — her skin was warm, her pulse steady. He shook her shoulder. "Major, wake up."

Nothing. Whatever it was they'd hit them with, it was powerful — he'd never felt anything quite like it. Definitely not a zat.

Sagging against the wall next to Carter, he kept his hand on her shoulder and waited. He could feel his body slowly recovering, but it wasn't there yet, and until they were both up and running no one was going anywhere. Besides, he needed to think and this was as good a time as any.

He flexed his tingling fingers and tried to pull his thoughts together.

Their situation was bad. Daniel — wherever the hell he was — needed urgent medical attention and the mission to Tollana was a little over twenty-four hours away.

Worse still, he felt like his team was falling apart, and he was starting to doubt that, even if they got out of this mess, he'd be able to rebuild the trust that had once bound them so closely.

He was tempted, so tempted, to drop the whole charade and just tell them everything. But Hammond's orders had been explicit: *No one can know, Jack. Not even your team. The future of the planet depends on the success of this mission.*

Jack knocked his head back against the rocky wall in frustration. Sometimes he wished he was more of the maverick everyone imagined him to be, but while there might come a time — and soon — when he felt it necessary to disobey Hammond's orders, he hadn't reached that point yet.

So he had to carry on. He had to keep up the jackass routine, get them home, save Daniel, betray his team and save the world. Again.

And after that? Hell, after that he was going fishing. And no one could stop him.

Beneath his hand, Carter stirred. She opened her eyes, winced in pain, and groaned.

"You're okay," he said, giving her shoulder a reassuring squeeze. "It gets better."

"Sir… ?" She blinked, rubbed at her face with clumsy hands. "God, what happened… ?"

"They shot us," he said. And what he wanted to add was, *You were right, by the way. We should have stayed at the camp, close to the gate.* But he couldn't — all part of the act — so he just said, "Daniel and Teal'c are missing."

"What?" She struggled to sit up and he helped her, resting her back against the wall next to him. "How long have they been gone?"

"I only just woke up," he said, watching as she started shaking the pins-and-needles out of her hands. "That'll take a few minutes."

She nodded, but didn't look at him. He hated that she was wary around him now. "That was no zat, sir," she said.

"No."

"But I'd sure like to take a look at one of those weapons."

A creak drew his eyes to the door. "You just might get that chance, Major," he said, pushing himself to his feet. She tried to follow, but he waved her back down. "Stay there."

He took a step forward as the door opened and Aedan Trask strolled into the cell. He was still armed, although the weapon dangled casually from a hand hanging loose at his side. "Ah," he said, smiling, "you're awake. How do you feel?"

"You shot us." Jack put himself between Aedan and Carter. "How do you think I feel?"

"Apologies for that," Aedan said, although he didn't sound very apologetic. "This is a dangerous world, eh? But no harm was done. The stunner only disables you for a short time."

Jack glanced past the man's shoulder but couldn't see anyone else. The door opened onto a narrow passageway and he could see more light at the end of it and hear a bubble of chatter. He wondered how hard it would be to rush the man, to grab his weapon. If Carter had been less incapacitated...

He heard her scramble awkwardly to her feet behind him, no doubt thinking along the same lines. Unfortunately, so was Aedan Trask. He lifted the weapon, aimed it loosely in their direction. "No need for any of that," he said. "You're not our prisoners."

"Really? Then I gotta tell you, your guest rooms suck."

From behind him, Carter said, "Where are our weapons?"

"In a safe place," Aedan said. "You'll have them again when you leave. In the meantime, your friends are enjoying our hospitality."

Jack lifted an eyebrow. "Are they, now?"

Stepping back from the door, Aedan gestured down the passage with his weapon. "See for yourself. Your friend, Teal'c, woke quickly from the stunner and we didn't use it on your injured companion. Meagan, our medic, is treating him. Come on." He flicked his head towards the door. "It's a cold night, but the fire's warm and we've food to share. You're welcome here, Jack O'Neill and Carter."

"It's Sam," she said, moving on wobbly legs to stand next to Jack. "My friends call me Sam."

Aedan smiled. "Sam," he said. "Come on, your friends are waiting."

With that he turned his back on them, leaving the door open, and headed down the narrow passageway. If they'd wanted to jump him, now was the perfect moment.

Jack looked at Carter, silently asking her opinion.

"I believe him, sir," she said with a shrug. "For what it's worth."

He wanted to say, *It's worth a lot.* But all he allowed himself to say was, "Me too." And then he headed out after Aedan, forcing himself to leave Carter, still woozy from the stunner, to follow as best she could.

"There." The woman — Meagan — sat back on her heels and admired her handiwork with a pragmatic eye. "You'll be more comfortable now, Daniel."

He lay on his back on a straw pallet, his shirt pushed up to expose the gash in his side. Meagan had washed out the FastClot and he felt better for it. There was no new bleeding either, which he took as a good sign. Then she'd covered his wound with a herbal poultice that she claimed would prevent infection — interesting, he'd noted through the pain, that she knew the word 'infection' — and redressed the wound with a sterile dressing from Daniel's pack.

As she tied off the bandage, Daniel opened his eyes. The worst of the pain was over now and he could concentrate on the world again.

"Daniel Jackson." Teal'c sat at his side, watching him with the steady focus he'd learned to interpret as concern. "Would you like me to administer a dose of morphine?"

Yes, he thought. *And no.* He started to tug his shirt down, but Meagan batted away his hands and did it herself with an irritated *tsk-tsk*. She was one of the oldest women in the group, although it was difficult to judge her age accurately in the smoky yellow light of their lamps. He thought he'd put her at about forty. Not old by American standards, yet she was clearly treated with the reverence of an elder here and it was unsurprising given that everyone else looked so young. Her hair was graying, braided and beaded like all the others, her eyes merry with lines around them that crinkled when she smiled. "Morphine?" she said, considering the word. "What is that?"

"It helps with pain," Daniel explained, wincing as he shifted to allow her to readjust his shirt. "But it leaves you pretty out of it."

Meagan frowned at the expression. "It clouds your mind?"

"Yes," he said, and glanced at Teal'c. "Maybe later?" He wanted to talk to these people while he was still lucid, first and foremost about the whereabouts of Jack and Sam.

Teal'c nodded and turned his eyes on the rest of the room. He was uneasy, but that was an improvement on his previous state of 'extremely pissed off'.

When Teal'c had woken from the stun blast halfway into the cave network, the confrontation had almost proven disastrous, but luckily Teal'c's reflexes had been fogged by the stunner and Daniel had been conscious enough to talk him down before he could do too much damage. Nonetheless, a couple of Aedan's men were sporting bruises and black-eyes and casting Teal'c wary glances from the far side of the room or, rather, the cave. Teal'c had set himself up like a sentry next to Daniel and, despite being unarmed, was watching the whole room as if daring any-one to challenge him. So far, no one had accepted that dare.

"Can you help me sit up?" Daniel asked Meagan.

"You're a stubborn one," she said, but not without approval. She nodded to Teal'c. "Take his other arm, help me."

In silence Teal'c did so and between them they eased Daniel upright. There was something solid behind him, like a heavy cushion, and he leaned against it for a moment as he adjusted to the new level of pain and then waited for it to recede.

Meagan watched through narrowed eyes. "I'll fetch you something," she decided, "for the pain and the fever. It'll not cloud your mind."

Daniel nodded his thanks, teeth gritted and still unable to speak. Next to him, Teal'c shifted restlessly.

"I am concerned for O'Neill and Major Carter," he said, his gaze turning toward the room to which they'd been taken to sleep off the effects of the stunner. "Why have they not woken yet?"

"Junior?" Daniel managed, with a feeble gesture toward Teal'c's stomach. It was the obvious explanation, but Teal'c didn't look convinced.

Meagan returned then, holding a steaming wooden cup in her hands. "Here," she said, offering it to Daniel. "It'll help."

He sniffed — it smelled herbal, faintly acrid.

"Are you sure that is wise, Daniel Jackson?"

Meagan frowned. "It'll do him good," she said, offended. "I've a fair bit of skill in medicine."

"I can tell that you do," Daniel said, smoothing things over. "And, really, thank you Meagan. For everything." He blew on the steaming liquid and took a tentative sip. It was soothing, if just for the heat alone, and he felt himself start to relax. "It's good," he said, taking another sip. "Very good."

Megan cast Teal'c a triumphant look and stood up. "When you've supped that," she said to Daniel. "You should rest."

"Okay," he said. "But first I was hoping I could ask a few

questions… ?"

Her head tipped to one side she said, "About what?"

"Um, well, everything really."

"Everything is a big subject."

He laughed a little, and then winced at the jolt of pain. Although, actually, it was more like discomfort now that he came to think about it. He eyed the drink with rather more respect and took another sip. "Let's say, your world then," he said. "What's it called?"

Meagan shrugged. "We've no use to call it anything of note. It's our home and nothing else."

"But what about when you speak of it to others?"

"Others?" She frowned, but then her face straightened into a sterner expression. "The only 'others' are the Devourers. And we don't speak to them."

There was that name again. Devourers. It sounded terrifying and Daniel wondered what sort of people it could describe. He hoped they'd have no call to meet them any time soon.

"But what about your lives, the history of your people?"

"Ah…" Megan gave a small smile, settling a little, her eyes creasing. "Then you should speak to Elspeth. She wastes her days learning about such nonsense."

Nonsense? Okay. He glanced around the room. "And Elspeth is… ?"

Meagan looked about and then called out, "Elspeth Burne!"

Elspeth was the girl from earlier, he remembered now, from outside the caves. She was sitting on the other side of the fire, eating one of the MRE's Daniel had dished out in exchange for their help, and looked up, startled, when Meagan called her name. "Come here, girl," Meagan said, beckoning her over. "The stranger wants to ask you about all that nonsense you peddle."

With a muttered word to the women she was sitting with, Elspeth stood up — taking the MRE pack with her — and made her way over to Daniel.

"Hello," he said as she came to stand in front of him, looking down with an appraising expression. "I'm Daniel. I, ah, didn't mean to disturb your meal."

Meagan made an impatient gesture and Elspeth sat on the end of the Daniel's pallet, crossing her legs beneath her. "You didn't," she said, and carried on eating. She glanced again at Meagan, and then at Daniel, and said, "What is it you wanted to know?"

"Everything," Meagan said, with a roll of her eyes. "So that should keep you talking all night." She gestured again to Daniel. "Drink it all, and then rest. You'll feel better tomorrow."

He watched her as she made her way across the room. Aedan had emerged from one of the passageways that led onto the room, and they stopped to talk together. This room, Daniel figured, was a kind of central point — a gathering place and living space for the small community.

"Meagan doesn't hold with tales of the past," Elspeth said, sniffing at a packet of crackers. "She thinks it's a waste of time learning them, she only wants to learn what she can use now. Like herb lore and so on."

"Well, she has a point," Daniel said, turning back to the girl. No, girl wasn't right. She was a young woman, hardened and lean like all her people. "But I think that stories of the past can help us too, they can teach us lessons — point in the direction we should travel."

"Aye…" She looked at him with surprise, eyes widening. "That's what I think, that's exactly how I feel. But no one here agrees, they say there's no time for that. They say I've a head full of dreams."

He laughed. "Oh, I can so identify."

The expression puzzled her, but didn't dim the light in her eyes. He recognized it at once, the pleasure of discovering a kindred spirit.

"So," he said, "tell me about your people. Meagan says this world has no name."

Elspeth pursed her lips and then said, "She's right in a way. You'll not find a soul in this room who'd give it a name, though

I've seen it called the Lallans."

"Seen it?" asked Daniel. "Where?"

"In the books," replied Elspeth, but then pressed her lips together as if she'd revealed something she shouldn't. Too late, though. Daniel had heard the magic word.

"You have books? Where? Can you show me?"

"I don't like to show them. Most people mock me. They don't understand."

"I promise I wouldn't mock you, Elspeth. I'd really like to see."

But it was no use; the girl shook her head, braids fluttering about her shoulders and Daniel knew that pushing the matter wouldn't help. He settled for the next best thing.

"Then tell me what you've found. Tell me about your past. Your people."

"*My* people?" she said with a speculative look. "Do we not share the same past, Daniel? Or do you truly come from the world beyond the Eye?"

Teal'c shifted, making his presence known, a reminder not to say too much.

Daniel cleared his throat. "Ultimately, we all share the same past," he said. "But some of us know more about it than others, and you strike me as someone who has a lot to teach."

Elspeth nodded, looking pleased, her braided hair swaying and the beads clattering together. "That's true."

Scholars were the same the world over, it appeared; academic vanity was always their weak point. "And I would be honored," he said, "if you'd share with me what you've learned."

"Very well, then," Elspeth said, settling herself. "The story of our people begins with the war."

"The war that destroyed the Stargate?"

"The war," she said, like she was telling a story, "that destroyed *everything*."

And this, he thought, with a sudden fierce joy, *this is why I still do the job*. After the trauma of losing Sha're, of losing his purpose, *this* was the reason he still got up in the morning.

"Tell me —"

"Daniel."

Startled, he glanced up to see Jack prowling into the room. Brow furrowed he was scanning the area with his customary vigilance, checking for exits and hidden dangers. Daniel could practically see his fingers twitching for lack of a weapon. "Jack," he said. "Feeling better?"

"I was about to ask you the same thing."

He raised his cup in salute. "Much better."

"Daniel…" Jack's frown dug deeper. "What have I told you about drinking the local brew?"

"I did endeavor to warn him," Teal'c said. "I was unsuccessful."

Daniel met Jack's gaze and held it. They were both smart men and they both knew the likely outcome if he didn't get home soon. "I figured, what's the worst that could happen?"

Jack just grunted in reply and moved further into the room, picking his way through the people gathered around the fire, eating and watching him with open curiosity. Eventually he reached Daniel and dropped down on the floor next to him. He stifled a groan as he did so, as if moving was an effort, and sat there for a moment flexing his fingers, shaking them like he had pins-and-needles.

"Where's Sam?" Daniel said, looking around. "Aedan said she was with you."

"She's coming."

And a moment later Sam appeared at the end of passageway, one hand braced against the wall for support, looking groggy and unstable on her feet.

Teal'c immediately stood up. "Major Carter." He flung a disapproving look at Jack. "You require assistance."

She tried to wave him away. "I'm fine."

But Teal'c ignored her, hurrying over to take her arm and lead her to a space on the opposite side of the fire. "Sit here," he said. "I will find you food and water."

With a grateful smile she eased herself to the ground.

"Thanks, Teal'c."

Jack said nothing, his angry glare apparently engrossed by the dancing flames.

Looking between them, Daniel couldn't figure out what the hell was going on. "Is she okay—?"

"She's fine," he growled. He jerked his head toward Aedan, who was still talking to Megan on the other side of the room. "You find out anything useful yet?"

Swallowing his irritation—and admittedly this wasn't really the time or the place to make a scene—Daniel resettled his glasses on his nose and said, "As a matter of fact, Elspeth was about to tell me about the war."

"When they nuked the gate?"

"I don't know. That's what she was about to tell me."

Jack gave a shrug as if to say, *Don't let me stop you.*

So he didn't. Elspeth was watching the exchange curiously, her inquisitive gaze darting between Daniel and Jack, as she steadily worked through the last of his MRE as if it were the finest meal she'd ever eaten. Perhaps it was. But she smiled when he looked at her again, licking gravy from her fingers.

"So," he said, "the war?"

She nodded, pushing the MRE container aside and settling down for the story. "Well, it happened long ago, when our parents' parents were young."

"Longer ago than that," Aedan corrected. He'd climbed up onto a ledge of rock halfway up the wall and sat there fletching arrows.

"It was in the time of the old gods," Elspeth said, ignoring the interruption. "They were beautiful, and very powerful, and our people served them and worshiped them."

"*Some* of our people..." Aedan, again.

Elspeth scowled but carried on regardless. "Then the Amam came—Devourers, as we call them now." She dropped her voice, adding a little extra drama. "It's said that they came in a single night, pouring through the Eye from the underworld."

"The underworld?"

Jack gave a disparaging grunt, but in fact the term made perfect mythological sense in the context of 'Amam'. Not that Jack knew that, of course. Or would care much, probably.

"And what — exactly — are the Amam?" Daniel said. "Are they people, like us?"

Elspeth shook her head. "They are the undead. They come from the underworld to devour the flesh of the living."

"Zombies." Jack raised an eyebrow. "That's new."

Daniel ignored him and smiled encouragingly at Elspeth. "Go on — the Amam came and… ?"

"And the old gods fought them. They sent every one of their mighty warriors against the Devourers, but they couldn't defeat them. You see, the undead cannot die. And so the war lasted for many, many years. It is said that millions of people died."

Daniel glanced over at Aedan, to see if he'd object to the exaggeration. He must have sensed Daniel's eyes on him, because he looked up from his work and gave a slight nod. "That much *is* true," he said. "No one doubts that. We find their bones everywhere."

And that was an image to keep you awake at night.

"The Goa'uld have been known to use tactical nukes," Sam chipped in, talking around a mouthful of the stew she was eating. She gave a little shrug, "If we're talking about WMDs and 'old gods'…"

Daniel nodded. It was pretty clear that the Goa'uld had been here at some point, and maybe they hadn't left. "So these Devourers, the Amam, they won the war?"

The girl's expression darkened. "Yes. They drove out the old gods and then there was no one left to protect us. The Devourers swarmed over the world like rats, feeding on flesh 'til they could eat no more. Some few of us survived, like this, under the ground where they can't find us. But others…" She looked over at Aedan, her voice less certain. "In the south, they say, there are camps where humans live penned like animals. The

Amam feed on them at their pleasure."

Aedan gave a curt nod. "That's true. I've seen it."

He said no more, his face closing down into a hard expression that wouldn't have looked out of place on Jack O'Neill. The room fell silent, everyone subdued, and suddenly Daniel realized that this wasn't mythology, it wasn't even history. This was a cold, dark reality. The thought raised a shiver along the length of his spine.

"What about the Stargate?" Jack said, breaking into the silence. "Do the dead guys still use it?"

"The Eye?" Elspeth said, glancing at Daniel for confirmation. He nodded. "Yes," she said. "The old gods tried to destroy the Eye, but they couldn't. And still the Devourers fly through it."

"Fly?" Jack threw a significant look at Daniel. "In ships, I presume. Not with... wings?"

Elspeth blinked. "Neither boats nor wings," she said. "They ride in fighters."

"Fighters?" Jack made a swooping gesture with his hand. "As in fighter aircraft? In the sky?"

"Death Gliders," Teal'c surmised from his place next to Sam.

"It's possible," she said. "Maybe they have some kind of onboard DHD so they can dial the gate remotely before they fly through?"

Jack nodded. "You ever see them land one of these things?"

"Never," Elspeth said. "When the Devourers are close, we stay inside and put out all the lights. Discovery means death."

With a soft clatter, Aedan dropped his arrows onto the floor and jumped down from his perch. "You can't travel through the Eye," he told Jack. "Only a fool imagines escaping this world. And there's only death for those who try."

"That's not true," Elspeth retorted, turning to face him. "People *have* escaped." She appealed to the rest of her people. "Haven't they?" Some of them shrugged, while others just shook their heads as if bored of an oft-rehearsed argument.

But she had one rapt listener. "How?" Jack demanded. "Tell

me how they escaped."

"The resistance, of course."

"And they are…?"

She looked at him askance, eyes narrowing. "Why do you pretend you know nothing of them when you're wearing their symbol on your arm?"

Jack's gaze darted to Daniel's. "This?" he said, touching his SG-1 patch.

Elspeth shook her head impatiently and pushed up her sleeve, revealing a tattoo on her arm. "This," she said.

The Earth glyph.

Jack's eyebrows rose. "Okay," he said cautiously. "Daniel, any ideas?"

"Well, think about it," he said, mind racing ahead to make the connections. "If you're looking for a symbol of resistance, of a place of safety, that's a pretty good one."

"You mean because of what happened to Ra?"

Daniel nodded. "Stories are powerful," he said. "They spread fast and they're almost impossible to stop. Over time they evolve into legends and myths, but there's usually a kernel of truth in there somewhere." He brushed a finger over Elspeth's tattoo. "And there it is."

"The resistance is no legend," Elspeth insisted, pulling down her sleeve. "It's real." She threw a defiant look at Aedan, as if daring him to object. "They're led by a man called Dix, and he's helped thousands to escape this world and join them."

"Through the Stargate?" Jack didn't sound convinced and neither was Daniel. No one was escaping covertly through a defunct Stargate, with no DHD, that was the only thing standing for miles around.

Elspeth shook her head. "I don't know how. I just know that if you find him, he'll get you out."

"Elspeth, stop it," Aedan said at last, weary and frustrated. "Stop your nonsense."

"It's not nonsense!" She turned back to Daniel. "Dix serves

the old gods," she said, "and the resistance is going to help them return and save us. The old gods will drive out the Devourers and we'll be free again."

"The 'old gods'," Teal'c said darkly, "will not free you. They will enslave you."

Elspeth folded her arms across her chest and fixed Teal'c with a hard look. "Well, I'd rather serve the old gods than feed the Devourers."

"Then you know nothing of slavery."

"And *you* know nothing of the Amam."

Teal'c glared at her and she glared right back. Daniel had to swallow a smile at the sight of this stripling girl going toe-to-toe with Teal'c.

"Easy there, big guy," Jack said, not bothering to smother his own amusement. "This one looks dangerous."

"Take no notice of her," Aedan said, glancing between Elspeth and Teal'c with a shimmer of concern. "Elspeth believes in fairy tales."

"Aedan," she warned. "Don't you —"

"It's a myth!" he snapped. "The whole Dix thing is a myth. How could he still be alive? The war was generations ago."

"The old gods can do anything."

"Nonsense! Everyone knows the 'old gods' weren't gods, they were just creatures from another world. And now they're gone and they're not coming back to save us. *No one* can save us." Aiden snatched up his arrows from the floor and headed for one of the passageways branching off from the room. He stopped at the last moment, fixing Daniel and Jack with a serious look. "I don't know where you've come from, but, trust me, it's better to hide and live than to fight and die. That's the reality of the world and anyone who thinks otherwise ends up dead."

After Aedan had stormed out, it wasn't long before Elspeth and the others started preparing to sleep. Sam was surprised when the colonel suggested they sleep back in the 'cell' until she realized that it had a door, which meant they could talk with a modicum of privacy.

So they dragged their kit inside, along with a straw pallet to help Daniel rest more comfortably, and made camp. Once they'd laid out their bedrolls Sam extinguished the lamp and groped her way back to her sleeping bag. It was almost pitch black, only the dimming firelight seeping around the door cutting the darkness. Crouching down, she misjudged her position and when she reached out for her bedroll, she hit a nose and part of a face instead.

"Ow! Carter!"

She snatched back her hand, wincing. "Sorry, sir."

Expecting another sour complaint, she was amazed when he just said, "Nah, it was only my eye. I've got a spare."

Bottling her surprise, not quite knowing how to respond, she found her sleeping bag in silence and crawled inside, pulling it up right under her chin against the chill of the cave. Away from the fire the damp stone seemed to be pressing in all around them. She shivered.

They were all quiet for a moment, lying close together in the darkness. Outside she could hear the muted sounds of their hosts settling down for the night, low voices and the rustle of their straw pallets. It was comforting, in a way, and she could feel herself start to unwind for the first time in days — maybe months. Aching muscles sank into the scant comfort of her bedroll, her eyes closing as sleep stole up on her. Next to her, Daniel yawned. None of them had slept much the night before and she felt safe here — the colonel hadn't even bothered to set a watch.

"So… zombies, huh?"

Despite the tension stacked up between them, Sam smiled; the colonel sounded like a kid telling scary stories after lights-out at camp. "Whatever they are, sir, I think we can rule out the cast of *Thriller*."

"It is most likely that they are Goa'uld," Teal'c said.

"Flesh-eating snakeheads?" The colonel gave an exaggerated sigh. "Is it me, or is this whole situation CATFUed, Carter?"

"What?" Daniel said, puzzled. "Cat food?"

Sam snorted a laugh, mostly born of stress and exhaustion, and then found that she couldn't stop.

The colonel didn't laugh, but she could hear a smile in his voice when he said, "No giggling."

And that made it worse, made it harder to stop laughing, and for a moment — a *moment* — it felt like old times, like things were normal again.

Shifting on his pallet, Daniel said, "Okay, what am I missing?"

"Carter? Care to translate for our linguist... ?"

It took her a couple of tries before she could get a grip on her giggles. "CATFU, Daniel," she managed at last. "C.A.T.F.U. Completely and Totally, um, 'Fouled' Up."

"Ah. Military humor. Ha ha."

"Cat food," Sam laughed again. "This situation is Whiskas, sir."

Daniel chuckled and even the colonel huffed a quiet laugh. Silence fell for a while as their laughter subsided, a good silence, as if they were all enjoying the rare moment of camaraderie. It was probably the first time they'd laughed together since before Edora.

But eventually the moment passed and Daniel said, "You know, I think Teal'c might be right about the Goa'uld."

"You think they're flesh-eating snakes?"

"Well, no. I mean, I don't know about the flesh-eating part, but I *do* know the term Amam."

The colonel shifted. Now that her eyes were used to the dark, Sam could see him loop his hands behind his head and settle in for the long haul. "Let's hear it then."

"It's quite simple really," Daniel said. "The Book of the Dead describes a set of demonic entities that harrow the dead in the between-realm of the afterlife. They're known as Devourers, or Amam, who feed on parts of the body and soul."

"Sounds like fun."

"Well, they *are* demons…" He cleared his throat. "Teal'c, have you ever heard of the Amam, or any kind of 'undead' creature?"

"I have not," Teal'c said. "But it does not follow that they do not exist. I have not encountered everything in this galaxy."

"True," the colonel said. "You haven't even encountered my lake yet."

"Is that an invitation to fish, O'Neill?"

"Maybe it is."

And maybe, Sam thought, it was something about this darkness that was lightening the colonel's mood because somehow he was more himself now than he had been in weeks. And she felt lighter for it too, because perhaps it meant he wasn't so lost to them after all.

"You know," she said, "these Amam could just be the Jaffa of a new System Lord who's come in here and wiped out whoever used to be in charge."

"That's what I was thinking." Daniel turned toward her, his glasses glinting in the faint light seeping around the door. "They're probably Jaffa mythologized into 'undead' creatures by whatever Goa'uld first ruled this world. Perhaps they've even taken on the persona of Amam?"

"And don't forget the sarcophagus," Sam added. "I mean, talk about rising from the dead…"

"Yes! I think we can say we're not dealing with real live — or is that real undead? — zombies."

"I hope you're right," the colonel said, "because *Night of the Living Dead* spooked the hell outa Teal'c."

"It did not, O'Neill."

"He's just saying that. He was watching through his fingers."

Sam grinned, she couldn't help herself. "At least one thing's clear, sir. Whoever these 'Devourers' are, they can use the Stargate network. And that means there's a way home."

"My thoughts exactly, Carter." He scrubbed a hand through his hair. "I can't believe I'm about to say this, but it looks like tracking down the flesh-eating-snakehead-zombies is actually our best chance of getting off this rock."

Sam smiled into the darkness and, after a moment, Daniel said, "You know, Jack, it's at times like this when I… I just…"

"…wonder where it all went wrong?"

"Yep, pretty much."

CHAPTER ELEVEN

HOPE was starting to fade, that was the worst of it. After three days without contact, or the slightest sign of SG-1, hope was starting to fade. He could do without a lot of things — sleep, food, good news — but hope was critical. Without it, everything started to collapse. And George Hammond could see hope fading in the faces around him every time the Stargate opened and SG-1 didn't walk through.

Take now, for example. Standing at a comfortable parade rest, his hands clasped behind his back, Hammond watched as SG-2 traipsed down the ramp and the wormhole fizzled closed behind them. Shoulders slumped, they looked defeated as Major Ferretti glanced up at the control room and shook his head: another hope dashed, another planet crossed off the list. There weren't many left.

Leaning forward, Hammond pulled the microphone toward him. "Welcome back, SG-2. Debrief in one hour."

Not that it looked like they had much to report, but he wanted every possible detail. You never knew what would become important.

Sergeant Harriman looked up from his station as Ferretti's team handed over their weapons to the SFs and trudged out of the gate room. "Sir?" he said. "We have a scheduled contact with Tollana. Shall I send 'Situation Unchanged'?"

"Yes, go ahead." Hammond repressed a sigh, preferring to keep his feelings to himself around his people. The less they knew about what was going on with the Tollan the better, but the base was full of smart people and he couldn't keep their frequent contacts secret.

He watched as the gate started to spin again, Harriman counting down the chevrons until the seventh locked and the wormhole erupted into the gate room. In a couple of moments the message had been sent and the wormhole collapsed. Another ten hours before the next update, and by that point they'd be half a day away from the trade negotiations that were meant to spark off the whole operation.

Come on, Jack. He sent the message out silently into the cosmos. *Get your team home.* But there was no response and the Stargate remained still and mute.

"SG-3 is due out at 1800 hours, sir," Harriman reported, interrupting his thoughts. "No scheduled activations until then."

"Thank you, son." He thought for a moment, then added, "Would you ask Colonel Makepeace to report to my office before he gears up?"

"Yes sir."

Leaving Harriman to his work, Hammond trudged up the steps to the briefing room. For the first time since SG-1 had gone missing he was starting to contemplate the idea that they might not be coming back, that they hadn't simply fallen victim to a glitch in the Stargate network and that something nasty, something deliberate, had befallen them.

Jacob's warning was still fresh in his mind: there *were* a lot of Goa'uld looking at Earth with hungry eyes. And if any one of them knew that their relationship with the Asgard was hanging by a thread — and that that thread was in the person of Jack O'Neill — then wouldn't it be in their interest to get him and his whole team out of the picture?

There was another option that was even darker, in its own way. But if Maybourne had somehow gotten wind of their plan, then what better way to sow the seeds of distrust between Earth and her allies than to abduct SG-1 and continue to steal from their friends? With the SGC's flagship team implicated in the collapse of their alliance system, the Pentagon would be more inclined than ever to adopt the aggressive policy toward off-world relations for which Maybourne and his ilk had long been pushing. The whole situation would play right into their hands.

Stomping across the briefing room into his office he shut the door and slumped down into his chair, letting it rock back under his weight. Truth was, if that happened, General Hammond wasn't sure he could continue to serve, because that policy would ultimately lead to destruction — not just of Stargate Command, but potentially of the whole planet. They had enough enemies out there without making enemies of their friends and, to put it bluntly, there was no amount of military hardware they could steal that would protect them better than the alliances they had spent almost three years forging.

Someone rapped on his door and he looked up to see Makepeace standing there.

"Come," he said, switching on his desk lamp to alleviate the gloom.

"You wanted to see me, sir?" Makepeace said as he stepped inside.

Hammond nodded. "Shut the door, Colonel, and take a seat."

A muscle in Makepeace's jaw tightened, a spike of anxiety, as he closed the door and perched tensely on the chair in front of Hammond's desk. Very different from O'Neill's studied nonchalance, he couldn't help noting. Makepeace managed to be at once hard and tense, like iron under stress. It was his strength, no doubt, but also a weakness. Hammond had always suspected that O'Neill's flexibility, his propensity to bend — the rules, his ideas, and his strategy — was at the core of his talent for leadership. But, that be as it may, O'Neill wasn't there and Makepeace was.

"Colonel," Hammond said, picking his way through the conversation carefully, "there is something I need to brief you about regarding SG-1."

"Sir?" His hands were fists, resting on his knees.

"Regarding the need to bring them home." Makepeace's brow furrowed, but he didn't say anything and Hammond continued. "You may have noticed that we are in close contact with the Tollan at the present time."

"Yes sir."

"That's because our alliances, both with the Tollan and the Asgard, are in a fragile state. We are trying to rebuild them, but it's proving difficult — especially without Colonel O'Neill. As you know, he is a particular friend of the Asgard."

Makepeace gave a curt nod. "Yes sir, I understand." A beat, then "Can I ask why our alliances are so fragile?"

Hammond spread his hands flat on the desk and tried to decide how much he could reveal. It made him angry, furious, that he should be forced to doubt his own people, that the treachery of one of their own had driven his allies to demand this secrecy. He looked across the desk at Makepeace, fixed him with a searching look, and made his decision: he couldn't keep his teams working in the dark any longer. "There have been some thefts, Colonel. Technology and weapons, stolen from our allies by a rogue off-world team operated by Colonel Maybourne."

Makepeace's face was like granite. "I see."

"The disappearance of SG-1 has only exacerbated the situation," Hammond continued. "Some among our allies suspect them of complicity, and they're using that against us, to justify ending their alliances with us."

A long silence fell as Makepeace absorbed the news. Stoic as ever, he didn't even look surprised. "Those alliances have always been a raw deal for us, sir," he said eventually. "Maybe we'd be better off without them, relying on our own knowhow instead."

"Better off without them?" Hammond repeated, aware of the edge creeping into his voice. "Colonel, those alliances are the only things that have kept this planet safe."

Makepeace nodded, but then said, "But maybe we relied on them too much, sir. Maybe we should have built up our own capability instead."

It was an old argument, he was weary of it. "Maybe we should have," he conceded with a sigh. "And maybe we relied too much on Colonel O'Neill's friendship with the Asgard. But we are where we are and it would certainly serve our enemies' interests if the Asgard withdrew us from the Protected Planets Treaty."

Makepeace shifted in his seat, uncomfortable. "But that's not an imminent danger, is it, sir?"

He hesitated before he answered, but there was no point in hiding the truth. "Colonel, if we don't find Colonel O'Neill soon, I believe it's a very imminent danger."

Makepeace stood up, paced the length of the room and back again. "What kind of timescale are we talking about, General?"

"We're talking days, Colonel."

"*Days?*"

"Our allies wanted O'Neill to —" He stopped himself before he said more; he daren't talk about the SGC mole. But, if they didn't retrieve SG-1 soon, all secrecy would be moot because there'd be a Goa'uld fleet in orbit and then everyone would know everything. Of course by then it would be too late and, instead of searching for SG-1, they'd be scrambling around looking for an Alpha Site and wishing like hell the Appropriations Committee hadn't put the kibosh on O'Neill's plan. He ran a hand over his head, trying to scrub away the panic. It was dangerous and only ever produced bad decisions. "Colonel," he said after a moment, "I'm telling you this because there's a chance that SG-1 has been abducted by those who would profit from the collapse of our alliances. And I need you to factor that possibility into your search."

"You mean the Goa'uld?" He stopped pacing and fixed Hammond with a probing look. "You think the Goa'uld might have done this deliberately, to damage our alliances?"

"The Goa'uld," he said. "Or Maybourne."

"Not Maybourne."

Hammond lifted his eyebrows at the colonel's vehemence.

"He —" Makepeace broke off. "He's a slime ball, sir, but he's not a traitor."

"Son, Colonel Maybourne is nothing *but* a traitor: self-serving, conniving, and unscrupulous." He cocked his head, studying Makepeace's unyielding features with sudden doubt. "Don't tell me you're sympathetic to his cause?"

"Absolutely not, sir, but he's an Air Force officer. He wouldn't harm his own people."

Hammond shook his head. "I don't know who his people are, anymore, Colonel. But there's too much at stake to rule out any possibilities."

Makepeace frowned. "Yes sir. I understand."

"Give it some thought," Hammond said, studying the troubled expression on Makepeace's face. "Anything your team can discover, or remember, that might shed light on the whereabouts of SG-1 will be valuable."

"I'll do everything I can to locate them, sir," he promised. "I'll—" He cleared his throat. "Everything I can, sir."

Hammond nodded. "I know you will, son."

After Makepeace had left, Hammond sat in silence for a while. On his desk, the red phone gleamed dully in the light of his lamp and he stared at it until it blurred. It had always looked ominous, recalling as it did those long fearful years when Earth had been poised on the brink of mutually assured destruction, but today it seemed to take on an even graver significance. If O'Neill wasn't back before the scheduled mission to Tollana then he'd have no choice but to make the call, but until then he was determined to cling to what little hope remained and to carry on believing that next time the Stargate opened it would be to welcome his people home.

CHAPTER TWELVE

HE'S DIGGING. There's something he needs, something he can't live without. It's buried and he can't reach it. He's digging, but earth is collapsing in on all sides, faster than he can dig it out, burying him in black, loamy dirt.

"Jack?"

Someone says ashes to ashes *and he can't breathe. He has to find a way out, he can't stop digging. Hands pull on his arms, dragging him away.* There's nothing you can do. I'm sorry, he's gone. *He fights them off, he wants to hit them, to scream, but his voice is locked in his throat and he can't make a sound, he can't —*

"Jack!"

He jerked awake with a gasp, and for a moment the only real thing in the world was the hand on his arm.

"You were dreaming," Daniel said, voice raspy.

Rigid from the nightmare, he had to force his body to relax before he could work enough moisture into his mouth to speak. "Sorry," he said, scrubbing a hand over his face. This happened sometimes, to all of them: bad dreams. Opening his eyes, he looked around, but could only see darkness and had to fight off a slight nightmare-induced panic when he remembered they were underground. Ripping the Velcro cover off his watch he looked at the time — 0300 hours MST, which didn't mean much here, but told him they had about twenty-four hours before the operation to Tollana began. He could feel pressure like a band tightening around his head, and that choked scream from his dream still clogged his throat.

"I think it's morning," Daniel said. "Sam and Teal'c went to find a bathroom about half an hour ago."

Taking a breath, easing the tension, Jack just lay there for a moment. At least he wouldn't have to try to sleep again. Rubbing the grit from his eyes, he sat up and reached for his flashlight and matches. Rustling across the straw-covered floor, he lit the lamp in the corner and the room brightened enough that he could see Daniel. The sight did nothing to help his dark mood; Daniel wasn't looking good at all.

"How you doing?" Jack asked, trying not to betray his concern as he dropped down onto his bedroll and started lacing his boots.

Daniel made a non-committal gesture which, given his propensity to underestimate, most certainly meant he felt as god-awful as he looked. Jack ran a hand through his hair, considering his options. There weren't many. "Maybe you should stay here? We'll come back for you when we find a way home."

Staring up at the ceiling, Daniel said, "I don't want to slow you down, but I think we both know that if there's any chance I can get back through the gate in the next twenty-four hours I should take it."

Jack closed his eyes and swallowed hard before he said, "That bad, huh?"

"Yeah," Daniel said shortly. "Definitely infected, probably verging on septicemia by now."

"I'll give you another antibiotic shot, we've got one more."

Daniel turned his head to look at him, his glasses glinting in the lamplight. "Thanks," he said. "But you know that won't be enough."

Jack nodded and reached out to press his hand against Daniel's forehead. He was burning up. "God, Daniel..."

"Dose me up with everything you've got left and let's just get home," he said with a weak smile.

Jack forced a smile of his own. "You know Fraiser's going to kick your ass for this, right?"

"At this point," Daniel said, turning to stare up at the ceiling again, "I'm actually looking forward to it."

Sam sat amid a small group of Aedan Trask's people with one of their weapons in her lap. Aedan himself stood a little apart, watching her through narrowed eyes. But he seemed relaxed enough about letting her handle the gun and just leaned one shoulder against the cavern wall, sipping at a steaming mug of the herbal infusion they called tea.

Sam had refused the offer of breakfast — these people obviously had limited resources — and instead shared out the content of her Apple Maple Oatmeal MRE pack. In return, she'd gotten this close look at one of their weapons.

It was like nothing she'd ever seen before and it was almost certainly not of Goa'uld design. There was something organic about its flowing lines, from the rounded muzzle through to the segmented handle.

"It has a stun setting?" she asked, looking for some kind of interface that might regulate the power output.

Aedan shook his head. "No settings," he said. "It's only designed to incapacitate." He shrugged. "Unless you're very weak. That's why we didn't use it on your friend Daniel."

That surprised her. "It's a non-lethal weapon?"

"The Devourers prefer to consume their prey alive."

She looked up to see if he was joking, but there was no irony in his face. "But they must —"

Her question was interrupted by a shout from the other side of the room. "Carter!"

The colonel was awake, standing next to Teal'c at the head of the passage leading from their sleeping quarters. Still buoyed by the thawing tension of the previous night, she waved in response and climbed to her feet. "Thanks for showing me this," she said, returning the weapon to the young lad next to her. "It's fascinating."

He grinned and colored a little, making Sam smile.

Then, with a nod to Aedan, she began picking her way through the people toward the colonel and Teal'c. "Sir," she said as she drew closer, "I was just looking at one of their weapons. I've never seen anything like it."

"Fascinating," the colonel said, without interest. "Now gear up and get ready to move out."

"Move out?" She glanced at Teal'c. "Where to, sir? Back to the gate?"

He ignored her question — so much for last night's bonhomie — and instead summoned Aedan over with the kind of curt gesture usually reserved for airmen.

Obviously irritated by the colonel's manner, Aedan muttered a few words to the people around him before strolling over. "Jack O'Neill," he said. "Good morning."

"These 'Devourers'," the colonel said, without preamble. "Where can I find them?"

Aedan gave a gruff laugh. "You don't," he said. "You hide from them."

"Say I wanted to find one," the colonel pressed, his patience clearly thin. "Where would I look?"

Aedan shook his head and sipped his tea. "Up," he said.

Sam frowned. "Up?"

Aedan gestured toward the ceiling of the cavern. "They fly," he said. "And if they see you, they take you. And then you die."

"Teal'c," the colonel said, "you think you could take down a glider with your staff weapon?"

"It is possible, O'Neill. But not easy."

And suddenly Sam understood his plan. "You think we'll be able to recover some kind of DHD from a wrecked glider, sir?"

"You said they probably had one on board."

"I was speculating," she pointed out.

"And yet it's the best plan we've got," he said, as if he was willing her to agree. But she couldn't, she knew there was a better plan. After a moment, the colonel turned back to Aedan and said, "Thank you for your... hospitality. We'll be leaving now and we'll need our weapons."

Aedan nodded. "You're strange people," he said, "not to know or fear the Devourers. I don't know whether to admire or pity you."

With a flicker of a smile, the colonel said, "Go with 'admire'."

Aedan's expression softened a fraction, but all he said was,

"Either way, if you seek out the Devourers you *will* end up dead." He nodded to Teal'c and Sam. "I will have your weapons ready for you topside. Elspeth will show you the way." Then he walked away and Sam watched him until he disappeared down one of the other passageways.

"Okay," the colonel said. "Let's grab our stuff."

He headed back toward their sleeping quarters and Sam followed, Teal'c at her shoulder. "Sir?" she ventured. "Are you sure this is wise?"

"I didn't ask for your opinion, Carter."

"No, sir," she said as they entered the small room where Daniel lay looking sallow and fevered. "But I just think the further we move from the gate the less chance there is of a rescue team finding us. And, sir, Daniel's really not well and —"

"I know!" He spun to face her, anger sparking in his eyes. "I know Daniel's sick. I *know*." He took a breath, calming himself. "That's why we have to go. We have to get home *today*."

"Sir," she said carefully, "our best chance of getting home is staying close to the gate and waiting for rescue."

His jaw tightened in the way it did when he was biting back words and he turned around and started to pack up his gear. "We have no idea if rescue's coming, Carter."

"But it is, sir." She tried another tack. "Think about it: if you'd left the vicinity of the Stargate on Edora your radio wouldn't have picked up our signal and Teal'c would have died in that cave. You'd still be there."

He didn't say anything for a moment, rolling up his bedroll with quick, angry movements. "Three months," he growled, stuffing it into his pack. "I waited three damn months on Edora, Carter. Do you think we have *anything* like that time?"

She didn't answer, couldn't quite think around that slap in the face. Didn't he know what those three months had been like for the rest of them, not even knowing whether he'd survived the fire rain? Not knowing whether all they'd bring home in the end was a body? She felt a swift flare of anger that she could barely control and dared not open her mouth to reply.

"God, Jack," Daniel sighed from where he sat propped up against his pack.

No one spoke for a while. Sam, furious and hurt, moved to her pack and started shoving everything back inside. It didn't take long and she was done before the colonel, which gave her a bleak moment of satisfaction. Still too angry to risk speaking, she silently began to help Daniel.

"We have one day," the colonel ground out. "Twenty-four hours or we are so unbelievably screwed, you wouldn't believe it."

Daniel frowned in confusion and Sam shared it. What was he talking about? But then Daniel's eyes widened in understanding. "Because of me, you mean?"

The colonel didn't answer. "You've got five minutes," he told them, hefting his pack over one shoulder and stalking out.

The tension eased once he was gone, but Sam searched Daniel's face in concern. "What do you mean because of you?"

He closed his eyes for a moment, then looked at her and said, "I'm not doing so well, Sam. I need a doctor. Soon."

"Okay," she said, swallowing a sudden surge of fear. He didn't need to deal with her worries on top of his own. "Okay, so we'll get you home."

"That's the plan."

Teal'c offered his hand to Daniel and between the two of them they got him onto his feet. Jaw set, he looked doubtfully at the pack on the floor.

"You cannot carry that, Daniel Jackson," Teal'c said.

"No."

Sam crouched and opened it up. "Tell me what's important."

"Ah, my notebooks, camera…"

"MREs, canteen, med-kit?" she suggested, pulling them all out. "Spare clothes. Teal'c, do you have room for his bedroll?"

It didn't take long to redistribute most of Daniel's belongings between the two of them and her pack only felt slightly heavier when she swung it onto her back.

"Okay," Daniel said, grim but determined. "Let's do this." With obvious effort, he started walking toward the door and Sam exchanged a worried look with Teal'c as they followed.

Bending his head toward her, Teal'c said in a low voice, "Daniel Jackson is strong. He will endure this hardship."

"I just wish he didn't have to."

Teal'c didn't respond to that and she figured there was nothing he could say about her futile wishes. All that mattered now was getting Daniel home.

At least it wasn't raining.

But it *was* cold, a dank kind of chill that crept into your bones. Crappy planet, Jack thought, squinting up at the white roof of cloud that served as the sky. Maybe the sun never shone here?

A few of Aedan's people had gathered to see them off, Elspeth among them. An older woman stood talking to Daniel, who was resting on one of the rocks and catching his breath after the climb out of the caves. In the daylight he looked even worse, dark circles under his eyes and skin like dirty snow. God only knew how he was staying on his feet; Jack knew plenty of soldiers who'd have given up by now. The woman put her hand to his face, shaking her head in a manner that reminded him of Fraiser — he figured she was the doc, or medic, or whatever they called her. Shame she didn't have more than a few herbs to work with.

"O'Neill." Teal'c called his attention away from Daniel and toward the iron door to the caves. It stood open as Aedan Trask and a couple of his men emerged holding all their weapons. Thank God for small mercies. They lay them carefully on the ground and stepped back.

"Thank you," Jack said, crouching down to examine their stuff. Their weapons looked untouched and he picked up one of the MP5s, turning it over in his hands.

"That's mine, sir," Carter said, holding out her hand for it. They all had their preferred weapons, the ones they'd check out of the armory first if they had the choice. His had a little nick on the forearm that was the result of a close encounter with the side of a cliff-face one dark night. Carter's had a scratch along the pistol grip.

He handed over her weapon without comment and she took it without thanks. Better that way, he figured. He'd let things get too friendly the previous night, too normal, and it was time to cool off. But it had been hard to resist that unexpected moment of camaraderie between them all, lying in the dark and feeling more-or-less safe for the first time in days. Maybe he shouldn't have let it happen, but he was getting so tired of the whole jackass routine and he missed his team, he missed the bond that had drawn them so close — especially now, when it felt like everything was going to hell. He wasn't too proud to admit he needed them.

Another twenty-four hours, he told himself, and he'd call it off. If they weren't home by then, the Tollan mission would be a bust anyway, and he wasn't keeping up this charade for a moment longer than absolutely necessary.

He picked up his MP5, slipped the strap over his head and cinched it tight, then holstered his Berretta. Better. He felt much better armed. Carter was doing the same and Teal'c was hefting his staff weapon with obvious satisfaction. Daniel hadn't moved, so Jack picked up his handgun and handed it to Teal'c; Daniel wasn't in any condition to fight and someone should make use of the weapon. Just in case.

So, this was it. They were ready. The question was, ready for what?

He glanced up, but the sky was empty. He figured they'd head for high ground and stay out from under any tree cover, looping back toward the Stargate. If there were some flesh-eating Goa'uld flying around up there, they'd get a good view of them and hopefully come close enough that Teal'c could take them down. If not, then maybe Carter would be right and they'd find a MALP at the Stargate and SG-3 scouting the area.

Crazier things had happened.

It wasn't a great plan, but it was *a* plan.

After their final farewells, Aedan's people watched in silence as they left. The only one showing any kind of agitation was Elspeth. She was fidgeting next to Aedan, looking from him back to Daniel, and up at Aedan again. Jack couldn't figure out if she was his sister, girlfriend, or just another member of the gang, but in the end she didn't say anything as Jack gave the order and his team moved out.

He took point, leading them back up the valley along a shallow incline. There was a ridge along the top that was nice and exposed and would give an easy view down over the valley and back toward the Stargate. He kept the pace slow because of Daniel, who walked with Carter. Teal'c brought up the rear. No one was talking. Specifically, no one was talking to *him*. He could hear Daniel's slow, breathless voice behind him and a few curt replies from Carter. He couldn't hear what they were saying, for which he was grateful. Eavesdroppers never heard anything good about themselves and he was quite sure he didn't want to hear Carter's opinion of her CO right now.

He kept his eyes on the sky as they walked. The clouds were high, a thin misty layer of darker cloud running fast beneath the impenetrable ceiling of white. Once he thought he saw something, a dark flash that was gone before it was there, but he couldn't be sure. It could have been a bird. "Teal'c," he said, glancing over his shoulder, "did you —?"

He broke off when he saw a figure running after them — one of Aedan's people.

Teal'c also turned when he saw Jack looking and then they all stopped and waited while Elspeth, braids dancing as she ran, caught up with them. Bracing himself to turn her down if she wanted to come along for the ride, Jack stalked back past Carter and Daniel so that he was the first one to meet her. "Did we forget something?" he said.

She shook her head, out of breath. "I wanted…" she gasped,

"…to tell you…"

Jack waited, almost patiently, while she caught her breath.

"South," she said, when she could speak again. She pointed off in the opposite direction from the Stargate. "You should go south," she said. "That's where the camps are. If you want to find the Devourers, they're there."

Jack shared a glance with Teal'c. "How far south?"

"Several days walk," she said. "But if you go north," she nodded in the direction he'd been taking them, "there is nothing beyond but mountains. Some people up there, yes, but little food. And when the snows come, they'll head south too."

Jack didn't bother telling her that they weren't planning to hang around for the ski season.

"Thank you, Elspeth," Daniel said, coming to stand next to Jack. "Um, did Aedan not want you to tell us? Will you be in trouble, now?"

She shrugged. "Aedan thinks the Devourers will take you before you get anywhere. And if you walk like this, in the open, they will. He thinks you're fools."

"He may have a point," Jack said.

But the girl shook her head. "I think you're unafraid and that's rare in this world. Aedan is no coward, but he's frightened. He's too frightened to do anything. But you…" Suddenly she seized Daniel's hand, squeezing it between her own. "If you find Dix, if you find a way to reach the resistance, promise that you will tell me. Promise you will come back for me."

"I…" Daniel threw Jack a helpless look. "Sure. Of course we will, Elspeth."

"Promise."

"I promise."

She looked at him closely for a moment, as if judging the honesty in his face, before she nodded in satisfaction and let his hand go. She glanced up at the sky, then back again. "I will pray that the gods will keep you safe," she said. "And that they'll guide you toward them and to safety."

Next to him, Jack heard Teal'c take a breath to object, but silenced him with a hand on his arm. "Great, thank you," he said. "You pray away."

Elspeth nodded, gave Daniel one more long look, and then took to her heels and started running back toward the distant line of rocks that marked her home.

"Did you see the way she checked the sky?" Jack said to Teal'c.

"I did."

"I thought I saw something earlier. Keep your eyes peeled, buddy."

Teal'c raised an eyebrow at the expression, but didn't comment. Carter said nothing, still resolutely pissed off, but her disapproval of his plan — such as it was — radiated out in cold waves.

With a sigh, Jack glanced at the ridgeline. He figured they'd get a better view from there — both north and south — and then they could decide which path to take. "Let's go," he said.

"I don't suppose we'll be able to come back for her, will we?" Daniel said as they started walking. "I hate doing that, making promises I know I can't keep."

"You gave her hope," Carter said. "That's something. And who knows? We might be able to come back."

If Daniel answered, Jack didn't hear and they walked on in silence.

Maybe half an hour later, they were climbing up the rocky incline toward the ridge. Daniel was struggling and Carter had her hand on his arm, helping him along. Jack stopped halfway up and looked back along the valley. At the far end, beyond the entrance to the caves, it swept around and he realized it joined with the Stargate valley — the whole area looked like it had been glacial several millennia ago.

Although the air was dank and cold, the white sky was weirdly bright and Jack pulled on his sunglasses to cut the glare. And that's when he saw it: a dark shape racing up the Stargate valley, banking right and streaking toward them, long and jagged like a dagger. And fast.

"Teal'c!"

Teal'c lifted his weapon, but the ship — whatever it was — was moving too damn fast. Then it climbed, almost vertical, and disappeared into the clouds.

"Okay," Jack said, "that was no glider."

"It was not," Teal'c agreed. His eyes were still on the sky and he pointed. "There, look."

O'Neill followed the line of his arm and saw it, another shape, swooping down through the clouds and then up again. "Huh," he said. "That *was* a glider."

"Indeed."

They kept watching the sky and suddenly the clouds lit up, orange then blue, before two shapes dropped down out of the clouds, one on the tail of the other.

"It's a dog fight," Carter said.

"The ship in pursuit is certainly a Death Glider," Teal'c said after a moment, his sharp eyes picking out what Jack's couldn't. "The other, I do not recognize."

"Whoever he is," Jack said, "the other guy's in trouble." There was a burst of weapons fire — definitely looked like a staff-cannon — and then the small ship was nose-diving, a trail of smoke streaming out behind. "He's lost power."

Jack winced as he watched the ship plummet toward the ground, but at the last moment its pilot managed to pull the nose up. Not enough to keep the bird in the air but enough to keep it from driving headfirst into the ground.

He heard the impact a few moments later and saw the curl of black smoke rising up on the far side of the ridgeline. Up above, the glider disappeared into the clouds and was gone.

"Let's go," he said, heading up to the top of the ridge. From there it was easy to see the crash site; it was about half a klick down into a valley on the other side. Despite the smoke hanging in the air, Jack couldn't see a lot of fire and it looked like a sizeable portion of the fuselage had survived the impact. It wasn't in pieces, at least, and for the first time in too long Jack felt a pulse of optimism. Maybe, at last, their luck was about to change.

"That is certainly not a Death Glider," Teal'c said.

"Nope. But whatever it is," he said, "it came out of the Stargate valley." He risked a glance at Carter. "Think it might have a DHD on board?"

"There's no way to tell, sir."

"Well, there's one way…" He turned to Daniel. "Okay to keep going?"

A tight nod, not even a smile, was his only response. Daniel was in a bad way, but this could be it — their way home. They couldn't stop now.

"Right," Jack decided, "stay sharp. We're gonna check it out."

CHAPTER THIRTEEN

COLONEL O'Neill led them slowly down the steep incline toward the smoking remains of the crashed ship. He moved with his customary stealth, but more slowly than was usual in consideration of Daniel Jackson's incapacity. Teal'c himself brought up the rear, his gaze roving between his teammates and the smoke curling black into the misty sky. He caught the acrid scent of burning flesh on the air and guessed that the pilot had not survived the impact.

High in the sky, he thought he saw more shapes darting in and out of the clouds. But they were too far away for him to be certain.

The terrain was rocky, as if some giant hand had scattered boulders across the landscape, which made it easy to conceal their approach. Here and there a few of the low, scrubby trees that populated the higher slopes also dotted the sides of the valley, and among those trees Teal'c thought he saw movement. He was about to alert O'Neill when the colonel lifted his fist to halt them, dropping to a crouch behind one of the larger rocks. He waved Teal'c closer.

Major Carter helped Daniel Jackson to sit down, and as he passed them Teal'c caught her eye. The look of sharp anxiety he saw there made him fear for his friend, whose skin now bore an unmistakable deathly pallor.

Preoccupied with his fears, Teal'c crouched next to O'Neill. His eyes were also fixed on Daniel Jackson, his mouth a tight line of concern. But when he looked at Teal'c all he said was, "I saw movement in the trees."

Teal'c nodded, "As did I."

Peering around the boulder, Teal'c scanned the crash site. It was now only a couple hundred meters away and he could make out a dark, wedge-shaped ship that was mostly intact.

A long furrow of scorched, overturned earth marked its landing trajectory, the sharp nose having come to rest amid a small copse of trees close to the edge of the valley. Smoke was rising from the rear of the ship and Teal'c thought he could see what appeared to be an open canopy. Someone, perhaps, had survived. He also saw movement, on the far side of the wreck.

He ducked back down and let his back rest against the boulder. O'Neill's face was closed and hard, his eyes once more fixed on Daniel Jackson. Major Carter was trying to persuade him to drink from her canteen, her expressive features unable to mask her distress.

"I believe," Teal'c said in a low voice, "that we will not be the first to reach the crash site."

O'Neill nodded. "We need whatever that ship uses to dial the gate," he said. "At any cost."

Teal'c understood his meaning. "We are well armed, O'Neill, and have the element of surprise."

With a curt gesture, O'Neill beckoned Major Carter closer. "There are people," he said, when she crouched down next to him. "Teal'c — go around to the nose of the ship, wait for my signal. Carter, you're with me."

"What about Daniel, sir?" She glanced back at him. "If we leave him here, he'll be vulnerable."

"Don't worry about me," Daniel Jackson said, opening his fevered eyes. "I'll catch up."

There was silence while O'Neill considered the question: Teal'c could tell he liked neither option. Daniel Jackson was too weak to fight, and they must move fast to keep other scavengers from taking or damaging the technology they sought in the downed fighter, but to leave him alone and unguarded also posed dangers. After a moment, O'Neill said, "Carter, once we've secured the ship, come back for Daniel." He looked over at Daniel Jackson. "And *you* stay put."

Daniel Jackson just closed his eyes. "You betcha."

Major Carter merely nodded, her hands moving to ready her weapon.

"Okay," O'Neill said, catching them both with one look, "I want this quiet, fast and with no fuss. Our only priority is the dialing mechanism — assuming there is one." He crept to the edge of the boulder, peered around it, and after a moment signaled for them to move out.

In a low run, they moved from cover to cover, crossing the remaining distance quickly. Teal'c could now see people moving on the far side of the ship — they appeared similarly dressed to Aedan's kin — and there was some commotion taking place in the trees beyond the crash site. As they drew closer, O'Neill signaled Teal'c to move left while he and Major Carter made their way around to the rear of the ship.

Keeping silent and low, Teal'c moved into the shadow of the fuselage. Seen at close quarters, he realized that even the material from which the ship was constructed was unfamiliar. If these were Goa'uld, they were like none he had ever encountered.

He could hear shouts now, rising up with the smoke. Jeers of anger, furious laughter. Rage. It was the sound of a mob and he did not like it.

With caution, he made his way around to the front of the ship, keeping his weapon ready. Crouching low near the crumpled nose of the fighter, he studied the scene before him. A dozen young men were gathered around a figure that lay prone on the ground. Teal'c could see little of him besides large, heavy boots. He assumed it was the body of the pilot, dragged from the wreckage. But as he watched he saw the boots start to scrabble backwards, sliding along the ground until they lifted up and he realized that someone had strung a noose around the man's neck and that the rope was slung over a tree branch.

Teal'c had seen much horror in his life, many things far worse than this. Yet he felt a cold revulsion watching the laughing, jeering men haul on the rope until the pilot's head started to rise above the mob as he struggled against the rope that was slowly hanging him.

Teal'c sucked in a breath, shocked when he saw the pilot's face. Whatever he had been expecting, it was not this. The man — if indeed it was a man — was monstrous. His skin was mottled green, gray-hued lips pulled back in a snarl over sharp, killing teeth and his long hair hung in lank and pallid strands around his face. He struggled in fury, spitting and growling, his hands tied behind his back and something black — blood? — seeping from a wound in his leg.

The humans were beating him now with sticks or pieces of the wrecked ship, cursing, venting their fear and fury on this wounded creature.

In his ear, Teal'c heard his radio crackle.

"Teal'c," O'Neill said, hissy through the static. "You seeing this?"

"I am," he said quietly.

There was a long silence. He knew the question with which O'Neill was wrestling and could guess the choice his friend would make; his stubborn adherence to right in the face of wrongdoing was the trait that had first drawn him to the man.

To aid his decision, Teal'c toggled his radio and said, "The men appear to be armed only with sticks, O'Neill."

A moment later, O'Neill spoke again. "Yup. We're gonna stop this. Look to your right."

Teal'c did as ordered and could glimpse O'Neill's leg and boot protruding beyond the wreckage. "I see you."

O'Neill moved further out of cover, crouching low, with Major Carter close behind him. He signaled *three, two, one. Go.*

They went.

O'Neill let loose a burst of gunfire wide of the mob, hammering bullets into the trees and knocking out chunks of bark and leaves. Teal'c did the same, sending two bolts from his staff down into the ground at the feet of the men, spewing up dirt, while Major Carter broke to her left and came to stand midway between Teal'c and O'Neill.

"Move back!" she yelled. "Move away from him!"

Half the men dropped to the ground, the rest bolted into the trees.

O'Neill stalked closer, his weapon leveled. "Go!" he barked at those who cowered in the dirt. "Get outa here. Go on! Run!"

They did not need to be asked more than once, scrambling to their feet and racing up the sides of the valley after their friends. Teal'c kept his eyes, and his weapon, trained on them until he could see them no more. Behind him, he heard O'Neill say, "Carter, go get Daniel. Now."

"Yes sir." And she was gone.

After a moment, O'Neill came to stand at Teal'c's side, lowering his weapon but not his guard as he studied the man — creature — still trapped at the end of the rope, but no longer in mortal danger. It looked like a wild animal, cornered, spitting and hissing at them. O'Neill glanced at Teal'c. "What the hell is that thing?"

"I do not know."

"Really?"

"I have never seen its like before."

O'Neill took a deep breath and shook his head, as he often did when about to do something of dubious wisdom. He clicked his weapon onto single shot and said, "Stay sharp." Then, in one swift move, he lifted his gun and made the shot, slicing through the rope that held the creature. It collapsed forward with a thump and laid there, arms and legs still bound, still snarling.

Teal'c aimed his weapon and so did O'Neill, watching the creature watch them through its strange yellow eyes.

"Okay," O'Neill said. "So I guess we wait for Daniel to come talk to the zombie."

By the time Major Carter and Daniel Jackson returned, the creature had maneuvered itself to a sitting position — clearly favoring its left leg, which appeared to be bleeding heavily.

"Sir," Major Carter said as she approached, and Teal'c turned to see her supporting Daniel Jackson as he limped closer.

But, despite his obvious suffering, Daniel Jackson's eyes widened when he saw the creature Teal'c was guarding. "Wow," he said. "I guess that's one of the Amam? I can certainly see where the name came from."

"See if you can talk to it," O'Neill said, jerking his head toward the creature.

"Can we untie him first?" Daniel asked, wincing as Major Carter lowered him to the ground. He did not look like he could travel much further.

"I don't think that's a good idea," O'Neill said.

"We have to build trust."

Getting back to her feet, Major Carter drew closer to the creature. "Sir, its leg — It's wounded."

"It's the teeth I'm concerned about," O'Neill said. "Devourer, remember?"

Apparently choosing to ignore him, Major Carter crouched down close to the creature and said, "Are you hurt? Can we help you?"

The creature just snarled.

"It can't understand you," O'Neill said. "And just move back, would you? I don't like the look in its creepy, yellow eyes."

The creature hissed again, this time at O'Neill.

"Oh," Daniel Jackson said. "I think he understood that."

O'Neill raised his eyebrows. "No offence?" he said doubtfully.

Ignoring him, Daniel Jackson returned his attention to the creature. "My name's Daniel," he said. "We're — God." Gritting his teeth against an apparent wash of pain he pressed his hand to his side. When he could speak again he rasped, "We're trying to get home. Through the Stargate. Do you have a way to open it?"

The creature just snarled, baring pointed teeth.

"Sir," Carter said, "I think it's in pain. I think we should cut it free."

"She's right," Daniel said weakly. "Build trust."

Teal'c kept his weapon trained on the creature, as did O'Neill. It watched them in return, wary, but intelligent. Teal'c suspected that Daniel Jackson was correct; the creature could understand their words.

"Sir?" Major Carter pulled out her knife.

After a moment O'Neill gave a curt nod. "Be careful."

The creature flinched back as Major Carter moved in, but she held up her hands and said, "It's okay, I'm not going to hurt you." First she cut the rope around the creature's feet, then moved around behind it and cut his arms free. She stepped back quickly, sheathing her knife and lifting her gun as she backed up next to Teal'c.

Behind him, Teal'c heard Daniel Jackson gasp as the creature rubbed at its wrists and flexed its hands. They were large and clawed, like they were intended for killing. Still watching SG-1, it climbed to its feet.

"Woah," O'Neill said, backing up a step.

It was tall, taller even than Teal'c, broad and powerful; even unarmed, there was no doubt that this was a dangerous creature. It sniffed the air, cocked its head as if listening for something distant.

"Ah, Jack?" Daniel Jackson said from behind them, his voice shaking.

O'Neill did not turn around, his gaze fixed on the creature. "The Stargate," he said. "Can you open it? We need to go home."

"Jack…" Daniel Jackson's voice was urgent, frightened. "Oh God…"

Teal'c turned around in time to see Daniel Jackson pull his hand away from his side. It was red with blood, a dark patch spreading across his jacket. His face was colorless.

"Daniel!" O'Neill dropped to the ground next to him just as Daniel Jackson's eyes rolled back in his head.

"Jack…" He collapsed backward and O'Neill caught him, lowering him to the ground.

Major Carter blanched. "Oh God."

"Daniel… ?" O'Neill tapped his face. "Daniel!" He pressed his fingers to his neck, moving them, searching for a pulse.

"Shit. *Shit!*"

"No…" Major Carter fell to her knees on the other side of Daniel Jackson, her hands on his shoulders, shaking him. "Daniel, please."

Teal'c felt his heart constrict, his jaw clenched in grief, but he fixed his eyes and his weapon on the creature. He was all that stood between this thing and his friends, and protecting them was all he could do to help.

The creature took a step forward. Teal'c raised his weapon, braced his feet for an assault. "Stay back."

It snarled, bared its teeth. And in a flash of movement it seized the end of Teal'c's staff weapon, pushing it up and away from its face. Teal'c tried to jerk the staff free, but the creature was strong and had the better angle, its clawed fingers curling tight around the weapon and holding fast.

"That one is dying," it said in a strange, sepulchral voice. "I can help him."

CHAPTER FOURTEEN

OVER the span of his forty year career, George Hammond had developed an instinct that was almost like second sight: the ability to read a room, an inherent sense of danger ahead, an intuition that told him when a situation was about to swing one way or another. As Harriman announced the incoming wormhole and the Tok'ra IDC, Hammond knew that this was one of those situations.

He uttered the words he'd said a thousand times, only this time they brought with them a heavy feeling of dread. "Open the iris."

It was Jacob. The video stream was irregular, the audio stuttering at times, and Hammond wondered from where in the galaxy he was transmitting. "What's the news, Jacob?"

But it wasn't Jacob Carter who spoke. "There is no news you will want to hear, General Hammond," came the reverberating tones of Selmak. "Our search for SG-1 has been unsuccessful. We have investigated the planet thoroughly, each crystal within the Stargate dialing device has been scrutinized, and we can come to only one conclusion."

"And that is?"

"That the last gate dialed was Earth's."

Hammond took a breath and closed his eyes, trying not to lose his patience. "Forgive me, Selmak, but hadn't we already established that? What we need to know is what went wrong? Where did it go if it didn't end up here?"

"I'm afraid we have no answer to that, General."

Hammond balled his fists and leaned against the control room console, feeling like, if he didn't lean on something, he was going to collapse under the weight on his shoulders. "So what now? What's our next move?"

Selmak said nothing for a moment, just glanced away. The

gesture was almost imperceptible through the static of the video feed, but Hammond caught it. And he knew. "There is no next, is there?"

"We are sorry, General Hammond. Truly we are, but our search revealed something else that was unanticipated. This attack by Hecate was not isolated. Her forces have recently been involved in a number of other skirmishes on planets close to that solar system. Part of an ongoing conflict between Yu and Hecate's ally, Nirrti."

Frowning, Hammond said, "Infighting between the System Lords is nothing new. Especially between those two."

"The fighting has just stopped."

Hammond waited, trying to figure out what Selmak was saying, feeling his heart hammer and hearing the hiss of sand falling through the glass. Then he understood. "They've stopped fighting because they have allied."

Selmak gave a solemn nod. "And they are not alone. Tok'ra agents report a number of ha'taks heading for what the Tau'ri call the Orion nebula. A fleet is assembling, General Hammond, and it is close. A fleet led by one far more dangerous than either Hecate or Yu or Nirrti."

His throat was dry as he asked the question. "Who?"

"The veracity of our intelligence is irrefutable. Apophis is preparing, General. All he needs is a target. Do not, under any circumstances, allow Earth to become vulnerable."

"But don't you understand, Selmak? Without SG-1 we *are* vulnerable! This is why we need help to find them." He was practically shouting now and could sense the concerned gaze of Harriman seated at his side, but this situation was desperate and sometimes a calm voice achieved nothing. He tried one other tack. "What does General Carter have to say about this? Why am I speaking to you?"

His expression changed, a subtle shift, and suddenly Jacob was looking at him through the flickering screen. He looked tired, strung-out and hopeless. "I'm here, George," he said. "And

God knows I wish there was something I could do."

"We can't give up on them," Hammond said. "You know that."

"It's too late, George. I'm sorry, but Selmak's right. The Tok'ra can't help you —"

"Or won't."

Jacob spread his hands, conceding the point. "Either way, the game has changed. You need to call off the search for SG-1 and bring your people home. You have to prepare, George, because Apophis won't wait. And when he strikes —"

The video feed stuttered and fizzed and then blinked out. Hammond turned to Harriman, who shook his head and shrugged. "Bad transmission, sir."

Yes, son, thought Hammond. *Bad transmission. The very worst.*

It was over. The last grain of sand, the last tick of the clock. The last turn of the wheel.

His heart felt like lead and his voice was just as heavy. "Sergeant, send a message to all teams currently off-world. Bring them home."

And, just like that, SG-1 was officially Missing, Presumed Dead.

Daniel was dead. Sam was sure of it. His skin was ashy, as if there wasn't a drop of blood left in his limp and unresponsive body. From the frantic look on the colonel's face as he pressed his fingers first to Daniel's wrist and then his neck, she could tell he hadn't found a pulse.

"Come on," he growled. "Damn it, Daniel, don't you *dare.*"

Sam let go of his shoulders, pulling back the neck of his shirt, and saw the telltale red spots of septicemia spreading, livid across his chest. Her gut twisted, tears blurring her vision. It was too late.

Somewhere Teal'c spoke, ordering the alien creature to stay back. It snarled, but Sam didn't turn round. All she could think of was Daniel. Dead. *Oh, God, Daniel...*

"That one is dying," said a guttural voice behind her. "I can help him."

She looked back over her shoulder, swiping a hand across her eyes. The creature was watching them, its hand clutching Teal'c's staff weapon in a manner that was almost casual, despite the strain on Teal'c's face as he tried to wrest it back. The creature's yellow eyes, with their narrow black pupils, betrayed neither concern nor malice. Sam didn't know how it could help, but if there was any hope... "Sir?"

"Not a chance." The colonel had his MP5 trained on the creature, unflinching in his stance, though his eyes flicked back to where Daniel lay prone.

"He hasn't done anything to hurt us, sir. And Daniel..." She didn't need to finish her sentence. There was nothing they could do to save him now.

"Why should I let you anywhere near him?" Colonel O'Neill said to the creature, which merely tilted its head.

"It is of no importance to me whether you do or not. You have assisted me. I can now assist you in return."

There was a moment that stretched. Sam, watchful, her hand on Daniel's too still chest; Teal'c, tense and waiting, ready to seize his staff weapon at the first opportunity, and the colonel, firearm steady, his gaze shifting from Daniel to the alien and back again. Noon was approaching, the planet's sun trying its best to burn a hole through the perpetual mist, it's strange, thin light casting a diffuse glow across the colorless landscape.

Daniel's chest moved.

"Sir!" She bent her head close to his mouth, and almost laughed in relief as she felt the tiny hairs at her temple stir with the faint exhalation that came from his mouth. "Sir, he's breathing but we don't have much time."

Another moment of hesitation, then...

"Alright, go!" Colonel O'Neill barked at the Devourer. "Help him." The creature moved forward, and the colonel let his MP5 drop to his side and pulled his Beretta from its thigh holster. As the Devourer bent on one knee next to Daniel, its movements unhurried, the colonel pressed the muzzle of the gun to the back of its neck. "One wrong move. Just one."

The Devourer gave no indication it had even heard the warning, never mind felt threatened by it. It merely pushed Sam's hand aside and pressed its own to Daniel's bare chest, extending its long talon-like fingers. It pushed down... and Daniel's eyes flashed open as he gasped in pain, arching his back up off the ground.

"Let him go!" shouted the colonel, but the Devourer swung its free arm back without even looking and sent him flying into a nearby boulder, stunning him. Sam grappled for her own weapon, heard the buzz of Teal'c's staff opening. As she pulled her handgun free, bringing it to bear, she saw the colonel, woozy, struggling to do the same. She aimed for the Devourer's head, finger tight on the trigger.

"Sam, no!"

She froze. Daniel's palm was an inch from the barrel of her gun.

"Daniel?" Colonel O'Neill's tone mirrored her own amazement. "You ok?"

Daniel's skin, while still ashen, was decidedly less death-like. Not to mention the fact that he was sitting up, his breathing normal, the look on his face concerned rather than pained. He was fine.

"I'm fine," he said.

"It actually helped you?" said the colonel, pushing himself up from the ground. He pressed a hand to the back of his head and winced.

"Yes," said Daniel. "*He* helped me."

Sam felt the tension leak from her shoulders and she lowered her gun in relief. "Thank God."

Daniel's brow furrowed, as if something had just occurred to him, and he pulled up his shirt, tugged off the bloody bandage, and ran his hand over his side. It was now entirely healed, only a faintly uneven patch of skin visible where his wound had been. "Wow, I guess he *really* helped me."

Sam exchanged a glance with the colonel and in that glance was the shared thought: *If it helped us with this, what else might it help us with?*

"Uh, thanks," the colonel said, "for that." He waved his hand at where Daniel was still scrutinizing his healed wound.

The Devourer watched them, its shoulders rising and falling heavily as if breathless; Sam guessed that the healing process had depleted its energy reserves. Otherwise, it looked unaffected. "The debt is paid. A life for a life." Its head snapped up, its reptilian eyes scanning the low sky.

"Yeah, about that," the colonel said, "we've been told you came through the Stargate and we need…"

But the creature wasn't listening. Still watching the sky, one hand moved to a device on its wrist. There was a sudden rush of air and a noise like an F-16 approaching the sound barrier. A beam of white descended from the sky, strands of light sweeping the ground, and before the colonel could finish his question, he was gone. Then Teal'c, then Daniel. Sam brought her Beretta around, but before she could squeeze off a shot, her weapon hand was gone — and so was she. The light had taken them all.

CHAPTER FIFTEEN

IT WAS a task that didn't get any easier, no matter how many times he had to do it. Normally it was news he had to deliver over the telephone, but when time and geography allowed for it, George Hammond preferred to have this conversation face-to-face. Although neither time nor geography was on their side on this occasion, the telephone was not an option and, after everything his father had done for the people of Earth, Rya'c deserved to hear this news in person.

"It's a lovely day, sir," said Janet, though there was sadness in her voice. Hammond couldn't disagree with her. The sun blazed in a clear blue sky as they made their way from the gate to the town square, and Hammond could smell the heady fragrance of whatever purple flower flourished in the nearby fields; the Land of Light was a beautiful planet on which to make a home and the weather made no allowance for grief.

He was glad that Janet had requested to come with him. She had cited her friendship with Teal'c as a reason, but he suspected she knew just how much he needed a friend by his side for this trip. The doctor was no stranger to delivering bad news, and he could rely on her to offer support when the time came.

A figure approached from the direction of the square and Hammond guessed who it was before she was close enough to make out her face. He had already broken the news to Drey'auc over a MALP link and, as she drew closer, he could see that she had been crying.

"General Hammond, Dr. Fraiser," she said with a short bow, "it is good to see you both, though this day is a sad one."

"Drey'auc," he said, inclining his head in return. "I can't tell you how much I wish this visit was for a happier reason. Does he know?"

Drey'auc shook her head. Her eyes glistened and he knew that she was struggling to hold tears at bay. "No, I was happy to grant your request and allow you to tell him. He is at home. Come."

He and Janet followed Drey'auc through the town, a picturesque collection of twin story buildings in some sort of stucco. The townspeople watched them pass with curiosity, and the occasional smile, but no suspicion. This was a good place to raise a family, he could tell, something that Teal'c would never know.

And there it was. The guilt. It was delayed this time, or maybe early, but he had known it would come. It always did. During the conversation with the parents who had been so proud of their boy, the sister who would say how much her kids had loved their aunt, and asked how was she supposed to tell them that she wouldn't be visiting on their birthdays anymore, the wife who smiled through tears and thanked him for coming, all the while left with a war widow's pension instead of a husband. The son whose father had left to fight a war in a far off place and had paid the ultimate price.

A hand on his elbow stopped him in his tracks and he glanced back to find Janet looking up at him. "We're the ones who give them the news, sir. They're angry and hurt and don't want to hear what you're saying, but we say it anyway and we take whatever they throw at us. Because we're the ones who give them the news."

Hammond swallowed the sudden thickness in his throat and nodded. He was glad Janet had come with him. Up ahead, Drey'auc waited outside a small house set back somewhat from the main square, watching them with quiet interest. They made their way towards her.

On most occasions, and for most people, it was clear from the very fact of the phone call or the visit from a high ranking Air Force general that something was wrong. Most people knew, he could always tell from the change in their tone of voice, or in the way their features fell when they saw the uniform. Hammond was not an unfamiliar face to Rya'c, however, and the boy had no frame of reference as to what this visit could mean. So when he came down the stairs, his expression was one of affable curiosity. Hammond could see how the boy had grown; a young man now — the man of the house.

"General Hammond, my mother did not tell me you were coming." He stopped, his feet mid-step between the first and second stair, and he looked over Hammond's shoulder. "Dr. Fraiser." His expression was puzzled now, wary. He glanced over at his mother. "Why are they here? Why… why are you crying?"

Hammond removed his hat and stepped forward. "Rya'c, I'm sorry to be the one to bring this news —"

"No…" Rya'c began to back up the stairs, as if distance could forestall the inevitable.

"— but I'm afraid your father has been —"

"No!" He pressed his hands over his ears and Hammond could see the young boy once more, the one who had come to Stargate Command a year ago, who had been saved by the man who was now lost to them.

"I'm sorry, son. He's missing. And we fear the worst."

Rya'c dropped, landing heavily on the stairs, his head in his hands, and his mother ran to him. He didn't weep openly, and whether that was from the Jaffa ideal that emotion was a weakness, something to be repressed, or from the simple shock at the news, Hammond didn't know. The boy let himself be guided to his feet by Drey'auc and led to the large wooden table and chairs in the center of the room. His mother sat down next to him, her arm around his shoulders.

"He was a good man, Rya'c," said Hammond. "A good warrior. You should be very proud of him."

When Rya'c finally spoke, his voice was choked with unshed tears. But also anger. "He should not have died for the Tau'ri."

Hammond had expected this, but still was unsure how to respond. "Son —"

"No!" His hand banged onto the table, and finally he looked Hammond in the eye. "He had his own people. His own war. Why did he leave us to fight for a world which cared nothing for the people of Chulak or the slaves of Apophis?"

Hammond said nothing. It would do no good to tell Rya'c he was wrong. Janet was right. He was the one who gave them the news. Let the boy's grief manifest itself in whatever way necessary. He had that right.

In fact, it was Drey'auc who tried to talk her son around. "Rya'c, your father fought for us all. You know that. If it was not fighting on the side of the Tau'ri, he could have died among the ranks of the Jaffa resistance. He died fighting for the freedom of us all. We should take solace from that."

Rya'c's lips turned down in a grimace of both sorrow and anger. "I will not."

"My son…"

"I will not accept this! Where is his body?"

This time it was Janet who spoke up. "I'm afraid we have no body, Rya'c. At this stage, Teal'c's official status is Missing, Presumed Dead. But the fear is… we think there may be no body to recover."

With a defiant lift of his chin, Rya'c said, "Then you have no proof that my father is truly dead?"

Every fiber of Hammond's being wanted to say *No, Rya'c. No, we have no proof and I don't accept it either. I know your father isn't dead. I know that he and the rest of SG-1 are still out there somewhere.* But he was a Brigadier General in the US Air Force, he spoke on behalf of the United States government, and he acted on behalf of the entire world. He could not let his own feelings, his own instincts, influence him here. So instead he said, "Rya'c, your father was more than a soldier to me, he was a friend. I can't express how much his loss will be felt. But I see him in you. I see his finest qualities handed down to his son. There is a lot I can't tell you right now, son, but know this. A storm is coming and it'll hit hard. We need fine men, Rya'c. We need leaders. No matter what happens now, I know you will live his legacy."

As Hammond spoke, calm came over Rya'c. He stood and

faced him, and it was only then that Hammond realized the young man was of a height with him. "You're wrong, General," he said. "A storm may be coming, and I will do everything in my power to ensure that my people weather it. But my father is not dead. He is out there, somewhere, and I shall not rest until he is found. One way or another, I will see him again."

CHAPTER SIXTEEN

DANIEL woke up slowly, a gradual return to consciousness that began with a thrumming in his head.

Images flashed through his mind, memories — pain, tunneling vision, the certain knowledge that death hovered near. The tight grief on Jack's face, Sam's eyes wide with fear, and then another face, fierce and inhuman, but ultimately the face that had saved him.

Never judge a book by its cover.

His eyes opened on the threadbare homily, but they opened into darkness. Not pitch darkness, though, and he realized he could see shapes and shadows, movement from the corner of his eye. He turned to look, or, rather, he tried to turn and that's when he discovered he couldn't move. Something was holding him fast, sticky — almost fleshy — tendrils were wrapped around his throat, body and limbs, and there was some sort of membrane close to his face. In revulsion, he jerked away from it, but there was nowhere to go.

"Yeah." Jack's voice drifted out of nowhere, familiar and reassuring. "Pretty gross."

Peering through the darkness, Daniel could just make him out on the other side of the narrow chamber. Or was it a corridor? Like him, Jack was held fast against the wall by thick fleshy bands, his face just visible past the skin-like membrane. "Jack?"

"Out of the frying pan, huh?" He looked as grossed out as Daniel felt. "One day," he said, "we're gonna catch a break."

"On the plus side," Daniel said. "I'm not dead."

Even in the darkness, he could see Jack's expression soften. "Yeah," he said. "There's that." He let a moment pass. "So, how're you feeling?"

He considered the question. "Well, aside from the obvious, pretty good actually." He shifted, trying to gauge the level of pain in his side. There was none. "The alien healed my wound completely."

"And then beamed us up and encased us in sticky snot," said Jack. "That's some mixed signals right there."

As Daniel's eyes adjusted to the low lighting he began to realize that they weren't alone. He could see at least a half dozen other people, all wrapped in this strange, sticky substance. But they were lifeless, either dead or comatose. He had a sudden, horrible image of giant spiders cocooning their prey to keep it fresh. He shuddered. "What is this place?"

"I was kinda hoping you could tell me," Jack said, struggling against his bonds with a stubborn, if futile, determination that was all Jack O'Neill.

Daniel tried to look further down the corridor, but his vision was obscured by whatever it was that bound him in place. "Where are the others?"

"I am here." Teal'c's voice came from further down the corridor to Daniel's right, but he couldn't turn his head far enough to see him. "I am glad that you are well, Daniel Jackson."

"Me too — you know, aside from being stuck in some kind of giant spider web."

"And Carter's right next to you," Jack said, his gaze fixing somewhere left of Daniel's shoulder. "She's still out cold."

Flexing his muscles, Daniel tested the bonds. They weren't budging so he decided not to waste his energy and concentrated instead on trying to figure out where they were. He could hear sounds in the distance, mechanical noises and a faint, but unmistakable, hum of technology. "Are we on a ship, do you think?"

With a grunt, Jack stopped struggling and let out an angry sigh. "Maybe," he said. "But if we are, we're not moving. And I don't think we're even in orbit."

"No," Daniel agreed. It was a subtle sensation, but you could always tell when you were dealing with artificial gravity. "So perhaps we're still on the planet?"

"You're right about that."

The voice, young and male, startled Daniel and it took a moment to locate the speaker. Then he saw movement on the same side of the corridor as Jack, but further down, closer to Teal'c. "Oh, hello," Daniel said. "I'm Daniel Jackson."

"Name's Hunter." The man strained forward in his bonds, far enough that Daniel could make out his face. Like all the inhabitants of this world he looked spare and hungry, although unlike Aedan's people his hair was cropped short. And as he brought his face into the dim light, Daniel sucked in a breath of surprise. Further down the corridor Teal'c did the same.

"What?" Jack said, struggling in vain to see. "What's going on?"

"Um," Daniel said, "he's Jaffa."

"He is not," Teal'c said firmly.

Daniel looked again at the symbol tattooed on the man's forehead. Teal'c must have a better view, but even from this distance Daniel realized that the symbol — not one he immediately recognized — was crudely drawn.

"You are not Jaffa," Teal'c said. "Why do you bear the emblem of their slavery?"

"I wear no such thing," the young man retorted. "Dix himself marked me with the symbol of the goddess, Hecate."

Dix? Now that was interesting.

The man — Hunter — nodded his head in the direction of Teal'c. "And you bear your own mark, friend."

"It is the mark of a *false* god."

"Apophis," Hunter nodded. "Ain't no one but Dix wears his mark no more."

"Daniel?" Jack's voice, pitched low, drew his attention. He threw a significant look in the direction of the stranger. "Any ideas?"

"Well, I've never heard of Hecate," Daniel admitted, frowning. "That is, obviously I've heard of Hecate within the Hellenistic tradition — uh, interestingly sometimes considered a goddess of gateways — but I've never heard of her in the, um, Goa'uld tradition."

Jack gave a curt nod, brow drawing down into a thoughtful frown. "What did he mean, just then, that no one but —" He broke off abruptly. "Carter?"

"Colonel… ?"

Daniel couldn't see her, but he could hear the woozy disorientation in her voice as she woke up. "Sam, I'm here," he said. "We're in some kind of… Actually, I have no idea what this place is."

He heard her trying to move, then "Urgh! What the… ?"

"Yep," he agreed. "It's gross."

"What *is* it?"

"Alien goo," Jack said from across the corridor. "Technical term." He let a beat fall. "You okay, Carter?"

There was a pause while she considered. "I think so, sir. Where's Teal'c?"

Jack nodded along the corridor. "Over there. Talking to a fake Jaffa."

"A *fake* Jaffa?"

"Oh, it's just getting weirder and weirder, Carter."

Daniel smiled, which was odd given the circumstances. Yet things suddenly felt more normal than they had in weeks and he couldn't quite put his finger on why, although no longer being half-dead and in excruciating pain certainly helped lift his mood.

"Sir," Sam said after a moment, "I think we were beamed up by that fighter. Did you see it?"

"Not exactly," he said, "but I figured."

"I saw it take you all. It just kind of swept us up."

"The question is," Daniel said, "now what?"

A dark laugh drifted along the corridor, a cynical sound from such a young man. "Don't you know what happens here?" Hunter asked, incredulous.

"Actually, no," Daniel said. "We're, um, new around here."

"That ain't possible."

"Apparently it is." He wished he were closer to the man and

could meet his eye; it was difficult to understand the subtext from this distance and in the dark. "Look, Hunter, it would really help us if you could tell us what you know about this place."

"Ain't nothing that can help you here," he said, "'cept the grace of the goddess."

Daniel tried a different tack. "It was the Amam," he said, "the 'Devourers' who brought us here, right?"

"We call 'em Snatchers."

"Right, okay. And we're their prisoners?"

Again, the dark laugh. "We're their food."

Across the passageway, Jack started struggling against his bonds again and Daniel could see the frustration in his face when nothing gave. "Damn it," Jack growled.

"When you say food," Daniel pressed, "what exactly—?"

"Shh! They're coming."

Daniel heard it too, the distant clank of heavy footsteps on a metal deck. More than one set of footsteps. A low moan rose up around them, as if the whole room had started whimpering, and he realized that not everyone trapped in here was unconscious. Terror had kept them silent and now even the young would-be Jaffa shrank back against the wall as if trying to hide.

Jack licked his lips, edgy. "If anyone's got a genius escape plan, now's the time. Carter?"

"Sorry sir. I've been trying to reach my knife, but I can't move an inch."

The footsteps grew closer and then stopped. Someone started crying softly, the pitiful sound doing more than anything else to coil fear tight in Daniel's stomach.

At the far end of the corridor, a door slid open.

"Ah, crap," said Jack.

SG-1 was officially missing. Missing, Presumed Dead.

Makepeace didn't know if he was the only one in the briefing room who understood the full impact of that fact, but there were no smiles among the SGC's senior officers. No banter. They waited for the general in subdued silence.

Hammond himself was still in his office. Makepeace could see him—they all could—standing behind his desk with the red telephone to his ear. Apparently the situation had escalated right to the top.

"You got any idea what this is about, sir?" Ferretti said, leaning his shoulder closer and speaking under his breath.

Makepeace shook his head—a lie among so many other lies. "Only that it's got something to do with SG-1."

"I can't believe they called off the search," Ferretti said with a shake of his head, fist tapping lightly on the table in frustration.

"I guess they have their reasons, Major."

Whatever Ferretti's response might have been, it was cut off when Hammond's office door opened and he stepped into the room. Everyone got to their feet and he nodded in acknowledgment. His face was grim, as grim as Makepeace had ever seen it. Something dark curled tight in the pit of his stomach, something like dread. Or guilt.

"As you were," Hammond said, taking his customary seat at the head of the table.

He waited until everyone was seated, his hands resting on the table, fingertips pressed together. He was the picture of control, of calm under pressure. Makepeace's fear kicked up a notch; he could feel his pulse racing, heart thumping in his chest.

"What I'm about to tell you," Hammond said gravely, "will come as a shock to most of you. I know it did to me." He swept his gaze over them all and Makepeace forced himself to meet those cool, incisive eyes without flinching. "Several weeks ago," Hammond said, "I was contacted by the High Chancellor of the Tollan Curia. She informed me that Colonel Maybourne had established an off-world base, and that he was running rogue teams from that base to steal weapons and other technologies from our allies."

The shock was palpable. Though he couldn't feel it himself, Makepeace could still see it reflected in the faces of his colleagues and hear it in their low outraged murmurs.

It's not like that, he wanted to say. *We're doing it to help, to make us stronger.*

Hammond held up a hand for silence. "Unfortunately, that's not the worst of it," he said. "It seems that someone in this command, someone in an off-world team, has been working with Maybourne to smuggle plans and stolen technology back to Earth through our Stargate."

This time, Makepeace didn't need to fake the shock that hit him like a left hook.

They knew. Hammond *knew.*

His hands clutched the table, knuckles turning white. He glanced at the door, but there was no way out, no way to escape this. Mouth dry, muscles like iron, all he could do was sit and wait for the ax to fall.

"Who is it?" Colonel Reynolds said, taut with anger.

"We don't know," Hammond said. "And that's the problem…"

Hammond was still talking, but Makepeace wasn't listening. The only sound in his ears was the white noise of relief, a blank space where thought used to be. *They don't know it's me. Thank God, they don't know…*

He took a breath, deep and slow, relaxing his muscles, returning to the room.

"…unfortunately," Hammond was saying, "and for obvious reasons, Colonel O'Neill has been unable to conduct that investigation. And it is my duty to tell you that, as a result, both the Tollan and the Asgard have withdrawn from their alliances with us." Hammond spread his hands on the table, pressing them flat as if to steady himself. "As of 1800 hours today, Earth stands alone."

"Sonofa —" Ferretti cleared his throat. "Excuse me, sir."

Hammond shot him a wry look. "Under the circumstances, Major, I concur with your sentiment."

"But the Asgard wouldn't abandon us," Reynolds protested. "Over one rotten apple? That's insane, sir."

"It appears," Hammond said, "that the Asgard have their own problems. And whatever we may think of their decision, the fact remains that Earth is no longer covered by the Protected Planets Treaty."

Makepeace cleared his throat, conscious that he'd been silent until now. "It's not like we're entirely helpless, sir," he said. "And if we're lucky, the Goa'uld won't figure out what's happened until we've had time to fortify our defenses. It's not like the Asgard are going to send them a memo."

That raised few, faint smiles around the room, but not for the general. If anything his expression grew bleaker. "Unfortunately, Colonel, we have reason to believe that Apophis is already aware of the situation. In fact, our contacts among the Tok'ra believe he's assembling a fleet."

"A fleet?" His heart jolted, skipping a few beats. "Already?"

"As we speak, Colonel. I've just briefed the President and he has authorized DEFCON2. Our immediate priority is mounting what defenses we can muster." He frowned, his glare turned inward. "Our most critical problem is that we have no established Alpha Site available. It won't be easy, but we will need to look at options for a full-scale evacuation."

Evacuation. DEFCON2. Apophis. This wasn't how it was supposed to go down. This wasn't why he'd risked his neck for Maybourne's operation. He'd wanted to make Earth safer, more self-reliant. Not weak, not vulnerable.

"Sir," Reynolds said, leaning forward across the table, "what if we dig out Maybourne's mole ourselves and hand him over? Hell, I'd be happy to beat the life out of the bastard myself. Sir."

Makepeace's mouth tasted like sandpaper, too dry to speak, as if it were trying to keep him from saying the words that would condemn him. *It's me. I confess.*

He could have admitted to it, could have handed himself over right there. But he didn't, he said nothing. He was too afraid.

"Even if we could discover the perpetrator's identity," Hammond said, oblivious to Makepeace's silent act of cowardice, "I'm not sure it would help. The Asgard have already made their decision. In truth, I think it was probably made some time ago."

"That's ridiculous!"

"Yes, Colonel, but it's also the reality in which we must operate."

Hammond got to his feet, everyone else following suit. "The President, Vice President and Joint Chiefs are already on their way here. The Pentagon is sending a strike team in with them, to coordinate their evacuation, and they'll brief you when they arrive. In the meantime, prepare your people and await further orders." He paused, and then added, "Needless to say, this information remains Top Secret. The President has yet to decide what, if anything, to make public at this time."

Dark looks crossed the room, stoic but bleak. This wasn't the first time disaster had threatened and they knew the drill. Even so, the tension in the room was sharp enough to cut steel.

"I won't pretend this isn't serious," Hammond said into the silence. "I won't pretend that our world isn't facing grave danger. But I do know that we have beaten the Goa'uld before."

"Yeah," Ferretti said, "but only thanks to SG-1. And they're not here."

Hammond fixed him with a look. "Son," he said, "we beat Ra way back when we had nothing but sticks and stones to throw at him. We beat him then, and we can beat Apophis now. Because we won't lie down, we won't accept defeat. We will fight — each one of us here, and every man and woman on this planet. And that gives me hope. It should give you hope too."

But it didn't give Makepeace hope. All he felt was alone and foolish — the Judas at the feast. And as he watched his friends and colleagues slowly filter from the room, exchanging words of grim determination, all he could think was *I did this.*

I'm the reason the Goa'uld are coming.

Daniel watched as a group of three Amam stepped into the room. They all looked similar to his eyes — the consequence of some kind of cross-species bias, he figured — and it was difficult to tell if the one who had saved him was among them.

They were all tall, powerfully built, and appeared to be male. Two had long white hair, braided in parts, but the third creature's hair was jet black. They stopped in the doorway, sniffing at the air, teeth bared.

Everyone in the room had gone silent and still. Daniel found himself scarcely breathing as, on some unspoken signal, the Amam stalked further into the room and the door behind them slid shut. Their yellow, alien eyes swept over the cowering prisoners as they sauntered past. Browsing, Daniel thought, with a sick sense of dread. Opposite him, Jack watched the Amam with tight-lipped intensity.

Two of the creatures halted close to Teal'c, but the one with black hair continued on toward Daniel. He stopped when he was in front of him, head cocked to one side as he studied him.

"Um, hi?"

"Daniel…" Jack, warning him to shut the hell up.

The Amam ignored them both, drew a step closer as it examined Daniel. It didn't speak, but reached out one taloned finger and scratched it down the side of Daniel's face. Teeth bared, it drew closer.

"Daniel!" Jack was cursing, struggling helplessly.

"Ah," Daniel said to the Amam, drawing back as far as he could. "Listen, maybe we can —"

A commotion at the far end of the room interrupted and the Amam pulled away with a hiss. Someone was shouting, begging. Daniel looked with horror as one of the creatures pulled a man free of the tendrils that held them all in place. Wiry and thin, the man beat at the Amam's arm until it let him go and he fell, knees buckling, to the floor.

"Please," he begged, scrabbling backward. "Please don't…"

The Amam stalked after him with slow, deliberate strides, like a cat toying with its prey. Desperate, the man got to his feet and started backing up toward Daniel.

"Please. Not me, please…"

He was crazed with fear and looked half starved. Daniel wondered how long he'd been in this place, what he'd seen here. The black-haired Amam in front of Daniel stepped out into the frightened man's path, waiting as he backed away from the creature advancing on him.

"Please…" Arms outstretched before him, warding off the enemy, he didn't see the Amam at his back until he bumped into him. In horror, he turned his head, his mouth open in a silent scream as the Amam bared its teeth and grabbed the man's arms, pulling them behind his back and holding him helpless as the other creature approached.

The man's mouth worked, opening and shutting until, at last, a hoarse scream escaped. "No!" he rasped, as the Amam lifted a hand, exposing claws and a strange mouth-like organ on its palm. "Help me!" the man begged, turning to Jack. "Please, help me!"

Jack's expression was grim as stone. "I'm sorry," he ground out.

But suddenly, like a flash, Daniel understood what was happening and he almost laughed with relief. "It's okay!" he said. "He's not going to hurt you. He's going to help you!"

The man looked at him as if he was insane, and in that moment the Amam closed on him and drove his hand hard against his chest. A scream of pain and terror tore from the man's throat, his head flung back against the creature that held him still.

For the space between two heartbeats, Daniel expected to see the man healed and healthy. But then something else started to happen, something hideous.

"Oh my God," Sam gasped, horrified.

The man withered. Before their eyes, his body aged and wasted until, after no more than a few seconds, he was nothing but a desiccated corpse. The Amam released him, throwing back its own head in a moment of ecstatic pleasure as the body crumpled to the floor.

Across the corridor, Daniel met Jack's dark gaze. He looked

as dangerous as a loaded gun and a hair's breadth from snapping. "Don't do anything stupid," Daniel warned, but Jack's expression didn't change and his gaze didn't waver for a moment.

The raven-haired Amam swung hungrily toward Daniel and he flinched, braced for the end. But when the creature struck, it didn't reach for him. It reached for Sam and dragged her from the wall, throwing her staggering into the center of the chamber.

And that's when Jack went nuts.

CHAPTER SEVENTEEN

"CARTER!"

Sam dropped into a low, wary crouch. Her firearms were missing, but her dive knife was still in its holster and she reached for it, moving slowly, as she watched the Devourer watch her.

The colonel was struggling, desperate but helpless. "Hey. Hey!" He yelled at the Amam, trying to draw its attention away from her. "Over here, you ugly bastard!"

But it didn't even glance in his direction. Its attention was fixed entirely on Sam as it took a predatory step forward.

She retreated, her knife raised. "Stay back," she warned. The Amam bared its teeth and she had the distinct impression it was enjoying itself.

Risking a quick glance over her shoulder, Sam found she was backing herself into a dead end; there was nothing behind her but more pods, more people. Damn it. Heart thumping, tuning out the colonel's increasingly frantic shouts, she tried to assess her options. There were three Amam and they were all armed. Black Hair was stalking her, the other two were watching from further down the corridor — standing between her and the only exit. They had height and weight on their side, and she remembered the way the creature on the planet had flung the colonel aside like a ragdoll, so she guessed they had strength too. Speed was an unknown, and she was fast. If she could somehow disarm the creature in front of her...

She took another step back.

"You do not fear," the Amam said. Its voice was precise, as if it was unaccustomed to speaking her language. "Your lifeforce will be all the sweeter for your resistance."

"Goddamn sonofabitch," the colonel growled, flinging himself against his bonds again. But it was hopeless and he knew it. "Carter…"

She licked her dry lips. "It's okay, sir."

"You can take him," he growled. "You can do it, Major."

"Maybe I should let you run," the Amam mused, closing in on her — forcing her to step back again. Soon, she'd hit the wall and there'd be nowhere left to go. "The hunt always enhances the final pleasure."

Sam let her vision narrow, her focus entirely on herself and the creature. She had one chance. Perhaps the colonel saw the shift in her, because he fell still and silent and all she could hear was the hammering of her heart and the rush of blood through her ears. If she let the Amam back her up against the wall, she was dead. She had to act and she had to act now. Without taking her eyes off the creature, she readjusted her hold on the knife. Her palms were sweaty but the rubber handle still gripped well. Subtly, she shifted her weight forward onto the balls of her feet. Her mouth was dry, her throat tight, but her vision was clear and her senses sharpened by the adrenaline flooding her body. It was now or it was never.

Without warning, she threw herself at the creature, barreling into it with her shoulder and thrusting her knife up in a gutting motion toward its belly. For a moment it seemed to lose its balance, momentum carried her forward and her heart jumped as she made a grab for its weapon. She was going to do it!

But triumph only lasted a moment.

A powerful blow struck her across the face, slamming her backward so hard she hit the floor with an *oomph* that knocked the breath from her lungs and the knife from her fingers.

She scrambled to her feet, fighting for breath, but the Amam didn't give her a moment. It was on her, large fingers curling into her jacket as it lifted her off her feet and held her dangling in mid-air.

"It has been too long," it hissed, "since I fed on one such as you."

And then it smashed her against the wall, holding her there with one hand at her throat as it raised the other to expose the feeding organ on its palm.

"Go to hell!" she spat, gripping the arm at her throat and trying to push it away. It was hopeless, but she refused to die without a fight.

"Carter!"

She couldn't turn her head, but, from the corner of her eye, she saw the colonel watching her in horror. She didn't want the face of her killer to be the last thing she saw so she held onto the colonel's gaze, let it anchor her as the creature snarled.

"I will savor you," it breathed, like a vile caress.

She shuddered, choking in a gasp past the fingers at her throat. "Sir…"

His eyes widened in panic. "Carter!"

And the creature struck, driving its hand into her chest and crushing her against the fleshy wall of the chamber. She screamed, flinging her head back as pain lanced into her heart.

Dimly, she could hear the colonel shouting and cursing but her ears were ringing, head swimming as her life was wrenched out through her chest. Her fingers were numbing, her legs jellifying and then —

It dropped her. Clutching its hand as if it burned, the Amam staggered backward, gasping for air as it fell to one knee.

Sam didn't wait to wonder why, she just acted. Forcing her body to work, she aimed a kick at the creature's chest and sent it sprawling onto its back. Then she was on it, pulling the stun weapon from its holster in one swift move and firing once, twice, three times. It jerked beneath the crawling electrical charge, and then lay still.

She spun, caught the second creature a moment before it grabbed her, and threw herself backward as she fired again. The third had its weapon drawn, but she dodged the first blast and landed two clean shots to the creature's head. They sent it to its knees and the third laid it out completely.

Only when all three were down did Sam let her own knees give way and she crumpled, gasping for breath, to the floor.

"Carter…"

She couldn't reply, just rolled onto her hands and knees and concentrated on breathing past the pain that still knotted her chest.

"Sam?" Daniel this time. "Sam get up…"

Just a few more breaths.

"Major!" It was an order and she responded instinctively, sitting back on her heels. At least the world had stopped spinning, even if her mind felt upside down. "Carter." The colonel was speaking to her like she wasn't quite there — maybe she wasn't. "Carter, you have to get the knife."

Yes, the knife. She shook her head, trying to clear it, and pushed herself back to her feet. Her knees buckled at the first attempt, but she gritted her teeth and forced herself to stand. The knife lay close to Daniel, hidden in the shadows. Her legs wobbled as she walked, but she was breathing easier now, although she still felt weak from whatever that thing had done to her. Grabbing the knife, she braced herself for a moment against the pod holding Daniel. Then, with visceral pleasure, she plunged the blade into the tendrils that held him in place, sawing at them and grimacing at the oily substance that leaked out when the blade sliced deep.

It didn't take long before Daniel was free and pulling her into a swift, fierce hug. "Sam, thank God," he whispered against her neck.

"I'm okay," she said, holding tight for a moment and then pulling back. "Go free the colonel. I'll help Teal'c."

She tried not to look at the faces of the other prisoners as she made her way over to Teal'c, and definitely didn't look at the withered corpse on the floor. But she saw enough to tell her that most were beyond help — comatose, maybe even dead.

"Teal'c," she said, focusing on his face and not the horror all around them, as she started cutting him free.

"Major Carter." He held her gaze, not looking away for a moment, as if aware that she needed his presence. "That was most impressive."

Sam shook her head. "I didn't do anything," she said, working the serrated edge through the leathery bonds. "It just let me go."

"Because you're blessed by the gods." Hunter spoke from behind her and she threw him a quick glance as she struggled to free Teal'c.

"What do you mean?"

"The gods are powerful. The Snatchers can't feed on them they bless."

Sam exchanged a look with Teal'c. "Jolinar?"

"It is possible."

At last Teal'c's arms were free, he pulled out his own knife and after that it didn't take long to get him out. Released from the cocoon, he put a hand on Sam's shoulder and gave it a brief squeeze. "Thank you," he said. "Once more, I owe you my life."

"Teal'c," she scolded gently. "I thought we agreed to stop counting?"

He gave a slight smile and then his eyes moved to Hunter. "We cannot leave him."

"There must be twenty other people in here," she said, glancing down the length of the chamber. They couldn't free them all.

The colonel was free now too, brushing the last of the gunk off his uniform. He stopped when he reached the unconscious body of the Amam who'd attacked her, crouched down and studied its face intently. Then he stood up, walked over to one of the other creatures and snagged the weapon from its limp hands. Turning back, he fired twice into the body of Black Hair, then twice into the other two creatures, and stood watching the blue energy fizz across their skin. None of them would be waking up any time soon.

He caught her eye when he looked up and there was something dark and furious there; it made her glad he was on their side. But all he said was, "We need to get outa here. Now."

"Yes sir."

Teal'c said, "We cannot leave this man, O'Neill."

"Teal'c—"

"I can help you!" Hunter broke in. "Please—I know this place. I can get you out, and I can get you to Dix."

The colonel shrugged, unimpressed. "And what's Dix?"

"Ah, not 'what'," Daniel said, coming up behind him, "who. Remember what Elspeth told us?" He looked at Hunter. "Dix is a man, right? A resistance leader?"

"He's *the* resistance leader," Hunter said, as if Daniel was stating the blindingly obvious. "First Prime to Hecate."

"First Prime, huh?" the colonel flung Teal'c a look. "How about that?"

Teal'c didn't respond, although his expression hardened.

"Sir?" Sam said. "If there's a Goa'uld here and this planet's gate is inoperative, that suggests there's a ha'tak in orbit. Possibly with a Stargate on board."

The colonel frowned, a deep line carved between his eyebrows. He obviously didn't like the idea, but what choice did they have? It was clear now that there was no chance of the Amam helping them. "This Dix guy," he said eventually. "Why would he help us?"

"I already told you," Hunter said. "Dix leads the resistance. He'll help anyone who fights the Snatchers."

"Most Jaffa," the colonel pressed, "want to kill us, not help us."

Hunter looked perplexed. "You ain't our enemy," he said. "It's the Snatcher's we're fighting."

"That's interesting," Daniel said. "My enemy's enemy… ?"

"If he's really their enemy."

Daniel lifted an eyebrow. "If?"

"I'm just saying it's a little odd. Why would they keep him alive if he's such a big shot in this 'resistance'?"

Hunter snorted. "Snatchers don't care what I am. To them, we're all just food."

"And we're not exactly in a position to turn down help," Daniel pointed out.

A long look passed between him and the colonel, a silent conversation, and then the colonel nodded. "Okay," he said, with a sigh that sounded rather more like capitulation than a decision. "Teal'c, cut him free, Daniel go grab that thing's weapon."

Daniel headed off and Sam moved to help Teal'c, but the colonel stopped her with his hand on her arm.

"Hey," he said, lowering his voice. "Good job back there."

Surprised, she just said, "Oh. Thanks, sir."

He nodded, but didn't let go of her arm, if anything his grip tightened. "You okay?" He made a vague gesture toward her chest. "I mean, does it hurt?"

"A little," she said, reaching up to touch the place where the creature had tried to feed. "But I think it's mostly bruising."

"That was—" He shook his head and blew out a long breath. "What the hell are these things?"

"I have no idea, sir. Not a clue."

He huffed a laugh and dropped his hand from her arm. "That's usually my line, Carter."

She smiled, partly at the old joke, but mostly because she felt like something had changed. Despite their precarious situation, the tension that had dogged the team since the colonel's return from Edora seemed to have disappeared. She was a little disconcerted by how relieved she felt.

"Um, Jack?"

Daniel appeared at the colonel's shoulder and behind him Sam could see Teal'c helping Hunter step free of the cocoon. She shuddered at the way the tendrils flinched and moved as if they were alive, and fixed her attention on Daniel instead.

He was watching the colonel with a familiar challenge in his eyes. "We're okay with leaving the rest of these people here?"

"No, not really," the colonel said. "But do you think we have a choice?"

Daniel made a face, like he really wanted to argue the point, but in the end he just sighed and said, "Maybe we can come back?"

With a sympathetic clap on his shoulder, the colonel moved past Daniel toward Teal'c. Sam watched him for a moment. "He seems in a better mood," she ventured.

"Yeah," Daniel said with a lift of his eyebrows. "Inexplicably, given the circumstances." Then he shook himself, dismissing the vagaries of their mercurial leader, and held out his scavenged weapon to Sam. "You take it," he said. "You're the better shot."

She didn't argue. "Thanks, Daniel."

"I'll take point," the colonel said then, handing the third blaster to Teal'c. "Keep an eye on your new buddy, huh?"

Teal'c nodded. "I shall."

The colonel grunted an acknowledgment as he headed for the door. "Carter?" he said, jerking his head toward the door controls. "Do the honors?"

"Yes sir." The door looked heavy and was made of the same organic material as the rest of the ship, but the interface appeared simple enough and, after spending a moment examining it, she was satisfied she could open it without a problem. There was no reason to lock these people in, after all. "Ready, sir?" she said, before she touched anything.

He nodded. "Do it."

She hit the release mechanism and the door slid open, but the materiel felt unpleasant beneath her fingers and she pulled them back quickly, with a muttered exclamation.

"Carter?"

"Nothing sir," she said. "It's just — It feels warm, like it's alive."

He pulled a face, but didn't comment. Glancing each way down the corridor, he made a quick decision and turned left. Daniel, Hunter and then Teal'c slipped out after him, leaving Sam to cover their backs as she followed her team out into the dark corridor beyond.

There was a patch of scrubland outside the entrance to Level 1, just dry grass and dirt where people sometimes came to smoke.

It was quiet, and right now Makepeace wanted quiet. He lit up a cigarette, taking a long drag as he gazed up at Cheyenne Mountain looming high above them. Just another guy taking a break, getting some air. He threw a casual glance at the guards on duty at the entrance, but no one was watching him, so he turned and walked quickly along the side of NORAD's administrative offices and past the giant fans sucking air down into the mountain complex.

Once he was hidden from view, and the hum and whir of the fans was loud enough to mask his voice from anyone trying to overhear, he stopped and pulled out the cellphone Maybourne had given him. He hit dial and pressed the phone to his ear, squinting against the afternoon sun.

After two rings, Maybourne answered. "You have news?"

Smoke caught in his throat, making his voice scratchy. "We have to stop," he said. "It's gone too far."

There was silence. Then, "What are you talking about?"

"They're coming," he said, dropping his voice. Beneath his boots, the dirt was dry and dusty. "The Goa'uld are coming and our allies won't help us because of what you — What *we've* done. Maybourne, we screwed up. We have to give back what we stole." He swallowed, ground out the rest. "And we have to give ourselves up."

Another silence.

"Are you listening? We screwed up, Maybourne. We have to fix it before it's too late."

"I never realized," Maybourne said at last, "that you were so short-sighted, Colonel. This is *exactly* what we wanted."

Makepeace kicked at the hard, compacted earth. "Are you insane? It's an invasion."

"It's a chance to prove our worth," he said. "Are they evacuating Stargate Command?"

"Yes, but I don't know where. There's no Alpha Site set up."

There was a pause, and then Maybourne said, "There's ours."

A shadow fell, the sun dipping behind the top of Cheyenne Mountain. Makepeace pulled on his cigarette to steady himself, blew out smoke. "You're going to tell the Pentagon where it is?"

"I'll suggest the option, so long as it remains under my command."

"Hammond won't accept that. None of them will."

Maybourne laughed. "Where else can they possibly go? The enemy is at the gate, Robert. And I have the key to the only back door."

"Was this your plan?" He licked his lips, knocked ash from the cigarette. "Is this what you wanted all along?"

"We're a little ahead of schedule but, yes," Maybourne said. "We have the means to fight, Robert. We just needed the right incentive for the Pentagon to authorize our tactics." He sounded smug; Makepeace could practically hear him grinning. "And now we have it."

"People will die," he hissed, struggling to keep is voice down. "Unless we stop this, people will *die*."

"People are already dying," Maybourne snapped. "Or hadn't you noticed the roll of honor at the SGC?"

"I mean civilians. Damn it, Maybourne, the point of this was to keep the planet safe, not —"

"The *point* was to take control." Maybourne's voice was shrill. He sounded like a man on the edge. "Fall on your sword if you want to, Robert, but don't expect me to do the same. This is *exactly* what we've been waiting for and I intend to use the opportunity."

With that, the line went dead. Makepeace stared at the phone for a long moment, then hurled it hard against the wall. The case split and the phone fell, broken, onto the dry ground. He'd been kidding himself to think that Maybourne would hand himself in or give back the tech they'd stolen. He'd see the world burn first.

And what about you? his conscience whispered. *Will you hand yourself in, walk up to Hammond and confess? Or will you watch the world burn too?*

The question made his chest tighten, his breath constrict, and he knew the answer: he would no more hand himself in than Maybourne would. He lacked O'Neill's propensity for self-sacrifice.

But it didn't mean he wanted to watch the world burn, and something Maybourne said had given him hope: they had an Alpha Site.

Whatever the hell this place was, Jack thought sourly, the sooner they were out of it the better. It was damp and smelled bad, a kind of musty odor that stuck in his throat, and it was too damn dark to see anything. Not that he wanted to see a lot of the detail, but all these gloomy corridors and shadowy alcoves made the hair stand up on the back of his neck. It didn't help that the alien stunner felt wrong in his hand, too smooth and slightly slimy, and he missed the comforting weight of his MP5.

He slowed as he approached a junction, holding up his hand to stop the others, and listened. There was movement to the right, but it was distant. No voices, though, which was odd. No barked orders, no idle chatter. Nothing.

He beckoned Hunter closer. "Which way?" he whispered.

"We can get out that way," Hunter said, pointing left.

Jack shook his head. "Weapons," he said. "They took our weapons."

Running a hand nervously over his short hair, Hunter said, "Not real smart to go deeper inside."

"No one ever accused me of being smart," Jack said. "You know where our weapons are?"

Hunter shrugged. "Know where they might be. Can't say for sure, though."

"I'll take a maybe." Jack gestured with his stunner toward the intersection. "So, which way?"

"I'll show you," Hunter said, with a pointed look at the weapon. "I ain't gonna run."

Jack gave him a level smile. "Makes me feel better." Then he nodded along the corridor. "Let's go."

Hunter led them on, creeping through the endless corridors. Through one open door Jack saw another room full of pods like those they'd been trapped in. It was a larger room going back so far he couldn't even see the end. He exchanged a glance with Daniel who just gave him a despairing shake of his head.

Whoever, or whatever, these Amam were, they scared the crap out of him. And not least because of what they'd tried to do to Carter. He had to fight to keep the memory of her screams out of his head, of that thing's claws buried in her chest; it was too dangerous a distraction from the here and now. But he'd fixed the face of the creature in his mind's eye, and if he ever had the chance he'd pump the bastard so full of lead he'd look like Swiss cheese. Assuming they found their weapons, assuming they ever got out of here alive.

After a while, Hunter called a halt, ducking into a corridor and signaling the others to come closer. "There's a room up ahead," he whispered, "where the Snatchers bring their discoveries, junk they find outside."

Daniel's eyebrows twitched in interest. "Oh? What kind of junk?"

"Daniel," Jack warned.

"What? I was only asking."

Jack gave him a quelling look, and then turned to Hunter. "You think our weapons might be in there?"

"That'd be my guess. But that place ain't safe, there'll be Snatchers close by — it's real close to where they do the experiments."

"Experiments?" Carter flung Jack an alarmed look. "What kind of experiments?"

Hunter shrugged. "We ain't figured that out exactly. But they're looking for folk with the right kinda blood."

"Nice." Jack thought for a moment, shifting the alien stunner in his hand. They only had three weapons, none of which were lethal. If they managed to get off the ship, they'd have no real way of defending themselves, no food, water or any of their other gear. And that really wasn't an option. Dangerous though it might be, they had to find their stuff before they escaped. "It's worth the risk," he decided and saw Teal'c give a slight, assenting nod.

Up ahead, a faint blue light drifted around the corner where the corridor snaked away to the left. "Is it down there?" he asked Hunter, shifting his position so he could see more clearly. Whoever built this place didn't go in for straight lines.

"Yup," said Hunter.

"Okay, let's check it out."

When they reached the corner, Jack peered around the edge and saw that the light was coming from a side corridor a little further up. He could hear noises too, footsteps in the distance. It was worth checking out, but not worth risking everyone.

He pulled back around the corner and whispered, "Teal'c, stay here with the others. Wait for five minutes, then follow if you don't hear trouble. Carter, with me."

They crept forward in silence. The corridor was empty, although the sounds of movement were louder now. He threw a questioning look at Carter, to see if she'd heard it, and she nodded, gesturing up ahead. She was right; the noise wasn't coming from the direction of the light. But it was close.

At the point where the corridor branched off, he stopped and poked his head around the corner. The corridor beyond was empty so he gestured for Carter to follow. Hugging the wall, they headed toward the light spilling from what turned out to be an open doorway. Jack slowed as they got closer, coming to a halt a couple meters away, Carter so close behind him he could hear her quiet breathing. There was sound coming from the room too, the soft hum and whir of technology that reminded him of every lab or control room in the galaxy. Crouching, ignoring the protest of his right knee, he edged closer and snuck a look inside.

The place was crammed with junk, weird machines and strange amorphous screens that glowed with a sickly yellow light. It was a technology like nothing he'd ever seen before, which was no surprise on this freaky-assed ship. On the plus side, the room appeared to be clear of bad guys — for now. Slowly, he stood up again and gestured for Carter to stay put. He took a breath, centered his concentration, and turned sharply into the room, trying to cover all directions at once.

Definitely no bad guys and, even better, he could see their gear dumped in a heap against the far wall. He let out a short sigh of relief and poked his head back out to summon Carter. Her weapon was aimed right at his head and he held up a hand in mock surrender. "Easy," he murmured, although he didn't blame her for twitchy reflexes.

Her expression was taut as she lowered her weapon. "Sorry sir."

He waved her apology away. "Come on," he said, and headed back inside. "You're gonna love this."

There was so much stuff in the lab he couldn't really take it all in, and as Carter followed him inside her eyes went wide. "Oh, wow."

"I knew you'd say that."

Jack covered the door, while Carter went over and collected her weapons and the rest of her kit. "Sir," she said, while she pulled on her tac vest, "I know we're just here for our stuff, but it's possible we could find something even more useful…"

"Such as a way to open the Stargate?"

"Maybe." She flashed him a quick smile. "I won't know unless I look."

"You've got five minutes," he said, resisting a smile of his own.

"Yes sir." Jamming the alien weapon into her belt, she got down to work.

One shoulder wedged against the doorway, Jack stood watch while Carter poked about in the lab. After a couple of minutes, he saw Teal'c peer cautiously around the end of the corridor. Jack lifted his hand in greeting as the others approached. "Hunter was right," he said. "All our gear's in here."

"Well that's lucky," Daniel said, sounding dubious. "Why does it make me feel like something's about to go horribly wrong?"

"Bitter experience?"

"Yep, that'll be it."

Hunter shook his head. "You can't be dawdling here," he said, glancing nervously back down the corridor. "Ain't safe."

"Here," Jack said, offering Hunter the Amam's weapon. "Take this. It'll make you feel better."

"O'Neill?" The slight question in Teal'c's voice was enough to suggest disapproval.

Jack shot him a look. "My enemy's enemy, Teal'c." He turned back to Hunter, layering his words with a tone of command. "He's not gonna hand us over to the zombies."

Hunter glanced down at the weapon, then up at Jack before he reached out and took it. "You can trust me."

For now, maybe. But he couldn't keep his gaze from the symbol Hunter wore on his forehead and all he said was, "Cover the corridor while I get my gear." He didn't have to ask Teal'c to stay with him.

While they took position at the door, Jack followed Daniel into the lab and retrieved his vest and weapons, leaving his pack until they were about to move out. He was relieved to see that nothing had been tampered with and he felt a hell of a lot better being properly armed again.

"Wow," Daniel said as he shrugged on his tac vest, "this place is amazing."

"Reminds me of your office," Jack said, glancing around the cluttered space. "Full of junk."

"Or fascinating artifacts and highly advanced alien technology?" Daniel suggested absently, his attention already caught by something he'd seen.

In the center of the lab was a bank of consoles where Carter stood gazing at something with her usual intent focus. Around the edges of the room, on a kind of work bench, there were numerous gizmos and gadgets, some of which were taken apart. Most looked as bizarre and creepy as the rest of the ship, but a few were more familiar and some were definitely Goa'uld. He spotted a disassembled zat on the far end of the bench and reached out to pick it up, turning it over in his hands.

"Daniel?" Carter said, glancing up from the console. "Do you recognize this language? At least, I'm assuming it's a language…"

Daniel was on the other side of the lab, but he headed gamely over to where Carter stood and peered at the screen. "Oh, it's definitely a language," he said with sudden interest. "Okay, wow, this is fascinating."

"It is?"

"Ah, yes. Yes, very."

As Daniel bent closer to the screen, Jack glanced down at the zat in his hands. It looked beyond repair, at least beyond his skill, and he dumped it on the bench and headed back to the door. "Teal'c," he said, "go get your stuff."

Back braced against the doorframe, he kept one eye on the corridor and one on Hunter. "You've been here before?" Jack guessed.

Hunter nodded, but kept his gaze fixed on the corridor behind Jack. "We're collecting intel," he said. "On the Snatchers."

"Intel?" Jack said, surprised by the word.

"For Hecate," Hunter explained.

"Right." For the Goa'uld — it was important to remember who he was dealing with here.

"Huh," Daniel said suddenly, standing up straight behind the console. "That's unexpected."

Jack waited for him to elaborate, but he either forgot he'd spoken out loud or got distracted, because he was bending over the screen again, squinting at the text. Jack glanced at Carter, who just gave a small shake of her head and a shrug.

"Daniel," Jack said. "What does it say?"

"Oh," Daniel glanced up over the tops of his glasses. "Ah, I can't actually read it."

Jack's eyebrows rose. "You can't read it?"

"No."

"And yet… ?" He gestured toward the console. "'Unexpected', you say?"

Daniel nodded. "Yes, I definitely wasn't expecting the language to be a derivative of Ancient."

"Ancient?" Carter echoed in surprise. "Really?"

"Oh yeah," Daniel nodded. "Without a doubt. Ancient was its root language — a long time ago, obviously."

"Obviously." Jack ran a hand through his hair, trying to quell his frustration. "So, what, these are some kind of flesh-eating zombie *Ancients*, now?"

"I have no idea," Daniel said, with obvious delight.

"Okay." He took a breath. "Carter?"

"I can't interrogate the database, sir. There's data streaming, but the interface isn't responding." She grimaced in annoyance. "I'm sorry, sir. I don't think there's anything here that can help us open the gate."

He acknowledged what he'd suspected with a nod. Not what he wanted to hear but there was no point in wasting time on a dead end. He headed back inside to get his pack. "Right," he said, "we'll move out and —"

"Wait!" Daniel's head was tipped to one side as he squinted at the screen. "Just — Okay, wait, I might have something. Huh…"

He'd disappeared down the rabbit hole again, but Jack figured they could spare a couple of minutes. If anyone could figure it out, it would be Daniel. "Two minutes," he warned him, slinging his pack over one shoulder. "And then we're outa here."

If he heard, Daniel didn't respond. Jack glanced at his watch, marking the time: he wasn't joking about the two minutes.

It was evening back home, he noted. The sun would probably be setting. Hard to imagine, in this place, that home was still out there, that its billions of people were still running about oblivious to the threat they faced from so inconceivably far away. Hard to imagine that he'd been one of them, once. Oblivious.

Perhaps because he was thinking of home, something on the cluttered lab bench caught his eye. Was that… ? He peered closer. It was. Half buried beneath something that might, once, have been a Goa'uld hand device he saw a familiar symbol: Earth. Reaching out, he knocked the debris away to reveal a small, square block that looked like it could have been made out of polished soapstone. Five of its sides were smooth and blank, and the only thing on the sixth side was the symbol for Earth. Weird, he thought, that it would be here. But then he remembered the girl, Elspeth, with the symbol tattooed on her arm. Resistance, she'd called it, a symbol of rebellion.

"Okay," Daniel said behind him, talking to Carter, "so the thing is, I don't think this is actually a spoken language at all. The syntax is impossible..."

Jack peered more closely at the cube. It looked harmless enough so he touched it, smooth stone beneath his fingertips. He picked it up.

"Anyway," Daniel was saying, "if I'm right then I think this, here in the corner, translates roughly as 'schematic'."

"*That's* a map?" Carter said, sounding dubious.

Jack glanced up at them, turning the block over in his hands. "A map of the ship?"

"Well, it's not Vegas," Daniel said, one eyebrow lifted.

"Funny." He nodded toward the console. "Can you see a DHD on there?"

"Just give us a minute..."

"I don't see it," Carter said shaking her head. "How is that a map?"

"Think of it more like an anatomical diagram of the body."

Both he and Carter were bent over the screen now. "Oh! Okay, so we're here?" Carter said, pointing. "That's — Wait. Are those life signs?"

Jack glanced over at Teal'c, who was back at the door with Hunter. "You see anything?"

"No," Teal'c said quietly, though he held his staff weapon ready for use. "I have seen nothing, O'Neill."

"That don't mean they're not coming," Hunter cautioned. "They can be real quiet. We should go."

Hunter's unease was contagious, but Jack schooled himself to be patient. They'd found a map and if there was a DHD they'd find that too. Maybe, at last, their luck was changing; maybe they'd get home after all.

Turning the block over in his hand, he traced his thumb over the Earth symbol with a sudden, intent longing. It felt cool and smooth to the touch but he wasn't expecting it to move beneath his thumb, for the symbol to slide slowly inward until it was flush with the rest of the cube's surface. "Oops."

Daniel looked up. "What 'oops'?"

"Probably nothing," he said, just at the moment a beam of white light shot up into the air and expanded into a giant holographic image of Earth. Then a female voice started talking — very loudly — in a singsong language he didn't understand. The lightshow filled the room and, almost certainly, the corridor beyond.

"Sir, shut it off!" Carter said in alarm, staring at the screen. "They're moving!"

He prodded at the block but nothing happened. "I'm trying!"

"What did you do?" Daniel asked, hurrying around the bank of computers.

"Nothing, I just —"

"O'Neill!" Teal'c shouted, backing into the lab in the face of a massive Amam. He opened fire immediately, but the staff blast just bounced off the thing as if it was shielded. It paused for a moment, head swiveling from side to side as it scanned the room, searching for something. Or someone, as it turned out. Its eyes fixed on Jack and it began to stalk toward him.

"Ah, okay," he said, taking a step backward.

Carter got off a couple more shots, but they just ricocheted away, sending Teal'c diving for cover.

"Hold your fire!" Jack barked. The room was too small for a semiautomatic.

Slowly, he backed up. He was trapped at the back of the lab between the bank of computers and the bench. He looked around for a way out, but there was nothing. And the creature was bearing down fast.

"Sonofabitch," Jack growled, pulling out his handgun. But the Amam slammed its hand down on his wrist and knocked the weapon from his fingers, sending a bolt of pain shooting up into his shoulder. "God…" That hurt.

Then the Amam seized his other wrist, holding it up close to its face as it stared at the block Jack was still clutching. The skewed, revolving image of Earth cast eerie shadows as it turned across the creature's face, but it didn't seem to notice as it gazed at the cube.

Behind it, over its shoulder, Jack could see the door was clear. The others could escape. He threw a look at Daniel who just shook his head in refusal. No.

So he glared at Carter instead, until she reluctantly nodded, grabbed Daniel's arm and hissed something into his ear as she pulled him toward the door. She knew, as well as Jack did, that backup would be on its way. They only had a few seconds.

Sure enough, at that moment, Teal'c stepped out into the corridor and fired several times back the way they'd come. "Major Carter," he yelled. "We must go."

Hunter joined him, glancing the opposite way along the corridor. "Come on! It's clear this way."

The creature holding Jack turned its head, but it didn't look concerned and its grip on Jack's wrist tightened further. His fingers were starting to go numb.

Too late for subtlety he yelled, "Carter, get them outa here!"

"Sir…" She looked torn.

"Just go!" There was only one way this was ending for him. "Find a way home."

Stricken, she turned, pushing Daniel ahead of her into the corridor as Teal'c covered their retreat.

The Amam didn't follow, as Jack had hoped it might, it just turned back to him, studying him like a hungry man might study a juicy steak.

"I warn you," he said. "I haven't bathed in days. I'm not gonna taste any good."

Ignoring him, the creature tightened its hold on Jack's wrist. He spat out a pain-filled curse and the block dropped from his fingers. Its light died as soon as it left his hand and the Amam watched it fall to the floor with apparent fascination. Then it looked back at O'Neill, head cocked to one side in a curiously human gesture. "You are Lantean," it said, forming the words precisely.

"I'm what, now?"

It bared its teeth. Maybe it was smiling. "You are of use."

CHAPTER EIGHTEEN

GEORGE Hammond had told himself that the current situation was just about as bad as it could get. He'd been wrong. He hadn't factored in the appearance of the man now standing in his office, but perhaps that was due to his own short-sightedness: vultures always circled while the carrion was still kicking.

"What do you want, Maybourne?"

Without waiting for an invitation, Colonel Harold Maybourne sat down in the chair opposite, tossing his hat onto Hammond's desk. "I'd say a more appropriate question would be 'what is it *you* want, General?'"

Hammond took a breath, biting back the reply that sprang to his lips. The worst thing you could do with men like Maybourne was play their game. "Can we dispense with the obfuscation, Harold? I have a planet to defend."

"Yes, I had heard that." Maybourne leaned back in his chair and crossed his legs. Though his expression was solemn, self-satisfaction radiated from him in waves; Hammond could practically smell it. "The situation, I believe, is grave."

"And how would you know about that?"

"I have sources."

"Not official ones. You are so far from this chain of intel, Maybourne, you might as well be shucking corn back in Iowa. So I'll ask again, how would you know about that?"

By rights, Hammond knew he should be sticking to the eyes-only directive for the current situation, but he couldn't resist prodding Maybourne, shaking him up a little to see what fell out. Besides, he was neither confirming nor denying anything. And by the looks of it, his little test had worked. Maybourne shifted in his seat, eyes flitting to the side as he realized he'd given away more than he should.

You think you're a big player in this game, thought Hammond.

Son, you're nothing but Little League.

But the colonel made an admirable attempt to recover. "I think, General, that we should focus on what's important here. The Earth is in trouble and something has to be done. I don't believe I'm speaking out of turn when I say that I may be the one to do it."

At that, Hammond's fraying temper almost snapped. Only one last tenuous thread held it together and that thread told him there was hope yet, that, against the odds, SG-1 might still make it back and put this whole damn thing to bed. A tiny fragment of hope, but there it was.

To reveal anything else to Maybourne at this stage would be unwise. But Maybourne, it seemed, was less circumspect.

"General, I've succeeded where Jack O'Neill failed. I've been able to set up an off-world base. An Alpha Site, if you will. Just say the word and we can begin evacuation immediately." He cleared his throat and had the good grace to look mildly uncomfortable. "Of course, there would need to be a... discussion about the chain of command. My people, however, have already proven more than resourceful in establishing an efficient operation. If you were to speak to the President–"

"Now just wait one damn minute, you slick son of a b–"

"No, General, I've already waited long enough. We all have. This entire planet has done nothing but wait, and now it's about to pay the price. That gate isn't simply an on-ramp for the intergalactic highway, George. It's a weapon. You and your teams might be happy to take your little hearts and minds trips around the galaxy, smiling at the locals, while the Asgard and the Tollan and the Tok'ra pull the strings and play you like puppets. But there are factions who believe that more... robust measures need to be taken to ensure the safety of this planet. You had a duty of care, General, and you failed. If we're waiting on anything, it's for the other shoe to drop."

Enough was enough. To hell with eyes-only, to hell with playing the cards carefully, this idiot had just pulled on

Hammond's one remaining thread. "You've got some damn nerve, Maybourne. You come in here and tell me how *your* people can save us? Do you have any idea why we're in this position? It's because of your people and what they've done. They've lied and they've stolen and they've turned our allies against us. You and your people put Earth in danger, and you've done so in the most underhanded way possible. Don't you dare accuse me of failing this planet; the blame falls firmly on your shoulders."

"The blame, sir, falls with the SGC and your command. The blame falls with your flagship team, always ready to play the heroes and take the glory. So tell me, General, where is SG-1 now? Where are your heroes?"

At that, Hammond rose to his feet, leaning forward and bracing himself on his desk. The lacquered walnut felt sturdy and solid beneath his knuckles. Maybourne met his eyes, but Hammond could see the unease there; you didn't get two stars on your shoulder without knowing how to intimidate. "I could have you arrested, Maybourne. One call and they'd bury you so deep you'd never see daylight again."

He feigned unconcern, but Hammond could see a shimmer of sweat on his forehead. "On what evidence?"

"You just confessed."

"Your word against mine, General. Besides, right now, I'd say your word doesn't stack up to a whole lot." Maybourne gave a serpent's smile. "You need to face facts, *sir*. SG-1 isn't coming back and you'll have to look elsewhere for salvation. That's exactly what I'm here to offer."

There was truth in what Maybourne had to say, of course. Hammond wasn't fool enough to deny the predicament they were in. There was a storm coming, a howling blue-norther ready to rip the very ground from beneath their feet. But Hammond would not allow a snake like Maybourne to have the upper hand. "Let me tell you a few things, Maybourne," he said. "First of all, I'd rather jump in a hand basket and ride it straight to hell than accept any help from you. Secondly, you may accept that the end of the world is a foregone conclusion, but I like to think that the human race has something left to fight for, and I sure as hell won't be giving up any time soon." He rounded the desk and picked up Maybourne's hat. "And lastly, I don't care if God has opened the heavens and unleashed the seven plagues of Egypt upon these lands; I am still a general in the United States Air Force while you're nothing but a pissant colonel. So when you enter my office you stand to attention until I say the words 'at ease'. Forget that again, Colonel, and I'll haul you up for insubordination and make sure you spend your last hours on this earth cleaning the filthiest toilet in Leavenworth."

Maybourne stood up as Hammond spoke, keeping the chair as a barrier between them. "You couldn't," he said.

"That phone doesn't dial Pizza Hut, son." Hammond held out the hat. "Now get the hell out of my office and off my base."

Maybourne took his hat, clearly struggling not to snatch it. "You hide behind this good ol' boy bluster all you want, General," he said, "but sooner or later you'll realize that I'm your last hope."

"Get out, Maybourne." He nodded to the two airmen waiting outside his office. "Make sure the colonel leaves the base without incident."

As Mayborne stomped out the door, he shouldered past Harriman, who'd just come running up from the control room. One glance at the sergeant's face and Maybourne was forgotten.

"What is it, Walter?"

"It's not good, sir. At just after 0900, a ship came out of hyperspace, just beyond the Kuiper belt. And then another and then —" He shook his head and swallowed. "General, Apophis's fleet has entered the solar system."

CHAPTER NINETEEN

TEAL'C took the rear as they made their retreat, Hunter leading them on a frenzied sprint through the ship's winding corridors. There appeared to be no direction to their flight, but
there was no time to question it. He must trust their new ally.

Teal'c laid down a series of covering blasts, a few of them
finding their target, but their pursuers were strong and difficult
to kill. Just when he thought he had felled the last of them, he
heard quick footsteps echoing along the corridor down which
they had just fled. They were far from safe.

Major Carter drew to a halt suddenly, causing Teal'c to col-
lide with her, back to back. "Major Carter, we must keep moving!" But when he looked over his shoulder in the direction
they were running, he saw why she had stopped. The door
ahead was sealed.

"Hunter?" she hissed. "Now what?"

"We gotta get through that door."

But at that moment three Amam rounded the corner behind
them, no more than twenty meters away.

"Major Carter," Teal'c said, warning her.

She turned. "Damn it."

The Amam stopped and assessed the situation, sniffing the
air. Hunters, with their prey cornered. Teal'c could sense their
triumph. He raised his weapon, Daniel Jackson and Major
Carter doing likewise. Prey, or not, they would not succumb
without a fight.

As one, the Amam lifted their weapons and began to stalk
toward them.

"On my mark," Major Carter said. Her voice was tense but
steady. "Three of them, three of us."

But suddenly a figure darted forward, low to the ground.
Hunter. In his hand he held a metallic egg-shaped object, which,

with a quick twist, he hurled down the corridor. There was a moment of silence, as the Amam watched the object sail towards them. Recognizing the weapon, Teal'c knew the outcome before it landed and cried out, "Cover!" He pulled Daniel Jackson to the ground, trusting that Major Carter would share his instinct.

The grenade went off, showering them with debris and what may possibly have been Amam body parts, but he did not look back to find out, for the door now stood open and the four of them fled into daylight. Hunter had fulfilled his promise.

"Keep going!" Hunter cried as they ran. "Into the trees!"

Teal'c looked back once, but there was no pursuit. Only the ship loomed behind them, alive and threatening, like a beast ready to swallow them back up.

The grenade had given them time, but they could not stop.

"Hunter?" he shouted as they ran. They were blind now, no sense of direction beneath the heavy sky, no destination even had they known the direction in which they were running. Everything relied on Hunter.

"This way," he replied, breathless but showing no signs of slowing.

Onward they ran, heading downhill toward a scrappy line of trees. They were free, they had escaped. But Teal'c felt no triumph, no victory, only a heavy sense of loss. And though he did not look at his friends, he knew their thoughts were one with his.

O'Neill, left in the grasp of the enemy. Perhaps already dead.

Grabbing him by the scruff of the neck, the Devourer marched Jack from the lab. Somewhere, further down the corridor, he could hear the echo of staff blasts and the rattle of gunfire. These life-sucking bastards obviously weren't happy to let their lunch escape so easily and Jack could only hope that Hunter was honest enough, or at least self-interested enough, to show his team how to get the hell out of this place.

Jack's own weapons were still back in the lab with the rest of his gear, and the thing holding him was huge, bigger than any of the other Devourers they'd seen so far, so he guessed that any attempt at escape would just land him a broken neck — or worse.

Despite his captor's size, however, Jack got the impression that it was just a grunt and that he was being taken to face whatever counted for higher management among these sons of bitches.

Eventually, they arrived at a door which slid open as they approached. Jack was thrown into a large room with a towering ceiling. Around the walls of the room and through its center sat tables with an array of equipment on each. None of it looked like anything SG-1 had encountered on its travels but, unlike the hodgepodge of tech that had been strewn about the laboratory he'd just left, all of this equipment had a similar appearance. He didn't have Daniel or Carter's expert eye, but Jack would have bet that it all had the same origin. Another difference he noted from the laboratory was that the tech in this room was very well cared for. Valuable, then.

"You are Lantean."

The voice was a hiss from the corner of the room and Jack spun towards it. From the shadows, walked a shape. A Devourer, slender like the others, clad in a buckled leather robe. Its skin was pallid, almost translucent in the ship's eerie blue light, and its ratted hair was white. Only with this one, something wasn't right. 'Walk' was the wrong word to describe the way it moved, this thing's movements were jerky, as if it hadn't mastered basic motor control. It crouched as it came forward, arms held out at its side. Jack tried in vain not to be seriously creeped out by the sight.

"You," it said again, with no inflection. "You are Lantean."

And there was that word again. Jack wasn't sure what it meant, all he knew was that it had so far prevented him from being turned into a human juice box. "From Minnesota actually, but I guess my accent's faded a little."

The thing closed its eyes and lowered its head, murmuring something under its breath. Jack strained to make it out and wished he hadn't when the words resolved themselves into a chant.

"Bloodbloodbloodbloodblood."

The Amam's eyes sprang open again and Jack recoiled, pinned by a frightening reptilian stare. It pointed a clawed finger at him. "You have Ancient blood."

Jack narrowed his eyes, considering that for a moment. There was of course the question of how it seemed to know what had happened in the lab without the grunt having said a word — Jack himself was still trying to figure out exactly what *had* happened — but that wasn't what struck him as being important right now.

Ancient.

Daniel had said their language was rooted in Ancient. And if they had some kind of connection to the gate builders then maybe they might also have the means to dial out without a DHD. It was worth pursuing.

But he knew he had to buy time, play this one carefully. If he just asked straight out, they were hardly likely to help him. "Well," he said, "I have *some* blood, and sure, sometimes it feels a little old–"

But the Amam wasn't listening. It jerked its head towards Jack's silent guard, its chin jutting upwards, and bared its teeth with a hiss. It was then that Jack realized what was so unsettling about this situation, what was so wrong with this creature compared to the other Devourers they had encountered so far. They had been cold, emotionless, calculated. This one was plain, tinfoil hat, batshit crazy.

Without a word, the grunt turned and left the room.

"Hey," called Jack, to its retreating back, "you don't wanna stay a while? Split a six pack? Watch the game? Not leave me with Charles Manson here?" But the door closed and he found himself alone in the room with Crazy. With a grimace, he turned back to face his new companion. "I'm gonna miss that guy."

Crazy rounded the table and came towards him. Jack tried not to recoil as it leaned in as if taking his scent. The thing drew back and cocked his head. It looked down and to the side, as if searching its memory for some forgotten knowledge. "You... hunger. You require food."

"Um, no," he replied, not exactly relishing this bizarre attempt at hospitality — Hansel and Gretel had probably had a similar offer. He ignored the sudden growling of his stomach at the thought of food. His last MRE had been in Aedan's camp and who knew how long ago that had been? "I never eat standing up," he said.

But evidently Crazy had either forgotten the offer or hadn't been that interested in Jack's response because it turned back around to the table of equipment and thrust out its hand, pointing at the space next to him. Jack took this as a summons and keeping as much distance between him and the alien as possible, approached the table. "This is some pretty cool stuff you got here," he said looking down at the array of gadgets.

Although, in truth, 'gadgets' was doing these objects a disservice, because they were quite beautiful, each of them rendered in exquisite glass and metalwork. He was sure Daniel would have had a field day, but for his part, Jack could at least appreciate how pretty they were.

The Amam ran his hand lightly across their surface, with something that looked almost like reverence. "Such beauty," he murmured, in a way that made Jack doubt that it was speaking to him directly. "The gods who left their children. They made them and then they left them. Salvation or damnation. The choice was simple."

"Look," said Jack, "I appreciate that you people are just trying to get on with... with whatever it is you're getting on with here." Crazy's head spun towards Jack, as if it had only just remembered he was in the room. Unnerved, Jack plowed on. "All I'm saying is, we don't want to intrude and I'm willing to forgive the whole 'imprisoning us and trying to eat us' thing if you can help me out. The Ancients. Do you know them? I mean, do you know who they were?"

The Amam squinted at him and for one weird moment Jack felt like the crazy one. It looked to the table and back to Jack, then reached out and picked up one of the objects that lay there. It was a transparent disc of colored glass about the size of a dinner plate, edged in metal. From the center, were radiating rows of characters that looked similar to the writing that had so fascinated Daniel on the screen back in the lab. Ancient, he guessed, or something like it. "Touch," said the Amam, holding out the disc. "I must see your blood. Touch."

"Oh, I'd better not. I'm sure you have some sort of 'You break it, you buy it policy.'" Crazy hissed, baring its teeth, and Jack recalled the even more vicious teeth on the palm of its hand. He took a breath and gingerly took the disc from the alien and turned it over in his hands. The writing on it was gibberish to him. Daniel, of course, would have been able to figure it out, but right now he was hoping that Daniel was at least a mile away. "Listen, I really think you've got the wrong guy. I just–"

The disc sprang to life. Beams of light spread across the ceiling of the vast room before contracting into myriad tiny pinpoints. He was no expert, but Jack knew a star chart when he saw one. He scanned the constellations, searching for any he recognized. He wondered if it was the Milky Way, and where among all those tiny points, Earth might be. That's where Carter would have proven useful.

I am so the wrong guy.

But, as his thoughts dwelt on home and where among the stars it might be, the light show began to move, like a ship moving at sub-light.

It's searching, he realized, *and I'm the one making it move.* With sudden alarm at where the star map might be headed, Jack threw it onto the table before it led exactly to the place he never wanted this crazy bastard to know existed: Earth. It landed with a crash in the midst of the surrounding artifacts.

The Amam snarled and Jack understood his mistake a second before he found himself knocked halfway to the door. Crazy stalked towards him.

"I'm sorry!" Jack said, holding his hands up. "I'm sorry. I didn't mean that." He pushed himself to his feet and shook the ringing from his head.

But as Crazy approached with its shambolic gait, Jack saw something that was even more unsettling than the threat of further violence. The Devourer was grinning. "You will be of use," it said. "You will lead us."

"And what use do you think I'll be?"

"I have not seen one with your power before," it said, and for the first time Jack thought he glimpsed some semblance of sanity in its expression. "The others of your kind are weak, control falters too often, and they are spent before any progress is made. But the blood… your blood is strong. You may be the one we have awaited. You will lead us, Lantean. You will let us fly."

Perhaps sanity was the wrong word to use after all.

CHAPTER TWENTY

THE FIRE burned bright, bringing warmth to Daniel's bones. Sam had objected to lighting it for fear that it would bring the Amam right to them, but Hunter had said it wouldn't make a difference.

It was true that their escape had seemed almost too easy. They had sprinted towards the cover of a nearby forest, downhill and away from the alien craft. Daniel had expected, with every passing moment, a clawed hand to close on his shoulder. But the only assault had come from the tree branches that tore at their clothes and exposed hands and faces.

"They won't chase us no further," said Hunter, once they'd finally slowed. "They've got what they want."

"You mean Colonel O'Neill?" Sam had almost spat the words.

But Hunter had been unfazed by her anger. "Right enough," he said. "But don't worry, they ain't gonna feast on him. He's safe enough for now."

"How do you know?"

Hunter had just smiled, though his eyes were hard. "'Cause I know Snatchers."

He'd led them then to a clearing, canopied by skeleton trees whose jagged branches cracked the darkening sky into brittle pieces of gray. From the snaking carcasses of roots that jutted through the hard-baked soil, it looked like this area might once have been densely wooded. Now it was just a filigree of death and dust.

In the near distance, the behemoth that was the Amam ship lurked on the mountainside like some brooding creature, and they sat in its shadow collecting their thoughts. Looking at his friends' faces, Daniel knew they were all asking themselves the same question: What now?

"Where did you get that grenade?" Sam asked Hunter. "How

did you know what it was?"

"Took it from one of the tables in the junk room. We've seen 'em before. We use what we can find and we've stolen plenty like that in the past. Sometimes we just find 'em in the dirt."

"The grenade appeared to be of Goa'uld design," Teal'c said, "although unusual. Most likely they were abandoned here during the war with the Amam."

Hunter just shrugged. "Dix provides."

His devotion to the mysterious Dix was fascinating, and Daniel wondered what role he played on this world. To Elspeth he'd been little more than a legend, yet to Hunter he seemed very much a living person.

"You said you would take us to him," said Teal'c.

Hunter just threw another bundle of sticks onto the fire. "If you lend me one of your knives, I could catch us a jacker. Some good eating in a jacker."

Sam grabbed his elbow. "Hunter, you said you would help us. We don't have time for this."

Hunter nodded and said, "I'll take you to Dix soon enough, but strangers can't just go walkin' in on him."

"Fine," said Sam, "then *you* take us there. Let's go. Let's go right now." She stood up, brushing the dirt from her BDUs, heading away from the light of the fire. Daniel could see how antsy she was to get moving and he could understand her impatience.

"No!" Hunter's shout split the night and Sam froze. Clearly she was as alarmed as Daniel was at the panic in the man's tone. It was more than just concern at them wandering in where they weren't welcome, though. It bordered on actual fear. Hunter took a breath and sat back, staring at the fire again. "No," he said again, quieter this time. "Ain't safe in the Shacks at night."

"Why not?" asked Sam. "What happens at night?"

"The Snatchers come."

"There is no safety in your home?" said Teal'c.

Hunter huffed a bitter laugh. "There ain't no safety nowhere."

"Then why do you remain there?"

He ignored the question, just fixed his gaze on the crackling flames, and said, "I'll take you to Dix, but in the morning. In the daylight."

"Hunter," said Daniel, "our friend is back on the Amam ship. We can't leave him there."

"Going back'll only get yourselves caught."

"Maybe," Daniel said, "but we don't have a choice. We'd like to know if Dix can help us."

"He will, but not in this. That'd put us all in harm's way. Your friend… the Amam won't hurt him none. You got time."

"How much time?" Sam said. "How do you know they won't hurt him?"

"'Cause your friend's Lantean."

"He's what?"

"Lantean. The Snatchers won't hurt him none, not till they're done testing him."

"Testing him?" said Daniel. "What do you mean?"

"Gods' truth. There are those the Snatchers take from among their harvestings, and test with workings like the one O'Neill touched. If they've the gift to work such devices, then they're taken to serve a purpose other than…" He swallowed and rubbed his hand over the center of his chest. Daniel saw Sam flinch, as if recalling the momentary pain she'd experienced.

"But to what end?" she asked. "What are they testing them for?"

"No one rightly knows. There's camp-tales, though, but most of them are nonsense."

"Tales?" said Daniel, unable to hide his interest.

Hunter sighed and rolled his eyes, as if being asked to recite a children's story for the hundredth time. "There're legends of a city that was once sunk beneath the ocean and lived in by a race of… I don't know, some call 'em gods. Seems that only the descendants of the gods — those of the Lantean blood — can restore the city and save us all."

"But you don't believe the legends."

Hunter shrugged and threw some more kindling on the fire. "Don't matter whether I believe it. What matters is that the Snatchers do. And so they search for Lantean blood, like that of O'Neill. Trust me, if he complies, then his fate'll be better than any other."

"Whatever that fate may be," said Teal'c, "I am certain it is nothing good. The Goa'uld often select slaves to become their own personal attendants and treat them, for a time, as the Tau'ri may treat a cherished pet. They are still slaves however, and when their master becomes weary of them, or is displeased in anyway, the slave is dealt an unenviable punishment."

As it always did, the memory of Sha're was sudden, still painful after all this time, blessed by Apophis in the form of a symbiote in her head. He could almost see the unnatural flash of her eyes in the flames of the camp fire.

Sam pressed her lips into a thin line. "Trust me, Hunter, Colonel O'Neill is not someone who'll 'comply' with the Amam's wishes. And I sure as hell won't be leaving him in their hands."

"Nor I, Major Carter," said Teal'c.

"You're foolish to go back," said Hunter. "It's sure death."

"Not really," said Sam. "They can't feed on me, remember?"

"The Snatchers have other ways of killing. You ain't safe. Your leader man is."

"We don't leave our people behind, Hunter," said Sam. "We're going back for him."

"Then we're decided," said Daniel. Not that there had never been any other option. "So when do we head back? First light?" But then he saw the grave expression on Sam's face and realized she'd come up with another option — one he wasn't going like very much.

"Not you, Daniel."

"What?"

"Teal'c and I go back. You take my pack and go with Hunter."

"Sam, no!" There was no way he was letting them go back

there alone. The stakes were too high and the idea of the four of them scattered across this barren planet filled him with unease.

"Daniel, it's the only way that makes sense. If we… if anything happens, you need to go find Dix and get a message home. You're the one who'll need to get help."

The fact that she was right only deepened his dismay, because it would be all the more difficult to talk her out of it. "Then we all go to Dix," he said. "We're stronger together."

"Daniel, you know we don't have time for that. Any delay could cost the colonel his life."

"But—"

"Daniel, it's the only way. Consider it an order." Her expression was resolute and Daniel knew it was useless to say any more. When Sam pulled rank on him, the argument was over. She nodded at his acquiescence. "First light, then. Teal'c and I go back to the ship. Hunter, can you take Teal'c's pack with you? We'll move faster if we travel light."

Hunter nodded, and seemed genuinely torn when he said, "I'm sorry I can't go with you, but I've a wife and a son."

Teal'c bowed his head. He, of all people, understood the decision.

"It's alright, Hunter," said Sam, less fervent now that the decision had been made. "Go back to your family. And thank you for your help. We couldn't have made it this far without you."

Hunter nodded. "I can't go with you, but I can still help you." He picked up a stick and sketched a few lines in the dirt. "Here, on the side of the ship where the light rises, you'll find an access hatch. Ascend two levels and you'll find the cells where the Snatchers are likely holding O'Neill. Here. And here. The prisoners they hold there are valuable, so you should expect much resistance. It won't be easy." From the way he shook his head, Daniel could tell that he thought it would be nigh on impossible. "If… if you make it out, follow the tree line along the base of the mountain. You'll find the Old Road. It's broken up and hard to see, but it's there alright. At the end of that's the Shacks. You'll be welcome in my home, Major Carter. And Dix'll help if he can. I'll wait for you."

"Our thanks, Hunter," said Teal'c.

"The gods' grace go with you," he said, but his tone was grim. He obviously doubted there was enough divine grace to cover what luck Sam and Teal'c would need.

Sam knelt down next to the roughly sketched ship schematics, focused and determined. "So, let's go over these plans again," she said, "and this time I have a few questions."

The ceiling of the cell was dark and featureless, cold, just like the rest of this godforsaken ship. Say what you wanted about the Goa'uld, at least they had some flair when it came to decor. This place felt like it had not so much been designed, but rather it had grown from some gruesome embryo. The cell itself was ordinary, more or less. Not the sticky pods from which he and the others had escaped, but a room enclosed by an intricate mesh of bars. He'd been escorted past a heavy guard presence and could still hear the steady tread of the regular patrols in the hallways. Here, though, he hadn't seen a soul for a couple of hours. *At least they didn't put me back in the pantry*, he thought grimly.

Although they hadn't fed him either, or given him anything to drink.

He'd made some obligatory attempts to find a way out, but the only thing he could see that even resembled a lock was too far out of reach. The Amam guards who'd brought him here hadn't even appeared to touch anything, the netlike bars simply parting in front of them. Despite the latent talent he'd just discovered for activating alien gadgets, Jack had been thus far unsuccessful in getting the bars to open for him. He thought back to Carter's grimace when she touched the door panel earlier and her comment that it felt almost alive. It was not a pleasant idea.

It seemed that even the Amam had forgotten about him for

the time being, which was just fine with him. Crazy hadn't hurt him as such. In fact, the thing had seemed completely ambivalent towards his wellbeing. It had spent what felt like hours forcing Jack to try and activate an array of weird tech. Jack had tried his best to prevent the tests from being successful, but it appeared that the outcome of each one was out of his control: some had worked, some had not. He wasn't sure what it meant. Then he'd been brought to this cell and left alone.

For now, he had no choice but to wait.

Wait for what? For rescue? Who's coming back for you, Jack?

He hated that little voice. It had been his constant companion on Edora too, until eventually he'd answered its persistent questioning.

No one. No one was coming for him.

That was what he'd thought and then his team had gone and proved him wrong. And he'd been angry. He'd been *angry*. What a truly ungrateful son of a bitch.

There was a time, long ago, when everything in his life was solid and certain. A time before Charlie and the sound of the shot that had cracked his world apart. He'd known his purpose and his duty then, and, yes, there had been times when he'd landed in situations to which hell had seemed an attractive alternative, but that was all on him. That was part of serving, part of the choice he'd made. Then everything had changed and he'd ended up with nothing. In those days, he *was* nothing. Until the Stargate. Only then had he realized that purpose and duty hadn't deserted him after all.

Sometimes, though… Sometimes he woke and felt nothing but old. And it was those times that made him wonder whether this was his game anymore. Did he still have the heart for the fight?

Edora. The place had tested his commitment and he'd come up wanting. Some days he truly wished he was back there, back to the simplicity of farming and fishing. Some days he wished there had been no rescue, that Carter hadn't been smart enough to find a way home. Some days he thought he could've lived with that.

Yet right here, right now, being on this godforsaken rock at the ass end of the galaxy made him realize how wrong he'd been. Maybe it was that old school Air Force ego kicking in, but all Jack could think about was how much he was needed elsewhere, and what might be going wrong without him and SG-1. He had a duty, to his people and to his team, to make it through this. He wouldn't forget that again.

This wasn't Edora. And this time there would be no rescue, because he'd ordered it so. Hopefully, Carter, Daniel and Teal'c were already on their way to see Dix, whoever he might be, and hopefully Dix would help them find a way off this miserable world.

If he made it out of this, he'd try and pick up their trail and follow on behind — no, *when* he made it out of this. Because right now Jack knew that he was the only hope he had.

CHAPTER TWENTY-ONE

DAWN crept into the sky, a vague brightness through the shroud of mist. Whatever sun stood at the center of this solar system, it brought little light and almost no warmth. Sam thought it would have been almost useless as a guide in most circumstances, but Hunter had said where the light rises, and that much, at least, was distinguishable.

They packed up their rough camp in silence, but when she suggested they get rid of the debris from the fire to hide their trail, Hunter shrugged and shook his head. "They won't track us here. They don't hunt in places like this."

"Why not?" asked Daniel.

"They have easier ways."

Sam stepped forward and touched his arm. "Hunter," she said, "if we can, we'll take them down for you."

Hunter only smiled, a beaten expression, and said, "You won't defeat them. There are always more." Then he headed into the forest, gesturing for Daniel to follow.

Sam, Daniel and Teal'c spared each other a moment, one that had passed between them many times. A look exchanged, a nod, a few brief, meaningless words that didn't — *couldn't* — capture everything they'd want to say if this was the last time, if one of them, or none of them, were coming back from this. The words couldn't be said out loud so they settled, as they always did, for the nods and the looks, and then they moved out.

The way back to the ship was harder than their escape had been the night before. That had been an all-out run across the open scrubland towards the forest. This time, Sam and Teal'c kept to the tree line when they could, making use of the sparse cover it offered, but it meant a harder uphill climb, with fallen branches and twisted roots to bar their path. The ever-present mist didn't help.

"Major Carter, do you believe that Hunter is being truthful in saying that the Amam will not hurt O'Neill?" asked Teal'c, as they hoisted themselves up and over a large rocky mound.

"Why would he lie?" replied Sam, though she'd harbored the same doubts. She focused on her footing, not wanting to consider the possibility of what might be happening to the colonel right now if Hunter was lying.

"I do not know. But his tale of a flying city would make his word seem less than reliable."

"He said himself that he didn't think those stories were true."

"He did."

"And Daniel would say that myths like that tend to be more elaborate versions of something that once was fact."

"He would."

"I don't think we have any reason to doubt Hunter's word."

"Indeed."

She stopped in her climb and turned to face him. "Why would he lie, Teal'c?"

"I am sure he did not." But Sam knew what Teal'c wasn't saying: perhaps Hunter hadn't lied, but perhaps he didn't know the Amam as well as he claimed. She picked up her pace, more eager than ever to get to the ship.

By her watch, it took them a further half hour to reach it and they headed around it counter-clockwise, as per Hunter's instructions. It unnerved her to be so close to the enormous vessel and she fought the prickly feeling that the thing was somehow alive and watching them. In truth, it probably gave them more cover than if they'd approached their intended point of entry in a direct line from the forest. This route also gave Sam a chance to scrutinize the hull.

"This thing hasn't moved for decades," she said, running her hand along the pitted surface that looked like no metal she'd ever encountered. "Look at how high the moss reaches. I wonder why they'd want to stick around on a planet like this. What's here for them?"

"The vessel may no longer be able to fly."

But Sam was thinking of the dark hints that Hunter had dropped, about the Amam's feeding habits and them having easier options than hunting. She wasn't sure what he meant, but it didn't sound like anything good. The sooner they found a way off this planet the better.

For that, they had to find the colonel first. Up ahead the ship curved around and from Hunter's diagram, she knew they were close. They rounded the hull and found the opening he'd spoken of: a narrow aperture covered by a mesh, about three-feet square, which led into a dark vent. It wouldn't be comfortable, especially not for Teal'c, but it would do the job. Sam pulled out her pocket knife and began to work the mesh free.

Hold on, sir. We're coming for you.

Hunter walked with the steady lope of a man used to crossing large distances by foot and Daniel allowed him to range ahead while he followed more slowly. Out in the daylight, away from the murk of the Amam ship, he could see him better and took the opportunity to study their new ally. Hunter was young, but his skin was weather-beaten and his body lean and wiry. Just like Aedan and his people, Hunter looked hungry, his youth already ravaged by the hard life he lived.

They walked downhill through the scraggy forest, its pine scent intensifying the lower they got and the denser the trees became. Daniel was no expert in forestry, but from the amount of dead wood rotting on the ground and the uniform height of the new growth, he could guess that this whole forest had burned at some point in the past — probably when the Amam ship had landed, back during the war Elspeth Burne had described. He wondered if there were bodies beneath the loamy soil, the bones that Aedan claimed they still found everywhere. The thought made him shiver in the cold morning air and he tugged his boonie lower, sticking his hands into his pockets.

Behind them, the Amam ship crouched against a mountainside that disappeared up into low cloud. The ship seemed to merge with the rock, its weirdly organic hull covered in lichen and clumps of scraggy grass. It almost looked like an abandoned crash site, except that there didn't seem to be any damage to the ship.

"Hunter," Daniel called, keeping his voice as low as possible.

Hunter turned, stopping and waiting for Daniel to catch up. "You doin' alright?"

"Yeah." He gestured back toward the ship. "Does that thing ever move?"

"Nope. Told you before, it don't fly."

"Because it can't?"

Hunter shrugged. "Just know it don't." He jerked his head in the direction he was walking. "Nearly at the Shacks now. C'mon."

He headed off again and this time Daniel kept pace with him. The descent was steeper here, the ground sometimes rocky, and occasionally Daniel thought he saw patches of some kind of paving. Probably the Old Road that Hunter had mentioned. He'd also spotted what looked like metal girders, twisted and misshapen, and the rough signs of structural foundations. There had been buildings here once.

After a while, Hunter reached out and touched his arm, slowing him as the ground levelled off and then fell away steeply ahead of them. The forest grew sparser again, and here and there Daniel noticed stumps where trees had been recently felled, ax marks biting deep into the blond wood. People foraged here, he guessed.

Hunter turned to the right, walking parallel to the trees that ran along the top of a steep escarpment. And through the trees, beneath the mist, Daniel began to see a camp emerge. The sight stopped him dead, stunning him with its sheer size. He'd been expecting something like Aedan's encampment but this was on a whole different scale.

He let out a breath. "Whoa…"

The milky sun was behind them and the mountain cast a

long shadow, reaching like a pointing finger across the valley below and the sprawling encampment that stretched out in all directions. It was vast and squalid, the worst kind of human misery, and even from where he stood amid the pine trees, Daniel could smell the rising stench of degradation.

Hunter spat on the ground as if trying to get rid of the foul smell. "They say it was a city once, but there ain't nothing left now. Just people on top of people, hoping they ain't the ones to be snatched."

"How many people?" Daniel said, his heart sinking with a sudden, overwhelming sense of despair. Like the people waiting to die on the Amam ship, there was nothing he could do to help these people, and it left him feeling angry and powerless.

"Dix thinks a hundred thousand."

Daniel shook his head. "I had no idea there were that many people on this planet."

"This ain't the only camp," Hunter said, giving him a sideways look. "Dix says they're all over the world. He can see, from up there." He glanced up at the sky.

"From Hecate's ship?"

Hunter nodded. "Dix says there's hundreds of thousands of people here. He says it's an army, enough to drive off the Amam."

Hundreds of thousands of people in camps like this? It wasn't an army — it was a catastrophe. "We can't let this carry on," Daniel said out loud, although he was talking more to himself than to Hunter.

But Hunter answered anyway. "We ain't gonna let it carry on," he said. "Hecate will help us, Dix will help us."

"And we'll help you too," Daniel added, determinedly ignoring his inner Jack O'Neill warning him against making rash promises. But this was an atrocity on a global scale and Daniel didn't give a damn what anyone said — he was going to ensure Earth helped these people if it was the last thing he did.

"Dix takes anyone prepared to fight," Hunter said, then nodded toward a narrow trail ahead. "That there's the way down.

Be careful, it's steep."

It was steep, but there were enough trees around to hold onto and the descent was at least fast. Then they were crossing an empty patch of no-man's-land toward the edge of the enormous tent city.

There was no barrier to the camp, no wire fence keeping people in, which surprised Daniel. Contrary to his first impression, it wasn't a prison camp. It was more like a refugee camp, with all the misery and desperation that entailed. Towers rose up at regular intervals around the perimeter, roughly constructed of wood with a large platform at the top — watch towers, Daniel thought at first, but he couldn't see any Amam patrolling them. They seemed abandoned.

"Not watch towers," Hunter corrected, when Daniel asked. "Feeding stations."

He felt his eyebrows climb. "Feeding stations as in… ?" He made a clawing gesture with one hand.

Hunter shook his head. "We're fodder to them, sure enough, but it don't do them no good if we starve to death before they eat."

"Wait…" It took a moment to process the thought. "The Amam *feed* the people in the camp?"

Hunter nodded. "Twice a week they send Snatchers to leave rations atop the towers."

Daniel felt his stomach turn with a deep nausea; these people were being kept like animals, like cattle. "Why do they stay?" he wondered aloud. "Why do they live like this?"

Hunter slipped him a look that said he should know better than to ask. "Because they ain't got no choice."

And that was the truth of it, he supposed. No one lived like this if there was an alternative. Across the galaxy, humans clung to life with a tenacity that sometimes defied reason. If it was this or death, they'd choose this — no matter how hopeless their lives had become.

"Now stick close," Hunter said as they approached the edge of the camp. "There's some here who'd stick you as soon as look at you if they think you've got a bite to eat."

Daniel let his hand come to rest on his weapon. "Don't worry about me," he said. "I can take care of myself."

Hunter looked dubious, but didn't argue and together they headed into the sprawling, stinking camp.

The ventilation chute was hot and cramped. Sam lay stretched out on her front, her arms folded beneath her. It was the same position she'd occupied for the past twenty minutes and for five of those she'd tried to ignore the pain that was creeping into her stiffening joints. Teal'c lay behind her, just as cramped, and she didn't want to guess what discomfort the large Jaffa might be suffering.

She watched the corridor, hidden from the patrolling Amam guard by only the thin mesh covering of the vent. She was anxious to make a move, but knew that rash action would mean an end to their plan before it had begun. Stealth was their biggest advantage. For now.

She checked her watch. By her count, a patrol was due to pass within the next ten seconds, and sure enough she heard heavy footsteps approach.

Wait, wait, wait...

Shadows passed over the grill.

Turning as silently as she could in the cramped space, she gestured to Teal'c, letting him know what was coming next.

Two grunts, heading clockwise, move out in 5... 4... 3... 2...

Sam pushed against the grill, which she'd already loosened with her knife, gripping it tightly so it didn't go clattering to the floor, and placed it inside the vent. Then she wriggled forward, dropping down softly. Teal'c followed, but his boots hit the ground with an audible thump and she cringed, looking up the hallway to where the grunts had disappeared around the corner. There was no sound to indicate they were coming back. If her count was right, she and Teal'c had three minutes before they returned.

Not very long for them to find what they were looking for, but it would have to do.

They pressed themselves against the wall, weapons drawn, and followed the curve of the corridor.

"Look for a screen like the one we saw in the lab," she whispered to Teal'c. "Hunter says it'll show us the brig."

After a few moments, they spotted another of the eerie yellow screens, this one emerging from the hull almost as if it had grown there. A quick check left and right, then she dashed forward, bracing her hand against the wall as she studied the screen. Once again she felt that awful sensation, that there was something alive within this ship.

Alive, but still rotting from the inside out.

She studied the screen and there it was — a collection of rooms almost identical to Hunter's improvised map. The brig.

It swarmed with yellow dots.

"One of those must be O'Neill," said Teal'c, and Sam prayed he was right, but her mind kept returning to the mawing hand that had been thrust against her chest, to the desiccated corpse of the nameless man on whom the Amam had fed.

"It's no use; we'll never make it through those sorts of numbers."

"Major Carter..."

"I know, Teal'c! I know."

The seconds ticked down. Somewhere along the corridor, the regular tread of heavy footsteps grew louder. The guards were returning, completing their circuit. Struck by a sudden idea, Sam thought back to the map she and Daniel had seen in the lab, conjuring the image back into her mind. Then she was moving again, down the corridor, a quick gesture to Teal'c telling him to follow.

She knew where they were going now, and it wasn't to the brig.

Teal'c followed Major Carter along the winding lengths of the Amam ship's hallways. They had fled from the approaching footsteps, finding a doorway through which to duck just seconds before the two guards had passed within inches.

Now they made their way to an upper level. They'd spoken little for fear of being heard by any Amam who might be close by, but Teal'c did not question the last minute change of plan. He trusted Major Carter and knew her judgment to be sound. Even in the most difficult circumstances, she never lost focus and was not prone to rash, emotional decisions. She took point now, her stride determined, though her manner watchful, while Teal'c covered their backs.

That was not to say that he was unconcerned, for her grim resolve held its own disquiet. This mission was fraught with danger and it was no exaggeration when Hunter had decried it as suicide. But they had faced worse and lived. And there was no question of them leaving Colonel O'Neill to whatever fate the Amam had in store for him.

The life-signs shown on the schematics panel were further cause for concern. During his watch in the forest, he had seen many of the small alien gliders return to the grounded mothership and he'd wondered if they'd been on patrol around the planet, or if they'd been engaged in battle with the Goa'uld on a larger scale than the dogfight they'd witnessed near Aedan's camp.

Whatever the reason, it meant that there was now a greater enemy presence on the ship and every level swarmed with Amam. To find O'Neill and escape would present a significant challenge.

Footsteps approached, rapid and uneven. Teal'c glanced around and then pulled Major Carter by the elbow into the shadows of a run-off corridor. The Amam who passed them was not a guard. He was of the same slim build as the one whom they had rescued from attack, and who had subsequently summoned the ship that had captured them. But there was a marked difference between the two.

The Amam who had healed Daniel Jackson had carried himself as one who was in control, exhibiting a cold, commanding presence. The creature that approached them now moved in an unbalanced, erratic manner. He was no less menacing for it however. He passed by completely oblivious to their presence, more concerned with the object he held in his hands.

Major Carter gave a start, clearly recognizing the object at the same time Teal'c did.

O'Neill's Beretta.

Even in shadow, Teal'c could see the expression on Major Carter's face. She wanted to follow this strange Amam, for he must know something of O'Neill's location, but she held back. This turn of events clearly did not alter her plans.

When the corridor was clear, they set off again, arriving shortly after at an intersection. Teal'c's eyes were immediately drawn to a series of marks on the wall. He grasped Major Carter by the shoulder and gestured towards the scorch marks which were obviously caused by a staff weapon — his staff weapon.

The major nodded. She knew this was the corridor down which they had made their original escape from the ship, the corridor that led to the lab where O'Neill had been captured.

Teal'c thought of the alien ordinance that had been strewn across tables within that lab and remembered how she'd quizzed Hunter the previous night. A grin threatened, the flush of *kalach-mek*, what the Tau'ri called adrenaline. A battle was due and his blood was burning for the fight. This day, the Amam would know what it was to challenge SG-1.

CHAPTER TWENTY-TWO

JACK slept. Not deeply, not in this place, but he'd been in enough situations where exhaustion had outweighed danger and he'd learned how to find the balance between sleep and vigilance.

His first realization on waking, therefore, took him more than a little by surprise: something was in the cell with him.

There was a faint regular scraping noise, the nature of which he couldn't make out, but he kept his eyes closed, wanting to gauge the situation before letting his guest know he was awake. Maybe he could work this to his advantage.

"Your breathing pattern is different," said a chilling, familiar voice. "Why does your kind sleep for so short a time?"

His eyes flashed open. *So much for that advantage.*

Jack pushed himself up from the floor, wincing as his joints cracked. He might not mind sleeping on hard surfaces in theory, but his body disagreed with him more and more these days. He eased out the kinks and looked around the cell.

The first thing he saw was the door. It was open.

Was this a test?

The low light of the corridor cast the interior of the cell into starker shadows and Jack blinked away residual sleep, trying to gather his bearings and decide whether it was worth making a run for it. Somewhere close by, the regular tread of the guard patrols echoed down the hallways. The scraping sound continued.

"Why?"

It was then that he saw it. Crazy hunkered in the far corner to the left of the doorway, crouched so that its chin was almost on his knees, like a vulture perched on a tree limb. Its fingers flexed in a rhythm, long talons scraping the floor, producing that strange whispering scratch. Jack fought the urge to shudder. "Why what?" he said.

"Sleep. What purpose does it serve you?"

Jack had no clue how to answer this bizarre question. "You don't sleep?" he said.

Crazy closed its eyes and, despite the gloom of the cell, Jack thought he could make out some semblance of a smile on the Amam's face. "*Sleeeeeep*," it said, the vowels long and drawn out, as if the very word was something to relish. "We slept, so long, so long, so long. And when we awoke, we fed." The thing raised its hand to its mouth and, to Jack's disgust, licked the maw on its palm, as if tasting again the poor bastards whose life it had sapped.

Its eyes were still closed, and so, slowly, slowly, Jack edged towards the open doorway. He leaned back, trying to get a look out into the corridor, but couldn't see any guards. This was too easy, but if he didn't take the chance now he might never get out of there.

"*You.*"

Jack jerked back, away from the doorway, hoping that Crazy hadn't seen what he was doing. But the Amam's reptilian eyes were suddenly fixed on him, alert where seconds ago he had seemed lost inside his own chaotic mind.

"Uh, yeah?" he said, when Crazy seemed content to just stare at him, claws scraping softly on the floor.

"You are different."

"Yeah. My blood. All ancient and stuff. You said that already."

"No, you are... unlike. You are apart."

Jack narrowed his eyes, wondering whether this creature could see inside his skull and read the thoughts he'd been batting around in there.

I am apart.

"Why do you try?" it asked. "Why do you think?"

Jack was tired, hungry, thirsty, and the wild mind of this creature left him unsettled. He sighed. "I don't know how to answer your questions."

The thing sprang to its feet. Jack fell back, heart in his throat as it came towards him, pinning him against the back wall of the cell. Something clattered to the ground as it moved, but Jack didn't get a chance to see what it was before Crazy's face was within an inch of his own. "Why do you *try*?"

"Because it's who we are!"

Crazy looked to the side, as if the answer made no sense. Jack didn't miss the irony of that. Out of this entire situation, it was *his* answer that made no sense. "Who are you people?" he asked wearily. "What is it you want with this planet?"

But Crazy only hissed, as if wholly dissatisfied with Jack's response. "You are small. A small worthless species. But you serve."

"As what? As food?"

"Barely worthy as that. Thin, meager, like dust on the tongue." It grimaced, as if tasting something bitter; the expression was hideous on such a face. "You huddle and cower. You *let* us feast."

Jack shook his head. He might not be from this planet, but he was just as human as its ragged inhabitants. "That's bullshit."

The thing merely stared, clearly not understanding the epithet.

"If these people are so worthless, then why stay? Why fight the Goa'uld for them?"

Crazy gave a snort. "Small, worthless gods to rule a small, worthless race. The parasites are nothing — like *iratus* larvae, easy to crush."

"From what I've seen, those parasites aren't going down without a fight." Defending the prowess of the Goa'uld? Well, *that* was something new.

God's honest truth, though, he'd rather go up against the snakeheads than these freaky bastards any day of the week and twice on Sundays. With the Goa'uld, you knew what you were getting. Devious and nasty though they were, they wore their villainy on their elaborately embroidered sleeves.

This creature, however, was cold, callous in the very truest sense of the word. For a thing to be evil, it had to want to be evil. But the Amam were something else entirely. Right now though, he just couldn't figure out what. "The question still stands," he said. "Who are you people?"

"We are Amam," said the creature. "We are Devourers and Snatchers. We are the Soul Burners and the Blood Eaters. We are *Wraith*. We survive. We feed. We *are*."

"And you'll destroy a species just to survive?"

"We are."

Crazy scuttled back to crouch in his corner and resume his aimless scratching at the floor. As it moved, the light caught the object that had clattered to the floor and Jack felt a beat of what was almost hope. His Beretta lay just a few yards from the open doorway.

This truly is too easy, he thought, and prepared to make his move.

From within, the camp seemed even more ragged and sprawling than it had when Daniel had looked down on it from the mountainside. Shacks made of nothing but scraps of fabric or wood leaned drunkenly together, a mishmash of shapes and sizes, and everything the uniform drab of dust and dirt. Between the shacks ran muddy, rutted tracks and here and there lay piles of refuse. The stench was appalling.

But poverty and misery aside, Daniel was struck by the huge ethnic mix he saw in the population. On most worlds they visited the people were pretty homogeneous — like Aedan's people — having been taken from just one location on Earth, sometimes from a single village. But here, there were faces of all different races and with no apparent distinction drawn between them. It was an ethnic fusion few places on Earth had achieved. Perhaps, he thought, faced with the inhumanity of the Amam, racial differences had ceased to have any meaning here? If you were looking for silver linings, he supposed that might be one.

Nevertheless, the camp was no nirvana. In fact it was the sort of place you'd expect to see on the evening news, with a camera crew and a scrolling plea to donate money to the emergency appeal. Except no one was coming to help these people, not unless Daniel could get home and somehow rouse the humanitarian instinct of the Appropriations Committee.

That, in itself, was a dismal prospect.

It took a couple of hours to reach Hunter's home, not least because he was stopped every few minutes by people astonished to see him alive, returned as if from the dead. Some embraced him, while others peered out cautiously from inside their raggedy shacks, but most simply touched two fingers to the center of their forehead in salute.

"I was snatched from the Shacks," Hunter explained as they navigated the labyrinthine alleyways. "People who get snatched don't usually come back again."

"But you did," Daniel said with a smile. "You came back."

Hunter touched the mark on his forehead. "By the grace of Hecate, I did."

Daniel didn't comment on that, it wasn't really the time to debate theology and in truth his mind was too distracted anyway. His thoughts were with his friends back on the Amam ship rather than with Hunter, and as the hours passed and his radio remained stubbornly silent he felt a cold weight of fear settle in the pit of his stomach. It had been too long, something must have gone wrong.

"Perhaps this was a mistake," he said, looking back over his shoulder at the Amam ship. Far away though it now was, its looming presence still dominated the camp.

Hunter glanced at him. "What do you mean?"

"I should have gone with them," he said. "I should be with them."

"Sam called it right," Hunter said, although he sounded distracted now, his attention darting ahead. "You'll do 'em more good finding help and talking to Dix."

"That's easy for Sam to say," Daniel grumbled. "She's not the one out here waiting."

But Hunter wasn't listening anymore. He'd stopped in front of an unremarkable shack, no different from all the others, with a scrap of fabric for a door and a lean-to roof. "My home," he said quietly. Despite his uneasiness about his friends, Daniel sensed Hunter's anxiety spike, heard the repressed emotion in his voice as he called out, "Faith? You here?"

There was a moment when nothing happened. Hunter looked like he was holding his breath and Daniel realized, with a rush of empathy, that Hunter probably didn't know what had happened to his wife after he'd been taken. Maybe she was dead too, fed on by the Amam?

"Faith… ?" Hunter called again, more urgently.

And then a flap of fabric flew back and a young woman, a child propped on her hip, appeared in the doorway. She stared at Hunter with wide, shocked eyes and then pressed a hand over her mouth and started to sob. Hunter ran to her, pulling both her and the child into his arms, burying his face against his wife's hair. "It's true," he said in a voice raspy with emotion. "It's me. I'm back…"

Daniel had to turn away from the scene, too affected by that single moment of unexpected joy amid so much abject misery. It didn't help that he had to fight down an unworthy surge of envy too; that happy reunion had been forever denied to him and his wife.

"Come on," Hunter called and Daniel turned, watching as the woman ducked back into the shack. "Come inside."

He forced a smile past the knot of helplessness, past the gnawing fear for his friends, and followed Hunter into his home. It was small and cramped, with a fire-pit in the center and smoke-blackened walls and ceiling. Daylight seeped in through gaps in the walls and roof, but at least it was warmer than outside and Daniel crouched by the fire, holding his hands out over the flames.

"Faith," Hunter said, "this here's Daniel. He helped me bolt from the Snatchers and I'm taking him to see Dix in payment." He lowered his voice and added, "One of his friends, he's a Lantean, an' the Snatchers took him. Couple of Daniel's kin went on back to fetch him out, so Daniel's waiting on 'em here."

"They went back to the ship?" Faith said, incredulous. "That ain't clever."

Daniel smiled to himself. "Maybe not," he said, "but it's kind of how we operate. We don't leave our people behind."

Faith exchanged an eloquent look with Hunter and then moved closer to Daniel, crouching next to him and reaching out a hand to touch his shoulder. Like Hunter, she was young but her face was gaunt and weary. "You got my thanks for bringing Hunter home, Daniel," she said. "And you're welcome to the heat of our fire while you wait."

"Thank you," he said and, cognizant of the hunger in this place, added, "I'd be honored to share my food with you, while I wait."

He shucked off his pack and dug out one of his last MREs. Faith watched in astonishment as he pulled it open and shared out the bounty between them. Although the short rations left him hungry, Hunter, Faith and their child ate as if it were a feast.

After the food was gone, the child curled up to sleep on a narrow pallet at the back of the shack, Faith sitting with him and stroking his head as she talked quietly with Hunter. It was impossible for Daniel not to overhear their conversation, though he sat as far away as possible on the other side of the fire.

"I went to Dix, after you was snatched," Faith murmured. "Like you said I should."

"Did they help you?"

She nodded, gestured to a few small packages next to the wall. "Zuri gave me rations and promised more. She said Dix would come by tomorrow, when he's back from up there."

"Good," Hunter said. "That's good to know." He tightened his arm around her and Faith suddenly pressed her face against his shoulder, as if her strength had cracked for a moment.

Daniel heard her quiet tears, muffled against Hunter's shoulder, and turned his eyes away, offering them at least the illusion of privacy.

He stared into the fire instead, watching its ever changing

dance. It had been over five hours since he'd said goodbye to Sam and Teal'c and still he'd had no contact. Sam had told him to wait ten hours, but with every moment that passed his fear grew. Sitting there, helpless and idle while his friends were in trouble, went against all his instincts. And it was tortuous, it was almost impossible.

He lifted a hand to his radio for a moment, willing it to jump into life, for Sam's voice to crackle over the airwaves telling him they were free and everyone was safe. But he heard only silence, the hiss of the fire and Faith's tearful breathing.

"Your friends are real smart and well-armed," Hunter said suddenly, as if guessing the path of Daniel's thoughts. "If anyone can evade the Snatchers, it's them."

He glanced up. "Yeah," he said. "I know."

"Don't you give up," Faith added quietly, wiping at her face with one hand. "You give up, you die." She leaned her head against her husband's shoulder. "Anyways, sometimes miracles happen."

"By Hecate's will," Hunter said and Faith nodded, reaching up to press two fingers against the symbol on his forehead and then her own. Like a blessing, Daniel thought, and remembered the salutes Hunter had received on their way through the camp.

He figured that Hunter must be a kind of miracle to the people in the camp: the man who'd returned from the dead. But while Hunter might credit divine intervention for saving him, Daniel knew that it was SG-1 who'd preformed the miracle and that gave him a little hope of his own.

Saving Hunter from the Amam wasn't the first miracle SG-1 had performed. He just had to hope it wasn't the last.

Jack tried to move without moving, a subtle shifting of his feet. Crazy's eyes were closed, its claws scratch-scratch-scratching. Blue light glinted across the black sheen of the Beretta. To reach it, he'd have to come within inches of the unhinged Amam, so when he made his move, it would need to be fast.

He glanced down at the handgun and then back up at Crazy. The thing was watching him.

Jack froze. But it was too late.

Crazy casually looked down at the gun and then reached out to pick it up. It held it by the grip and sniffed along the barrel. "This object, a weapon?" It regarded the gun with an expression of doubt. "Inefficient. Rudimentary. Yet it makes you feel safe?"

It would if I could get my damn hands on it and shove it down your throat.

"Why would you shun the might of Lantis for such simplicity? With such blood as yours you could be the destroyer of worlds."

"Like you did to this planet?" asked Jack, wondering how far he'd get along the hallway before Crazy was on him. Would he make it to the next doorway? Even if he could, by the sound of the footfalls beyond, there was a heavy guard presence. His odds were slim, but that open door was so damn close.

Crazy laughed, a dry, hacking sound. "We did nothing to this planet. So many souls, such abundance." The thing stood up, smacking its lips, then began stalking towards Jack. He backed away, disgusted. "Why would we destroy it?"

"Then who... ?"

A loud boom echoed through the ship, shaking the ground beneath Jack's feet. Along the hall, the steady sound of footsteps had turned to running. Crazy darted to the door and, for the first time, Jack saw genuine alarm on its face. Something had happened, something the Amam hadn't bargained on.

Jack's stomach lurched, a good feeling, one that got his blood up, knowing instinctively who was responsible.

SG-1.

Crazy marched out into the hall, started scrutinizing a panel that had appeared in the wall. A huge area glowed red. The creature wailed, rage and despair in the one sound. It whirled on Jack, but he was already moving. He smashed his fist into the thing's face, driving it backward, but not to the ground. His Beretta dropped from Crazy's grasp and Jack grabbed it.

Only then did he realize his mistake, something that had escaped him in the gloom of the cell. The gun wasn't loaded.

A bright blossom of pain exploded through his temple, as Crazy cold-cocked him, sending him flying across the floor. Jack shook the ringing from his head, determined not to lose whatever advantage he had.

He pulled himself to his feet, acting more dazed than he actually felt. His earlier fatigue had gone. Rage and adrenaline fuelled him now. Crazy advanced, but Jack was ready. One way or another, he was getting out of this.

Sam sprinted through the hallways of the ship, hoping her sense of direction didn't fail her now. Smoke bloomed through the winding corridors and dark shapes came at them through the murk. She took them down with her MP5, while Teal'c handled any threat from the rear.

The lab had gone up like a firework and Sam wondered what sort of explosive power the alien ordinance within had contained. They'd scavenged what they could before lighting it up — including the colonel's pack and MP5 — and, thank God, the explosion had packed a big enough punch. The next part of the plan depended on it.

Two Amam guards came out of the smoke to her left. She spun, spraying fire, too close to take proper aim. The guards just kept coming and Sam felt a searing pain along her upper arm.

No time to check it out now, she'd deal with it later.

"Teal'c! This way!" she called, darting off to the right. The brig should be around there somewhere, but with the smoke and the chaos she started to worry they'd got turned around somehow. Was it this — ?

Something barreled into her, knocking her to the floor, pinning her down and knocking the gun from her hands. She heard the hiss of Teal'c's staff weapon opening...

"Teal'c! Don't shoot — it's me!"

"O'Neill."

Adrenaline high, Sam almost laughed in relief. Colonel O'Neill's weight disappeared from her and she grabbed up her weapon as he pulled her to her feet. "Colonel, how did you — ?"

"Later, Carter. My escape isn't exactly one hundred percent complete."

"*Lanteaaaaan! I will hunt you!*" The banshee wail came from somewhere in the colonel's wake, a nerve-shredding sound. "*I can smell your blood!*"

"I suggest we depart this place, O'Neill."

"Ya think?"

A shambling figure rounded the corner, inhuman in every sense. Behind it, Amam moved in the smoke, gathering to strike. Sam swallowed and took a step back, lifted her weapon.

"Carter?" the colonel breathed. "Run."

They ran.

CHAPTER TWENTY-THREE

DANIEL was on his feet and out the door in a flash. A dull boom still ricocheted around the mountains as smoke billowed from one side of the Amam ship.

"Sam," he breathed. He wasn't sure whether to be pleased or terrified by the development, but at least *something* was happening.

"You think your people done that?" Hunter said, following him outside.

"I just hope they meant to."

There was a beat of silence while they both watched the ship, waiting for the next explosion. But nothing else happened. "You know," Hunter mused, "one day I'm gonna watch that whole darn thing burn."

Daniel couldn't help smiling at the certainty in his voice. It was a young man's certainty, the kind that hadn't had its optimistic corners knocked off yet. He remembered when he'd felt like that himself. "Listen," he said, glancing at Hunter. "I need to help my friends now. If they escaped the ship, they'll be heading down to the camp and I need to show them the way."

Hunter turned his gaze from the smoking ship and back to Daniel. "I'll take you out to the boundary," he said, "but we gotta hurry. It's dangerous outside after dark."

Daniel glanced around at the other people who stood staring at the smoke drifting in the misty evening air. "Because people might attack us for food?"

Hunter shook his head. "Because at night the Snatchers come to hunt."

Daniel took that in, nodded, and then glanced past Hunter toward Faith who stood in the doorway to their home, watching her husband with a tense expression. He looked again at the Amam ship pouring smoke into the sky, at the steep mountainside down which they'd walked this morning and then back at Hunter. "You stay here with Faith and your son," he said. "I'll go alone."

"You won't find the way," Hunter objected.

Daniel allowed himself a slight smile. "You think I won't be able to see that Amam ship from anywhere in the camp?"

"And to find our home again?"

"Trust me. I have a good sense of direction."

"But you—"

"Hunter," Faith said from where she still stood in the doorway. "Please."

Daniel reached out and put his hand on Hunter's shoulder. "You've done enough for us," he said. "And I can do this myself."

Hunter looked torn for a moment, but then nodded. "If you're not back by dawn, I'll come lookin'."

"Okay," Daniel agreed. "Now go be with your family."

The journey back out to the perimeter was much faster than the journey in, partly because Daniel was running and partly because no one was getting in his way. Everyone was hunkering down inside, a sense of anxious expectation pervading the whole camp. Daniel doubted the explosion on the ship had done much to steady anyone's nerves and there was certainly no sense of celebration in the camp. It made him wonder about the relationship these people had with the Amam — both the givers of life and the bringers of death.

As the feeding station grew closer, he slowed to a walk to catch his breath. Stealth, he thought, might be helpful too, although so far he'd seen no sign of the Amam and he'd heard no tell-tale rattle of gunfire. Both of which could either be good or bad news, but he didn't dare break radio silence to find out.

The feeding station was on his right now, the shacks thinning out the closer he got to it and to the edge of the camp. He tried to imagine what it must be like on the days when the Amam delivered rations — did the people fight for them, or had they organized a fair way of distribution? Perhaps this Dix character was involved in the running of the camp? Faith's story of going to see him, and of being given some kind of food after her husband was taken, seemed to indicate that a social structure existed, although—

His train of thought was abruptly derailed by a flash of blue energy up on the mountainside, halfway down the slope. A moment later came the distant report of an MP5. His gut tightened: they were off the ship, they were fighting.

At least, some of them were.

He made his way beyond the last of the shacks and took cover behind a stub of something that might once have been a wall. It was full dark now and Daniel didn't dare risk his flashlight, but he ran his hand over the surface and it felt like old brickwork. Someone might have lived there once, he thought, before the war that had destroyed this city.

If there was a moon in orbit around the planet, the clouds hung too low to let it shine. The only light came from the strange bio-luminescent glow of the Amam ship and the snatches of firelight escaping from the camp behind him. But his eyes were used to the dark and he could pick out the tree line that marked the edge of the mountainside's sparse forest.

He checked his watch. Ten minutes since the brief firefight and no contact. Nothing. They could be dead. They could be some-where in the trees. All he could do was wait.

Cold, a real mountain cold that was sharp and bitter, made his breath mist in front of his face. He thought with regret of his Parka back at the SGC, but his adrenaline was high, everything on full alert, and that was enough to keep him warm for now. Nevertheless, he was aware that he couldn't sit there all night. If they didn't come soon, he'd have to find shelter or succumb to hypothermia. He pulled his hands from his pockets, blew on them to warm them, and then froze.

There was movement in the trees, a flash of something. Slowly, Daniel reached down and pulled his Beretta free of its holster. His mouth was suddenly dry, too dry to swallow, as he rested his hands on the brickwork and trained the weapon on the trees. Blinking against the dark, he strained to see. Had he been mistaken? No, there it was again, movement in the trees along the ridge where he and Hunter had stood and first looked out across the camp.

SG-1 or Amam? Possibly both.

He could hear footfalls now, a skittering of rocks as if someone had slipped or stumbled coming down the slope. Daniel licked his dry lips, tightened his grip on the gun. And then there was a figure in the dark, emerging from the trees. Daniel flicked off the safety, the click sounding loud in the night.

Someone called out, "Hold your fire!"

Heart hammering, it took a moment before the voice penetrated the sound of blood rushing through his ears. But he didn't lower his weapon, peering through the darkness as two other silhouettes materialized from the trees.

"Daniel?"

"Oh thank God." Relief washed through him at the sound of Jack's voice, his gun sagging against the rock and his finger slackening on the trigger. "Over here," he said, and climbed to his feet, holstering his Berretta.

Jack appeared from the darkness first, looking weary but unharmed. Sam and Teal'c were a step behind. "Hey," Jack said, laconic as ever, "thanks for not shooting."

"You're welcome." Daniel glanced past them, up toward the ship. "You didn't bring any friends?"

Jack shrugged. "A couple tried to tag along. We changed their minds."

"It is possible," Teal'c said, "that more will pursue us."

"Likely, in fact," Sam added with a wary glance over her shoulder. Her arm, Daniel noticed, was bandaged. "We need to hide," she said. "And the colonel needs to rest."

"We *all* need to rest," Jack corrected.

Daniel smiled. "Well, I know just the place."

Daniel seemed to have a good idea where he was going, which was lucky, because Jack was too tired to do anything but follow him as they picked their way through the ramshackle camp. "Hey," he said, touching Daniel's shoulder. "Check that out."

He gestured off to their right, squinting through the crowding darkness to where he could just make out the distinctive shape of a Death Glider's wing that had been co-opted into the lean-to wall of a house.

"Interesting," Daniel said. "I guess Elspeth's stories about the 'old gods' had some truth in them after all."

"Yeah. And maybe not-so-old-gods, if Hunter's right about this Dix character."

Daniel nodded, mulling over the idea as they walked. "He seems to think that Hecate would help us — that the Amam are her enemy."

"Yeah, well, I'll believe that when I see it."

"Could she be Tok'ra?"

Jack shook his head. "With her own Jaffa?"

"Okay," he conceded. "But that doesn't mean she won't help us. It wouldn't be the first time a Goa'uld has done a deal with their enemies when faced with a common threat."

Jack grunted. "And that always ends *so* well…"

They lapsed into silence, Daniel still up ahead and Teal'c walking close to his shoulder with his staff weapon at the ready. They looked tense, but Jack didn't feel any fear or hostility coming from the people around them — just curiosity.

Mostly there was a weary kind of resignation in the faces that watched them pass, and not a spark of hope anywhere. He wondered how long the people of his world had lived like this, in thrall to the Amam. A generation or two? More, perhaps.

A small child ran across their path and was snatched up by a young woman who might have been her mother or sister. Jack gave a tight smile, like he always did when there were kids around, but kept on walking. He couldn't engage with these people, he had no way to help them. He couldn't even help his own people.

He yawned — God, he really was tired — and scrubbed a hand

over his eyes; it was getting harder to think straight.

"Sir?" Carter nudged his elbow and held out a power bar. "I'm guessing the Amam didn't feed you?"

"Hey, I'm just glad they didn't feed *on* me." He glanced at the bar. "Have we got enough of these?"

"It's yours, sir. We ate this morning."

That was good enough for him, and after a couple of mouthfuls and a good sugar hit, he felt the weariness recede a few steps — not far, but enough. "There's a lot of weird technology back in the ship," he said between bites, throwing Carter a look. "Apparently it's Ancient — capital A."

"Really?" Daniel turned around again, fascinated as always by anything touching on the gate builders. "What kind of weird technology?"

Jack shrugged. "I don't know — star charts, gizmos, all sorts. Crazy had me testing a ton of it."

Daniel blinked. "Uh, 'Crazy'?"

"My freaky friend." He frowned, remembering something. "They don't speak to each other," he said. "You notice that?"

"Yeah," Daniel said. "Actually I was wondering if they have some kind of telepathic ability, because their written language is literally unpronounceable."

"Telepathy, huh?" Jack stuffed the rest of the power bar into his mouth. "Handy." He chewed, swallowed, and said what was really on his mind. "So I'm thinking that where there's Ancient stuff there has to be a way to open the gate… ?"

Daniel raised his eyebrows. "You want us to go back into the ship? *Again*?"

He opened his mouth to argue the point, but Carter got there first.

"Actually, sir," she said, "it might not be as simple as finding a way to dial the gate anymore."

He sighed. "I ask you, Carter — when is it *ever* simple?"

With a slight smile, she said, "Sir, I think we may have been transported a significant distance away from the Stargate." She glanced at her watch. "The first night here, I reset my watch to 1800 hours at sunset — it's arbitrary, I know, but I wanted to measure the planet's day/night cycle. That night lasted sixteen and a half hours."

"Wow," Daniel said, his hand moving involuntarily to his side. "And I thought it just *felt* like forever." Jack could still see the bloody splotch on Daniel's jacket and felt a ghost of the fear that had dogged him since they'd arrived on this rock with Daniel practically bleeding out in front of him. The wound beneath the blood was healed and Daniel was fine now, but he'd been healed by an Amam and Jack had no idea what that might mean.

"The thing is, sir," Carter continued, "last night the sun set at 1200 hours, by my watch, and when I measured the hours of darkness they only lasted twelve hours and twenty minutes."

Jack frowned, he didn't like where this was going *at all*. "So you're saying we're in a different time zone?"

"Yes sir." She gave a small shrug. "I mean, there's no telling exactly how far that would be on this planet — but on Earth it would equate to a couple thousand miles."

"A little more than a stroll, then?"

"It would be a long walk," she agreed. "And that's assuming we could figure out which direction to go and that we're even on the same continental mass, because the —"

He held up a hand to stop her. "Any good news, Major?"

She shook her head. "I just think this Dix guy might be our best shot, sir."

"Yeah," he sighed. "I knew you were going to say that."

Not long after that, Daniel and Teal'c drew to a halt a short distance from a flimsy wood and cloth shack. "Looks like we're here," Jack said, instinct moving his hands to rest on his gun. Hunter served a Goa'uld, after all.

With a quick glance at Jack's weapon, Daniel said, "He has a family — a wife and a son."

"Then let's hope he knows how to keep them safe," was all he said.

Daniel just nodded and approached the rickety shack. "Hunter?" he called in a low voice. "Hunter, it's Daniel Jackson."

After a moment, the cloth drew back and Hunter appeared in the doorway. A grin flashed across his face when he saw Jack. "Looks like you're right hard to kill."

"So I'm told," Jack said. "Mind if we come in?"

Hunter's home was little more than a dirt floor, a smoky fire-pit, and some bed rolls. A couple of cooking pots hung on the wall and some shabby clothing was draped over a nail nearby. With everyone crowding in, the place felt cramped and claustrophobic.

"Um," Daniel suggested, "shall we sit down?"

It was better with them all sitting, although no one was small and it felt like there were long legs and booted feet everywhere. The weapons didn't help much either, but Jack wasn't about to leave them outside. At last, after a substantial amount of shuffling around, they all found a seat by the fire. Toward the back of the hut, Hunter's wife and child sat together on one of the bed rolls, the child's head in his mother's lap as he sucked his thumb and drifted drowsily toward sleep.

Jack didn't allow his gaze to linger there, instead turning his attention firmly back to Hunter who crouched close to the fire, feeding a few sticks to the flames. "So," he said, "you can take us to see Dix?"

"Yup." Hunter sat back on his heels. "At first light."

"Why not now?"

Hunter shook his head. "'Cause Dix won't be back till mornin'."

"Back from where?"

Hunter turned his eyes skyward, "From speaking with the goddess."

Jack followed his gaze to the ceiling before exchanging a glance with Teal'c. "She has a ship in orbit?"

"You'll see," Hunter said. "I've already said more than I should."

Jack was about to object when Teal'c said, "O'Neill, it would be prudent to rest while we are able."

He rubbed a hand across his jaw and considered the point. He *was* exhausted — he'd missed at least one night's sleep, maybe two — and Teal'c was right, he needed to rest and eat. They all did. But with Daniel no longer at death's door, Teal'c didn't realize how urgent it was that they get home. Beyond urgent at this point, it was critical, the whole damn alliance system could already be falling apart.

"Sir, there's nothing we can do tonight," Carter added, weighing into the discussion. "And if the Amam are looking for us we should probably keep our heads down."

Another good point; there'd been no real sign of pursuit so far but he couldn't dismiss Crazy's threat about hunting him down. And as far as places to hide went, this was a good option. He didn't like it, but there was no real choice. Reluctantly he said, "Yeah, okay, we'll stay here tonight." He cast a glance at Hunter. "We'll need a place to crash."

"Um, he means a place to sleep," Daniel clarified.

Jack threw him an irritated look.

"What? You think the whole galaxy speaks idiomatic North American?"

Ignoring him, Jack glanced around the small space. "A couple of us could stay in here, maybe?"

Hunter nodded. "You'd be welcome. I owe you folks my life and that ain't a debt lightly paid."

"Nah," Jack said, waving away his thanks. "It was nothing. A walk in the park."

Except that it was anything but nothing. He glanced over at Carter, noticing the way her expression tensed. They'd almost lost her, they'd almost lost Daniel. And he'd almost lost himself — in more ways than one. No, whatever this place was, it was no walk in the park.

He pushed the grim thoughts aside. There was no point in dwelling on near misses and might-haves, right now was all that mattered. "Teal'c," he said. "You okay to take first watch?"

Teal'c nodded. "I am."

"Okay. Two hour watches — Teal'c, me, Carter, Daniel."

"Um, how about Teal'c, *me*, Sam and then you?" Daniel said. "We all got some sleep last night, Jack, while you were up playing with Crazy and his toys."

"Daniel's right, sir," Carter chimed in. "You should take the last watch."

He considered arguing, but the huge yawn that stopped him from speaking did a good job of undercutting his case. So in the end he just grumbled "Fine" and accepted the fact that being too tired to argue probably proved Daniel's point.

In the end there hadn't been enough room for even three of them to sleep inside Hunter's tiny shack so Jack had just unpacked his bedroll outside, buried himself in his sleeping bag, and was snoring before anyone could object.

And with Teal'c also outside on watch, it left Sam and Daniel just enough room to bed down close together on the opposite side of the fire from Hunter and his family.

Like Jack, Sam was soon fast asleep, but Daniel had yet to master the skill of instantly switching off and his mind was racing as he lay in the dark, gazing up at the heavy fabric that constituted one slanted wall of the house. The fire still burned, its light casting dancing shadows over the material and its smoke drifting up and out through cracks between the wooden slats.

In some ways, it took him back to Abydos — the canvas, the firelight. But his home on Abydos, although primitive by Earth's standards, had been nothing like this. It had been warm and dry, full of laughter once Ra had been driven out and the Abydonians had been free to live as people again. He wondered if these people would ever be free, whether there was a way to save them from the Amam in the way they'd once saved Sha're's people from the Goa'uld.

"Hunter?" he asked quietly, thinking back to the question

he'd asked earlier. "Why do so many people live here, dependent on the Amam? I mean, we've met others, people who hide from them and live free."

"There's some as choose to live in the wilds," Hunter admitted, his voice drifting with the sparks up into the cold air. "But there's thousands in the camp and how many d'you think could live off a few jackers in the mountains? Truth is, most camp folk don't have the knowhow or the plucks to run, so they stay here where there's food and family and pray that when the Snatchers come they don't get took."

"You could run," Daniel said. "With your family. You have the skills."

"But I won't. I won't run and I won't hide," Hunter said, adamant. "I'm here to fight and, by the grace of Hecate, drive those Snatchers out."

Daniel bit back his instinctive reply — that the Goa'uld would give no one their freedom — because, caught between the devil and the deep blue sea, what choice did Hunter's people really have? If a Goa'uld offered their only chance of escaping the nightmare that had overtaken their planet then they'd be fools not to take that chance.

But the question it left behind, dancing like firelight through his mind, was whether he could give these people a better option. Because if Earth stood for anything, and Daniel thought it stood for a lot, then it stood for freedom.

Jack might disagree, and it wouldn't be the first time they'd argued over the real purpose of the Stargate Program, but Daniel was certain that it was their responsibility — their moral duty, in fact — to come back to this world and offer these people something better than an alliance with the Goa'uld.

CHAPTER TWENTY-FOUR

"MR. PRESIDENT, I'm requesting DEFCON 1."

General Hammond spoke calmly into the red telephone, his gaze fixed on the far wall. There was a pause, then, "Yes sir, I will. Thank you, sir."

Janet felt sick at the reality of it all and glanced over at Colonel Makepeace who sat, stiff-backed, next to her. His hands were tight fists on his knees, and he looked even tenser than the general.

As Hammond carefully put down the phone, his steady gaze met Janet's. "Are your people ready, doctor?"

"Yes sir." As ready as they could be for a Goa'uld invasion, but it felt like standing by for a medevac with nothing more than a Band-Aid to hand. "I've had Cassie brought onto the base," she added, swallowing a swell of fear at the thought of her little girl. "I don't know if she'll be any safer here, but at least I can keep an eye on her."

General Hammond nodded. "I've told my family to head into the mountains. They've got a cabin up there."

There was silence in the room, because they all knew that if the Goa'uld came there'd be no hiding — in the mountains or anywhere else. Hammond's expression darkened, his mouth making a hard line of anger. "We have no Alpha Site," he said, as if to himself. "The Pentagon shut down Colonel O'Neill's plan and now we have no Alpha Site."

"Bureaucrats," Makepeace growled. "They've hamstrung this operation from the start."

The colonel's bluster wasn't exactly helpful so Janet ignored him and said, "I'm guessing the Tollan won't take us in?"

Hammond made a dismissive noise in the back of his throat. "They have 'no capacity', apparently, to house refugees from 'non-allied worlds'."

Janet just shook her head — how could you even answer an attitude like that? "The Asgard?"

"Out of contact. And the Tok'ra certainly won't give us the address to their secret base with a fleet of Goa'uld ships parked overhead." He slammed his fist on the table, once — a controlled measure of anger that sent ripples over the cold coffee sitting in a mug next to his keyboard. "I should have fought harder for the Alpha Site," he said. "Colonel O'Neill knew —"

"Colonel O'Neill isn't here," Janet said, and then added a hasty, "sir." She considered Hammond for a moment, took in the lines furrowed in his brow and the tense set of shoulders that bore the weight — almost literally — of the world. "And if he was, General," she said in a softer tone, "I think he'd tell you there's no point in dwelling on should-haves or could-haves."

Hammond gave a tight smile. "You're right, doctor."

Sitting forward in her chair, hands folded on Hammond's desk, she said, "Sir, there must be another world we can evacuate to? A safe world, somewhere we can regroup."

"Yes, of course," he said, "there are plenty of worlds. But we'll have nothing, doctor — only what we can carry with us through the Stargate. We'll be a rootless, homeless people with no way to resupply and no back-up." He shook his head. "I'm not sure it will save us, doctor. It might save a handful of individual lives, but I doubt it will save our civilization."

"General Hammond?" Makepeace got to his feet, his hard face intent and serious. "There is another option."

Hammond frowned up at him and, from the taut look on his face, Janet suspected he knew what was coming. "Which is what, Colonel?"

Makepeace shifted on his feet, scratched at his jaw. "Colonel Maybourne's off-world base, sir."

"No." Angry, Hammond got up from his desk and paced to the other side of his office. Through the window, he gazed out past the briefing room toward the Stargate and Janet watched the rapid rise and fall of his shoulders as he struggled to rein in his temper. "That man is why we're here, Colonel," he said at last. "His greed, his paranoia and lack of faith in our allies — that's why we've found ourselves friendless in a hostile galaxy. And I won't let him —"

He broke off, chewing on his words, and Janet could almost hear his inner conflict. To accept help from Maybourne's shadow operation, the very people who'd brought this disaster down upon them, left a bitter taste indeed. But… "General," she said quietly, "do we have a choice?"

He turned on her, leveling an angry finger. "That base, doctor, represents everything which I oppose — on a military, moral, and personal level. If we evacuate there, then God help us."

"It doesn't mean we have to become like them, sir," she said. "Maybourne won't be in command."

"Won't he? Do you think he'd give us the address on any other terms?"

"Sir, we'd be evacuating the President and the Joint Chiefs — not even Maybourne has that much chutzpah."

"Don't count on it, doctor," Hammond said darkly.

Silence fell again and Janet felt a cold, sinking sensation. The general was making a mistake, he was letting his anger get in the way of the only pragmatic choice, and she didn't know how to change his mind.

"For what it's worth, General," Makepeace said, "I think we have to go with Maybourne's base. At this point, it's our only option."

Hammond continued to glare out at the Stargate and Makepeace watched him with a forbidding, unreadable expression on his face. Carved out of stone, that man, Janet thought. It wasn't really fair to compare him to Colonel O'Neill, because O'Neill was a one-off, but nevertheless the contrast was stark. There was a hardness about Makepeace that she didn't like. He was too austere, too bleak, unable to see hope in dark places and, given their current circumstances, they could do with a dose of O'Neill's spirited optimism rather than Makepeace's grim practicality. But on this point, at least, Makepeace was right — and Colonel O'Neill, had he been there, would probably have backed him up.

"Sir, I think Colonel Makepeace is right. Distasteful as it is, it's our only choice."

Hammond was silent for a moment. "And what if Maybourne won't give us the address?"

"He will if it's his only way off the planet."

"General, let me bring him in," Makepeace said, his voice thick with anger. "As soon as we get the address we can start the evacuation — we can save lives, sir."

Hammond didn't turn around, but she could see him struggling with the decision as he ran a hand over his jaw, shaking his head. He had no choice, not really, but Janet knew this must feel like defeat — after all the times he'd fought for the integrity of Stargate Command, he was being forced to accept that Maybourne's shady operation was the best hope for saving their people. The very outfit that had brought about this catastrophe was going to claim to be their saviors. Her own disgust was visceral.

With a heavy sigh, Hammond turned around and she felt heartsick at the bleak look he directed at Makepeace. "I suppose you know just where to find him, do you, Colonel?"

It was an odd question, but it made Makepeace flinch. His hard features grew harsher, his skin grayer. He swallowed. Janet watched his Adams apple bob up and down. "I can find him, sir," he said stiffly. "Let me bring the bastard in."

For a long beat the two men just stared at each other, locked in silent communication, and then Hammond gave a slight nod. "Do it," he said in a leaden voice. "And make it fast, the attack could start at any moment."

"Yes sir. Thank you, sir."

"We'll lock down the mountain in two hours," Hammond added. "Make sure you're back."

"Count on it, sir." And with a curt nod to Janet, Makepeace was gone.

She watched him stride across the briefing room, running down the stairs, and let the echo of his footsteps fade before she stood up and moved to stand next to General Hammond. He'd turned back to his contemplation of the Stargate and as she joined him she could just glimpse its arc through the briefing room window — still hopeful, even now.

"Do you think they'll come back, sir?"

He gave a slight smile, but didn't look away from the Stargate. "SG-1 always comes back."

She nodded. "What about you, General? Will you take command of the alpha site?"

"No. My place is here." Folding his arms behind his back at perfect parade ground rest, he straightened his shoulders and looked exactly as he always looked during the long wait for his people to come home. "I'll keep a light on for SG-1," he said, "even if I have to die trying."

Janet nodded because that's exactly what she'd expected to hear. Turning her eyes back to the Stargate, emotion tightened her throat as she said, "With permission, sir, I'd like to stay too."

"Doctor —"

"SG-1 *are* coming back, General, and I want to be here to see it."

"To welcome them home?"

She threw him a sideways glance. "To kick their asses for being so damn late, sir."

It was quiet in the camp, and dark. The moonless, starless sky hung black and featureless overhead and the fires of earlier in the evening had burned low despite the cold. The sounds of shifting, shuffling humanity were all around, the distant cry of an infant quickly hushed, the soundscape of sleep. But no one was out; there was no movement, no campfire discussions, no laughter. Everything spoke of fear and of hiding from the monsters under the bed.

Except here the monsters were real.

She'd been dreaming of it — the creature's hand stabbing into her chest, its bared teeth inches from her face — when Daniel had woken her for her watch, his concerned face half hidden by shadows cast up by the dying fire. And even now she could feel the burning on her chest that should have meant her death, that would have meant her death if it hadn't been for Jolinar. How strange, she thought, that *that* nightmare had protected her from this one.

She sat outside now, her sleeping bag wrapped around her shoulders against the biting cold, and looked up at the Amam's ship. It was almost the only thing she could see in the black night, an eerie light seeping from where it squatted on the skirts of the mountain. But as vile as it was, Sam was drawn to the mystery it represented. These creatures were like nothing they'd ever encountered, their weapons and their technology were completely new and she itched to take one of the stun guns apart and figure out how it worked. It was the organic component, of course, that made it so different from any of the technology she'd encountered before. She was hopeful that Janet would be able to help her figure out the biological and technological interface because, if she could do that, then who knew what kind of uses it could be put to? Not only in weapons technology but potentially in medical —

"Carter?" The colonel's gravelly voice rose from somewhere inside his sleeping bag. "You were meant to wake me for my watch fifteen minutes ago."

She glanced at her watch and realized he was right. "Sorry, sir, I lost track of time."

"You lost track of time?" he said, sitting up and scratching his hand through his hair. "Sitting in the dark, freezing your ass off, you lost track of time?"

She smiled and hitched her sleeping bag up around her shoulders again. "I was thinking."

"Oh, well, in that case..." he said and then shivered. "Damn, it's cold."

"Yes sir."

It was too dark to see his face, but she heard him yawning, fidgeting and rustling around in his sleeping bag. "Sir," she said, "I don't want — That is, I don't think I'll get back to sleep again tonight, so if you want to grab some more shut-eye I'll take your watch."

He stopped moving. And the thing she'd learned early on about Colonel O'Neill was that when he went still you were in trouble; it meant he was paying too much attention.

"Bad dreams?" he said.

She sighed because there was no point in denying it. "A few, yes sir."

There was more shuffling around and a moment later he came to sit next to her, his sleeping bag draped over his shoulders too, and close enough that she could see the hard lines and shadows of his face even beneath the bill of his cap. "You want to talk about it?"

"What's to say? It tried to kill me, it failed."

"And then you kicked its butt."

She gave a faint smile. "That was just luck," she said. "I think it's because of Jolinar, sir. I think it might have to do with the naquadah in my blood."

The colonel gave a soft laugh. "So you're indigestible, huh?"

"Maybe."

"And according to Crazy I'm a 'lantern'," he said with a sigh. "Carter, is it me or is this one of the freakier places we've ended up?"

"It certainly ranks in the top ten, sir."

"Oh, at least."

"Not as weird as PJ2-445, though," she said. "Remember the singing plant people… ?"

"How could I forget? This is scarier, though."

That went without saying and her gaze drifted back to the sickly light of the Amam ship.

"Does it still hurt?"

"Hmm?"

He nodded towards her and, looking down, she realized she held her hand to her chest, as if rubbing away a phantom sensation.

"Oh, no, not much." She gave a rueful smile and tapped her head. "Up here, mostly, I think."

"It's been a tough few days."

"A tough few *months*," she snorted, and then winced because she hadn't meant to sound so bitter. "Uh, I just meant—"

"I know what you meant," he said, staring out into the darkness.

Not sure what to say next, Sam opted for saying nothing and the awkward silence between them grew deeper. High overhead she thought she heard a thin whine, but when she glanced up she saw nothing but night.

"Listen, Carter, I know I've been acting like an ass since I got back from Edora and I—"

"Sir, it's fine," she said, cutting him off. She really didn't need to hear his reasons.

"No," he said, "it's not fine."

"Sir, I understand why you had mixed feelings about coming home. It must have been a wrench."

He shook his head. "That's not it. Well, maybe. Maybe some of it, but—"

"Colonel, I—" From the corner of her eye, she thought she saw movement—a flicker in the darkness—and glanced over to her right. But there was nothing there, only shadows.

"Carter?"

"Sorry, sir," she said. "I thought I saw something."

He followed her line of sight. "Over there?"

"It's nothing."

"No," he agreed after a moment. "No, I don't see anything either." His attention returned to her and he said, "Look, Carter, I just wanted to say thank you for getting me home. I know how hard you worked and I—" He trailed off. "I might not have *appeared* grateful, but I was. I am."

"You weren't," she said, feeling a rise of anger and looking back out into the camp, trying to tamp it down. "I know you weren't happy to leave."

"That's not true."

"Oh come on, sir, you've been —" She broke off, searching for some politick language. "You've obviously been out of sorts since you got back and, well, it's pretty clear why."

"Carter, it's not what you think." He sighed, sounding frustrated. "There's a lot more going on here than you know about."

She looked at him, feeling a new pulse of anxiety. "What do you mean? What's going on, sir?"

He blew out a long breath, considering his answer. For a while he said nothing, but she could see the frown furrowing his forehead and knew that, whatever this was, it was serious. Eventually, and in a low voice, he said, "Something's wrong — at home."

Her heart rate kicked up a notch. "At home?"

"I can't — I'm under orders — not to tell you about it. I shouldn't even have said that much, but given our current situation…"

A new fear struck her, nebulous and uncertain, but even more terrifying than the Amam. "Sir, is it the SGC? What —?"

"I can't tell you," he warned. "Swear to God, I wish I could. You'll just have to trust me, Carter, when I say we *really* need to get home fast —" He broke off suddenly, eyes darting past her shoulder. "What was that?"

Turning, she saw it too, a flicker of movement in the shadows, the same as before. Something there, then gone again. A sliver of cold ran up her spine. "I saw it." Slipping the sleeping bag from her shoulders, she grabbed her weapon and rose slowly to her feet.

Behind her, the colonel did the same. "Easy," he murmured, "there are people behind every damn wall."

"Yes sir."

Something else moved, like a shadow within a shadow. She shook her head and blinked. It didn't feel real, somehow, everything felt skewed.

"I don't like this," the colonel said.

"No sir."

Then a sudden shaft of familiar white light shot down from the sky a couple hundred meters to their left, followed by two more, even closer. Something whined overhead, the backdraft rattling the camp. The colonel followed it with the nose of his weapon, but didn't fire. "Fighter," he said.

And suddenly there was screaming and running feet coming their way. Panic in the dark.

"Uh-oh," the colonel said, backing up closer to Hunter's shack.

"It's the Amam," Sam realized. "They've come to feed."

"Convenient," he growled.

She darted him a look. "What do you mean?"

"Crazy said he could trace me." There was a cold kind of self-recrimination in his voice. "I've brought them right here."

"Sir, you don't know that."

"Well otherwise it's just a huge damn coincidence, Carter, and I don't believe in those."

The running feet and panicked screams were getting closer now, the ominous sound of a mob in flight. Sometimes, Sam thought grimly, there was nothing more dangerous than people.

"Sir, we have to get out of here."

"I *know*! Daniel, Teal'c—"

The canvas flew back and Teal'c was already there, staff weapon in hand. Daniel stood behind him, talking urgently to Hunter, whose wife was kneeling on the floor, pulling up several old planks to reveal a shallow hole in the dirt. To hide the child, Sam realized, with a jolt.

"Mob," the colonel said. "We need to go."

"Hunter says it's safer to stay," Daniel said. "The Amam like to hunt so if you stay quiet they'll usually pass by in search of, uh, livelier prey."

"Not this time," the colonel said. "I'm the one they want."

"Sir, you don't know—"

"Teal'c," he said, barreling right over her objection, "you're with me. Carter, Daniel — stay with Hunter. We'll get back to you when we can. Maintain radio silence."

And with that they were gone, disappearing into the dark just ahead of the vanguard as the panicking horde spilled like floodwater through the myriad alleyways of the camp.

Sam backed up into Hunter's fragile shelter. Crouching at the entrance, her weapon trained, she watched people stagger past, desperate and frightened. Behind her, she could hear the child whimpering and Daniel's quiet, reassuring voice talking to Hunter.

But outside people were screaming and her chest tightened in pain; she knew how they were dying and it horrified her.

CHAPTER TWENTY-FIVE

COLORADO Springs was burning.

The attack had begun before he left the base, dull booms echoing down into the mountain, rattling lights and turning frightened faces up to the ceiling.

Topside, things were worse. Death Gliders, flying in pairs, dropped out of the clouds and flew in long strafing runs across the city. From the direction of the Air Force Academy, Makepeace could see plumes of black smoke, but there were fighters in the air too — F-16s, scrambled from Peterson, roaring overhead to engage the enemy.

It was like something out of a movie and, despite everything he'd seen off-world, Makepeace couldn't quite make himself believe that this — here — was real. No more than he could accept that his own actions had brought the catastrophe down on their heads. It was simply too enormous to be true, his mind rebelled against the reality of it.

But there was one thing he did understand, one simple human thing, and it was the flash of disbelieving shock he'd seen in Hammond's eyes in the moment he'd understood the truth. His grievous disappointment, his hurt, cut deep and Makepeace knew that, somehow, he had to try and make amends. So he blocked out the sight of his home in flames, ignored his guilt — so enormous it could swamp him — and just kept on driving.

The road down the mountain was empty, but he could see that I-25 was jammed as the whole city tried to flee before this unknown terror. He tried not to imagine those people, the frightened men, women and children dying at the hands of the Goa'uld, but it was impossible to ignore as another wing of gliders screamed overhead. In the far distance, a fighter fell from the sky, impacting in a ball of flames somewhere in the city. He couldn't tell if it was one of the enemies or one of their own. To the people below, it wouldn't matter; they'd be dead either way.

The city was lost from view for a moment as the road curved around and down, and then it spread out again before him as he rounded another corner. He could see the overpass now, where he had arranged to meet Maybourne. He just hoped he'd made it; if the bastard had died without giving up the gate address for his Alpha Site then everything was lost.

As he got closer to the highway, he started to hear the frantic blare of car horns, the wail of emergency vehicles stuck in traffic, and the screams of panic and anger as the road clogged up. There were people running along the highway, cars abandoned. It was chaos.

He pulled off NORAD Road before he reached the overpass, not wanting to get trapped in the traffic jam. He reached into the back seat, slung his MP5 over his head, and started running. Above, he felt rather than heard the gliders approach and dropped to the ground before the compression wave knocked him down, hands over his head as staff-cannon blasts peppered the scrubby ground around him and the road behind. He was back on his feet and sprinting as soon as they were gone, and didn't spare a look for the people behind him even though he could hear their cries for help. There was nothing he could do for them but this.

"Hey!" Someone grabbed his arm, dragging him to a halt—a middle aged woman with blood on her cheek. Her car was jammed in on the highway and Makepeace could see a man crouching next to it, holding two small children, their faces pressed into his shoulders, dazed with horror and disbelief. He felt sick. "What's happening?" the woman said, staring at his uniform like it meant salvation. "What is this?"

Makepeace shook off her hand, catching his breath, and backed up a step. "Alien incursion," he said. "Get off the road."

"What?" She stared up at the sky. "That can't be true…"

"Get off the road, ma'am. Take your family and head into

the mountains."

Owlish, glasses knocked askew, she looked like she was an accountant or a lawyer, maybe. "The mountains," she repeated, as if Makepeace had suggested she go to the moon.

"Get as far from the city as you can."

And with that, he started running again, dodging between the cars stopped on the onramp, over more dry grass and under the overpass. "Maybourne!" he yelled, his voice echoing against the concrete. "You bastard, where are you?" As his eyes got used to the comparative gloom, he saw a dark sedan pulled off the road further under the bridge. "Maybourne?"

A figure rose from where he'd been hiding behind the car. "What?" Maybourne said. "No military escort?"

"I'm it," he said roughly. "Let's go."

"Wait a second."

As he moved, Makepeace recognized a gunmetal glint in Maybourne's hand. "You have *got* to be kidding me," he said.

"I need assurance I won't be prosecuted."

Makepeace stared at him. "Prosecuted? Have you seen what's happening out there?"

"I won't just hand myself in," he said, moving out from behind the car with his pistol leveled. "I want assurances."

"Fine. If you stay here, you'll die," Makepeace growled. "How's that for an assurance?"

"You can't —"

The scream of an F-16, followed by the wail of a Death Glider in pursuit, cut him off. Weapons fire impacted on the road overhead, gliders strafing the length of the highway, sending chunks of concrete crashing down around them, filling their lungs with dust. Above, a crack ran across the bridge, widening as it snaked through the concrete. Makepeace could see daylight expanding through it. "Move!" he yelled, grabbing Maybourne's arm and hauling him toward the light as the overpass began to collapse.

Cars, people, everything fell and Makepeace kept running,

kept his fingers locked around Maybourne's arm, as dust and debris bloomed out around them.

Coughing, streaked with dirt and gasping for air, they eventually made it back to his SUV. Maybourne was wheezing so badly he was retching, bent double, so he didn't see the shadow fall. But Makepeace saw it and his stomach sank into his boots.

"Oh God," he breathed as a huge, dark shape descended. He grabbed Maybourne's shirt, hauling him upright, making him watch. "Look," he hissed, as the ha'tak landed on Cheyenne Mountain, sending an avalanche of boulders and rock cascading down its sides. "This is on us, Maybourne. We did this."

Coughing, wiping his mouth on the back of his hand, Maybourne shook his head and spat concrete dust out onto the ground. He fixed Makepeace with a hard look. "It's not over yet, Colonel."

There were three Amam, Teal'c saw, and their business here was pleasure.

He had seen Jaffa stalk with the same hungry intent through the slave camps of Apophis, although the appetite they had sought to slake had been of a different nature.

They walked in silence, these Amam, one taking the lead and his seconds — Teal'c had no doubt of the power structure — a step behind at either shoulder. Their white hair gleamed like bone in the darkness, their pallid skin almost luminous, long coats flaring out behind them.

At his side, O'Neill stirred uneasily; he was afraid that these creatures could sense his presence.

"They hunt for sport," Teal'c assured him.

"Yeah, and I'm the moose."

Teal'c did not fully understand the reply but did not query it. The Amam were close now, passing within an arm's reach of the place where they crouched, concealed. He slowed his breathing in the manner Master Bra'tac had taught him many years ago, letting the air flow in and out of his lungs like the tide flowed in and out of a river mouth. O'Neill simply stopped breathing.

The Amam's heavy boots crunched into the earth, their eyes scanning the camp for movement. They were one step past them, two, walking on until Teal'c could only see their backs.

O'Neill released his breath in a low sigh that would have given him away had the enemy not moved on. Looking at Teal'c, he gestured that they should circle back toward Hunter's house and Teal'c nodded. But before either of them could move, a terrified voice shouted out — an inarticulate cry of fear — and a young boy bolted from under a piece of fallen wooden paneling that lay almost beneath the feet of the Amam.

O'Neill made a strangled noise as the boy — perhaps ten years old — tried to run. He was not fast enough and one of the Amam snatched him up, its clawed hand seizing the child's shirt and lifting him off his feet. It held him up, legs kicking, close to its face.

The boy was sobbing, clutching at the creature's arm. "Jem!" he wailed. "Jem!"

O'Neill rose to his feet, but Teal'c grabbed his arm, holding him back. "You cannot."

And then someone else appeared, a thin girl — older than the boy, but not full grown — with wide, frightened eyes and tears on her cheeks. She held a large stick in her shaking hands, as she emerged from her hiding place to stand before the Amam.

"Let him go," she said in a trembling voice. "Put him down."

The leader of the Amam hissed at her, its teeth bared. She flinched, let out a wretched sob, and fell back a couple of steps. But she did not run.

"Jem…" the boy was still yelling. "Jem!"

"Please," she begged. "Please, let him go. He's only little."

The Amam took another step forward, but the girl held her ground despite the stick in her hands shaking so violently that she could hardly hold it.

"Screw this," O'Neill snarled.

"O'Neill —"

"No," he said, shaking off Teal'c's hand. "I have to."

Teal'c inclined his head toward the girl. "I will circle around behind her. Wait until I am in position."

O'Neill gave a short nod of thanks and in two steps he was out in the open, moving around to the back of the Amam, his gun trained on their commander. "Put him down," he yelled and the Amam turned in surprise. "You heard me. Put the kid down or I'll blow your goddamn head off."

Its expression was curious more than fearful, head cocked to one side as it turned away from the girl and moved toward O'Neill. Teal'c made use of the distraction to creep through the shadows toward the girl, placing the Amam between himself and O'Neill.

"You need a demonstration?" O'Neill asked, and with no further warning he fired into the ground at the startled Amam's feet. It jumped back; perhaps it had not seen a Tau'ri weapon before? "Let him go," O'Neill repeated.

"You are the one?" the Amam said in its strange, guttural speech. "The Lantean?"

"Let the boy go."

Teal'c was close to the girl now, who stood watching O'Neill with terror and astonishment. The boy was limp with fear, dangling from the Amam's hands as if he were no more than a toy. The creature's strength, Teal'c thought, must be significant.

Crouching down, he took a moment to prepare. When O'Neill opened fire on the commander, Teal'c would need to take out the two Amam who stood behind their leader. From this range, it would not prove difficult, but the girl was directly in his and O'Neill's line of fire.

"Child," he hissed quietly. "Child, come here!"

She did not hear, too focused on the drama unfolding and on the boy whom he imagined to be her brother. He swallowed a moment of frustration but dared not speak more loudly for fear of alerting the Amam. Surprise was his most valuable weapon.

"Jem!" he whispered, making an assumption about the name,

but still there was no response. The shock of the situation had robbed her of her senses.

"I'm telling you," O'Neill was shouting. "One more step and I'll blow your brains out." The Amam stepped closer and still O'Neill resisted opening fire, afraid of hitting the girl, afraid that Teal'c was not in position.

Teal'c had no choice but to act. Moving as quietly as he could, he surged to his feet and grabbed the girl. One hand went over her mouth and nose to stifle any sound and the other wrapped around her thin body. "I mean you no harm," he hissed into her ear as he dragged her silently into the shadows. "I am a friend, but you must be silent."

"Hell yeah!" O'Neill yelled, clearly having seen Teal'c move. "You ugly bastard, I am *so* gonna enjoy this!"

The girl's weak struggles abated and Teal'c risked loosening his hold on her mouth. "Make no noise," he cautioned again.

She nodded and he let her go. Turning around, she stared at him with bright eyes, frightened but full of intelligence. When they fell on his mark of Apophis, they widened even further and something like a smile touched her lips. Her mouth opened, but Teal'c put a cautionary finger to her lips to keep her quiet and she nodded, only mouthing the word 'Dix?'

Teal'c didn't answer the silent question, just gestured for her to hide herself. With a nod and a backward glance at the boy she moved off, but not far. She was, however, out of the firing line. Lifting his staff, Teal'c took aim and gave O'Neill a slight nod. They were ready.

"Okay," O'Neill said. "Time's up. Drop the kid."

The Amam holding the boy exchanged a look with the commander — and, perhaps, a telepathic communication — then bared its teeth at O'Neill and lifted its feeding hand. The boy screamed, the girl stifled a cry of her own. O'Neill opened fire.

Jerking backward, the Amam commander danced under the impact of gunshots that should have shredded his body. But it did not even knock him from his feet.

"Oh crap," O'Neill hissed and retreated a step.

Teal'c shared the sentiment. Lifting his staff weapon, he took aim and fired two bolts into the back of the commander and another two into the Amam who held the boy. He was relieved that they proved more effective than O'Neill's MP5.

The commander fell forward, onto his hands and knees, and the Amam who held the boy staggered hard to the right, losing his grip on the child. The boy hit the ground and scrambled to his feet, looking wildly in all directions.

"Kid, over here!" O'Neill yelled, opening fire again on the commander. But the boy stood between him and the other Amam who was already recovering from the staff blasts. Teal'c fired again, knocking him sideways, and then sent two bolts into the third Amam who was pulling his stunner free of its holster. He got off a shot in Teal'c's direction before the staff blasts knocked him back, but it went wide and Teal'c did not even need to duck.

Meanwhile, O'Neill was edging his way past the commander toward the boy. "Come here!" he was shouting. "Kid, run!"

His barked order penetrated the child's fear and he started running toward O'Neill who reached out as soon as he was close enough and dragged the boy behind him. "Stay down," he snapped, opening fire on the Amam again. This time the bullets put the creature down and Teal'c began to realize that the Amam were not impervious to their weapons, it simply required more firepower to do significant damage.

The third Amam was back on his feet, but Teal'c took aim and blasted the stunner from its hand and then fired again into its chest. This time, he did not think the creature would rise.

"Teal'c!" O'Neill yelled, and he looked over to see that the commander and the remaining Amam were closing on O'Neill. He was backing up, the child cowering behind him.

Taking aim, Teal'c fired again into the Amam and he dropped to his knees, back arching in pain. O'Neill finished him off, loosing a burst of gunfire into the creature's head that sent a spray of black blood up into the air.

That left only the commander. Teal'c advanced slowly and, realizing it was now vulnerable, the commander backed up, trying to watch both him and O'Neill. Then his hand moved toward the device on his other wrist, a gesture Teal'c remembered from the Amam who had healed Daniel Jackson. He had done the same to summon the fighter that had snared them with its transporter beam.

He opened fire on the creature's arm at the same moment as O'Neill. The creature's hand flailed, burned and came away from his arm. The Amam roared in pain and Teal'c fired at its head, twice, until it fell silent on the ground.

The grizzly business was done, and over the prone corpse, he met O'Neill's grim gaze.

"That was fun," he said.

Teal'c lifted an eyebrow but did not comment.

From behind O'Neill, the boy emerged and it was only when Teal'c took in his ashen face that he realized dawn had crept upon them.

"Hey," O'Neill said to the kid, putting a hand on his shoulder. "You okay?" The boy just stared and O'Neill ruffled his hand through his hair. "You'll be fine." He looked over at Teal'c. "Where's the girl?"

Looking back to where she was hiding, Teal'c lifted his hand and beckoned. She was running toward them in an instant and, when the boy saw her, he started running too until they collided together in a tangle of hugs and tears.

O'Neill cleared his throat, sniffed, then glared at Teal'c — daring him to comment. He did not dare.

"Hey," O'Neill called over to the children. "You two got a home to go to?"

The girl looked up over her brother's head. "We live in the Way Back."

"Parents?"

She shook her head. "Just me and Bryn."

"Then get outa here," he said. "They might send back-up."

With a nod, she took her brother's hand, but before she led him away she turned to Teal'c. "You're him, aren't you?" she said, gesturing toward his forehead. "You're Dix."

He exchanged a look with O'Neill who just lifted his eyebrows and left it to Teal'c to answer. He chose to let the girl draw her own conclusions and simply bowed his head in silence.

She gave a short bark of laughter. "I knew it," she said, bending down to talk in her brother's ear. "Dix saved you, Bryn. How about that?"

The boy looked up at him, his tear-swollen eyes going wide as the girl, Jem, pulled him away.

"You kids take care," O'Neill called after them, his voice tight with frustration. Teal'c understood his feelings; they could not protect these children, nor any of the thousands who lived here. The next night, perhaps, the Amam would come again and they would be taken — or the night after that.

O'Neill shook his head and stared down at the bodies at their feet. All around them Teal'c sensed people emerging with the morning light, staring in shock and fear at the fallen Amam.

"I'm not sure we did these people any favors," O'Neill said, looking about with obvious unease. "Someone's gonna come looking for these guys."

Teal'c followed his gaze, but alongside the fear, he saw something else in the faces watching from the shadows. It was not exactly hope, but perhaps it was something that could turn to hope.

"It will do these people no harm," he decided, "to learn that the Amam can die at their hands."

"They've got no weapons, Teal'c."

"Not yet," he said. "But if they value their freedom they must learn how to fight for it." He lifted an eyebrow and fixed his friend with a serious look. "This is not our battle to win, O'Neill."

He gave a tight nod, accepting the point even if he did not like it, and then slapped Teal'c on the arm. "Come on," he said, "let's get back. The sooner we get off this rock, the better."

Hunter was right and the flood of people washed past them. Daniel watched, sickened, through a gap in the canvas as three Amam stalked after their prey — driving the panicked population ahead like frightened sheep.

After the Amam were gone, they tried to eat. Daniel broke open one of the MREs in Sam's pack, sharing out the content, but the wretched screams continued and no one had much of an appetite. He flinched when he heard a man shrieking in the distance, trying hard not to imagine that it was Jack or Teal'c.

"How often does this happen?" he asked Hunter, as much to distract himself as anything else.

Hunter sat hunkered with his wife, the child still sleeping in the hide they'd created beneath their shack. "A hunt?" He shrugged. "Depends. Sometimes they hunt the same place every night for a month. Other times weeks go by without a sniff o'them. Hunting's just for sport, though. When they want to harvest, they use the Snatchers." He glanced at his wife, who pressed her face into his shoulder with a shudder, and drew her closer. "That's how they got me."

"You mean the beams of light?" Daniel said, wiggling his fingers to illustrate a transporter beam.

Hunter nodded. "We call 'em Snatcher beams."

"I can see why. That's how they got us too." He glanced over at Sam who sat guarding the entrance, as if her weapon and the scrap of canvas could keep out the Amam. He supposed it made her feel like she was doing something while they waited. "Hunter?" he said, in a voice loud enough for Sam to hear. "Have you ever heard of an Amam healing someone who was dying?"

Sam glanced over at him, gave a slight warning shake of her head.

"No," Hunter said. "Why would they? We ain't nothin' but livestock to them." He scratched a hand over the stubble on his jaw. "There are the Feeders, though," he added, "people who slave for the Snatchers. Heard it said they get fed." He made a clawing gesture with his hand. "Instead of taking life, they're given more."

"Really?" He resisted the urge to touch the place on his chest where the Amam had healed him. "I wonder what kind of affect that has on them?"

"They say their bodies live forever, but they ain't got no soul left inside." Hunter grimaced. "Makes me sick just thinking about it."

"Yeah, it's certainly… a disturbing thought," Daniel said, meeting Sam's alarmed look with one of reassurance. He wasn't going to admit to anything. "So, um, you've never met anyone it's happened to?"

"If I ever met one of the Feeders I'd kill him, not talk to him."

"Right," Daniel said, ignoring the 'shut-the-hell-up' looks Sam was throwing in his direction.

"Probably just camp-tales anyway," Hunter added. "Can't believe most of what people say around here."

"But Dix is real?" Sam said from the doorway, changing the subject. "And the resistance?"

"Yup," Hunter said. "They're real, for dead sure."

"I wonder," Daniel mused, unwilling to be distracted, "why they'd do that — the Amam, I mean. Why would they heal people?"

Hunter shrugged. "Who knows? They're monsters. Why do they do anything?"

But Daniel didn't believe in monsters and whatever these Amam were, they were intelligent and rational creatures. That meant they could be explained. He rubbed a hand absently over his chest, where the Amam had touched him. Unlike Sam, he felt no lingering pain. *A life for a life*, the Amam had said, which meant they had the capacity for moral thought. For altruism, perhaps. They might look like monsters, they might act like monsters most of the time, but that was too easy a way to dismiss them — and, perhaps, to underestimate them.

"It's getting light," Sam said, opening the canvas a crack with the tip of her gun.

In the distance someone started screaming again — it sounded like a child.

She grimaced, moving into a low crouch as she opened the gap wider. He saw her recoil a little, and in a grim voice she said, "There are bodies out there."

Hunter nodded. "There always are."

"Do they only hunt at night?" Daniel said.

"Yes, mostly. They see better in the shadows. You saw how dim their ship was — I think they see differently to us."

"Photosensitivity," Sam said, still watching the creeping dawn. "It explains the shape of their pupils."

"I wonder —" But Daniel's question was cut short by the distant but familiar rat-tat-tat of an MP5.

Sam was on her feet in an instant and out the door, Daniel only a couple of steps behind her. Weapon raised, she was scanning the area, but the sporadic gunfire was at least half a mile away.

"It's coming from over there," Daniel said, gesturing off to their right.

"Yeah." She lowered her weapon, jaw clenched tight. "I hope they're okay."

It went on for at least five minutes — swift bursts of gunfire and beneath it the sizzling sound of a staff weapon discharging. Then, after a longer and more intensive firefight, it stopped.

They waited, but nothing else happened.

"It's over," Sam said tightly.

But who had won? Daniel reached for his radio but Sam shook her head.

"Radio silence," she reminded him with a grim expression. "The colonel will contact us when it's safe."

Behind them, Hunter emerged into the thin light that was starting to lift the shadows from the camp. He looked around with caution and then his eyes fell on something Daniel hadn't noticed in his concern for his friends: two desiccated bodies, crumpled together amid the trampled shacks opposite. Daniel's gaze automatically flinched from the sight, but Hunter walked toward them and dropped to his knees at their side. Head bowed, he sat in silence and Daniel wondered if he'd known these people. He supposed that he must have.

At the doorway to the shelter, Hunter's wife appeared with their son on her hip, his sleepy head resting on her shoulder. She too looked over at the bodies, and all around, Daniel realized, people were emerging from within the ragged camp.

Lifting his head, Hunter reached out his hands and rested one on each of the bodies. "Oh Hecate," he said, loud enough for his voice to carry, "you are the beginning and the end, Mistress of the Crossroads and keeper of the Gateway. You guide us on our path to the world hereafter. Hail, Goddess, and attend to this our sacrifice."

Sam glanced at Daniel, but her usually bright curiosity was tempered by anxiety and her attention quickly returned to scanning the camp for signs of Teal'c and Jack.

Hunter rose to his feet. "That's done," he said. "Hecate will avenge them in the time to come."

"You mean the afterlife?"

"I mean," he said, "when we drive out the Snatchers."

You and whose army? Daniel thought, but kept his skepticism to himself. After all, at first glance, no one would have thought the Abydonians could have overthrown Ra.

"Daniel?" Sam said suddenly, "I'm going to go check —"

Static burst out of their radios, making them both jump, and then Jack's scratchy voice said, "Carter, Daniel, report."

With a grin of relief, Sam toggled her radio. "Good to hear from you, sir. All okay here. What's your status?"

"Heading your way, Carter. Have Hunter ready to move out."

"Yes sir." She hesitated a moment. "Colonel — we heard gunfire."

There was a pause, another burst of static, then, "The bastards are hard to kill, Carter. See you in five. O'Neill out."

Sam smiled at Daniel, then Hunter. "You heard the colonel," she said. "It's time to go see Dix."

Rocks, dislodged by the ha'tak, blocked the road up to the Cheyenne Mountain Complex so they had to abandon the SUV and walk the last half mile.

They were in the shadow of the ship now, where it perched on the mountain like some great, ugly bird of prey. Death Gliders swarmed around it, returning to base.

"Ground assault," Makepeace said, thinking aloud. "That's why they're calling the gliders home."

Maybourne glanced at him. "Then we'd better get inside."

There were two Marines on the gates; Makepeace recognized them both from the SGC. Nonetheless, he approached with caution, hands raised. He didn't want to risk anyone's jittery trigger finger. "Major Jefferson," he said with a nod. "Lieutenant Booker. Draw the short straws?"

Jefferson gave a small, tight smile. "Something like that, sir." His eyes darted to Maybourne, disheveled and out of uniform, then back to Makepeace. "General Hammond said to look out for you, sir."

"How considerate," Maybourne said.

Makepeace ignored him. "You still got comms, Booker?"

"Yes sir, I'll tell the general you're on your way down."

He disappeared into the guard post and Jefferson came forward. Twenty-something and hard as nails, he'd been assigned to SG-5 for the past three months. He jerked his head toward the city. From this entrance you could see smoke rising over the trees, but the city itself was hidden from view. "What's it like down there, sir?"

"Bad," Makepeace said.

Jefferson shook his head. "Glad my folks are still in Austin."

Makepeace didn't answer that, he doubted anywhere would be immune from this by the end.

"Sir?" Booker called, stepping out from the guard post. "General Hammond said to get down to the gate room as fast as you can. They're—"

The unmistakable sound of a ring-transporter activating cut off his words. Behind Booker, between the gates and the tunnel leading into the complex, Goa'uld rings dropped down and lifted again to reveal six Jaffa.

Makepeace opened fire immediately, took two down before the others had time to lift their staff weapons. "Get into the tunnel!" he yelled as another set of rings activated, depositing a further six Jaffa between them and safety.

Jefferson and Booker both dived to the side, firing from the shelter of the guard post, while Maybourne scurried behind them like the rat he was.

"Frag out!" Jefferson bawled, pitching a grenade with precision.

Makepeace turned his face away, ducked as the detonation threw up sharp pieces of stone, taking out half the Jaffa. "Nice!" he yelled at the major. "Got any more of those?"

"Yes sir!"

But the remaining Jaffa weren't giving up. "*Kalach shal'tek!*" bellowed one as he advanced, leaping over the bodies of his fallen comrades. Staff weapon raised, he fired. Makepeace pressed himself against the wall of the guardhouse, felt the heat of the plasma scorch past him, as Jefferson yelled a warning and threw his second grenade. The detonation flung the Jaffa forward, face first into the dirt. Makepeace heard his neck break, saw the dead-eyes staring up at him. Jaffa or human, dead was dead.

"Colonel!" Booker shouted, gesturing with his weapon; there was a clear path to the tunnel.

"Go!" he barked. "Get the blast doors closed. Maybourne—" He turned just in time to see more rings activating behind them. "Damn it."

Six, Jaffa appeared. Twelve. "*Rak'lo najaquna shel're hara kek,*" hissed one of them, raising his staff weapon.

"Whatever," Makepeace said and lifted his own weapon.

"Maybourne! Get behind me."

He did, scrambling to his feet as Makepeace took a step backward.

"You can't hold them all!"

"You better hope I can." He tightened his finger on the trigger. "Now run!"

He opened fire, sweeping backward and forward across the Jaffa as he slowly retreated, Maybourne sprinting for the tunnel behind him. Then he heard Booker and Jefferson open up. He hoped they'd taken cover in the tunnel entrance, but couldn't look around to see.

The Jaffa scattered under the onslaught, diving for cover, and Makepeace could feel the cold of the tunnel at his back. He'd made it. But, at the last moment, a staff blast came blazing from somewhere on his left and clipped his arm. He yelled, the force of the blast spinning him around, and he fell hard onto the ground. Something popped in his left knee, pain shooting up all the way into his gut.

"Colonel!" Jefferson called.

He tried to stand.

"Stay down!"

Pressed into the dirt, he watched as another grenade flew overhead, impacting almost before it hit the ground.

And then Booker grabbed his arm, hauling him to his feet with one hand and firing with the other as he half dragged him into the tunnel. At the far end, light spilled from the complex but the huge blast doors were already closing.

"Come on, sir," Booker said, as Jefferson grabbed his other arm. "We can make it."

For a moment, Makepeace almost felt worthy of these brave men's loyalty. But then he saw Maybourne darting past the closing doors, running ahead of them into the safety of the SGC, and he remembered the truth.

He'd betrayed these people. He didn't deserve anything from them.

It felt like they'd been walking for hours. No, scratch that. They *had* been walking for hours, weaving their way through the endless labyrinthine shantytown. If they were following a path, Jack couldn't make out where it went. But Hunter didn't pause, didn't waver, he just kept on going, leading them deeper and deeper into the camp.

Not wanting to stop and eat, Jack had pulled open a breakfast MRE on the road, so to speak, and eaten everything that didn't need rehydrating. He was still working his way through the chocolate chip pastry when Daniel said, "So, Hunter, how big *is* this place?"

Hunter glanced over his shoulder, gave a shrug. "Maybe ten miles across?"

"Ten *miles*?" Daniel echoed in surprise.

"Big," Jack agreed, but he'd seen that from the mountainside on the way down. The camp was vast.

"Most folk live on the boundary, near the feeding stations. But we're heading deep, to the Way Back."

He'd heard the name before — it's where the kids had come from — and he felt a clutch of guilt at the memory of sending them back there alone. But what else could he do? He couldn't offer them any safety. "The Way Back is the interior?" he said. "The center of the camp?"

Hunter nodded. "Way back from the ship," he explained.

"Safer?"

"Ain't nowhere that's safer," Hunter said, and walked on.

Reaching for his canteen to wash down the cloying taste of the pastry, he took a long swallow and then wiped his mouth on his sleeve. Daniel was frowning as he walked along next to him, his features contracted into an expression that usually meant he was puzzling over a particularly intractable problem. Jack nudged him. "What?"

"Huh?" Daniel said, looking up. "What?"

"You're thinking."

"Uh, yeah?"

When he didn't seem about to expand on the point, Jack said, "Care to share?"

"Oh. Uh, I was just—" He gestured toward Hunter and dropped his voice. "He said this place was ten *miles* across."

"Yeah? It's big."

"No. I mean, yes it's big, but *miles*?"

Jack shook his head, genuinely confused. "I don't follow."

From behind him, Carter said, "I think Daniel's talking about the unit of measurement, sir, rather than the actual distance."

"Exactly," Daniel said, still talking quietly. "Since when have the Goa'uld used 'miles'?"

Jack lifted an eyebrow. "You think the Goa'uld went metric?"

"No, the point is—"

"I get the point." He threw a glance at Hunter. "He is a *fake* Jaffa, remember?"

"I guess," Daniel said. "It's just unusual—"

Just then Hunter stopped suddenly, turning to face them with excitement in his eyes, and for a moment Jack was struck by just how young he was. Early twenties, maybe? "We're here," Hunter said, arms spread wide.

Jack glanced at the tumbledown shacks all around them, at the people crouching in the doorways, watching them as they cooked over meager fires. No different to anywhere else in this place. "I was expecting something... bigger," he said.

With a cryptic smile, Hunter only said, "Follow, but don't say nothing. I'll speak for you." Then he turned and slipped behind a wooden panel that was propped up against a stub of crumbling wall not much more than six feet tall.

"I do not believe we will find any assistance here," Teal'c said in disdain. "This is not the abode of any First Prime."

Jack had to agree and even Carter looked a little crestfallen. Only Daniel's optimism remained intact.

"Come on, Teal'c," he said, pushing past him to follow Hunter. "You know what they say about good things and small packages."

"I do not."

"Oh. Well, Jack can explain," Daniel said, and ducked under the planking after Hunter.

Jack threw up his hands. "Don't look at me. I don't know anything about small packages."

That earned him a snort from Carter and a dubious eyebrow lift from Teal'c, and he had to bite back a smile as he waved them both toward the entrance. "Come on, let's keep Danny outa trouble."

If he'd been expecting something grander inside, he'd have been disappointed. The shack looked pretty similar to Hunter's own — small, cramped and with a smoky fire — except that it also came with three other fake Jaffa hanging out inside. With the four of SG-1 crammed in as well, it was downright cozy. If this was Dix and the resistance they'd had one hell of a wasted trip.

"You can't bring strangers here," one of the men said, getting to his feet. He was big, with a bullish face. Trouble, Jack thought, and let his hands come to rest on his weapon.

"Dix'll wanna want to see these folk," Hunter insisted. "This one?" He gestured to Teal'c. "He wears the mark of Apophis."

The other man's eyes lifted to Teal'c's face, where the firelight made the gold of his brand glimmer. He frowned and then turned back to Hunter. "Where d'you find them?"

"In the larder."

He grunted. "Heard you'd been snatched."

"And freed." He brushed his hand over the top of his right arm and said, "You see what they wear."

The big guy looked and so did all the others. His eyes widened for a moment before his expression crashed down into a frown. "Take 'em in."

"Uh," Jack said, pushing past Daniel and Carter to reach Hunter. "What just happened?"

Hunter met his gaze. "You're gonna meet Dix."

"I don't think so," Jack said, tapping the SG-1 patch on his arm.

"What does *this* have to do with it?" As if he didn't know. Every damn System Lord out there wanted to get their hands on SG-1.

He brought his weapon up fast, backing up a step and cursing the cramped space. Behind him, Carter flipped off the safety on her weapon and Teal'c primed his staff as they both took up defensive positions. The fake Jaffa jumped to their feet in response, Amam stunners appearing in their hands, and just like that they had themselves a regular Mexican stand-off.

"If you think we're going to let you hand us over to some Goa'uld," Jack said, "you've got another thing coming."

Hunter raised his hands. "Hecate won't hurt you."

"Bullshit."

"Sir?" Carter said. "A ha'tak with a Stargate could be our best shot at getting home."

"She's right, Jack." Daniel stepped forward — typically, he was the only person in the room without a weapon in his hands. "Hunter," he said, "we want to trust you."

"Why wouldn't you?"

"You serve a Goa'uld," Daniel explained, indicating his SG-1 patch. "And most Goa'uld we meet want to, um, hurt us. A lot."

"Not Hecate," Hunter said. "Not Dix. I swear on the life of my boy, they won't hurt you." He touched the mark on his forehead and looked at Teal'c. "Dix wears the mark of Apophis, too."

"Though he serves Hecate?" Teal'c said.

"Apophis is dead, my friend. Now Hecate is Mistress of All."

Teal'c didn't answer and into the silence Daniel said, "Jack, do we have a choice? We could be thousands of miles from the Stargate and we still have no DHD."

Out of the corner of his eye, Jack threw a quick glance at Carter but her gaze was fixed firmly on where she was pointing her weapon. He knew her mind had to be running in the same direction as his, though. They should have followed protocol and stayed close to the Stargate, because now they didn't even know how to find it again. But there was no point in dwelling on should-haves, so he pushed the thought to the back of his mind and focused on the decision at hand: take their chances with Hecate's First Prime or head back to the Amam ship and try to figure out a way to get back to the Stargate and dial home.

Daniel was watching him with a steady gaze, Carter standing tense at his side while Teal'c remained as still and silent as always. They were all waiting for him to choose their fate, trusting him to make the right call. After everything the past few months had thrown at them, after the way he'd been forced to treat them, they still trusted him to get it right. It was a heavy responsibility, but it was a weight he was glad to shoulder; nothing was more important to him than the trust of his team.

Taking a breath he made the decision. "Better the devil you know," he said, lowering his weapon and flicking the safety back on. "Carter, Teal'c — stand down."

Warily, they lowered their weapons and Daniel let out the breath he'd been holding in a whoosh of relief. "Good," he said, rubbing his hands together in satisfaction. "So, Hunter, which way now?"

Hunter smiled. "Down."

Daniel's eyebrows shot into his hairline. "Um, down?"

Stepping aside, Hunter revealed a heavy metal panel on the floor — a trap door.

"He lives in the basement?" Jack said, flinging a doubtful look at Daniel. Who the hell was this guy, Dracula?

Two of Hunter's men grabbed a crowbar each and levered open the metal plate until it fell with a dull clang and a cloud of dust onto the dirt floor. A waft of dank, chill air rose up as Hunter grabbed a bundle of sticks and thrust them into the fire. They lit, guttering and spitting, before settling into a serviceable torch. "Come on," he said. "We've a ways to go."

Peering over the edge of the hole, Jack fished his flashlight out of his vest and shone the beam down into the darkness. It bounced off the crude metal rugs of a ladder and glistened on a damp, rocky floor. "What's down there?"

"You'll see," Hunter said, lowering himself onto the ladder.

"Dix can answer all your questions."

Yeah, Jack thought sourly, *right before he shoots us.*

CHAPTER TWENTY-SIX

THE DESCENT down the ladder was perilous. The concrete of the shaft was old and rotten, the rungs more rust than metal. The narrow space was dark and musty, and the dust clogged Sam's throat. She wanted to spit, but Hunter and Colonel O'Neill were below her.

Whatever this place was, it was nothing like any Goa'uld lair SG-1 had previously encountered. Another difference, of course, was that their previous incursions into System Lord territory had usually been covert. Allowing themselves to be led into the HQ of a First Prime could rank as one of the stupidest moves they'd ever made.

But despite her misgivings, Sam knew that they had no choice. According to the colonel, time was not a commodity they had in great store. Something big was happening. She knew better than to press him for information — the way things stood, she wasn't on the need-to-know list — but his word was enough. They needed a way home and they needed it now.

And there was something else that nagged at Sam, one thought that kept repeating in the back of her mind like the line of a tune she'd heard on the radio, seemingly pointless but persistent nonetheless. Something that told her to think about the light.

Sixteen hours thirty and twelve hours twenty. Sixteen. Twelve.

"Teal'c, do you remember how long we walked for that first day here?"

A sudden crash from above sent a shower of debris down on Sam's head. When she looked up, she was alarmed to see Teal'c hanging by one arm from a rung that dangled precariously from the wall. She grabbed his foot to help him find purchase on the ladder again and thanked whatever Jaffa workout had given him his upper body strength.

"You guys ok up there?" called the colonel from somewhere below.

"We're good, sir."

"Teal'c?"

"I am fine, O'Neill. The ladder however has seen better days."

"Yeah, Hunter. Would it kill this Dix guy to get an elevator put in?"

"A what?" Their guide's voice was even further away, the echoes of the shaft making the distance between them difficult to gauge.

"Nothing," grumbled the colonel. "Just… are we nearly there yet?"

"We've a way to go yet, O'Neill," answered Hunter. "Dix's chamber's real deep underground."

It made sense, thought Sam, in more ways than one. If this was the hideout of the resistance against the Amam, the last thing the alien creatures would expect would be to have it beneath their very noses. Hiding in plain sight was a common insurgent tactic. By the same token, caution was still a watchword and having the base so deep underground would ensure that the Amam didn't stumble on it during one of their hunts. Obviously, though, it hadn't been built by the Goa'uld, but rather adopted for their own purposes.

The colonel's chain of thought had clearly followed the same path as her own. "So what exactly is this place, Hunter? Some kind of mine?"

"Your what, Colonel?"

"Huh? No, I mean a mine. An underground mine."

"I don't get your meanin'. We're too deep to plant explosives."

"No, not a *mine*! I mean–"

"Jack, I think we can assume that the people of this planet have no mining industry. I've yet to see anything that would indicate they have any economy based on production and–"

"Daniel?"

"Yeah?"

"I just meant that this is a really deep hole."

There was a beat of silence and then, "Yeah."

Sam pressed her lips together to keep from laughing and kept climbing down.

After what seemed like another age, she heard booted feet hitting rock and a few seconds later a light shone up the shaft. "Careful, Carter," said the colonel. "Ground's a little uneven down here."

Moments later, she stepped from the ladder into the circle of illumination cast by his flashlight and tried to shake the ache from her arms and shoulders. They had reached a small chamber slightly larger than the shaft down which they had just climbed.

"Where now?" asked the colonel.

Hunter nodded towards a nearby wall that had collapsed in on itself, forming a large hole. "Through there. I can't go no further."

Sam frowned and peered through the hole. The passage beyond was dark and rubble-filled, just another rotten place on this rotten world. "But, Hunter," she said, "you said you'd take us to Dix."

"Yeah, Hunter," said the colonel, peering through the hole. "Jesus, it's like a war zone down here... Which, I realize, it probably is."

"I ain't Inner Circle," said Hunter. "From here, you go shadow."

"Shadow?" said Daniel.

"Yup," said Hunter. "Means you go alone." He glanced at each of their faces and Sam guessed he was seeing the same reluctance on each. "Don't worry," he said, swinging himself back on to the ladder. "Follow the red. Follow the red and they'll find you."

"What's the 'red'?" she asked, not liking the color connotations and hoping it was just an irrational instinct.

"You'll see," he replied, his voice already an echo in the darkness. "They'll find you."

The four of them stood staring up the shaft for a while longer, as if he would suddenly reappear, but when the only sound was the receding clang of boots on metal, Colonel O'Neill looked back down at the hole in the wall. "Follow the Yellow Brick Road, huh?"

Sam took a breath. "Sir, are you sure about this?"

He pulled his cap off and tucked it into his vest, scrubbing a hand through his mussed hair. "Nope, not really," he said, and stepped through the hole.

The passage was barely that. Crowded and knotted up with rocks and fallen debris, they had to watch their footing and scramble through narrow gaps. But these weren't the rough-hewn caves of Aedan and his people. The debris had a distinct manmade look about it, fabricated with metal rods which would have posed a nasty hazard if not for their flashlights. Daniel noticed the same thing.

"I wonder what this place was built for," he said, picking his way over fallen masonry.

"Must be some kind of bunker," said the colonel. "I guess they knew the war was coming."

"It doesn't look like it offered much protection."

"Not if they had bunker-busters. Wouldn't matter how deep underground it was then."

"It was most likely a strategic location then, O'Neill," said Teal'c.

"Probably."

Sam kicked at the crumbling concrete in her path. "I don't know, sir."

"Carter?"

She cast her light over the low-hanging ceiling and then down at the floor. There was another story here, another clue to be found.

Sixteen hours thirty. Twelve hours twenty.

"This damage seems to radiate from the ground up," she said. "It's almost as if…"

"As if they self-destructed," Colonel O'Neill said; he wasn't asking a question.

"I guess they had no option."

"They must've been pretty desperate."

Just like us, she thought.

"Red!" Daniel pointed his flashlight at a clear space in the middle of the floor, and sure enough there, visible through the dust and rocks, was a streak of red. Just paint, from the look of it, contrary to the gruesome image Hunter's instructions had conjured in her head. Scuffed and faded, but definitely red.

The colonel pushed away some of the rubble with his boot. "There's more of it up ahead. Is that another passage?"

It was a passage, barely noticeable amid the wreckage around it.

"I guess this is our turn off," said the colonel, and set off into the gloom.

CHAPTER TWENTY-SEVEN

THE STEEL doors to the mountain closed with a clang, the noise echoing along the rest of the tunnel. Propped with his back against the wall, Makepeace fought down nausea as Jefferson hurriedly bandaged his bleeding arm. There was nothing he could do about his blown knee.

"Booker," Makepeace said, spitting words through gritted teeth, "get Maybourne down to the gate room."

Booker glanced at Jefferson, uncertain. "Yes sir."

Something impacted on the door, ringing it like a gong. "Staff blast," Jefferson said. "Those doors won't hold them long."

Behind them the tunnel opened up into a parking lot and behind that was the security point and the elevators down into the complex. There were people there too, a last and hopeless line of defense. Makepeace looked up at the ceiling as another staff blast impacted on the doors.

"I don't know why they're bothering with the door," Maybourne said. "They can use ring transporters to get in here."

"But no deeper into the base," Makepeace said. "Not without a ring platform. They'll have to fight their way in from here."

Maybourne glanced toward the elevators. "The sooner we get to the Stargate, the better."

Makepeace stared at him, at his jowly face, at the arrogance he still saw in the man's eyes — and the cowardice. Maybourne was still running but Makepeace wasn't, not anymore, it was time to pay the price for what he'd done.

"Jefferson," he said, "help me up."

The major hauled him upright, and Makepeace took a moment to let the dizziness pass. He could only stand on the one leg, but that would be enough. "How many explosives can we get our hands on?"

He saw Jefferson exchange another glance with Booker. "How

much do we need, sir?"

"Enough to blow the tunnel, to bring this whole thing down on top of their heads."

"Are you insane?" Maybourne protested. "That would—"

"Shut up, Maybourne," he snapped. "Booker—get someone to take this piece of shit downstairs. Then bring me every stick of C4 you can find in the next five minutes."

In the end, it took almost fifteen minutes to rig the explosives. Enough time to send all the other personnel down in the elevators. Only Makepeace, Jefferson and Booker remained.

"Give me the detonator," Makepeace said, holding out his hand to Jefferson.

He handed it over with a frown. "Sir, we could rig it remotely—set a timer."

"Sure, if we knew exactly when the bastards were going to show up."

"Colonel, let me do it," Booker offered, with all the bullish bravery of the young. As if it didn't matter, throwing your life away before you hit thirty.

Makepeace shook his head. "You need to make this count. Get Maybourne and the Alpha Site address to Hammond and get through the gate," he told him. "Both of you. This fight isn't over."

"Sir—"

"That's an order, Lieutenant. Major." He settled himself against the wall, eyes on the steel doors, mostly hidden from view. He could see a sliver of light between the doors now as the Jaffa continued their assault. And it was only a matter of time before the first set of rings activated. Makepeace figured he could hold out for maybe ten minutes, let as many Jaffa as possible gather here for the assault on the base, before he detonated the charge.

He glanced up at Booker. "Go," he said.

"Yes sir," the lieutenant said, snapping off a crisp salute.

Makepeace reciprocated. Not because he felt that he had the right, but because the kid needed this moment. "Major?" he said then, turning to Jefferson. "Give General Hammond a message for me?"

"Yes sir."

"Tell him…" He considered his words, but there wasn't time for a full confession and even if there had been he wouldn't have known where to start. So, instead, he simply said, "Tell him this is a better death than I deserve."

"Sir?"

"He'll understand."

A screech from the steel doors echoed along the tunnel and, at the same moment, the first set of transporter rings dropped from the ceiling.

"It's time," Makepeace whispered, one hand firm on the detonator and the other on his gun. "Go. That's an order."

"Yes sir." There was nothing else to be said.

He didn't look around, but he heard the elevator doors open and close and knew that he was alone. Unobserved, he watched as the steel doors were pushed apart and daylight flooded back into the tunnel, along with ranks of Jaffa. Ring transporters continued to drop, depositing the enemy piece by piece as they massed for the assault on the SGC.

And Makepeace waited, finger on the detonator. He waited for just the right moment; he waited for his shot at redemption. It didn't take long to come.

Eyes open, Makepeace tripped the detonator.

By Jack's watch, they'd walked about ten minutes, although 'walked' wasn't an entirely accurate term for their progress. They'd climbed, crawled and often stumbled through a warren of tunnels too low for them to stand fully upright, following the odd patch of red paint on the floor. He was glad of the bread-crumb trail because, without it, he wasn't confident they'd be able to find their way back.

Just behind him, Daniel cursed as some rocks gave way beneath his feet and Jack looked back to find him flat on his backside. He bit back a grin. "You should probably watch your step there." Daniel cursed again, but not at the rocks.

If there was one thing that Jack was glad about in this whole rotten mess they were in, it was that he'd decided to let go of the asshole act. He couldn't control much of what was going on around them right now, but he could control that, and to have kept it up any longer would have risked the whole team. A weight had been lifted since he'd told Carter as much of the truth as he dared, especially because she'd accepted his word on it, knowing that there were certain things he just couldn't say. He looked up to see if she'd found Daniel falling on his ass as amusing as he had, but she wasn't even looking in their direction. She was sweeping her flashlight across what was visible of the floor and then up to the ceiling, peering through the debris that hung low above them.

"Everything alright, Carter?"

"Yes, sir, I think so," she said with a frown. "It's just… how many hours of daylight did you count before we got here?"

He shrugged. "Three? Three and a half? Why?"

She shook her head as if clearing a troublesome thought. "Nothing. I'm just trying to work something out. I don't know…"

Jack let it go, although normally, when Carter was concerned about something, they should all be concerned. He knew that it was best to let her work it out on her own; when she wanted to tell him, she would, so instead he turned to set off back down the passage.

A face was staring at him out of the darkness.

"Whoa!" Instinctively, he brought his weapon round to bear. Behind him, he heard Carter and Teal'c do the same. Their new companion, he noticed, did likewise. "Easy," Jack said. "Hunter sent us here. To see Dix. He said he could help us."

The man's eyes scanned each of them in turn and he frowned. Jack guessed they must stand out like a sore thumb in their BDUs when the locals seemed to prefer the grubby rags look. This guy was also sporting a Jaffa tattoo on his forehead, and looked slightly better fed than the folk on the surface. Getting in with a Goa'uld obviously paid well.

The man's gaze came to rest on Jack's MP5. He didn't seem hostile, just suspicious, so Jack decided to take a gamble. "Look," he said. "We're here as friends, and to prove it we'll put our guns down." He let go of the MP5, letting it hang from the shoulder strap — within easy reach should things go sour. "Carter? Teal'c?"

"Yes, sir," replied Carter following his lead. Teal'c took a few more seconds before closing his staff weapon.

"Who are you?" asked the man.

Daniel stepped forward. "We're from a place called Earth. We came through the Stargate… the Chappa'ai… but there's no dialing device to get us home. We were told that Dix may be able to help us. My name is Daniel and this is Sam, Jack and Teal'c. We really don't mean any harm to you."

As Daniel had been speaking, the man's expression had grown more and more perplexed. If it hadn't been for his question, Jack would have doubted that he even spoke English. But just when he'd started to think that there was no chance of this guy taking them to Dix, the man gestured with his head and said. "I think you'd better come with me. Zuri is going to love you."

The four of them exchanged a glance and then followed the man, who introduced himself as Slade, further into the tunnels.

Eventually, they reached a large hole in one wall, about the size of a double doorway. A huge sheet of rusted metal covered it from the other side. Slade banged out a rhythm on it and after a few seconds it slid back to reveal a large cavern, manmade by the looks of it, and clear of debris. After the cramped tunnels they'd just crawled through, this place felt like Grand Central Station. Soft light came from a series of lanterns, which hung above orderly rows of chairs and tables. The room had a definite military feel, reminding him of, maybe, a mess hall.

He turned to say as much to Carter, but she was frowning again, lost in thought.

"Who the hell are these fools?" barked a voice from across the room. A woman, tall and dark skinned, with close cropped hair, had risen from one of the tables and was approaching. "Slade, no one enters the Inner Circle without Dix's authority. You know this."

"I didn't think he'd say no to these ones, Zuri," said Slade. "Take a look at their sleeves."

The woman glanced at Daniel's jacket, and then, with a frown, grabbed the sleeve and pulled him closer, her eyes on the SGC badge.

"Um, okay!" said Daniel, and tried to pull his arm back, but Zuri held it fast.

"I was right," said Zuri. "You *are* fools! Why do you come here brazenly wearing this mark?"

"They say they are SG-1," said Slade.

Jack cursed silently; he should've thought to take off their arm patches. Zuri's reaction, however, wasn't what he'd expected.

She gave a derisive snort of laughter and let go of Daniel's sleeve as if she'd just discovered she was holding used toilet paper. "*You* are SG-1? Is this some kind of joke?"

"If it is, the punchline sucks," said Jack, his patience wearing thin.

"I assure you, Zuri," said Teal'c, "we intend no joke. We are in need of your help and must speak with Dix."

When Teal'c stepped forward, Zuri's expression turned from scornful to pensive. "You are true Jaffa," she said.

Teal'c inclined his head.

Zuri crossed her arms and stood as if in thought for a moment. "You will wait here," she said, before marching through another door at the opposite end of the hall.

"I guess we wait then," said Jack.

As it turned out, they didn't have to wait long and she returned within minutes.

"Will Dix see us?" asked Jack.

"Dix is here," she replied. It was only then that Jack noticed a figure standing in the shadows of the doorway behind her, watching them.

They stood in silence for a few moments, but, when it seemed clear this guy wasn't going to break the ice, Jack cleared his throat and said, "Hey there. Dix, I presume? I'm Colonel Jack O'Neill and this is —"

"I know who you are, Colonel O'Neill," said Dix.

"Well that makes a change…"

Dix walked into the light of the lanterns, revealing a tall, broad-shouldered Jaffa, perhaps just older than Teal'c, with a dusting of gray in his black hair — and the mark of Apophis on his brow.

Jack frowned as a flicker of recognition passed through his mind, as if he'd seen this guy somewhere before. "Do we know each other?" he asked.

But Dix wasn't looking at him. He was watching Teal'c, and to Jack's astonishment he saw a film of tears in the man's eyes. "I knew you would return," Dix said. "I knew you were not dead."

Teal'c stepped forward, almost stumbling.

Beside him, Jack heard Daniel mutter, "Oh my God."

"Am I missing something here?" said Jack, looking around, but Carter too was staring open-mouthed at the scene unfolding between Teal'c and this strange Jaffa.

"No," whispered Teal'c. "No, it cannot be."

"I always had faith that you would return to us, father."

And then, of course, Jack understood. But understanding set off a clamor of denial in his head because somehow, impossibly, this man, this soldier, was Rya'c — the young boy he'd last seen only a few months ago in the Land of Light.

CHAPTER TWENTY-EIGHT

IT SHOULD have been the best and the brightest, Hammond thought as he stood in the gate room and watched the frightened, tearful procession tramping up the ramp and through the event horizon. But instead they could only evacuate those who had reached the base before the attack began: mostly military, some civilians, a few bewildered children. Politicians, inevitably.

There were plenty on the list who'd refused to go, for whom the dual revelations of extra-terrestrial invasions and Stargates were simply too much to process, and there were others who didn't have the damn right but were going anyway. Maybourne was top of that list, though the wrongness of it almost choked Hammond. But then, if the colonel hadn't appeared on the base, sniveling and cowed and all too ready to give up the Alpha Site address, it was doubtful that they'd have been able to save even this many. Hammond took a grim satisfaction in the fact that the man's hubris had been knocked from him by whatever he'd witnessed topside. There had been no triumph, no I-told-you-so, just a small man desperate to escape. But the sight had offered little real solace.

As for the rest of the politicians, Hammond reserved judgment. They'd better damn well learn to fight or farm, because partisan politicking was the last thing this fragile human outpost would need. It was exactly that kind of scheming that had gotten them here in the first place.

He was still having a hard time accepting that it had been Makepeace all along. The man who had sat in his briefing room and listened to Hammond deliver the bleak sit-rep, knowing the precariousness of their situation in the galaxy and yet saying nothing. He was gone now, a last gasp attempt at redemption perhaps. By Jefferson's account, it was thanks to the colonel's sacrifice that Jaffa weren't swarming through the SGC's corridors already. Makepeace had bought them time to evacuate, but it was still a bitter pill to swallow and Hammond didn't think he was ready to forgive him yet.

Far above, something impacted the mountain and the whole base shook. Frightened faces lifted to the ceiling and the pace of the evacuation picked up a notch.

Stargate Command's power and communications had been knocked out in the first wave; they were operating blind now, limping along on generators. It was barely enough to power the gate. Dust sifted down from the ceiling as the assault on the mountain continued and the dull rumbles and thuds penetrated even into the gate room.

What the state of the surface was like, he dared not imagine. He just prayed that the enemy were concentrating their assault on the mountain, because he had one final role of the dice to make if he could find someone brave enough to take a risk on his last gambit.

All around him, the men and women of Stargate Command prepared to leave, dragging as much kit as they could find into the gate room. Dr. Fraiser was marshalling her own people and it looked like she was trying to send every nut and bolt from the infirmary through to the Alpha Site — God knew, they'd need it all and more. She caught his eye from the opposite side of the gate room and lifted a hand to wave. He nodded, but didn't disrupt her work. Every second counted. Once the gate shut down there would be no guarantee they could redial fast enough to prevent the Goa'uld from dialing in. They'd been lucky twice; he just prayed their luck would hold a little longer.

"Sir?" He turned to find Colonel Dixon standing at his side.

"Colonel?" Dixon's Pentagon Strike Team had been parachuted in to oversee the evacuation, so he was surprised to see the colonel still in the gate room. "I thought your team had gone through with the President."

Dixon nodded. "Yes sir, they did." He looked uncomfortable. "Sir, requesting permission to stay Earth-side."

Hammond didn't know him well, they'd crossed paths only once before, but he knew Dixon was a good man and this request was unexpected. "Why, Colonel? They need you out there on the Alpha Site."

Rubbing a hand across his face Dixon said, "Lainie, my wife — She's expecting our first child in a couple months, sir."

Hammond closed his eyes for a moment, as if that could block out this one small tragedy among so many billions of tragedies. "And you want to be with her," he said and didn't add *at the end*.

But Dixon shook his head. "No sir, she was in DC when the assault began." His face went tight and hard; they both knew that Washington must have gone already. "I want to fight, sir. I don't want to run from the bastards." He jerked his head up toward the skies above the mountain. "There are good men and women dying up there, sir. I want to join them."

It was a sentiment Hammond fully understood, but sometimes dying was the easy option. He considered Dixon for a long moment, tried to take the measure of the man in the few moments they had together. What did he know about him? He'd served under Frank Cromwell and had led the Pentagon Strike Team since Cromwell's death here at the SGC. Dixon had an honest face, but it was full of banked rage and grief and he was burning to fight back. He might just be the man Hammond needed to put his plan — worthy of O'Neill in its reckless optimism — into action. "You really want to fight, Colonel?"

"Absolutely, I do, sir."

"You know we can't win."

"We can die trying."

Hammond nodded, folded his arms and issued the challenge. "What if I said there was something else you could do? It won't turn the tide — nothing can do that now — but it could save lives. A lot of lives."

"I don't want to run," Dixon reiterated. "Lainie deserves more than that."

"It means staying on Earth," Hammond said. "I'm talking

about resistance, son."

He shifted his feet. "How? Doing what?"

"It's a crazy plan," Hammond warned. "In all likelihood it won't succeed and you won't survive."

Dixon gave a bleak laugh. "It's the end of the world, sir. What have I got to lose?"

That made Hammond smile, made him think that maybe his last stratagem might pay off. "There's a C-5 at Peterson," he said. "It's fully crewed and waiting for orders — assuming the base is still standing, of course." That was the first roll of the dice. "You'll have to get out of the mountain first and over to Peterson. When you find that bird, I want you to take her to Groom Lake."

"Area 51, sir?"

Hammond nodded. "Retrieve the Beta gate and its DHD and take them as far away from here as possible. Find somewhere remote — perhaps with one of our overseas allies. Somewhere secret, somewhere no one who's compromised by the Goa'uld would know about. Get the gate working, keep it working for as long as you can, and send as many people as possible through to the Alpha Site." He gestured to the forlorn procession of evacuees. "These shouldn't be the only people with a chance, Colonel. Humanity needs more than them if it's to survive."

Dixon's face had blanched, but he was a good, solid man and he was up for the fight. Hammond might just have laid the salvation of humanity on his shoulders, but he wasn't going to buckle under the strain. "I'll make it work, sir. We'll resist these bastards all the way."

Hammond nodded. "Yes we will, son."

"What about you, sir?" Dixon said. "Won't you come too?"

"No," he said. "My place is here until the end."

Dixon took a breath and nodded. "Understood, sir." Drawing himself up, he offered a sharp salute. "Good luck, General."

Hammond returned the salute. "Godspeed, Colonel."

And with that, Dixon turned and started weaving his way

through the orderly chaos of the gate room, breaking into a run as he left through the blast doors and disappeared into the emptying base. The dice were rolling now and Hammond knew he'd never find out how they landed, but he had faith in his people — in Dave Dixon and the crew of the C-5, in humanity as a whole. They might be down, but they weren't out yet. And if Dixon could offer mankind a chance, a way of enduring and fighting back, then maybe these would not be humanity's final days on Earth. At the very least, Dixon could offer them hope and sometimes hope was the most powerful weapon of all.

Shocked silence filled the room.

More than shocked, Jack thought, it was a kind of breathless incomprehension. How could this man be Teal'c's young son? His mind felt like it was struggling to change gears, struggling to process something so impossible.

"How?" Teal'c said at last, voicing the question they all shared. "You were a boy when last we were together."

Dix — or could it really be Rya'c? — nodded. "So I was, but that was close to one hundred years ago."

Daniel's breath left his lungs in a rush of disbelief. "*What?*"

"Oh my God," Sam gasped.

Jack just pressed his lips together in a hard, skeptical line. *Bullshit.*

Teal'c seemed to share his opinion. "Why should I accept your word on this?"

"Because it is the truth and you are my father and must know your own son." Dix drew a step closer, further out of the shadows, and Jack couldn't deny that the man bore a striking resemblance to Rya'c.

But Teal'c wasn't convinced. "Your assertion is insufficient," he said.

Zuri pushed herself forward, chin lifted with an angry cynicism that rivaled Jack's own. "Dix," she said, "surely you can't think these people are really who they pretend to be?"

"I know my own father!" His flare of anger was familiar and Jack was disconcerted to see Teal'c react to it, as if in that unguarded moment he saw the boy he'd known. Rya'c had always been fiery.

Zuri wasn't cowed, however, and cast her gaze over Teal'c and the rest of them without conviction. "How is it possible that they appear unchanged? This could be a Wraith trick."

"Yeah, a trick is exactly what this is," Jack insisted. "If you're Rya'c, then I'm Rip Van Winkle."

"Sir," Sam said quietly, "theoretically it *is* possible. This wouldn't be the first time the Stargate has connected with a gate in a different time."

"And we've woken up in the 'future' before, Carter, and found ourselves in Hathor's happy place."

"But we were unconscious then," Daniel pointed out. "This time we were awake all along. At least, you guys were, right?"

Jack acknowledged his point with a shrug, although it didn't really prove anything, and for a moment there was nothing between them all but silence.

Daniel made the most of the opportunity. "Why 'Dix'?" he said. "Why do you call yourself that and not Rya'c?"

Dix gave a tight smile. "Because 'Dix' is a legend."

"Yeah, we heard. He leads the resistance, apparently. Is that you? Is this… ?" Daniel gestured around them. "Is this the resistance?"

"In a manner of speaking, yes." He glanced at Teal'c. "I adopted the name 'Dix' because it has meaning here. I need these people to trust me."

"By usurping their legends and impersonating their heroes?" Jack said, not bothering to hide his contempt. "Sounds familiar."

"Huh." The snort came from Zuri. "*You* can hardly object to that when you —"

Dix put a hand on her arm, quieting her. "I have done what I must, O'Neill."

"Oh, I bet you have."

"Jack—"

"No, Daniel, this is bullshit. All of it." He turned to Dix. "Look, I don't know who you people are, or what scheme you've got going on here, but you clearly know us and I'm willing to bet you know how to get us back to Earth." He didn't raise his MP5, but he swung it around, letting everyone in the room know how this scene could play out. "So if your boss has a Stargate, *Dix*, then I suggest you take us to it. Now."

Dix exchanged a silent look with Zuri, before saying, "I understand why it is difficult to believe me, O'Neill, but there is something you need to see."

"Dix, no," Zuri protested. "You can't—"

"I must." With a serious look at Teal'c, he said, "It is the only way."

For once, Teal'c's emotions were easy to read and it was obvious that he wanted to know more about the man who claimed to be his son. Jack couldn't begrudge him that, even if he couldn't trust this Dix character any further than he could spit.

Hathor had proven that, when it came to Goa'uld plans for galactic domination, no scheme was too elaborate and no detail too small. But if this was a trick, Jack didn't know where it started and where it finished. Planet-wide nuclear destruction seemed over-the-top, even by System Lord standards, so whatever had happened to these people—the war, the enslavement, the invasion by the Amam or Wraith or whatever they wanted to call themselves—all of that was real.

The fact was that, wherever—and whenever—they were, their priority was still getting back to Earth. And Hecate's hat'ak remained their best shot at finding an operational Stargate. So, for now, he was willing to play along and see how far this game took them.

Dix turned and pulled a lantern from its hook on the wall. "Follow me," he said, his gaze fixed on Teal'c. "Then you will understand."

As Dix walked from the room, Zuri on his heels, Jack glanced across at Carter.

The unease on her face mirrored his. "What if he's telling the truth, sir?"

"We'll burn that bridge if we get to it, Major. For now, let's just find a way home." Pushing all other considerations from his mind, he focused on Dix's lantern as it lit the way through the ruined tunnels. "Stay sharp," he said as they headed out after him. "I've got a bad feeling about this."

The rubble had thinned out here, and the way was clearer and easier to navigate, but Jack didn't like how the lantern light bounced off the walls; the shadows stirred something queasy in his gut, a sense that this planet was wrong to its very core. Here and there on the ground, he saw a swathe of the same red paint they'd followed here.

Dix led them onward, until they reached a wide hole in the ground. From somewhere far below, a sound echoed like metal on stone. "Sounds like a dig," murmured Daniel, but he too seemed anxious as he peered into the darkness of that pit.

"What's down there?" said Jack, fighting the urge to draw back from the edge.

"You asked me to help you return home." He gestured to the hole, and Jack saw that a rope hung over its edge. "Now you must trust me."

They'd come this far and in the end it was nothing, a swift rappel down a long, sheer drop, then an awkward crawl through a narrow gap hewn into a wall.

They emerged into a large cavern, where men and women worked with hand tools, chipping away at the rocks and excavating them in hefty woven baskets. At first, Jack couldn't understand exactly what it was he was looking at. High above them was a panel with shattered windows, the remnants of some burnt out technology barely visible in the darkness beyond.

"Oh my God," whispered Carter, her voice stricken in a way that Jack didn't want to acknowledge. It was a desperate whisper, an awful sound.

"No, Carter…" But the back of his throat was acrid and bitter; he'd seen what was slowly emerging from the tumbled rocks of the cavern.

"The time, sir, the daylight hours. If I'd been able to keep count, I would have known. I would… I would have realized."

"What is this —?" said Daniel, but his words broke halfway.

Stone by stone, one hammer blow at a time, a curve of gray was being exhumed from its resting place. Familiar symbols gleamed in the torchlight, one of them a two sided pyramid topped by a circle, frozen in time. Frozen for a century, just like the Stargate on which it was engraved.

"You wish to return home, Colonel O'Neill?" said Dix. "You see now why I cannot send you there."

And in a moment of shock, of shifting reality, Jack's eyes suddenly made sense of the fractured world around him. They couldn't go home, because this *was* home. This was Stargate Command.

This was Earth.

EPILOGUE

NEVER had he seen the SGC so still, cold as a tomb without the lifeblood of its people pulsing through its hallways. George Hammond wondered what it looked like topside right now. There had been no weather report that day; every channel had run with only one story until they'd dropped off the air. What was the point of knowing whether rain would fall, if tomorrow wasn't guaranteed? He imagined, though, that the sky was clear, the night air crisp, the stars perfect and unchanged. This was what he wanted for his last night on Earth, therefore in his mind's eye, it was so.

Hammond got up from his desk and switched off the light, walking out through the briefing room and down the spiral stairs into the control room. The event horizon rippled, casting its blue light across the walls, making the stone come to life. Not long until the thirty eight minutes was up, but by then it wouldn't matter. The blasts from above had become less frequent, and Hammond knew it was because the Jaffa had already made their way deep into the mountain. As if to reinforce the point, the sounds of an explosion echoed from somewhere just two or three levels above and he felt a tremor beneath his feet. The wolf was at the door.

The gate room was deserted. The last of those lucky enough to have made the list for the Alpha site had ascended the ramp and passed through the event horizon some time ago. It was on that ramp that he had said goodbye to Tessa and Kayla. He hoped that, one day, they'd come to understand why he couldn't give in to their tearful pleas to go with them, why he couldn't promise that he'd see them soon. But he wouldn't think of that now. They were safe and that was all that mattered.

The Stargate itself stood like a lone sentinel; it was fitting that it should be his last companion.

"Sir?"

Almost his last companion.

He smiled at the voice, though he was tired and heart-sore. The loyalty and bravery of his people never ceased to amaze him, and the woman who walked into the control room was no exception. "Doctor, I thought I'd told you to leave with the last wave."

"And I thought I told you I'd be here 'til the lights went out."

Hammond glanced out of the control room window. "Just one left to turn out."

Janet's mouth tightened in some semblance of a smile, though when she spoke her voice trembled. "I'm not leaving, sir."

"What if I said it was an order, Captain?"

"Then I would say consider me insubordinate, General."

Hammond nodded. She would change her mind in a moment, but for now, God help him, he was thankful for the company.

Another explosion sounded and Janet looked up at the ceiling. "How long, do you think? Until they come?"

Hammond followed her line of sight. "Ten, fifteen minutes, maybe less." So little time, but time enough to complete the work left to him. He thought of this planet, his treacherous, maddening, beautiful, precious home, and the true nature of all that would be lost.

"Have you ever read Whitman, Janet?"

"Walt Whitman?" She shrugged. "In college, I suppose…"

"When I was younger, I had *Leaves of Grass* hidden beneath the mattress on my bed, because my father called him a commie — and worse — and wouldn't allow it in the house. I guess he just plain didn't get it." He closed his eyes and let the verse come to him. "*As onward silently stars aloft, eastward new ones upward stole.*"

"It's beautiful, sir. I didn't realize you loved poetry."

He smiled. "If ever there was a time for poetry, doctor."

"Yes, sir."

With a deep breath, Hammond strove to shake the sadness

that had settled over him. Their last minutes were counting down. "Time for you to go, doctor."

Janet looked between him and the gate, shaking her head. "I told you, sir. I'm not going anywhere. I won't–"

"Cassie's there."

With a startled gasp, Janet tilted against the control panel, as if needing the support to keep her upright. Tears spilled down her face. "But they said… they said there wasn't a chance Cassie could go. They said there was no place for her on the list."

"I made arrangements. So you see now that you haven't got a choice. Go through the gate, Janet. Take care of your family."

Still she hesitated, and Hammond knew that she was torn, that her loyalty to the base, and to Earth, made this an unbearable choice. But in the end, really, it was no choice at all.

"Thank you, General Hammond," she whispered. "Thank you, sir." She ran from the room, appearing seconds later in the gate room. She was halfway up the ramp when Hammond was gripped by a sudden, desperate impulse. Hope, it seemed, was a tough bastard to kill.

He punched the button on the PA system. "Doctor?" She stopped, whirling back to face him. "If there's a chance… If any of us survive this, will you come back? Will you come back and fight for us?"

Janet's shoulders shook, but without a radio her words were trapped behind the barrier of the glass. She nodded, raising her right hand and pressing it to her heart, before executing a perfect salute. He returned the salute and, in the next second, she was gone. The gate fell, for the last time, into darkness.

And so Hammond was left to finish this vigil strange, the Earth above him his fallen comrade whom he'd tried so hard to save and whom he would not abandon, even at the end.

One minute was left to him now and he would use it well. Opening up a deep space channel, he sent the final message, hoping it would be enough, wondering if anyone was even listening.

The countdown ticked on.

"This is a distress call from planet Earth. We are under attack and in need of assistance. If you have ever called yourselves our friends, we ask that you help us now. But if we must stand alone, we will stand strong. Though we may fall, we *will* fight. Though we may be outnumbered, we *will* endure. And for those who have abandoned us, know this: we will never forget. And we will never forgive. This is Major General George S Hammond, signing off."

Far above, on the bridge of a vast ship cloaked against the blackness of space, two gray figures watched the bright flower of light that burst across the area that was called Colorado. The final words from a dying planet echoed through the corridors of their vessel.

"We should have intervened," said one.

The other turned and walked away from the viewing window, and there was sadness in his step. "You know we could not."

Against a backdrop of stars, unseen by the ships that advanced towards Earth, the *Beliskner* retreated, leaving the lonely blue planet to her fate.

ABOUT THE AUTHORS

Sally Malcolm is the commissioning editor at Fandemonium Books and has overseen the production of almost fifty novels based on *Stargate SG-1*, *Stargate Atlantis* and *Stargate Universe*.

Sally has written *Stargate SG-1: A Matter of Honor*, *Stargate SG-1: The Cost of Honor*, *Stargate Atlantis: Rising* (novelization). She has also penned four audio dramas for Big Finish Productions: *Stargate SG-1: Gift of the Gods* starring Michael Shanks, *Stargate Atlantis: Savarna* starring Teryl Rothery, *Stargate Atlantis: Perchance to Dream* starring Paul McGillion, and *Stargate SG-1: An Eye for an Eye* starring Michael Shanks, Claudia Black and Cliff Simon.

She also wrote two episodes of the video game *Stargate SG-1: Unleashed* which were voiced by *Stargate SG-1* stars Richard Dean Anderson, Michael Shanks, Amanda Tapping and Chris Judge.

Stargate SG-1: Hostile Ground is the second novel Sally has co-authored with Laura Harper. The first one, *Stargate SG-1: Sunrise* was published under the pen name J.F. Crane.

Sally is currently working on Fandemonium's first Stargate short story collection 'Far Horizons' which will be published in October 2014.

And her first original novel will be published later this year by Choc Lit UK.

Laura Harper co-authored *Stargate SG-1: Sunrise* with Sally Malcolm, writing as J.F. Crane. *Stargate SG-1: Hostile Ground* is her second novel for Fandemonium Books.

Laura is currently working on an original novel and book two of the Stargate SG-1 Apocalypse series.

STARGÅTE SG·1.

STARGATE ATLÅNTIS

Original novels based on the hit TV shows STARGATE SG-1 and STARGATE ATLANTIS

Available as e-books from leading online retailers

Paperback editions available from Amazon and IngramSpark

If you liked this book, please tell your friends and leave a review on a bookstore website. Thanks!